The Maste

"She'll never make an operative." Simon propped his arm companionably over John's shoulder and watched as Josie sheepishly recovered from a stumble.

"She's my wife, not one of your lot." John clamped his mouth into a line and rolled his eyes, a habit he seemed to be borrowing lately from Josie. "But you're right. An operative she will never be. I'm just glad she's learning to hone her skills at defending herself. Clumsily, but still…"

"There's that," Simon agreed with a shrug then suppressed a chuckle. "And now, thankfully, she looks more the part so her cover will stand."

Though he'd never let on, Simon did like her. She was a bit crass, rude, nosy, and childishly naïve, but she'd somehow managed to tame his best friend's turbulent heart and reawaken his humorous nature. And, she had the uncanny ability to make John swoon like a girl, something that was practically unheard of until she came to live at the Citadel.

"At least now she won't second-guess her own strength and abilities," Simon continued.

At best, she and Simon resorted to a friendly banter of words and insults that sometimes erupted into violent outbursts of temper. But generally, they enjoyed the insults and would never openly admit—to themselves or others—that they were actually quite fond of one another.

With a final twist of the torso, a pivot and a lunge, Josie completed a rather difficult counter-attack kick on the sparring droid, successfully upturning it. Then, rather childishly, gave it a final below-the-belt kick, not that it mattered much to the droid. She huffed off and strode determinedly toward the two men who watched.

"Temper, temper." Simon clicked his tongue, not quite masking the impressed nod of approval as he mentally rated her performance.

T.K. Toppin

Champagne Books Presents

The Master Key

By

T.K. Toppin

This is a work of fiction. The characters, incidents and dialogues in this book are of the author's imagination and are not to be construed as real. Any resemblance to actual events or persons, living or dead, is completely coincidental.

No part of this book may be reproduced or transmitted in any form or by any means, electronic or mechanical, including photocopying, recording, or by any information storage and retrieval system, without permission in writing from the publisher.

BURST
www.burstbooks.ca
A Division of Champagne Books
Copyright 2011 by Tomomi Kaharabata-Toppin
ISBN 9781927454473
July 2011
Cover Art by Amanda Kelsey
Produced in Canada

BURST
#35069-4604 37 ST SW
Calgary, AB T3E 7C7
Canada

Other Books By T.K. Toppin

The Lancaster Rule

FEB 03, 2017

To Marc + Sue,
And again! :)

Toppin

One

"She'll never make an operative." Simon propped his arm companionably over John's shoulder and watched as Josie sheepishly recovered from a stumble.

"She's my wife, not one of your lot." John clamped his mouth into a line and rolled his eyes, a habit he seemed to be borrowing lately from Josie. "But you're right. An operative she will never be. I'm just glad she's learning to hone her skills at defending herself. Clumsily, but still…"

"There's that," Simon agreed with a shrug then suppressed a chuckle. "And now, thankfully, she looks more the part so her cover will stand."

Though he'd never let on, Simon did like her. She was a bit crass, rude, nosy, and childishly naïve, but she'd somehow managed to tame his best friend's turbulent heart and reawaken his humorous nature. And, she had the uncanny ability to make John swoon like a girl, something that was practically unheard of until she came to live at the Citadel.

"At least now she won't second-guess her own strength and abilities," Simon continued.

At best, she and Simon resorted to a friendly banter of words and insults that sometimes erupted into violent outbursts of temper. But generally, they enjoyed the insults and would never openly admit—to themselves or others—that they were actually quite fond of one another.

With a final twist of the torso, a pivot and a lunge, Josie completed a rather difficult counter-attack kick on the sparring droid, successfully upturning it. Then, rather childishly, gave it a final below-the-belt kick, not that it mattered much to the droid. She huffed off and strode determinedly toward the two men who watched.

"Temper, temper." Simon clicked his tongue, not quite masking the impressed nod of approval as he mentally rated her performance.

"Tell that to the stupid fucking droid," Josie retorted out of breath. "And I just bet it was *you* who programmed that last fancy bit of arm-work." She mimicked with a series of hand movements that made her look like a cartoon martial arts fighter. "Hah! But I beat it, so there." She flashed John a wide grin, who couldn't help himself from grinning back.

John had to admit, he'd gotten used to the amount of swearing that came out of his wife's mouth. It offended him at first but she was from another time, another century, it couldn't be helped—no matter how hard she tried. In fact, he had to admit again, he even started to use choice bits of expletives himself, though it unsettled him somewhat.

Josie was born in the 2006. It was now 2334. She'd been living in the future for nearly two years. When she was twenty-four, she stepped into her father's stasis pod—and slept for just over three hundred years.

Though she was but a shadow of the person that awoke two years previous, in her mind, she still sometimes thought herself to be simply Josephine Bettencourt, a fledging portrait artist with the rest of her life to live—the possibilities were endless.

But never in her wildest dreams would she have imagined just how far those possibilities would take her away from her simple, idyllic life. A life where the most exciting thing to ever happen was winning ten dollars in a scratch and win lottery ticket, and where the saddest moment was discovering that your grandfather had died in his sleep.

She'd survived three hundred years in suspension and came out of it looking like an anorexic cadaver. She'd been kidnapped and threatened with death by fanatical extremists, suspected of being a terrorist and then marked for assassination. She'd even stepped before an exploding human-bomb to save herself and her future husband. Later, she had no choice but to kill at least three people, and then finally, married the World President of the United Europe and Americas, John Lancaster, and discovered what love really meant.

And what living really meant.

Josie stood tall. Her body lean and sculpted now, and not at all like her once skinny and frail frame. The long months of physical training with her tutor and body-assistant Trudi—Mrs. Trudesson, who was also Simon's wife—had helped build her stamina and strength. Sometimes a specialized trainer assisted to condition her body and mind for specific combat techniques. The outcome was plain to see, her fighting skills were now passable enough to keep her alive. Even her knowledge of weapons and battle tactics seemed to be improving.

Her narrow face was capped with brown hair that scraped just along her shoulders. Her nose short and neat, her lips full, and tended to pout naturally if not sullenly. But it was her eyes that struck people when they first met her. They were a startling and vibrant emerald green, vivid and bright with brilliant marigold yellow at the centres that contrasted wildly with the black pupils and the thick dark frame of lashes. Slightly large for her face, her eyes dominated and carried with them a multitude of expressions and thoughts that never failed to amaze and intrigue John.

Josie yanked a towel resting on a shelf and scrubbed her sweaty face with enthusiasm.

"What time is it?" she asked when she surfaced, flinging the towel over her neck and cocking her head to John.

"Nearly three," he replied quietly and smiled, head bowed in his usual manner.

"You've enough time to get cleaned up, dressed, and be transported to Toronto," Simon said helpfully. Then, he grinned. "And scrub extra hard, you're a bit smelly."

Josie rolled her eyes and snorted. "Well at least I'll smell clean at the end of it, unlike you, who's just naturally stinky." A lame retort, but she had to say something appropriate.

John shook his head good-naturedly, hooked an arm through his wife's and tugged her along into the elevator that would take them to their kitchen a floor above.

"Come along," he said. "We've also a little time to grab a quick bite to eat before we head off."

For the heck of it, Josie turned her head back and stuck her tongue out at Simon, who laughed loudly with amusement as he followed them.

"Does he really have to come with us?" Josie glanced up at John, who stood a few inches taller.

"Someone has to keep an eye on you," John replied with a smirk. He winked at her and squeezed her arm. "Two days is not long, but it's long enough for you to get into any amount of trouble."

She titled her head up dramatically and let out a groan. "I *promise* not to get into trouble!"

"Promises, promises," Simon muttered from behind them as the elevator doors opened and they filed out into the large kitchen.

One of John's automated housekeepers busily cleaned the cooking range and turned to offer them a polite smile. It was designed to look middle-aged, soft-featured with greying hair like everyone's favorite aunt.

Josie still wasn't accustomed to having automated droids around, especially those that looked all too human—waxy, artificial complexion aside. She returned a squint-eyed stare and gave Crocker—John's wry sense of humor in naming the cooking droid after the legendary Betty—a wide berth before planting herself on a kitchen stool.

John instructed Crocker to provide them with refreshments and a light snack. With a small inclination of the head, Crocker obliged cheerfully. Josie rolled her eyes again. She still hadn't spoken directly to any of John's droids, preferring to defer that task to John himself.

"So," Josie said and cleared her throat. "After the big do tonight..."

John glanced at her and nodded, his head still bowed as he stood resting against the kitchen counter. He did, after all, promise. It would be hard for her to see the place again, but he supposed that if it were him, he'd want to do the same.

"You're sure?" he asked quietly.

Josie nodded, clearly looking distracted.

Three hundred years was a long time to see your hometown

again. It had changed—vastly—but she had to see it.

Just had to.

Holographic images and pictures of the city were one thing, but to actually be there was another. It would pain her greatly to see it once more, to see what once was, was no longer. But it was something she needed to do.

The street she'd once lived on was gone, replaced by a massive shopping centre to cover the ruins of a war that had once taken place nearly two hundred years previous.

The world had turned—as time and history predictably kept repeating itself—into a turbulent, dangerous, and terrible place.

Soon after she went to sleep in 2030, technology had bounded forward in massive leaps, to be then followed by a devastating economic crash that affected the entire world. Though it had been predicted to happen, people were still blindsided by it. Poverty and famines, segregation between the powerful super-rich and the poor was great; it encompassed everything from individuals to countries. Then came the civil and urban street wars, world wars, and finally, two hundred and fifty years later, Dane Lancaster emerged to bully his way into becoming the World President. The world had been ripe for the picking, and Dane Lancaster used it and abused it.

Dane had intimidated, had killed, had stolen, and had overthrown countless countries and their world leaders and political heads. He'd built a massive citadel in the Swiss Alps, which he then declared as the world capital, and dictated his ruthless regime for nearly thirty years—followed soon after by his son Baird.

But Baird had relented from the tyrannical rule fifteen years before he died. A horrible incident that involved the death of his sisters and a direct threat to the life of his son, John, altered the view of his rule. He realized that he was becoming his father—after all, it had been Dane Lancaster himself who had molded Baird to become just like him. But Baird felt different. He'd made changes, tried his hand at leniency, and began stripping away the secrets that shrouded the Lancasters by attempting to open the mind of the world that had become closed, scared, submissive, and distrustful of authority.

And then his eldest son, Adam, murdered him.

John assumed leadership by making more changes, vowing

to change the world for the better, and never to repeat what his grandfather had created. It was hard, and like his grandfather before him, John bullied and intimated those who stood in the way of progress.

But the world wasn't quite ready for change. After nearly two generations of fearsome rule, people were scared. And with oppression, there came a rampant birth of brutally vicious acts of opposition. And a new breed of terrorists.

Before becoming president, John had been happily assuming the role as head of security and anti-terrorism with his best friend Simon at his side. But after his father's sudden death, John reluctantly assumed the role he'd been trained and schooled for—born to do.

And then Josie stepped into his life.

Josie knew all too well what followed afterwards, when John took over and resumed where his father had left off. She'd been a part of it—had become a part of it. Sometimes she thought if she weren't here, now, maybe it would never have happened as it had.

But she believed in the unchangeable course of destiny now more than ever. That her life; it was always meant to bring her to this very place, this very life. It was beyond imagination, yet here she was—home, where she always belonged.

And sometimes she wondered that if by her coming to this future, she didn't help to bring disaster and destruction. Like a plague from the past, disrupting the natural order of time.

As it stood, by her very existence in this future, Adam Lancaster had been exposed and exiled into a life of seclusion within the Citadel walls. By a strange twist of fate and chance, Josie had been present to witness Adam's involvement in a plot to overthrow the government, led by a maniacal extremist who called himself Uron Koh. Koh appeared on the scene and wreaked destruction and murder in order to take over the Citadel, trying to assassinate both herself and John, and anyone else that stood in the way.

And this Uron Koh, he just happened to be someone that Josie knew—Max Wellesley.

Max was the son of the man who had saved her life after she'd been kidnapped and scheduled for death by fanatics. These were fanatics, calling themselves Naturalists, who abhorred pod-survivors by branding them abominations of nature. Pod-survivor was the term used for people who'd preferred to sleep away the oppressive years during the first Lancaster rule in stasis pods.

However, no one had counted on coming across Josie, who'd been only helping her father's primitive yet vital experiments three hundred years ago. And it had been Dr. Peter Bettencourt's initial research into stasis technology that the world used now, in every day life. Whichever way she looked at it, her role in this future seemed indelibly linked to her past.

~ * ~

"There she goes again," Simon muttered conspiratorially to John. "Lost in her thoughts."

"Oh, shut up." Josie snapped her attention back to the present.

She tilted her head to John who gave her a curious look, watchful and worried, but also mildly annoyed. She returned a look that clearly said 'what?'

John held her gaze a moment longer then averted his to the floor, clamping his lips together in his habitual way. "I can only accompany you in the afternoon."

Josie nodded, flicked a glance at Simon's deeply chiseled face, taking in its square, angular lines. Everything about Simon was straight and sharp, from head to toe. He stood with the proud, strong bones and face of a Viking. A short crop of red hair hugged his scalp, matching eyebrows and lightly paler lashes framed small but intense blue eyes. It was almost as though he was the light to John Lancaster's dark and mysterious. Complete opposites.

He and John stood shoulder to shoulder in height, and Josie knew from experience, that both moved with lightning speed and lethal power. Both had mastered the art of combat until it had become like a second skin, a second thought.

"I know, you said, and I get *Thor* here as a babysitter," she snorted sullenly, still looking at Simon with distaste.

John nodded, a frown building between his brows. "And as I said before, I don't think it's wise to go to Prince Edward Island. There will be nothing there to see anyway."

Why not? Josie wanted to retort but held her tongue. She knew it would sound petulant and petty. And they had discussed it to no end. *Why does he keep reminding me?*

Prince Edward Island had been where her brother and young family once lived, on a farm growing potatoes and producing alternative fuel for the island. It had also been where Josie's father ended up secreting away her stasis pod. With her sleeping form within, Dr. Peter Bettencourt had tucked her into the dark and damp cellar amid bags of potatoes and stacks of jams and preserves.

How and why she'd ended up there was a complete mystery to her. She'd probably never know, and it was something she tried hard to accept. And now, no one was alive to tell her. Her father died—documented as killed mysteriously—soon after he'd hidden her, but not before his works were published and pandemonium spread throughout the scientific community. Suspended animation was here to stay!

The fate of her brother and family were also another mystery; one she loathed to know yet curiosity tweaked incessantly, begging her to find out. Had they also been murdered? Or did they live their lives out naturally? Did the world's economic downfall and famines affect them? Were their descendents still alive? Did she still have family? She wanted to know—but at the same time, she didn't.

"I know..." Josie replied quietly.

She and John had talked about it before—argued hotly.

Prince Edward Island was now home to one of the worlds' most highly sophisticated and ultra-secret defense posts for the Atlantic Basin—a facility run by the Lancaster government. What happened there, stayed there. Lethally adept and specifically trained operatives emerged from its training facilities, a place touted loosely as where Josie herself had come from. Close enough to the truth, yet wildly fictitious that even she had trouble keeping the 'facts' straight. Posing as an operative had its downfalls when it came time to being truthful. As it was, she'd now learned to keep her manner aloof and her mouth shut. But that didn't stop people from talking about her with keen interest.

It had been during the final stages of building an additional facility to the defense post when the giant earthmovers came across her stasis pod. There she lay, tucked away in the depths of a dilapidated farmhouse's basement cellar, covered in dust and cobwebs and the cool dank stench of long-decomposed potatoes and vegetables. No one gave it a second thought and just followed the expected routine procedure by calling upon the world's most renowned pod rehabilitation specialists, Quin and Madge Aguilar. And Madge, because of who she was and what she did, she was now dead—killed by the very fanatics who'd also kidnapped Josie. Josie's only crime had been of sleeping in a pod. And Quin now lived in hiding.

John continued to watch her with that all-seeing Lancaster stare.

"I know," she said again. "I said I won't go."

It pained her heart, but John was right. There really was nothing there for her, nothing familiar. Prince Edward Island was military base, nothing more. Cold, stark, deadly and secret, and any trace or memory of what the Island once was or had, was no longer.

With a sigh, she looked away, inspecting her reddened knuckles.

John gave her arm a quick and light squeeze to bolster her spirits. He didn't like to see her sad or troubled with those shadows in her eyes, it clotted his thoughts and made him worry unnecessarily for her.

Crocker returned with a tray laden with small savory treats and began dishing them out on a round table in a small breakfast alcove that overlooked a lush forest of mountain pines. With the table set, Crocker inclined her head in the direction and offered a selection of refreshments to choose from. John ordered three mineral waters and followed Josie to the food—her stomach never failed to dictate her actions before all else.

"But I'm still going to my old neighborhood," Josie announced, already stuffing a savory meat pie into her mouth. "I don't care if it's a hyper-super-whatever-mall, I want to see it. And I want to cruise up Yonge Street—at least *that's* still there."

~ * ~

John Lancaster reclined into his seat and groaned quietly. The shuttle had been in the air not ten minutes and already Josie and Simon argued about something quite inane. In a quiet corner at the rear of the shuttle, his aide, Loeb, discreetly and pointedly studied the prepared speech.

Whatever thoughts that ran through Loeb's mind regarding

Josie, never showed. He kept his face professionally and neutrally bland. Loeb was quite fond of Josie, considering both her and the president part-and-parcel of his job. But her abrasive manner had been known to grate upon his refined sensibilities.

John ran a distracted hand through his dark hair. It had been recently trimmed, a bit too low that his scalp felt exposed. His hair was a glossy, brownish-black and formed a small widow's peak at his forehead. His body, tall and slender, tapered like a diver's. His movements were lithe and fluid which only sharpened his predatory look. Dark and brooding in manner, he was a man completely comfortably in his own skin, accustomed to the power that he wielded as if it were second nature. He held his movements and actions in check, tightly reined in to contain some wild elemental force. He was a man always consciously aware and in control of his emotions. But sometimes, he could be afflicted with random outbursts, especially when something affected him so deeply that the only outlet was to roar. And roar he did.

All his life, he'd grown accustomed to being observed with loathing and with awe. Because of this, he'd learned to keep his face in control, his thoughts private, head bowed. He was young, thirty-seven, and just beginning to show the strain and stress of leadership around his eyes and mouth. His brows, thick and dark, moved as if by their own design by expressing a multitude of emotions that his face seemed incapable of expressing. And finally, dark hazel eyes set deep into his face that tended to glow with a dark menace—predatory.

When Josie first met him, she'd been chilled to the bone by his appearance. He was a contradiction; gentle yet wild, handsome yet marred, young yet ancient. John's deathly quiet nature, the way he held his head low, keeping his thoughts secret, and the habitual way of compressing his mouth only added to the powerful persona he exuded. Even his pale skin, the small and slightly upturned nose—delicate but brutally male—the sharp cheekbones and strong jaw, embodied the fearsome presence that was John Lancaster.

Josie still had so much she didn't know about him. Everyday she learned something new, whether good or bad—and he, likewise. To them, the other was vital an element to living, like oxygen. They rarely parted for extended periods, and even then, would remain in close contact with one another. They'd become to depend on each other. A unit.

John cracked open an eye, stealing a glance at his wife. The woman both frustrated him and fulfilled him so completely that his own life no longer seemed as important as it once had been. He knew she felt the same way about him, and that frightened him deeply. How often had she proved that fact was obvious enough! Too many times. Like taking bullets and hits from assassin's missiles for him, risking her life thoughtlessly, just to save his sorry ass.

Their brief marriage, not three months old, was already filled with danger and death. But it seemed somehow fitting that it should be so, considering the circumstances of how they met.

Josie had been suspected of being a terrorist and held against her will by none other than John himself. They had developed a begrudging friendship based on trust and honesty. A friendship that turned to love that sometimes, even he, was confused by. He couldn't imagine a life now without her in it—let alone how he managed to exist before without her.

He had been blindsided by it. He wasn't looking for love but got it full in the face like a brutal slap. It toppled his perfectly contained world on its rear end and he was still spinning from it—and grinning like a lovesick fool.

It had been her honest nature that first drew him in. Her curiosity, naturally so, but brought on by the circumstances of finding herself in a future she hadn't anticipated. These traits intrigued him until every thought since their first meeting ended up about her.

At first, he didn't know of her past and didn't realize just how 'old' she was. When he finally did find out, it had knocked him flat—senseless. And when his mind came reeling back to accept it, he felt protective and proud for her. He was determined to keep her safe, secret, and all to himself.

Mine, he'd heard himself say. And he continued to say it, every time he looked at her.

But by God, she could be stubborn and foolishly so, that it annoyed him to no end. Sometimes, he was tempted to knock her over the head and tie her up in a corner with a gag in her mouth. This marriage business seemed like nothing short of hard work...very hard work.

And what on earth are they nattering on about now?

"Oh, for fuck's sake. You're such an asshole, you know that?" Josie snapped with a frown.

Loeb could be heard clearing his throat in discomfort. People hardly—or simply didn't—swear in this future. He'd been vaguely briefed on Josie's past, the key dates and elements having been omitted. As far as anyone was concerned, she was a pod-survivor from fifty years ago, just as the first Lancaster took control of the world. The story went that when she'd been resuscitated and 're-trained' to serve as an operative for the current Lancaster. This would account for her crass, old-world behavior.

In the time of Dane Lancaster's rule, he'd implemented a strict new law—or death would ensue—that forbade the use of expletives among other things. It was a law that enforced the proper use of language, including the instillation of old traditions of formality, etiquette and behavior, and the resurrection of strong familial values that over the centuries had run askew.
And now, generations later, old habits died hard.

Loeb shifted uncomfortably in his seat, trying desperately to ignore Josie.

"Josie," Simon grumbled but obviously enjoying himself. "I'm not taking you to eat at some fast-food outlet. They serve nothing but poison in places like that—processed poison."

"I don't care. It's my stomach! And Fried City is *still* around. That's fucking unbelievable."

"What is this obsession with food?" Simon frowned.

"I do not have an obsession with food. And since when do you care about what I eat?"

Despite her fretful manner, she seemed touched to know that Simon cared by allowing a quick tug of a smile at the corner of her mouth.

John smiled despite himself as he glanced over at her. He knew that Simon's taste for the brutally vicious *Venom Cocktail* that he indulged in bothered her like a fussy mother. Apparently, it was known render the drinker insensible for hours.

But theirs was a special friendship, based on insults, so, John noted, Josie struggled to fix her face to look annoyed.

"If Aline heard you'd eaten some processed junk she'd have a fit."

"Only if you told her, and I bet you'd love to rat me out to her. You tell her everything, even if I stub a toe! And the next thing I know, I'm hauled off into Casualty with a bandage the size of a motherfu—"

"And the security measures alone will be a nightmare—let's not forget *that* aspect." Simon cut her off before she could finish her rant. Then informed her with procedural drivel about having a fleet of his operatives needing to do a sweep of the surrounding areas several hours beforehand, during, and after, to ensure the safety of the president's wife.

"And don't even think of hopping onto a public transport," he warned with narrowed eyes.

"Well," she mumbled sullenly. "I wouldn't do *that*. But don't tempt me or I just might."

"Will you two just shut up?" John sighed from his seat. Just listening to them was giving him a headache. He'd noted that Josie seemed high-strung for the last few hours. Nerves, he told himself. It must not be easy to be going back to your place of birth after three hundred years.

And then there was the function they had to attend.

In fact, he sighed again, *she must be downright petrified.*

She was.

Two

It was the first official outing for me. In the three months that we'd been married, this was the first time I would accompany John to a public function, with dignitaries and important people...and the media.

Touted as an Arts Expo to promote the unification of arts and culture across the world, John, as World President was scheduled to make a short welcoming speech then officially open the one-week exhibition and festivities. This would be followed immediately by a gala function that required me to mingle with the guests and dignitaries. I nearly choked on my own breath when I heard what I had to do.

For nearly a year, I'd been safely tucked away in the confines of the Citadel. Aside from quick and informal trips to the space station in Greenland—not that I was ever allowed to go off-planet—a secret getaway in Britain and Germany, and a quick and necessary ordeal in Bali, this would be the first time that I would leave Switzerland in an official capacity.

Two weeks prior, I'd been given the full crash-course in proper etiquette and social skills that were expected from a woman in my position.

I failed miserably.

Half listening and completely deaf from nerves, I fumbled my way through the proper responses required should a question be directed at me. Also on my list of required necessities was how to ignore the media and obtrusive individuals; how to talk about absolutely nothing and do so convincingly; and, most importantly, not to swear in public. The latter part had been written in big, bold capital letters.

I'd been given a full two-page agenda—hard copy for my benefit—since my computing skills with the ever-popular *Slide* personal units were still somewhat lacking. Each item listed, and they weren't many, had detailed instructions of what would be expected of me and what I was supposed to say and do. No variations unless in dire straits or threat to life.

Fantastic!

After appearing publicly with John for exactly three occasions, I was also expected to perform one photo opportunity with the press—solo—while the Home Guardian Foundation presented me with an honorary master key. Apparently, my name had been unanimously selected as the figurehead to represent their cause, which was for the protection, safety and defense of home, families, and loved ones. I wasn't required to say anything expect "Thank you, you are most kind," and then smile demurely.

Aside from the countless committees, boards, associations and groups that wished for my presence and name—and they were quite numerous—it was my identity and who I was that intrigued the public more. I was a mystery woman who'd appeared out of nowhere and stolen the heart of the president. Some speculated that I was an assassin, a deep-sleeper biding my time to then assassinate the unsuspecting world leader. Others lauded me for my amazing and daring feats—all exaggerated, of course—during the recent siege, and placed me on some platform like an idol. Had they known that I'd been scared shitless throughout it all, and winged through most it, they might have reconsidered.

And many still looked at me as if I were some deadly disease, a ghost brought back from the dead to raise havoc and mayhem the moment their backs were turned. *A hideous abomination* or *pod-survivor* could be heard in hushed tones or muttered whispers the minute my back was turned from people. It annoyed me sometimes, but I'd been learning to ignore it. It was, after all, the truth.

Abomination was a term used now to suggest anything that was, to be perfectly honest, unnatural. Like freaks of nature, a category into which I conveniently fell. And in this future, there was much that was unnatural. And unnatural they thought I was, a preserved relic. While they didn't know the absolute truth, a mere fifty-year old pod-survivor still turned the edges of most people's noses. If only they knew the truth!

But whatever the situation or suggestion, I was still talked about. People still wanted to see me.

John was strict and adamant that I remain unseen as much as possible. He constantly feared for my safety. The less I was exposed to the general public, the less chance of my being in harm's way. And, the less chance of him going into catatonic shock.

Once the official functions were dealt with, I would be allowed free time to do as I pleased, watched by none other than Simon. This, however, didn't mean that I'd be free of the ever-watchful eyes of the media. Best behavior at all times had been the directive Simon drilled into me in every other sentence during his detailed instructions about the events to come.

My wardrobe was given a drastic facelift as well. Having arrived initially with nothing more than a manky sweatshirt, oversized pants, and men's running shoes, I'd soon progressed to a standard-issue uniform—specifically for women detainees. Basically, I was primarily a prisoner when I'd first arrived to the Citadel. When my position changed from detainee to guest—honored guest—my wardrobe changed once more to a casual selection of the current trendy modes of fashion.

Now, as the wife of the world president, my wardrobe metamorphosed into something completely foreign. Elegant evening dresses, sleek suits, neat and tidy casual wear were just a few of the selections I had to choose from. However, John insisted that I maintain a more masculine persona while performing public duties to instill the fact that I was initially a former operative, which, of course, I really wasn't.

Direct, strong, and unafraid was how I was supposed to speak. Lethal, quick, and in control was what my actions and body language must portray.

Ignorant, hyperventilated, and scared shitless was what I actually was.

Borrowing the cool, calm, and sometimes cold manner that John usually plastered upon his face, I muddled through the first two of the three official duties required of me. I kept my features bland, my mouth shut, and head inclined to a twenty-degree bow—just as John did—and watched with minute and detailed care everything and everyone around me. John usually stood two feet to my right and Simon two steps behind us both—*en garde!*

I wore a specially made evening dress for the gala function. A halter-top for wardrobe security—in case of combat—that molded discreetly to my body in a simple and elegant column. The dress was made of a lightweight black material from a type of fabric I'd never seen before. It had muted silver trimmings to keep the theme of subtle military authority and power.

I was also armed to the teeth with weapons, a body-shield, and at least two explosives tucked into my pinned-up hair. The stiletto heels of my shoes each had concealed within a refill cartridge for my Snare Gun 3 that I'd holstered just above my left knee.

The design of the dress had been made exactly to John's specifications, where he insisted that it expose my scars. Along my right shoulder was a network of still-pink scars from the explosion some months back. Peeking up from my side, the wickedly straight line from a throwing disc—both were marks left to me for life when I saved John's. He was proud of them, as I was.

Secured to my left wrist, in a sleek, black holster made to look like an elegant cuff-bracelet with intricate designs in muted silver and gold was my krima stick—my *light sabre!* as I used to call it. I never left home without it. It was the one weapon I knew well, and used well. It also gave me the most feeling of comfort and security. I didn't care who saw me with it, nor did I try to hide it. After all, were it not for the krima, I wouldn't be here now. People knew this, saw this, and looked at me with a certain amount of awe, if not respectable fear. It kept them at a distance.

The krima—it *was* me—like a trademark.

And just what was a krima stick? Short for an eskrima stick, it was loosely based on the ancient Filipino stick-fighting weapon. A stick about two or three feet in length, brandished with skill and blinding speed to bring down enemies in close-range combat. The krima, as it was simply called now was *vastly* modified and modernized. About seven inches in length, and thick enough to hold comfortably, it used contained laser beams that shot out over a foot from both ends—making it a lethal and destructive weapon. It sliced through flesh and bone as well as some solid materials with precision and efficiency. It was *effective*, to say the least. These were the standard versions. I had a compact, mini-version, which shot out three-and-a-half inch beams on either side. Even the handle was smaller, thinner, and easier to hold.

John was likewise outfitted though he preferred the Snare Guns, or his own two fists, as opposed to the krimas. And I don't even want to know what Simon was packing.

Loeb, too, was similarly attired. Aside from his duties as personal aide to the president, Loeb had been trained as a Second Level operative and sometimes served as Simon's second-in-command during public outings such as this. He was one of Simon's shadows, though Simon obviously didn't need any help. He was, after all, a First Level. And First Levels rarely needed any assistance.

As I dumbly nodded and greeted a blur of dignitaries and guests, Loeb murmured their identities discreetly into my ear—no handshaking in case of contact explosives or poisons—I was pointedly directed through the sea of people to a safe and more secure area of the large reception hall. John's firm grip at my elbow kept me on a tight rein, yet he positioned himself so that with one quick pull, I'd be catapulted straight into Simon, who stood behind us, and then on to safety.

John was also a First Level in the art of combat. Both he and Simon could move like the wind, sail through the air defying gravity and blend into the scenery as if they belonged there. They were like the elements, calm and serene, silent and deadly, wild and brutal. They were lethal and adept, and they were legendary…

Their training, loosely based on the ancient Japanese art of Bushido, they were Bushi—the warrior class. Though no one ever mentioned it, or categorized it, that was the code they lived by, as did many others in this century. It was a different time now, a different world. People fought for their lives with skills learned from childhood, and thought nothing of it. It was a way of life—fight to survive, literally.

And death and danger ruled our lives; it had been this way since the day John and I had met. Now was no different from any other. I'd become more accustomed to the daily threats to our lives, if that were at all possible. My brief and rushed training in self-defense had taught me the extreme basics of survival and combat, but it was still something that froze me to the core when I least expected it—the constant fear and uncertainty.

Could a person ever get used to it? Looking at John, with his calm and cool composure, I supposed one could. He was, after all, born into a life already riddled with danger and threats. He'd been conditioned from birth, it would seem, unlike me, who'd been thrown into this life by the circumstances of my fate.

But would I hesitate to dispense the lethal knowledge I'd acquired? No. Not for a moment. It definitely was a different world from the one I'd left behind. And I, too, had changed.

John directed us to a spot close to the approved and designated exit, located behind a large potted palm. A secure area, crammed with five operatives, two discreetly posed as invited guests while the other three stood severely at their posts near the exit. They were dressed in black suits with red trim, the mark of Simon's Elite team. On their faces, they wore near transparent headgear and goggles that monitored and screened every miniscule movement and individual around.

With our backs turned to them, we watched the flow of people before us. Loeb and Simon stood in front as a buffer. People came and went in a reserved manner, greeting us formally, politely. I let John do the acknowledging while I stood composed, aloof and cold, to any who saw. I was grateful for the fact that John insisted from early that I shouldn't be allowed to speak, or behave like some docile and charitable wife of a president. He wanted me to portray someone of power and disdain to keep the simpering politicians and 'beggars' at bay. It worked.

Yes, death and danger lurked everywhere in our lives, and today was no exception.

Regardless of all the tight security measures and screenings, danger still managed to slip through.

A portion of the glass-domed roof broke away like the crashing of a crystal chandelier. It showered us with tempered glass and metal fragments, muting the initial explosion that preceded it. I felt myself being hurtled behind John, caught deftly by one of Simon's men, then pushed sideways into the arms of another. I barely had time to register people screaming and chaos erupting, before I was out the exit and standing with one of the Elites in a quiet corridor. He talked rapidly to someone through his headgear.

John, Simon, and Loeb joined us not three seconds later. John grasped me by the arm, his face tight and severe.

"Time to go," he said in a clipped tone. "You'd better cancel your tour tomorrow."

Did he sound somewhat pleased when he said that? I couldn't be sure. Ignoring my plans for tomorrow, I matched his stride as we walked briskly down the corridor to another exit, and then into a waiting transport vehicle.

"What just happened?" I asked.

"Clumsy saboteurs," Simon said helpfully as we hopped into the vehicle.

What the vehicle was, I wasn't sure. It was something like a tank with the interior of an air shuttle, and the speed and agility of a Formula One race car.

"It's just an arts expo. Why would people want to sabotage it? What's the point?"

"Takes all kinds to cause a stir," Simon chuckled. He was accustomed to the point where he no longer flinched at these minor disturbances. "The local police can handle it. Nothing to do with us."

Both Simon and John once headed the world unit for counter-terrorism. They were a deadly combination, managing to shut down and eliminate numerous organizations. Whatever they did to achieve this goal, they never talked about nor did I care to know. So a simple aerial disturbance with an unclear cause was nothing to raise a brow over. It was business as usual.

"But just to be on the safe side," John said from beside me, already leaning back into his seat and getting ready to enjoy the ride back to our hotel. "You'd better stick close by tomorrow."

"I heard you the first time," I snapped tersely.

He flicked me an annoyed glance and then looked away, working his mouth into a compressed line.

"I'll take you myself another time. I promise," he said quietly, so only I could hear, but he wouldn't look at me. He glowered at the floor instead.

I glared at him for a moment longer than necessary. "I'll be holding you to that—you can be sure of it." Then, I settled back into my seat, snaking my hand out to hold his.

Pesky little saboteurs or not, it still rattled my nerves.

~ * ~

Josie lay in bed, tossing and turning most of the night feeling fretful and annoyed. Though she told herself it was pointless to get all worked up over it, safety being the priority that it was, it still didn't take the sting out of being disappointed. Seeing her city once more had been practically the highlight of the entire trip.

Meanwhile, sleep eluded her.

John, next to her, grunted his displeasure with each restless toss.

He said nothing. To say anything now would start another of their raging arguments. Not that they argued a lot. Like most couples it was about the usual things, only their arguments were notably...notorious. Also, he hadn't quite forgiven her for snapping at him like an ill-tempered horse.

He told himself that it was only because Loeb had been there to witness it, and that Josie should've used some measure of discretion. But of course, that wasn't it really. He was unaccustomed to being spoken to so abruptly. No one ever dared speak to him in that manner.

Until he met Josie.

Besides, John thought, this argument would be absolutely pointless. He knew well enough that she knew it too. But it was her nature to grumble about things like this just to prove a point. Very childish, in his opinion.

"All right," he muttered to her, knowing full well that she was wide-awake. "I'm sorry, but you know the situation. A disruption during the gala with us both present is just too close for comfort. For you to then go gallivanting around the city would be just plain lunacy. You know that, don't you?" He stared up at the dark ceiling imagining what her expression would be like. Murderous, was the first thought that came to mind.

Josie sighed and rolled onto her back. "Of *course*, I know that. Don't speak to me as if I'm a child. I'm not stupid. Just upset, is all. Disappointed..." She wouldn't pout, she told herself, but found it hard not to. Thank God, it was dark.

"And I said I'll take you once things quiet down. Maybe in a couple of months, we'll come unofficially. No one needs to know."

"I know. You promised." It sounded too much like an accusation. She cringed in the dark.

John heard it, chose to ignore it—his mind was on other things. He rolled to his side and propped his head on his hand. "So can we just get to sleep, then? Our shuttle leaves first thing in the morning." He reached a tentative hand to touch her stomach. "And I never said you were stupid."

"Yes, you have. Countless times." There was no sarcasm in her voice. She wriggled up closer then turned her back to him and jumped. "What the fuck is that?"

"Hmm?" he murmured. His erection, at full mast, poked her back.

"Don't you ever get tired?"

"Well, I figured that if you weren't sleepy and keeping me up—pardon the pun—we might as well make the most of the night. Dawn *is* still a long way."

Josie giggled despite herself and snuggled even closer, shifting slightly so that John would have a clear path to get between her thighs. His quick and clever hands were already investigating her there, causing her breath to hitch. She tilted her head back to find his mouth, he kissed her hungrily and brought her to climax with his hand before she even had a chance to take in another breath. Then, in one quick and sure move, he took her from behind.

It was fast, hard, and desperate. The frustration of the day working its way out, and it was what they both needed now. Afterwards, they lay still joined, breathing heavily and clinging to one another.

"I'm sort of glad not to see it just yet," Josie said quietly. Her throat felt ragged from the exertion. Her lungs ached for more air and John's heavy arm draped around her didn't help. "I don't know why. Maybe I'm a little scared to see it again."

"It's changed quite a bit, I've seen the old archive images." John kissed the back of her neck and gave her a light squeeze. He was close to dozing; the scent of her body furred his mind. He willed himself to pay attention but it was a losing battle. Even his speech slurred slightly.

"That, it has." Josie sounded distant. "Would you go back if it were you? To see?"

"Yes, I would." He ran a hand over her shoulder. "And you want to, I know you. I'll be there with you when you're ready...you won't have to reminisce on your own."

"I know." She smiled in the darkness. "I know."

~ * ~

The door sensors rang, causing them both to wake with a start. Josie muttered something that sounded very close to the smallest animal in a litter while John shook his head to clear it. He could've sworn he was only just resting his eyes for ten minutes.

"Who is it?" he called out knowing that only Simon would dare ring so late at night. He was up in a flash, stepping into his pants. Something urgent must've happened in order for Simon to come calling. He gave Josie a quick cautionary glance, waited for her to cover herself up clumsily then opened the door.

Simon looked tense. He had a hand pressed against the doorframe and gave John a dour look. John nodded and stepped aside for his friend to enter.

Josie muttered some more and struggled with the covers, tucking them securely about her.

"We've a situation," was all Simon said, quietly.

Josie felt something greasy slithering through her stomach. How many times had she heard him say just that before something horrible happened? She bit back an oath and stared silently at Simon.

"Michael Ho."

After a moment's silence, John ran a hand through his hair. "Where?"

"Direct link to us. He wants to talk."

"What the fuck for? He's still alive?" Josie blurted. A cold clutch of fear gripped her heart. "I thought he was supposed to be dead."

"It was never confirmed—just suggested." John's face was grim. "Did he say what he wanted?"

Simon shook his head. "We'll find out in the morning. I've prepped everyone and the shuttle is ready. We leave in one hour." He looked at Josie with a wink and a click of the tongue. "I suggest you get dressed but I'm sure the media wouldn't mind you naked. Me, personally, I'd rather see a warthog having a crap while standing in a fly-infested cesspool."

Josie snorted, gathered up the sheets and headed straight to the en suite bathroom.

Simon plucked at John's arm to stop him. "He wants to talk to Adam as well."

"Does he now?" With slow deliberate movements, John pulled a jersey over his head and smoothed it over his body, thinking of something. "Now, I wonder why?"

"My thoughts exactly."

"What time is he meaning to chat with us?"

"Nine." Simon flicked a glance at his watch. "More than enough time to get back."

Josie padded out, fully dressed. It didn't take her long to throw on a sweatshirt, pants, and soft shoes. She held a large bag that contained all her other clothes and toiletries. She traveled light.

"I heard. I thought no one was supposed to have known Adam's circumstances." Josie dropped the bag by the door and walked back to the bedside table to retrieve her personal unit, which she dropped into her pocket. She'd only just gotten it from John, and had yet to work out all of its functions. She'd hoped that during the quieter moments of their trip, she'd have a chance to do so. Called a *Slide*, the preferred choice of personal communication devices, it was a modernized mobile phone and personal computer all in one. Only three inches in width and about four in length, a simple press of a button on its side and it extended another few inches on either side. That much she figured out how to do.

"Which means there is either a leak or Adam has been in contact," Simon replied.

"Whichever it is, I intend to plug it up." John answered in a low voice.

"How can there be a leak?" Josie asked and hoisted the bag onto her shoulder, ignoring John's extended hand and offer to carry it for her.

"People talk, they see things, no matter how careful we are," he said simply. "I *will* find out."

Three

Adam Lancaster was a sick man. He'd been sick all his life. For as long as he could remember, he was either in a hospital or confined to a bed, receiving one treatment after another until his body and mind no longer focused upon it. He could remove himself to another place, a place where no pain existed, no suffering—a place where he alone was in control.

He did that once, and what followed was a madness that nearly killed him as well as his family. And it had made him kill his own father. It was a poor excuse, the reason to murder, but it was so.

He was a very sick man.

Adam blinked away that thought, took a breath, and concentrated on calm. These last few months in exile seemed to bring out his melancholy side. He found he'd far too much time to reflect on what could have been, should have been. Some days, his mind confused and tricked him.

Funny, since his mind was what made him. Made him successful. Alas, such was the existence of a man in exile.

Yes, he regretted what he did. It sickened him now to think that he could've done such a thing. What was it that drove a son to kill his own father? Greed and power? Some envy?

No, sickness, he reminded himself. Or, maybe it was hate, plain and simple.

He'd done it because he wanted to. And then he'd killed again because he had to—that day, when the boy who became Uron Koh killed his own father, Lorcan, who'd been Josie's protector. And then Koh turned to kill Josie. So Adam had to kill the boy, stop him.

To stop the madness that created the madness. Yes, he was, indeed, a sick man.

His mind swirled with images and voices, bright slashes of colors and sounds. He felt confused and calm at the same time, alert and numb.

Too much time to think.

Penance? A little atonement? No. Punishment? And this was his purgatory.

It was all of the above. He paid for it now, and he welcomed it with a certain pride.

Pride. When nothing else was left in a person, pride was the one thing that they couldn't take from him. Whatever he did in life, he always did it with determination and pride.

And acceptance.

He'd accepted the fact that he was sick and found ways to work around it, to use his mind. He'd accepted that he wasn't suitable to lead the world, and chose to follow a different path, again his mind. His mind was the strongest part of his body. He trusted his mind more than he did his heart. His heart confused things, made him weak and vulnerable—tempted him.

His heart was in love and it shamed him that he could be weakened so. It had been his heart that brought him back to the Citadel. He was a fool. A sick fool. To think a woman like her would ever return the love he had for her. He knew better than to indulge in such wishful thinking.

Yet, pine for her, he did. And hope. His heart kept tricking his mind with promises.

From the first moment he'd seen her, she had stolen his heart—wrenching it apart and twisting it like a giant clawed hand. She didn't know who he was then. He'd been a mere shadow, a figure in the dark, a frightful menace.

But he saw her.

And his world stopped making sense. He had to follow her, and follow her he did, straight into the waiting arms of honesty and retribution. He'd convinced himself that he would play it out and see where it led him. After all, he'd done wrong—he knew that. Life in exile wasn't so bad, considering what the alternative could've been.

Confessing to the conspiracy to overthrow the government—

and to murder—didn't hurt him as he thought it would. In fact, he felt very liberated by it. As though he had a new clean slate upon which to work. But, like most confessions, his had come too late. And she was already in love with his brother.

Now, she was married—untouchable. He would never dream of acting upon his thoughts or desires. To do so would somehow stain and dirty the image he had of her—the pedestal he'd put her on. She was pure, she was the light, she was a mystery; like a diamond with a multitude of gloriously lighted facets.

His mind had accepted this fact, but his heart still betrayed him every time he saw her, as it betrayed him now when he smiled broadly as Josie walked through the door and greeted him.

She'd become a lot like John now, Adam mused. Like forgetting to knock, doing so on purpose. She used to knock or announce herself before but no longer did. And it was so like her to ignore what people thought of their friendship, especially his brother John, who disapproved strongly.

Adam was a prisoner, in exile within his own country. His sole purpose was to be sequestered, to be used for his mind when called upon. He had been a strategist and was good at it. He'd also been required to assist with the rehabilitation of those injured or maimed during the siege—but he found his phobias prevented him. He did try, very hard, but it left him ill and unable. His sister Aline had intervened, John remained nonplussed. Adam no longer existed to him.

Josie visited him regularly, or as regularly as she could. He knew she was still very disturbed over the fact that he'd killed his own father, and betrayed John—lied. They never spoke of it, yet it hung over them like a dark and suffocating cloud. He was almost glad for it—it allowed him to keep his distance. And he knew she would never cross over that particular bridge.

She belonged to John.

Adam watched as Josie strode into the room, looking upset over something. How well he knew her, her mannerisms. She occupied his mind at almost every hour of the day, and even infiltrated his dreams.

Yes, something bothered her.

"How was your trip? Did you see everything you wanted to

see?" Adam asked. He would've touched her, but his phobias prevented him. He was an obsessive-compulsive, and human contact was just one of many things he didn't do.

~ * ~

Adam cocked his head, and appeared to take note of the tense look about her. Josie knew her face gave her away, even to her, it felt strained.

"We had to cut it short," she simply said.

Josie glanced over her shoulder to look back at the door. They were in Adam's private rooms, located in a very secure and out-of-the-way enclosure just west of the Citadel's southern sector where she and John resided. Adam had been allowed a small apartment that faced a glorious view of the mountainside with a stingy glimpse of the famous Doucet Falls.

The apartment was simply furnished, very basic. He wasn't allowed the use of any communications equipment or devices. In fact, he'd been ordered to live like a hermit—a monk—with nothing but himself to keep him company, not even books or television to pass his time.

His sister Aline visited often and sometimes brought food and small treats. Besides Josie, Aline was the only other person who visited regularly. Sometimes John walked in, mainly to consult Adam's intricate mind or ask questions regarding the strangling members of the group who had tried to overthrow the government. That was the extent of Adam's contact with the outside world. And even then, they weren't supposed to talk about current events in any detail.

"What is it?" Adam asked with a slight frown.

"They'll be coming round shortly to see you. I told them I'd come here so you could get dressed and ready, I know how you love surprises." Josie shrugged, remembering John's sullen face when she told him that she wanted to see Adam before the appointment with Michael Ho. He wasn't pleased though he didn't ask why. He'd learned to not question Josie's motives for wanting to continue a friendship with his brother. To be perfectly honest, she didn't know herself why she was drawn to Adam. Maybe she felt sorry for him. Or maybe because, like her, he was an outsider—had become an outsider.

"I sense trouble." Adam extended a hand, offering her a seat in one of the terrace chairs.

Josie knew that Adam preferred to spend his days on the terrace, gazing out at the view. It was lush and green as the last breaths of summer bloomed in full across the Swiss Alps. The mountains were capped with brilliant white snow, the air crisp and clean with the sharp tang of pine needles. The weather screens were up to buffer the UV lights and purify the air, but they didn't spoil the pristine view in the least.

It was early morning, not yet seven, and Adam still lounged in his robes. Solitary confinement had somewhat diminished his strict wardrobe habits, causing him to spend half the day in his sleepwear before he showered and made himself ready for evening. Dinner was still something that he made sure he was properly attired for—despite eating alone.

Josie ignored the chair and propped instead against the wall of the terrace. She idly plucked a leaf from a trailing vine and directed a calculating look at Adam.

"How does Michael Ho know you're here?"

Surprised, Adam simply stared at her for a moment. "I don't know."

He sat as if the wind had knocked him. He looked pale, sallow. Over the months of confinement, he'd lost more weight, causing his already stooped shoulders to curve inwards. Adam, nearly ten years older than John, but now looked closer to thirty years his senior. His once lightly greying dark hair, so much like John's, had turned light with silver. The face, also similar to his brother's, only longer and more elegant, was now hollowed and creased with worry lines around his mouth and forehead.

"Has he been spotted?" he asked. "I would have sworn he'd been killed."

"Yeah, me too."

Josie watched Adam, beginning to recognize his mannerisms and habits, enough to know that he was just as surprised as she was about the news of Michael Ho.

Glancing about his spartan rooms, she also knew that he had no device to transmit messages. The fact that the entire area was shielded with a deflector signal that repelled and prevented any form of electronic signal from coming or going also compounded this. He wasn't even allowed paper or writing materials, yet was allowed free access to sharp utensils like cutlery and glassware. To help him terminate himself, should he wish to do so? And therefore easing the problem and burden of keeping him sequestered like the deep, dark secret that he was.

John knew that Adam would never resort to self-termination. He knew is brother, knew enough of his phobias and quirks to know that to commit suicide, you had to bleed, hurt, or suffer. And Adam didn't like any of those. He would choose poison over anything else. But even that would mean he either had to ingest something foreign that wasn't food, or stick himself in the arm. Adam was already his own prisoner, the apartment, merely the vessel he hid in.

"He's asked for you—by name."

"Me?" Adam frowned and cocked his head abruptly to her. "But he doesn't even know the real me. I'd always been careful to disguise myself. And I'm sure that Uron—I mean, Max—did not divulge my secret to him. Ho was merely a pawn. An important pawn, but dispensable all the same."

"I know what your answer will be, but I have to ask. You know John will, too." Josie felt a little uncomfortable for thinking of it, but she knew it had to be said.

"I did not contact him. How could I?" Adam raised his arms dramatically about him to indicate his living situation. "The fight has left me, Josie. You know that best of all."

She nodded. He sounded deflated, tired—like a shriveled old man living in a younger body, a body worn and beaten from sickness…and shame.

"John thinks there's a leak."

"He would think that. He may be right—oh, a problem to solve!" Adam replied with widened eyes.

He appeared to go on alert. Josie could imagine his quick mind darting erratically, his blood pumping with excitement. She knew he loved to solve problems. It was something he was good at.

"But from where, Adam? Everyone's been very careful. People think you died that day. And there's only the droids that secure this area. Even if you've been seen, no one really knows or remembers what you look like, or will think that you're John's brother."

"Droids can be hacked into." Adam shrugged mildly. "And as I recall, Max used a lot of techs to help him get into this place. If I remember correctly, quite a few of them managed to escape."

"True. That's why I don't trust those fucking things," she muttered.

"Josie!" Adam looked annoyed. It upset him greatly that she swore like an outdated pirate.

Adam knew she was a pod-survivor, though he didn't know the full truth. It was the one thing that John insisted she never reveal to Adam. Knowing what Adam was like, she agreed, but sometimes she nearly forgot herself. It was very hard to keep a secret like that, especially when the handful of people who did know, were the people she saw most regularly and talked to the most. Besides Simon, Aline and her partner Rand knew, and so did Trudi. Of the fours others who also knew the truth, three were dead.

"Sorry. You know what I mean." Josie stood to pace the confines of the terrace. "But can they access the droids here?"

"Anything is possible. The Citadel is the most secure place in the world, yet it was broken into and taken under siege. John has weeded most of the infiltrators, and we know some have managed to slip through his fingers. Max had a long time to prepare for his day in the sun. Some could still be living among us. The leak could come from inside. Or…" Adam appeared to be mulling over an interesting thought. "Or, Ho could just be bluffing. Guessing. Whatever he is, he is not stupid. I think maybe we should insist that I am dead—call him out and frustrate him. Confuse things a bit. Make him uncertain."

"And is that the mind of a strategist at work?" The cool voice of John called out from behind them.

Adam sighed and turned in his chair. Josie merely looked annoyed.

"Good morning, John."

"Adam." John inclined his head stiffly and his mouth clamped tightly together. He refused to look at Adam, his head bowed lower than usual and he appeared to be rolling something bitter on his tongue.

Josie noted that he was angry at something, possibly at her

for wanting to give Adam a heads up before the meeting. She recalled the brief argument they had earlier. John had wanted to catch Adam unawares, to see his reaction—for himself. But Josie, for some inexplicable reason, wanted to tell Adam herself.

"You have to admit, what he suggests makes some sense." Josie said matter-of-factly from next to Adam, watching closely as John worked to control his agitation.

"And as he implies, Ho is not a stupid man. If he wants to talk to Adam, then he must know he lives. And if by showing off Adam, he tells us what it is he wants, then that is what we will do." John directed a cold glance at his brother. "This is not a game we play here."

"Isn't it?" Adam gave his brother an airy shrug. "Everything is a game. We just have to know the rules...and bend them to suit."

"Get dressed, Adam." John turned his back to his brother and looked into Josie's cool green stare. She seemed to be regarding him with a mixture of amusement and wariness. He squinted back at her. "We're going sub-level to meet with Ho."

Adam silently obliged but not before huffing out a sigh. He gave off the appearance of someone who'd become quite accustomed to life in solitude, and leaving it was nothing short of a mild annoyance.

"What is it?" John asked Josie in low and quiet tones.

"Nothing," she replied with a raised brow.

She noted the coldness in his voice; it seemed to match the mood he was in. She realized that there was still a great deal that she'd have to learn about her husband—his moods could turn in the blink of an eye, sometimes for no apparent reason. His mood earlier, after their argument, seemed much milder than what she saw now. She could only assume that something had happened since then.

"You speak to him like as if he were a piece of shit," Josie continued.

"You know I no longer trust him," he replied simply, as if that explained everything.

Josie made a derisive noise. "He's still your brother. He lives alone like a fucking shut-in and he said he was sorry. Can you not see the regret on his face? How sick he is? He needs help, not your scorn."

John sighed with something like impatience.

It was an argument—a sore point—that they replayed over and over again. It varied slightly with each venting, but it was never resolved. Today, it held a note of finality. And the black mood John was in now, he wanted it done. Over with. He still hadn't gotten over the sting he felt when Josie *insisted* she see Adam before the meeting with Ho. They didn't have a raging fight over it this morning, only a mild disagreement, but it had certainly felt like a slap in the face to him.

Like a betrayal.

John regarded his wife with what he hoped was a cold glower. He forgot sometimes that she was still quite young, somewhat innocent and impetuous, if that were the correct words for her naiveté. She still saw the good in people, at least, good enough that they could be forgiven from whatever evils they had committed. Forming a friendship with Adam, however odd it seemed to John, to her, was the most natural thing in the world. While that wasn't a bad trait to have, and the main reason he'd fallen in love with her, it threatened to blind her to dangers.

"Yes. He is my brother, unfortunately. That cannot be changed. But I no longer care to hold any ties with him. You know where I stand on the matter." John turned away in annoyance. *She has a lot to learn about people.* "Why are we even discussing this?"

"No reason," Josie snapped, bringing John's attention back to her. "At least you still have a brother."

John flinched. He could hear the bitterness in her voice. He knew, more than anyone, the hurt she'd suffered, the loss she felt. Maybe, too, he could see her needing this argument and needing an Adam in her life. Her mind, of late, was on her family. He immediately felt remorse for being so brutishly cold to her.

"This is not about you." He hoped it sounded sincere enough, but even to him, it sounded harsh and brittle.

"I never said it was." She leveled her eyes on him. "It's all about you
and how you can't forgive your brother. Okay, it's a big *thing* to forgive, what he did, even though he's sorry, but you'll forgive me if I want to maintain some form of contact with him. You seem so bent out of shape by my even speaking about him—let alone visiting him.

He *saved my life* remember? I owe him a friendship, at least."

John compressed his mouth and looked away. How could he ever forget? He'd been frozen with fear—lying on the floor injured and bleeding—when that madman Max stood poised over Josie, ready to impale her with her own krima stick. If Adam hadn't shot Max, Josie would've been lost to him forever. It had been the one reason—the only reason—that his brother still lived. Under normal circumstances, he would've been tried then immediately executed for treason, conspiracy, and patricide. And John would have done it himself, personally.

"Josie, you don't need to ask for my forgiveness. And there is nothing *to* forgive," he said finally, carefully. "I have faith…what I mean to say is, I understand your motives and your reasons for wanting a friendship with Adam. Regardless of what I think or feel, your instincts are always good. I trust you more than I trust myself. You know that. It has never failed you, or me, before—it should not in the future. I just…" John took a controlled breath. "I just wish that you were more…careful." He bit off the last words with much difficulty.

"Less trusting in others, that's what you really mean." She folded her arms across her chest and regarded him coldly. Her voice sounded icy.

"Yes," John replied harshly. Relenting, he shook his head and raised a hand in apology, but saw the anger still in her eyes. He lowered his hand. "Josie, I just ask that you be wary."

"I'm not some gullible fool, you know."

"I know that." He hissed in anger and returned her icy stare. He took a step closer and nearly snarled. He wanted to reach out, grab her, and shake her until some form of sense was knocked into her. "The man has killed—murdered. Calculated and methodically planned and executed. Not the clean death of combat, in defense or even in honour. It was dirty, cowardly, and unnecessary. Murder is murder. I do not care how much regret he has or shows. What he has done cannot be undone. He has lied and manipulated us to save his own sorry skin and you wish me to forgive him? I cannot—not him. Do what it is you must—I'll not question it. Just *be careful*. For me. He deserves whatever punishment he gets. The more he suffers, the better. And don't expect me to lose any sleep over it."

John stared hard at his wife for a moment longer. *Enough of this! She needs to learn that people aren't all good—the sooner she learns, the better.*

Josie gave him an unreadable expression, a crooked twist to her mouth like she had eaten something off.

"Right," Adam cleared his throat from across the room and presented them with a good-natured smile. "Now that we've gotten that off our chest, shall we go?"

Four

The holographic image of Michael Ho—lifelike and actual size—cast itself into the centre of the room. His neat black hair was slickly combed back against his scalp. His mixed-Asian features were smooth, creamy, and composed in his accustomed pose of faux pleasantness. He looked like an enlightened spiritualist, hands clasped before him like a monk.

We were in a private and secure communications room in the secondary sub-levels, deep in the bowels of the Citadel. It had been a home away from home for both John and Simon, having spent a number of years living and working underground, seeking out the many factions of terrorists. They knew this place like the back of their hands…and then some.

We arrived through a secret elevator and passageway, unseen and therefore unquestioned. The secrets of the Citadel were simply too great and so vast, that everyday I discovered yet another wonderment.

I stood off to one side, out of range from the transmitter's scanners. The cold manner in which John had spoken to me earlier still irritated me. But there'd been a mild ring of truth to what he said. I *was* a bit too trusting, I couldn't help it. Like trying to unlearn a mother's lesson—it went against my grain not to be trusting. John was right, this wasn't the same world I'd come from, dangers lurked everywhere. I had to adapt. But he could've at least expressed himself a little more eloquently that it didn't make me feel like a complete dimwit.

Adam, too, positioned himself out of sight. Simon stood

before the transmitter and glowered menacingly at Ho. To Simon's right, also out of view, John appeared to be inspecting the form of Ho with disdain, like one would to a mound of cow shit. Any disagreement we had earlier, he appeared to have forgotten all about it.

Seemingly aware that he was under this close inspection, a world away, Ho stood aloof and impassive. He had a composed and smarmy smile pasted onto his face. Every so often, he raised his head as if to look up to the heavens for inspiration.

"Michael Ho." Simon regarded him coldly.

"As I said before, I do not wish to speak with you." Ho sighed with a resigned smile. "Where is Adam Lancaster?"

"What do you want?" John stepped into view. No doubt, from Ho's perspective, he appeared as though entering a stage from its side.

John stood before the transmitter, dark and brooding. His head bowed low like a bull before he charged, and those dark eyes stared down at Ho from beneath his brows.

"President Lancaster." Ho seemed pleased to see him and broke out into the beaming smile that never failed to make my skin crawl. It made his cheeks rise, causing his eyes to slant even more. "And how is Josie? Your charming wife."

"Knitting," John replied with a flat, low voice, slightly bored.

"Indeed," Ho continued to smile. "She has become very domesticated, I see."

"Indeed."

I felt a flush of anger on my face. *Domesticated? What an insult!*

I remembered Ho from when I lived with Lorcan Wellesley, it seemed like a lifetime ago. I'd never liked him then and never trusted his unctuous demeanor. My feelings hadn't changed.

"Is she there? Oh, of course she is. I hear she rarely leaves your side these days."

"I ask again, what is it you want?" John clamped his mouth tightly and seemed to be controlling the urge shout. I could see he'd grown impatient with this game.

"Adam. Let me see him."

"He is dead."

From beside me, Adam raised a brow and looked at his brother with interest. So did I. Sometimes, I wondered exactly how the mind of John Lancaster worked. What was he playing at now? At other times, I marveled at how alike both Lancasters were—how tricky and sneaky they could be. Regardless of their differences, when it came to protecting the Citadel and its inhabitants, their own, they stood surprisingly united. They come from the same tree, was all Simon would say, shrugging as if it were the most obvious thing.

"Come now, stop telling tall tales." Ho showed a slight hint of annoyance. He brushed at a speck of lint from his sleeve. Long, graceful fingers smoothed the fabric with deliberately slow and careful strokes. His face completely composed now. "You may have fooled the world at large, but you have not fooled me."

"It was not my intention to fool you," John replied, he allowed himself a small purse of the lips. "We had heard that you yourself were dead."

"Alas, no." Ho beamed with another of his brilliant smiles. "I am like a cat, with many lives to spare."

"It would appear so. But that can be fixed, if you like." Simon, showing his distaste, curled a wicked smile on his face and took a step closer. "Come now, stop wasting our time. What do you want?"

Ho inclined his head as if conferring with someone at his right. He paused a moment in thought. "Josie," he called out, still facing the mysterious person on his right. "How badly do you wish to meet your dear great niece? Or shall I say, your great niece…seven times removed."

A hushed silence followed for exactly five seconds, where John merely frowned and Simon seemed to be doing some mental calculations with a perturbed look. I shook my head, positive that I must've heard wrong. I looked to Adam, as he was closest, to find him with eyebrows raised high upon his brow. He cast me a suspicious look, the beginnings of some realization seemed to dawn on him.

Simon was first to recover, his dour expression having never changed. "You amuse us, Ho. You are obviously playing a game that you alone know the rules to."

"Indeed, it would appear so." Greatly pleased with the effect that his statement had made, Ho continued to beam at us.

"You will enlighten us, no doubt." In a quiet voice John stepped forward, past Simon, to glare at Ho. They stood feet apart. Ho was a full head shorter than John.

"Of course," Ho said. "You see, after Wellesley fled his home, I had the house to myself. I found some very interesting discs of recordings…"

Shit!

My stomach dropped to my feet. The blood left my face and an involuntary gasp from my mouth. Adam moved a fraction closer, but didn't reach out for fear of touching me.

Until recently, I'd worn a pendant that contained a copy of these recordings. It told the story of my entire life, created by my father three hundred years ago. The pendant was now safely stored in a vault in our bedroom, but I still instinctively put a hand around my throat.

Before that, I carried with me a chunky image-bank unit that Quin Aguilar had stored all the original discs onto. The original discs were then returned to me during my time with Lorcan Wellesley. Quin by then had gone into hiding and saw to it that I had these as keepsakes. Of course, as I couldn't control the rapid series of circumstances that brought me to the Citadel, those same old discs had been completely forgotten about—until now.

"…very old recordings," Ho continued, bringing my mind abruptly back to current issues, "on very *primitive* discs. And what should I discover?"

"So, the secret comes out—as all secrets eventually do." Simon shrugged nonchalantly. "What of it?"

"What indeed." Ho seemed very pleased. "I took it upon myself to do some research. It took some time, and a great deal of effort and funds, but
I have located Josie's family. Her sole remaining family."

"And how is it that you were able to find something we could not?" John asked.

"You simply did not know where to look."

Where had we heard that before? Adam himself had once said that when we questioned him a few months ago regarding a graphic novel that featured a character called Uron Koh—a character that eventually overthrew the evil empire in its fictitious world. And Max Wellesley had fashioned himself in the likeness of this character. John and Simon had spent long months in search for his identity, and came up with nothing.

And now...this. I couldn't help but wonder if the resources of the Lancaster government were slightly lacking.

"Then where is this so-called niece of my wife?"

"She is with me. And she would dearly like to meet her great aunt."

"Introduce us, then," John dared in his silky, low voice.

"In good time, she is a little shy. Like your dear wife."

"So the question, yet again, is what do you want?" Simon asked.

"I want Adam," Ho said simply. "And if I don't have him, I will not only expose the truth to the world at large—and make a great amount of money selling it off—but you can be assured that it will make your wife's life very uncomfortable. Oh, and I'll kill her only remaining family. It's your choice."

"That's not much of a choice you've given us, now is there?" Simon snorted. "Two threats in one, either way, you're going to do one or the other. Try again."

Ho sighed. "Adam. I want him."

"Why?" John looked down his nose at Ho's image. He appeared to be enjoying his height advantage, like a schoolyard bully tormenting a small child.

"Because he took something from me. And I want it back."

Despite the tight control over his face, John cut Adam a sidelong glance that was cold, icy, and laced with fury. "Did he, now?"

Adam, who took this as his cue to appear, cleared his throat and approached the transmitter. His hands were tucked behind him and he smiled with easy effort; practiced and regal like one born and bred to behave so, which he was and which sometimes, I tended to forget.

"Michael, a pleasure as always," he said.

Ho returned his smile and inclined his head. "Adam, or shall I say Mr. Jones The Expert. Good to finally meet you at last, without your disguise. Obesity did not become you. But you're looking a bit ill. Does life in imprisonment not agree with you?"

Adam shrugged sheepishly. He'd worn, because he was Adam and had his quirks, a disguise when he'd met with Ho. This had been before he knew for certain who Ho represented, and what the real agenda was—so he had claimed. But we knew, through his own admission that he, Adam, had helped to create Uron Koh from the very beginning. And Max Wellesley had hired Michael Ho to be his representative. You could say, almost, that it was a reunion of conspirators.

"Not as agreeable as I had hoped but at least I do not have to worry about life's everyday hassles. I feel quite liberated from the stress. Rigid rules do have their uses."

Ho inspected Adam. "You are not as young as I imagined you to be." Then, sharply, "Where is it?"

"I have no idea what you are referring to." Adam feigned an air of puzzlement. "Age is merely a number. You would be surprised to know my actual age."

"I care not for a person's age. Only their worth and use." Ho twitched an annoyed eyebrow. "And right now your use is the only reason I wish to speak to you. I want it back."

Ho started to show a hint of impatience. I could see John lean forward just a bit to absorb this new bit of weakness in Ho. Simon could be seen curling a small smile on his thin lips. Obviously, I'd missed some vital point in this repartee.

"If you are referring to the bit of money I filtered out of your European accounts, I'm sorry to say, it's gone." Adam shrugged again. "I had to give it away. It was part of the requirements of my…exile."

"I have enough money. That is of no importance to me." Ho clicked his tongue. "I refer to something else."

John and Simon exchanged a quick look between them. Ho's agitation seemed to please them. I wished I knew the secret language they spoke.

"Well, get on with it then," Adam huffed. "No point with these guessing games if you don't give us any hints. I've no idea what you are talking about."

"The code," Ho said flatly. "Where is it?"

"The...code?" Adam look utterly lost. I knew his face and mannerisms enough to know that he didn't have a clue what was going on. Nor did the rest of us.

"If you have it," John spoke to Adam in a voice that was low and dangerously patient. "Give it back."

Adam gave his brother a befuddled look. It was returned by a tight frown.

"John..." Adam said, shaking his head. "I've no idea what he's on about."

"Enough of this," Ho interrupted. "Give me the code or by tomorrow, the world will know who Josie Bettencourt really is. And if I still do not have the code, I will kill her niece."

"Prove to us first that this person really is my wife's niece. Or no deal," John replied coldly.

I'd been quite unsure of what I felt up until that point. If, indeed, I had a niece—a family member still alive—then, yes, I would most definitely want to meet her. But this revelation coming from Michael Ho was questionable in itself, like trusting the word of a known liar. Or placing your head between the jaws of a crocodile and hoping it wouldn't bite.

Was he telling the truth? Did he really find a relation of mine when all efforts by John and Simon—with their immeasurable resources—had failed? A small part of me wanted desperately to believe him, to feel connected once more, to be part of something that made a whole. Another part told me Ho was bluffing so I'd better not get my hopes up, and that this was all in an effort to draw us out. To be brutally frank, relative or not, she was just a person I'd no idea of or any attachment to other than blood. She would be a complete stranger.

But I did wonder. Could it be?

"Proof?" Ho cracked a crooked smile. "If it's proof you require, it is proof you will receive. DNA, however watered down through the generations, does not tell lies. Expect a sample to be delivered in a few moments."

John raised a brow. "An electronic sample?" he actually laughed. "Come now, those can be tampered with."

"A delivery, expect it any moment. A man by the name of Xiang will be found detained in your Main Entrance Hall. He speaks very little English—he is ignorant. He carries with him a vial with a single strand of hair. If he does not hand over the vial directly to either you, or your lackey Simon, he has been conditioned and instructed to kill himself. If I am not mistaken, he would be right this moment creating quite a fuss with your security guards."

Simon snorted but pulled out his personal unit and made a call.

John cast Ho a lazy glance. "And I take it he'll still kill himself or be killed once he has delivered this vial?"

Ho only smiled broadly in return. "Even if you question him, he won't know anything. His main purpose for living was to deliver the vial and that alone. You can do with him as you like. He is just a messenger."

"Where has this niece of Josie's been all this time?" Adam called out.

"You will find out in due course. Who knows, when I receive the code, I may decide to let her visit with you, and she could tell you herself. But then, I have grown quite fond of her. She has the most charming disposition—quite like Josie, in a way. The resemblance is...uncanny."

"I still don't know what code it is you speak of."

"Come now, Adam, enough with the lies. I know you have it, you took it from me in Korea."

Adam scoffed. "I've not been to Korea in years. You mistake me for someone else."

Just then, Simon made a growl and gave John a look as he marched out of the room. Ho could be heard chuckling to himself.

"Tomorrow at noon," Ho called out and waved once.

The transmission ended and left us blinking at where his image had stood.

Five

Xiang, the messenger, a fifty-odd year old mentally retarded man had been detained, questioned, found insensible, and sent to the clinic's head trauma unit for observation. No one could've guessed that in two days time, he would be found dead in his room from a slow-working poison.

"What do you mean? Are you sure?" John rose from his seat and strode to face his sister.

Aline regarded him with a withering look. She was six years older and used each of those years as a weapon over her brother.

"Of course I'm sure. I've run it three times *to be* sure."

Aline was the Citadel's most respected physician. Regardless of who she was, she earned her current status on merit alone. She ran the main clinic, which was specifically for the presidential family and government officials. Like her brothers, she shared their dark hair and pale skin. Her manner was a mix of both, taking from John the stubbornly quiet calm, from Adam the quick mind, and what was all herself, a bossy and forthright nature.

And like them both, she had a habit of clamping her mouth into a line and administering that Lancaster stare of thorough inspection and calculation. Josie felt it upon her now.

"So, it appears you've got family after all," Aline said. She wasn't being spiteful, just her usual blunt self.

Josie merely stared back, uncertain of what to say or do. What could she do? What was there to say?

John reached out to take his wife's arm and gave it a quick and reassuring squeeze. Their eyes met in understanding. He would feel for her, it said. He would take the brunt of whatever happens next so she'd be spared.

She nodded and turned away feeling numb and unsteady. Whatever he did, it still didn't take away that awful feeling of excitement mingled with disappointment. What if it were all a hoax? She shouldn't get her hopes up, for them to come crashing down as the joke was revealed. But it was three hundred years—that was a very long time. Any number of things could've happened.

They were in Aline's office. A roomy and comfortable space, furnished with soft colors to calm the soul and light trickling noises from small water fountain ornaments to soothe the mind.

"What I don't get is how he managed to find this relative when we couldn't." Simon fretted from a corner. Obviously too restless to sit still, he stood propped against a filing cabinet lightly drumming his fingers upon it. He glanced across at Josie with a slightly worried look.

Despite the strong front she put up, Josie was still very fragile. Still healing from her 'ordeal'—that was about the only word any one could summon regarding her past and what happened since she'd come to the Citadel.

Simon creased his brow and seemed to be remembering when Josie plummeted to her lowest, when her mind was all but shattered at having lost everything—her past, her friend Wellesley, her life as it was so far in this new future she'd stumbled upon, the uncertainty of what was to come...

Simon opened his mouth as if in an attempt to raise her spirits by offering a sarcastic remark, but caught the look on her eyes. It was hollowed and distant. He closed his mouth instantly.

John, too, watched her. His expression grim as he took in Josie's pale face while it struggled with realization. With each passing moment, his face became more stony and angry. He thoughts were written plainly on his face, especially the desire to wring Ho's skinny little neck for causing this distress and uncertainty in his wife. And if it turned out to be all a lie, he'd break it clean with no regrets.

"And what's this code he talks of?" Simon called out with a frown.

John jerked visibly, as if Simon's voice cast away his fantasies of breaking Ho's neck.

"Josie?" Simon continued. "In your time at Wellesley's, was there any mention of a code?"

She shook her head absently and wandered aimlessly to look out a window. It showed a brilliant expanse of the clinic's gardens. Immaculate lawns dotted with benches, flowering hedges and shrubs with a winding pond that weaved through. Small wooden bridges and stepping-stones stretched over the pond and burbling water fountains spouted out lazy, fat trickles of water.

She needed to calm her mind, clear it. The vista before her may have helped, if she could see to be influenced by it. But her mind was miles away.

She considered her brother, Kellan, for a moment. For a very long time since awakening, she'd wondered if her brother and family had survived, having known that her father was later murdered after she'd stepped into the suspension pod. Her father had moved her pod to Prince Edward Island, but why she'd never been resuscitated was the mystery.

Did the people who killed her father, also kill her brother? If they didn't, then did the famines and economic crash affect them? Did they live out their lives, procreate and die at a nice, ripe old age?

All of these questions that came with no answers. And just how *did* Michael Ho get the answers that she and John had been trying for months to get?

She knew that during his spare time, John secretly ran his own investigation into the matter. She pretended not to notice, but she knew. In a sense, it was John's way of trying to make her feel connected to something, to give her an identity, a family—a sense of belonging. She'd said it didn't matter anymore and that John was now her family—she needed nothing more.

But now, she wasn't quite sure of herself.

Surely if her brother had lived, he would've known about the suspension pod and would've tried to reawaken her once it was safe to do so. He was a scientist, in a manner of speaking, and would've known what to do. She simply assumed that he'd died before being able to take care of that. After all, why then was she left lying there, forgotten for all those years?

What she rarely considered was that maybe he'd lived, and had decided to keep her hidden for her own safety—and for the safety of the pod and its design, it being the prototype. But then, her father's research documentation and publication had been released soon after his death. The world knew all the secrets already—there'd be no reason for her to remain asleep, hidden. So surely Kellan and his young family met some misfortune. That would be the only explanation. It made no sense to leave her sleeping all those long years. If she knew her brother, he would've at least tried to reawaken her, or left instructions and arrangements for this to be done if he couldn't. Kellan, if anything, was a perfectionist. It would've grated his sensibilities to have unfinished business that needed to be attended to.

Unless he was prevented...

Josie worked it out. Seven generations, that sounded about right. If her young nephew and niece, her brother's children, who'd been five and a year old respectively when she went to sleep, had grown and had children of their own...yes. It was about right, give or take a few incarnations that had children later in life. Seven generations.

But how did it come to be that only one survived? What horrendous misfortunes occurred through the ages at there was only one?

Josie held no attachment to this new niece. How could she? She'd no idea who this niece was, if in fact, she really was a blood relation. Blood relation, maybe, but definitely watered down through the generations. Watered and thinned out so far that this person was a complete stranger. A foreigner. So far distant from Josie and her brother that she may as well have come from another planet.

Josie made up her mind in that instant. Suddenly, she no longer felt confusion or longing. Instead, she felt a distant anger that bolstered her spirits. She was angry with Ho, for bringing her to this point where she found herself uncertain. To protect her sanity, she would convince herself that it was trick. Denial was sometimes much better, safer, than acceptance.

And there was something else that bothered her.

"*Why* would he try to find a relation of mine?" Josie spun around with a frown on her face. She startled John, who was rarely surprised, that he blinked a few times. "Was it out of curiosity? What's the purpose of revealing this niece? Surely, if he wanted to expose me, he'd have done so regardless. He has the fucking discs to prove it—why drag a niece into the mix? Why the double threat? To make sure we give him this stupid code when he's going to expose me anyway? I don't get it."

"Very nicely put." Simon smiled broadly, and seemed glad she'd come out of her funk.

"I hadn't thought of that." John frowned, looking disturbed that she'd once again out-thought him. Before he'd met her, his mind had been clear and focused. Now, he found himself befuddled. Love was a dangerous element. "But, yes. Why? And if we could not find anything, how did he?"

"There might have been a way..." Aline spoke up. She had a hip propped on the corner of her desk and a thoughtful frown on her face. "Not much people would know and not much people *could* gain access. It's strictly for select members of the medical profession and even then, it has its restrictions in place for good reasons. Only certain groups can gain access. The medical DNA banks, it's a more detailed variant to what the security authorities use. You would need specific passwords and authorization to log onto it and access the information, and even then, the amount of information you want is limited to a specific sample and its links. But with some effort and a very good hacker, anyone could probably get in."

"But we've scanned all DNA banks," Simon said.

"Yes, but not the detailed *medical* banks. These would hold key tags and specific markers, even shadows and blips that are indicative to the original DNA source—like a fingerprint that determines the dominant characteristics in a DNA strand. The authorities, what you would have used to source information, would have just an overview, with the strongest spikes and tags as markers. This would work if you were trying to source something a hundred years old. But after generations of blood mixes, you would need a more detailed method of tagging someone. Ho could easily have used any number of samples from Josie that he picked up from the house, used it as a base to screen for any similarities in the DNA banks now. If he tagged something remotely alike, he'd have investigated further."

Josie didn't even bother to ask how it was that a DNA bank existed for all the citizens of the world. The world had changed so much—some for the better, some for the worse—that a simple process of owning up ones own basic core identity, like your DNA, hardly mattered. There were strict privacy issues, yet she knew that the world now spied upon everything in microscopic detail. In fact, the Citadel alone was living and working proof that such things as privacy did not happen but only in one's own imagination. Deep in the bowels of the Citadel, where Simon and his Elites ruled, was a networked hive of surveillance technology and god-knew what else.

"Why is the medical DNA bank so different?" John asked in annoyance.

"Please, John," Aline groaned. "Because it is for *medical* purposes."

Exasperated, John compressed his lips. "Explain."

"Your DNA banks would only mark topical similarities—the main points—for identification purposes. That's perfectly fine and works well and very foolproof. And like I said, would only give you a hundred-year space to work within before things start to degrade, so to speak. But the medical banks would show more detailed markers. We need them to identify diseases and irregularities in a person's genetic makeup and history. Sometimes, we can even pinpoint the exact time and point where these irregularities occurred, and fix them in the newer DNA strands, therefore eliminating future sickness, deformities or irregularities…what have you."

"Like stem-celling?" Josie piped up, thinking here was something she knew a little bit of.

In her time, stem-celling had already gone mainstream. She herself had been told that her mother had relinquished her umbilical cord at birth for storage, to be used later in case of serious sickness or disease as a core sample to work from. She never paid much attention to it, though a lot of her father's work and research was based originally on genetics. Now, she listened to Aline with rapt attention.

"Uh?" Aline looked at her with distraction. "Something like that. Anyway, our banks only go about two hundred years, and those original samples were sketchy to begin with since the whole process was quite new. Now, we've got millions upon millions of samples, the majority already tagged back to the originals—so you've got a sort of family tree going on here."

"You mean you've a complete family tree of the entire world? A DNA tree?" Josie gaped.

"Something like that."

"Is mine in there?"

"It is now. Or I should say, if Ho has been using it, it will automatically update and tag your sample as the original, making it the base sample with the most and strongest amount of unique marker tags and spikes that all the others have, only not as strong. Ho would have used your original sample to access the others samples. You see, those markers—your unique markers—would've been the key to unlock all subsequent samples he has supposedly connected you to. Like a magnet, the other samples would have come to yours, guided by those specific markers. Got that?" Aline smiled brightly as Josie shook her head in incomprehension. "So, what we do now, is check the database and see if you've been tagged."

"Do it then." John looked grim.

He knew nothing of this databank, of how detailed and structured it was. How was it that he didn't know any of this? Secrets upon secrets that some knew of—and others didn't. Too much like how his grandfather ran things. It needed to stop. People needed to know that they had control over their lives. That 'parts' of them were not stored for later use. It was too close to how the suspension pods were later used and abused—and too close to how cloning breached its ugly head before being outlawed.

Though he did agree to the practicality and the benefits of having a DNA bank—medically speaking—it still felt rather invasive. What was next? Body parts preserved for salvaging later...the re-emergence of cloning? He shuddered mentally. He knew people tinkered and experimented, even though such practices were banned. He hoped that when he did die, the only parts left of him were his progeny, not a piece of tissue or dot of blood in a freezer or a detailed electronic data file. But he knew that wouldn't happen. He wouldn't be surprised if a tissue sample of his was already in cold storage—to be used in case he needed a new brain! He already knew he had his own blood stored. It was mandatory for government officials, in case of emergency transfusions, so that physician could manufacture replications of it. John frowned at the floor uneasily.

"John," Aline called again. Her brother seemed lost in his thoughts. "I said, as soon as I get the information, I'll let you know. Now leave so I can get some work done. I do have other patients to see."

"Fine," he replied. "Just where are these DNA banks?"

"Iceland," Aline chirped cheerfully. "Pardon the pun. But that's mostly for original samples. The mainframe for the electronic data is in Russia."

"Could Ho have cloned my DNA?" Josie asked suddenly.

Aline smiled widely at Josie. If there was one thing in a person that Aline liked most, was how a person's mind flitted from one thought to the next, the more random, the better. It showed that the person was a thinker—alive and running amok with curious bits of information and thoughts. And she liked Josie.

"That's very possible as well. Trickery? Possible. If that's the case, we're back to the first question. Why? But whatever the case, he means to hurt you. Watch yourself, Josie."

~ * ~

"You didn't know about this, did you?" I asked later as we walked down a courtyard passageway that connected to John's offices.

After leaving Aline, we'd gone back to his offices and spoke in detail about how we would approach this new development. Whatever the situation, good or bad, the so-called niece would be treated just like any threat to me—primarily—and to the Citadel.

Aline confirmed later that someone had been messing about in the DNA databanks, and sure enough, I was there like an immaculate conception.

John shook his head. "Not a clue."

"Sort of scary, isn't it? Having parts of you floating about in the computer networks? But I suppose that's how the world advances, right? It's kind of good to have it, don't you think? A world history of its people—detailed and concise."

"Mmm," he murmured.

"You're just pissed off that you didn't know about it," I said in a taunting voice.

He smiled slowly, looking abashed. He looked tired as well. I remembered then that we really hadn't slept in close to twenty-four hours. It was now late evening, and as I thought of it, we hadn't even had any food since leaving Canada, which had been just before dawn.

To change the subject I began a new, more pressing topic—one that we'd forgotten about completely. The code. It perked John up to the point we veered directions and headed straight to our house.

He was hungry.

When Crocker greeted us with her replicated smile that sent the usual shudders down my spine, John ordered up some steaks and good, old-fashioned French fries smothered with gravy and ketchup. To add a bit of civility to the meal, he opened a bottle of red wine. We wolfed down the meal, barely speaking save a few satisfied grunted responses, then, we sipped our wine. We were on a terrace off the kitchen, similar to the breakfast alcove, only outdoors.

"I don't know anything about it. I've searched my brain and still don't know," I said as we discussed the code again. "It's obviously something quite important for Ho to be so hard-pressed for it."

"And Adam isn't saying—or won't." John compressed his mouth into a line, pushing away from the table to lean back. He smothered a burp behind his fisted hand.

"I think he's telling the truth. I know he's good at tricks like the rest of you Lancasters, but he's not that good."

John chuckled at my reference to his family traits and regarded me with a sneaky look. "Whatever it is, if we don't come up with it by noon tomorrow…"

I nodded. "The world gets to know a lot more about me. And I lose the only living family member I have. Sucks all kinds of ass, doesn't it."

John laughed. "That's a new one. Did you just make that one up?"

"Nah, I heard that ages ago. Way, way, before your time."

We grew silent for a moment. I opened my mouth to say something, then, closed it, not knowing just how to say it.

"What is it?" John asked.

"I dunno." Shaking my head, I sighed. "Just that if I am exposed, how badly would it look, or be? Would people believe it?"

"There would be doubters, you can be sure of that. They

would insist on a thorough background check as proof. All the while the media would have a field day. As to how it would look—bad. It would come across that the government has, once again, tried to cover up things. And once its proven that you are the real deal, you can be assured that your life will never be the same again. You'll have people coming from all corners, and from all walks of life, wanting to be your best friend. That aside, you'll also attract the attention of every known extremist group who oppose the use of stasis pods, and they will try to kill you—as you no doubt have once experienced. And if you go into hiding, it will look as if we're cowardly and cannot bear to face the issue." John sighed. "Whichever way we go, it will look bad. Whatever we do, it will not be easy."

"We could make it look like a big hoax," I suggested. "Or bite the bullet and confess before he does."

"Would you really put yourself through that?" John gave me a hard look. "It's bad enough what they're saying about you now, but to add to it…"

"What other alternative is there? We have to diffuse Ho's threat."

"I will not let you go through that. And what about this niece? He'll still kill her."

"No, he won't. If he does, then he doesn't have any more cards to hold."

"True," he seemed to think on this and worked his mouth into a line again. "But…what if we were to create a hoax of our own? Fabricate our own wild and ridiculous story about you—I mean, what's one more story going to do? Then publicly denounce it—like we usually do. Simon has already had to create some fictitious footage of you in our Prince Edward training facilities—for official records. We could elaborate on those and use them as proof that you're not a three hundred year old relic."

"Relic, gee, thanks for that," I snorted. "Didn't you already have that fed to the media after we got married? Minus the three-hundred bit, of course."

"I did," he nodded. "And there were the doubters and skeptics. Simon has been very careful and selective with the amount of information we've leaked about you. As it is, your 'history' is solid. But I can't predict what the revelation of those discs will do to it."

John had watched those discs already in its compressed form from a memory stick. Over the months we'd spent together, we watched it again, while I did a running commentary of who was who, what was what. Like going through a modernized photo album, we sat companionably while I pointed, laughed, and reminisced.

Lorcan Wellesley, as a gift to me, created a special pendant with a memory stick inside that contained all the discs that my father had recorded for me. It was the history of my life, from birth to suspension. It showed a compilation of my family in various snapshots of time and life, video clips, messages from my father—his confession of what he'd done and why he tricked me into helping him—his thoughts and fears. But mostly, it was about my family, from old black and white stills of my ancestors, my parents younger days, my childhood...right up to the day I went to sleep. It was my entire life before waking up to a new future. My father had been thorough. He'd even sneaked through my personal computer and its files to gain access to some images. He then copied and burned them onto disks and secreted them away in a compartment of my stasis pod.

And these images were solid—un-doctored and raw—genuine. Any idiot could determine that just by looking at them.

By attempting to expose me to the world, it was pretty obvious that Ho was desperate, or just ruthless and cruel. Which he was. Whatever this code was, it held the key to something massively important. Money alone couldn't be the motivation for Ho. We knew his financials—what we could uncover—and they were vast. He had fingers in many pies, some known and others unknown. During his time affiliated with Max Wellesley, while Max was just a young boy, Ho represented his face and body for business transactions. There was just no telling how much money Ho had accumulated for Max and himself. And, if Max had the resources to buy entire armies for his use...

This code he spoke of, it could be anything from the mother load of weapons or the key to taking over the world, the latter being everyone's favorite first choice since before the reign of the Lancasters.

"Well, let's do it then. Expose me, but on our terms. Let's create something on our own—say that I'm an impostor—play it up like how your mother was. Make it sound cruel and ridiculous. Then when and if Ho decides to add his two-cents worth, it'll look like everyone's on the bandwagon again, coming up with any old thing about me. It'll look stupid and people will start to doubt. Then play out my fabricated past that Simon's created and act as if we're insulted."

John regarded me with a stern look. He looked hesitant. "You're sure? It would be absolute mayhem, especially for you. You won't be able to leave this place, let alone the Citadel, for a while. The in-house media will harass you to no end and Loeb would want to murder me because of it. And you'll have to speak to the press at some stage—you won't be able to get out of that one. It will just look as if we're covering."

"I'm sure," I said flatly. "Let's put Ho in his place. So get Simon and have him do his magic and make something up about me. The ridiculous the better."

"You've been spending too much time with Adam," John said through narrowed eyes. "Fine. It'll be done."

"How is your mum these days? Still spelunking in Mexico?"

"She's in Australia now," John cocked his brow with an amused expression. "Catching crocs for an eco-farm and communing with the Aborigines."

"Cool."

Griet Lancaster was a First Level body-assistant before she married John's father, Baird. For her entire married life, she'd been dogged with speculation and suspicion that she was trying to assassinate her husband. Baird had no choice but to exile her from the Citadel—yet they remained married and secretly continued their love affair. For Baird, there was no other woman but Griet.

She was innocent; Baird knew this, as did almost everyone else. But the smear campaign on Griet continued by those who opposed the Lancasters. To maintain her innocence and to protect her, she agreed to the exile and then 'disappeared' from the public eye. That didn't stop her from being mother to her children, which she'd been at almost every point in their lives. How she managed this, she never said a word. But John had said he could remember her presence throughout his childhood. But, the public never once saw her, or ever heard from her ever again.

To John, his mother was like a mythical warrior. Always there when he needed her, and even when he didn't. Her presence was strong, mysterious, and everywhere. He loved her and couldn't imagine a life different than how it was. It was just so.

When John became president, he lifted the exile on his mother and dared anyone who opposed it to show themselves and pretty much give him a reason not to hurt them. No one did. However, Griet refused to come back, claiming the Citadel held too many painful memories for her. Instead, she amused herself with wild and fantastic adventures. I was yet to meet her, but coveted her lifestyle and hoped that one day, I could be like her. In her late sixties, she was still active and dare-devilishly wicked. She could still vanish like the wind and fight like a demon—so I was told.

On the day of our marriage, I received a coded message from her. Her words were simple and straight to the point. *'Better you than me,'* it had said. I liked her immediately.

"Josie? Are you all right? You look very tired." John reached out a hand and touched mine.

Suddenly, I did feel very tired. His touch alone seemed to break my resistance. I sighed weakly. "Yeah."

And with that, I burst into tears. I felt the entire day come crashing down upon me. From the disappointment of not being able to visit my hometown, the revelation—however sketchy—of having a family member still alive, the threat of being exposed; it had mounted up.

So I cried, long and loud, and barely noticed that John had gently tugged me to him. I sat straddled across his lap like a young child, crying my eyes out. Living in the future was anything but easy. Compared to my idyllic past, everything now was one extreme emotion and situation after another.

And none of it would've been remotely bearable if it wasn't for John. He was the immovable rock that held my sanity in check. Slumped now as I was over his shoulder, I spilled my anguish out until the hitching sobs became soft snuffles. We sat silently, not needing to speak for a time. It felt good just to connect. Whatever this future held, I knew without a doubt, that here was where I was always meant to be.

    With a sigh that touched my heart, he cupped my face as we made ready to create a lie, and call it my past.

Six

"It's done," Simon said matter-of-factly and gave Josie a friendly wink. "Get ready for the fallout. I've a ratty old umbrella I could lend you."

With a pursed mouth, Josie grunted. It was early morning and news of her 'past' had been leaked to a small but reputable media house in Australia.

"I hope you made it look good."

"Please." Simon faked a pained expression. "It's me remember."

"Don't remind me." Josie rolled her eyes.

It wouldn't have surprised her if he'd altered and tweaked it to make her look like a simpering fool. In any other circumstance, she would've expected it, but considering the serious nature this was, she knew he wouldn't mess about. Whatever Simon was on the surface, he was honest and fiercely loyal to those he cared about. She'd never admit it to anyone, but if the tables were turned, she'd do the same for him.

Seventeen minutes later, they were still in John's offices when the first of a series of calls bombarded them. John's assistant, Aida, expertly fielded these with an affronted and cold, "Absolute rubbish!"

Within the hour, Loeb held a press conference to answer questions and dismiss the ridiculous stories about the President's wife.

As it was, the story had played up on Josie's already fabricated past. She was, it had said, indeed a pod-survivor, but linked to anti-government groups that had been bent on destroying the Lancaster regime. Her birth date was not seventy-odd years ago, but over a hundred. She was a full-fledged operative, ordered into stasis to await the moment when a very young Dane Lancaster would come of age, as he'd already been marked for manipulation by her handlers. She was then awakened when Dane was but a fledgling wannabe dictator, then, sought out to seduce him. But her identity and purpose were discovered, so her handlers ordered her into stasis once more. And now, she was reawakened to gain access into the government and bewitch the current president.

Select footage from her true past were used to show her as a young girl, these of course showed nothing to associate her to any particular place or time. There were images of Josie riding a horse, in a dress rehearsal for a school play, and simple face shots that appeared to be from school files. Other images were added—these being the 'footage' from her days at the Prince Edward Island training facilities. They were intentionally made to look grainy and dodgy, as they were purportedly stolen archival footage. Then others still were pasted together, recent images of Josie holding weapons, training, and seen in the company of suspicious individuals.

The initial 'leak' was said to have come from a source within the PEI training facilities. This individual had compiled and acquired information about Josie over the last year. It had been made to appear like an envious colleague, an ambitious but temperamental trainee that had been overlooked for promotion. And it was made to look fake.

At the press conference, Loeb's cool and composed face betrayed nothing of the ruse. With just a hint of amusement and a carefully placed frown of indignation on his face, he methodically countered the barrage of questions and accusations that came holographically via remote feeds. One reporter, obviously a stay-at-home-father, could be seen in shorts and ratty T-shirt with a young toddler at his knee while he asked his questions.

Yes, Loeb had said, Madam Lancaster was an operative—extreme deep cover—that was no lie, and in fact, common knowledge. She was also from a quiet family, a family who'd been long and dedicated supporters of the Lancaster government, but for security reason, they lived under a fabricated name. Dane Lancaster chose her himself because of her dedication and intellect, and her expert abilities to blend in. Yes, she was a pod-survivor. Furthermore, she was born 2260, not 2209 as the preposterous allegations indicated. What did people think? Loeb could be heard sounding incredulously amused. That she was some ancient relic from a century ago? That was absolutely ridiculous as no one could *possibly* survive in stasis for so long!

Loeb continued by saying that it had been her ordeal during the stasis process that proved her dedication to service and impressed her superiors by the lengths she'd go to expose the truth. She was deep cover, even then, trying to source the key players in a conspiracy to overthrow the first Lancaster. Though retired now, she'd proven to be a loyal operative. Her track record alone should stand; saving many lives during the recent siege, including the life of the President, her husband. She'd single-handedly delivered and exposed the key players in the recent attempt to overthrow the government, and the world, and her reputation and credibility were indisputable!

And so it was, amid the media chaos, John, Josie, and Simon sat across from Adam an hour before midday in the communications room.

Supposedly oblivious to what was happening outside, Adam, like a monkey, merely picked fastidiously at imaginary dust specks on his sleeve. If he put these dust bunnies in his mouth and nibbled them, no one would've raised an eyebrow.

"I've racked my brains and still cannot think of any code," Adam said wearily. He brushed his fingers together to remove the dust only he could see. "I thought I had some ideas, but they were too obvious and could be easily attained. Code or not, some things can be broken into quite easily."

"What were they?" John asked. He looked down, realizing Josie's hand was still in his since they left his office. She looked grim this morning—jumpy—so for the entire journey to the communication's room, he held her hand, giving it small squeezes to reassure her.

"There was some mention while Max directed the show, of vaults of money that some corporations kept within their buildings— in case of another economic crash, you know. They horded their funds and Max had once expressed an interest of liberating them of it. It was just idle talk. Ho was eager; the more money the better was what he said. But Max wasn't keen as it seemed too childish a venture. Then there was a plan to gain access into the banned inner-city districts from the former big cities. Especially the New York, London, and Paris emigrants since they were closer, and use their resources—or manic tendencies—to destroy the Lancaster government."

"What's that?" Josie looked blank. "I don't follow. What inner-city districts? Street gangs you mean?"

Simon cleared his throat and directed his attention to her. "The slums and inner-city gangs and armies from the urban wars were cleaned up and cleared out a couple centuries ago, then relocated to other cities, smaller more secure cities. Some cities were even created specifically for them. It was considered more humane to relocate them than execute them. The majority of terrorist and extremist groups were then spawned in these banned districts—for obvious reasons."

Simon shrugged mildly and continued. "At the time, the governments of the world were unstable and in upheaval. It was before our time, actually. Another war was starting, people were hungry, angry, scared. These banned districts, even the bravest never ventured into them. They became, through the generations, a sort of sub-culture species. Oh, they *are* still human, but the way they live has affected them—developed them into this scary and vicious breed of men and women, even children. No person, however bent on trying to take over the world, would ever dream of using them to help win the war. They do their own thing. They'd turn around and kill you before you even had a chance to think twice. As it is now, they kill each other for no reason other than to kill. They live like a wild pack of savage beasts."

"And these cities and districts have a lockdown code." John remembered once having to venture close to one to these districts when he'd been a young trainee in the military—just outside Rio de Janeiro. It had taken all his training and knowledge of fighting and survival to keep from losing his mind. Petrified wasn't the word used to describe what he'd felt. It had been a deep, dark, bowel-loosening fright—a basic revulsion to evil that near froze him.

They were no longer part of the human race. They were evil. It was a stain that they'd been allowed to live and fester for so long. Short of dropping a mega-bomb into the areas and eradicating them, under the governmental guidelines of the world, they were still categorized and considered human: living, breathing, Homo sapiens. And now, John was President, and still they lived and breathed among the sane. It was a perpetual problem that was easily solved by sweeping it under the rug until another day. He knew, that one day, it would have to be dealt with—effectively.

"Lockdown code?" Josie gaped. "Jeez, like in mental asylums? Prisons?"

"Similar." Simon nodded. "The general idea is to keep them away from us. For most of the time, they're happy enough where they are. They have their own cities or clans within their cities, their own rules and regulations, a way of life. However harsh and oppressive it is to live there, they have acclimatized to suit. It's just the extremely agitated who slip out and cause trouble—oh, there are ways to get out. Even with the three-layer lockdown system, they always manage to get out."

"I take it that this code is always in place?" Josie asked. Like someone listening to a scary ghost story around a campfire, she shuddered involuntarily.

"Usually, yes," Simon nodded. "But that's the thing. There isn't any one person who holds the master code. It's a series of computer generated codes and sequences that are random, so it cannot be hacked into easily. It changes quite regularly and there are numerous fail-safes in place in case of power failure—it's all automated, but with manual overrides. But again, no sane person would dream of letting loose a wild society like them."

"Max wasn't sane," Josie said flatly. "You don't think that he could've gotten into that system? Get the code?"

"He could possibly have, it's heavily guarded, but not so heavily guarded that it's unbreakable. People—even terrorists and extremists—prefer to leave them be. But as Adam suggested, Max didn't seem too keen. They are, at the best of times, very difficult to control." Simon seemed to be mulling over something. "If I were Max, as tempting as it would have been to raise an evil army to fight his cause, I would not have raised them. Our rules do not apply to them, you see. They may as well have come from a different planet and speak a different language. And if I'd been successful in overthrowing the government, it would still leave the problem of getting rid of them once the job was done, or keeping them in check. Because to turn them loose into a normal society would cause more of a headache to a new dictator than the existing population. Whatever Max was, I never pegged him as a stupid boy. It must be another code Ho is referring to."

"I'll ask him," John said flatly. "And if he doesn't want to cooperate, we won't play by his rules." He looked across to Simon. "Did you have any luck with the search?"

"Nothing too clear." Simon stood, frowning. It appeared waiting for noon to come irritated him. "But it's close. Moorjani is set up, ready to track him again. We think he may even actually be in Switzerland and bouncing his signal all over the place to fool us. It's just too confused and scrambled, as if he's making a point of trying to fool us when he knows he's right under our noses."

"We need to tag him and shut him down." John clamped his mouth tightly and then scowled at the floor, deep in thought.

Adam had been quiet all this time, silently musing. He gazed intently at the wall, barely breathing, as if to do so would distract his thoughts. It appeared that something quite disturbing ran through his mind, where he processed it and analyzed it the way only Adam could.

"What?" Josie looked beadily at Adam. Because she understood him, his silence meant he'd thought of something.

John looked annoyed that his wife gave so much of her attention to his brother. He made a distasteful face that wasn't lost on Simon, who watched him with something like bemusement.

"I was just recalling…" Adam's voice sounded thin and tinny. "The banned districts had spurred an idea. It's a bit wild, but it might have been what Max had in mind. Also, Wellesley and Ho were arguing—Ho was nearly crimson in the face—about communications and shutting down the worldwide networks. Wellesley insisted it was a bad idea and no amount of convincing changed his mind. He said something about 'over his dead body' would he agree to something like that. Now, when did this happen? It was during the first few meetings I had with Ho, when I first posed as Mr. Jones, The Expert. Before I came across you, Josie. I can't understand why he was so opposed. I mean if the intention is to overthrow the government, then shutting down the networks is a reasonable method of ensuring control. And, am I correct in assuming that there is a master code for the communications network?"

"You would be correct," Simon replied grimly, he looked suddenly pale. "But it can be easily rerouted to run independently. That aside, there is a master code for shutting down and reactivating the three satellites that is home to our off-planet military bases. And these bases not only house the majority of our military personnel, but it's the mainframe for every security network, surveillance monitors, communications, and defense protocols for the *entire* world. It's like our mother ship. Shutting it down would cripple us. All our secrets would be out. We'd be thrown back into the dark ages. And if I were Max, *that* is where I'd want to concentrate on and try to get into."

"For fuck's sake!" Josie stood up in horror. "What's with all these master codes? Haven't you ever heard of Plan B? Tell me there's a back up plan?"

"There's always a back up plan, Josie," John replied tersely. He stood to join her, clamping his mouth into a line. "How could Max Wellesley have gained the access codes? The codes are guarded and secret. Combined in the right order, they make the master code work."

Adam turned to look at him. "He was very resourceful. And he did have several key people within the government in his pocket. You've sought out and tried the majority, but there are still a great many out there who've the good sense to keep quiet about their former affiliations. Max had been planning this for a very long time, he could have acquired this code any number of ways."

"Three people hold the access codes. One is dead, so now I have it. And the other two, I will trust my life with them. And to the best of my knowledge, I did not entertain Max in any conversations about codes." John seethed in anger. "*How* did he get it and *where* is it now?"

Adam stared at him. "Apparently, me, according to Ho. And he now thinks that it belongs to him—rightfully, as he thought himself as Max's second."

"Why would he think that?"

"Well, you see. I think he realized that Max had been confiding in me. Maybe he was jealous. It was, after all, under Max's urging that Ho hired me to consult. Ho, of course, did not know who I really was at the time or the influence I had over Max. Nor did I realize who Ho was at first. But my influence on young Max had started to wane by then. He'd grown too…mad."

"Why would Lorcan oppose something like this?" Josie asked. She knew Lorcan and was fond of him, still. There had been a time when she loved him too. She'd trusted him and also his instincts. But he was dead now, killed by his own son, Max. If Lorcan opposed something, he probably had a very good reason for it.

"Shutting down the world's communication and security networks would cause absolute madness," Simon supplied helpfully. "We're talking mayhem. Wars would erupt—people would kill each other just to protect themselves. Identities would be lost, countries would be lost—everything would be lost. And we'd all be under the control of one person, as opposed to the united front it is now."

"You mean we're all under the control of *this* government, and it's all fair and just." Josie cocked a brow at John with a wry expression.

He nodded, seeing her point.

"It is," John said. "Whatever it sounds like, it is fair. It is the combined effort of the entire group of world leaders, including me. Control lies with everyone. Nothing is passed or agreed upon unless it's carefully investigated, tested, and thought out. What is in place now, is in place because everyone involved has agreed to it. But to have that taken away, for one person to control, that would be like given your soul to the devil and asking him not to corrupt you."

"But now someone supposedly has it and Ho wants it back. What's to stop this person from using it and fucking Ho over?" Josie glared at everyone. "And how do you know the person who's dead wasn't the one who spilled the beans and told Max in the first place? Who was he?"

John made a sudden growling noise and spun around to face his brother. He looked absolutely feral. Adam flinched involuntarily.

"He *told* you, didn't he?" John curled his lips into thin slivers, bared his teeth. "What an idiot I've been!"

"He told me nothing—I swear to you." Adam was out of breath, a sudden realization rushed to his face. He stood weakly to his feet and made as if to approach his brother. John stood hunched, ready to pounce and squeeze the life out of his brother.

"Except…" Adam swiped a hand roughly across his mouth. He looked ill. Horrified. "He gave me this—insisted I take it." He raised his left hand to present the ornate onyx and platinum ring.

His eyes focused onto it, just as the three other sets of eyes were now riveted upon it.

"The other person…the one that died," Josie whispered hoarsely. "It was your father?"

Seven

John, still reeling from the revelation, had to turn his back on everyone to give himself a moment.

Adam too was stunned. He seemed to be struggling with conflicting emotions, and the idea that he could've—all this time—been in possession of the most important master code there was. He'd all but wrenched the offending ring from his finger and flung it at John like it was some mortal disease.

Adam babbled about not wanting it anymore and the fact that he'd no idea. That he'd never been quite that privy to all the secrets that made up the Lancaster regime. John had rounded on him, accusing Adam that he'd lied, that he'd always coveted such knowledge, secrets. Adam admitted it might've been so, but not anymore.

In frustration, John, his rage still unchecked and bubbling under his skin, needed to press his hands and head against the wall to control himself. Josie didn't dare make a move, let alone a sound, not matter how badly she needed to speak.

It bothered her, yes, that Adam had all this time probably known what the business with the code had been all about. But his reactions towards it had told her that, he too, was horrified. That he didn't know. Yes, Max could've forced Adam to kill his father to gain access to his portion of the code, but then why not know about it, and acquire it while killing off his father?

John had his father's portion of the code. Which meant it had been written down somewhere for him to have inherited it. She didn't doubt that the other person was Simon. John trusted Simon more than he trusted himself, so he would be the obvious second person. Whoever the third was, most likely they were a lot like Simon. So if no one talked, and no one shared, how was it that the master code came to being in one place?

Simon had taken the ring from Adam immediately and disappeared with it. The anticipation of waiting, of finding out if it contained the code, was tortuous. Adam looked ready to die on the spot. He held his chest as if in pain. John still faced the wall and appeared to be trying his best to breathe evenly. Josie decided to help Adam first, risking her life by attending to John made no sense.

"Sit down Adam," she said without physically touching his arm, her tone brisk and matronly. He nodded blankly and sat heavily. "Try to breathe normally. Can I get you anything?"

He shook his head. He looked tired, ashen. "I'll do."

"It was Father's idea to have three people hold the codes," John called out from his wall. He sounded nasal, strained. "As insurance in case something happened. No one person ever knew what the other had. But each person that held their portion of the code needed a second, a person they trusted to take over should something happen to them. I was Father's second. Each of the codes can be anything, a symbol or a series of numbers, and entered in the right sequence, it made a whole. The master code. When they were created and first installed, these persons who held them, individually entered them into the mainframe computer and the sequence was locked in. In order to change the sequence, or the codes, you have to re-enter the codes in the same order to access them. After Father died, we changed the codes and chose our seconds to ensure security. Did you know this, Adam?"

"I keep telling you, I did not know. I *still* do not know."

"He's telling you the truth, John. Can't you see that?" Josie rounded angrily on her husband.

John cut her a lethal look. It said to butt out.

"It is impossible," John said slowly, "that one person has the complete master code. Each of us does not even know what the other has. Only our seconds know what our share of the code is."

"So you keep saying," Josie pressed on, hands on her hips. "But obviously, Ho thinks someone has. And until he comes on through that thing," she pointed to the hologram transmitter, "we don't know for sure if *that's* the code he's after."

"You can be sure it is," Adam said weakly. "It's a big enough reason for him to risk exposing himself, to risk being involved. If anything, Ho is a careful man but he has great designs—big expectations."

"But you don't know for sure," Josie insisted. "The code could be anything." She glared at Adam. "And what's this thing he's going on about Korea?" She spun back to John. "What if this has absolutely nothing to do with Max? What if it's all about Ho and something *he's* been planning?"

Simon returned to find the three people he'd left squaring off and glaring at each other. He shook his head with something close to relief, which made John's shoulders visibly relax.

"Nothing is there but dirt and grime." Simon casually flung the ring back to Adam. "You should clean it more."

Catching it with a fumble, Adam merely stared at it for a while. "There was nothing?"

Ignoring Adam, Simon tugged John's arm. He whispered something inaudible. Josie squinted suspiciously at them.

"My thoughts exactly," John muttered. He absently rubbed his left hip, an injury caused by Max during the siege; it still bothered him now and again.

"I'll set it up. We've time before Ho drops in."

"Do it," John replied. His face, set like stone, but a glimmer of amusement danced across his eyes.

"You're going to change the codes, aren't you?" Josie folded her arms across her chest, propped on one leg; the other tapped the floor. "And give him the old code. Don't you think he'll know that you've changed them? He's not an idiot."

"I don't care what he is." John coldly returned her stare. "He's not getting anything of ours."

Striding towards the door to follow Simon, John stopped and glanced at Josie again. His face had changed; it was softer and showed a little remorse that he spoke so harshly to her.

"When Ho comes, entertain him for me, won't you? Show him some of your rare charm." And with a smile that was pure mischief, John disappeared through the door.

~ * ~

Adam and I sat silently, for about three minutes. I decided to broach a subject that I'd skirted around for a long time. But it wasn't like as if we were going to talk about the weather or share a recipe for chocolate chip cookies. With a bracing deep breath, I opened my mouth to speak. Then found I didn't know how to start.

Adam glanced up. He'd been sitting with his head bowed for some time. He'd not bothered to replace the ring on his finger, but instead gazed at it as his fingers turned it around. He seemed to be inspecting it, absorbing the detailed work of the gothic dragon with its gaping mouth and its talons clutching a round black ball of onyx. The body of the dragon twirled and circled to form the hollow of the ring.

There'd been a time that the sight of that ring, and what those fingers did, froze my heart like stabs of icicles. Adam had a strange habit of tapping his fingers in an odd rhythm—a rhythm I remembered seeing and hearing when I lived with Lorcan. It was this action that caused me to expose Adam for what he really was. It was hard, too, to forget that it was only just under eight months ago when we learned the truth about him.

"You want to know why?" he said quietly, emphasizing once again that strange Lancaster trait of reading minds.

I shrugged. "You said the reason was because you wanted to take over from your father."

"Yes, that was it for a time. And of course, Max threatened to expose me and tell the world of my connection to him and all his intentions. I was scared, of course. But you know all that already." Adam nodded, more to himself. "John is right. I did plan it—right down to how I was going to get away with it. I'm a dangerous man—evil. You *should* be careful."

"If you were truly evil, then you won't feel any remorse. And I'd be already dead. You've had many chances and ample time to see to that—if that's what you wanted."

He laughed. "Point taken. Is that why, when I injected Father, I cradled him until he died? Of course, by then, I could not *undo* it. It was too late. Did you know he nodded his head to me, as if in understanding? He knew what I was capable of. How could a father not know his own son? He knew my weaknesses better than I knew myself. And he always knew that John was the stronger son, the good son."

He paused, staring off to remember before continuing. "I think he knew, that day, what my intentions were. He *offered* himself to me, in a way. He did not resist. He did struggle, but that, I think, was just reflex. I've played it over in my head so many times and wondered if I could have stopped myself in time. I see too, that Father gave me openings—chances—to stop, but I never took them. Yes, he knew and he was ready to die. Better to die by the enemy you know, right?"

I didn't know what to say. What could I say in return? "You think if he didn't understand, didn't know, you would feel the same way?"

"I'd feel worse, if that were at all possible. At least he knew it was coming." Adam laughed again, a hollow sound.

It was so like him to say something like that, to separate death into little compartments. After all, in his eyes, to die like a warrior, standing on your own two feet facing the enemy, was far better than cowering in a corner while death fell atop you.

"Listen to me—to us—speaking of murder as if it were an everyday topic of conversation. And me trying to justify my feelings like an excuse. I'm a murderer, nothing more." Adam shifted uncomfortably in his chair.

It wasn't often, but there were times, like now, where his guard dropped and I could see the real Adam exposed. He looked vaguely scared, like he'd seen his true self, a mere glimpse, and what he saw—a murderer—frightened him.

I'd killed too, and I'd do it again without hesitation. I wasn't proud of it; it was necessary. Was it really that different? Not really. I'd killed to protect myself, to protect John. According to the codes that the Lancasters and everyone in this future seemed to live by, to take a life to protect another was quite acceptable, just like facing your death like a warrior was. It was a modernized version of the old Japanese Bushido code, the way of the warrior—bodies to deflect the negative by using combat, minds to see with clarity and, above all, honor to keep things in balance. Another code. The world seemed full of them now.

"Why?" he said again as if answering my unasked question. "Because I wanted to. I felt empowered by it—the physical, actual, doing of it. For all my life, I was helpless and at the mercy of my sicknesses. But this one time, I was in complete control. And I liked it. I felt invincible."

With an audible gulp, I stared at him. "And...now?"

"Now? You need not be afraid of me. Now, I'm just an idiot. A murdering, sick idiot."

As if the words exhausted him to say, he slumped in his chair and fell silent. Quietly, he slipped the ring on his finger and continued to stare at it.

He looked like a man that was truly his own prisoner. He'd no need for bars or restraints; they were already in place, within his own mind. I felt sorry for him without quite understanding why. No, not sorry. I felt pity.

A metallic ping sounded. Michael Ho had announced his arrival.

I stood and made ready to entertain him like a good wife.

~ * ~

Michael Ho looked agitated. Upset and angry were too harsh a word to describe his controlled manner. He looked like an actor on stage, struggling with himself to achieve the right level of emotion to please the director, the audience. A slight sheen misted over his brow to suggest that something bothered him. But the gleam in his eye told Josie that he'd like nothing better than to pounce on her, and kill her with his bare hands.

Josie smiled beatifically, exaggerated enough to show her even teeth right to the molars. "Ho-ho-ho," she called out. She couldn't help herself, it just had to come out.

Ho inclined his head in that oily feign of politeness. "Josie, how very pleased I am to see you once again. I see you are well. The images of you on the media do not do you any justice."

"I've gained weight too, since the last time we met. Not a bag of bones like before—so I'm told." She shrugged mildly. "I'm here to keep your company for a moment. Everyone's just too busy that they've no time for you, I'm sorry to say. You'll forgive me if I'm a bit abrupt—they don't let me socialize much."

"I am sure the stories they have made up about you has them busy. How very smart of you. Congratulations are in order. My efforts to discredit you will now look like I'm on the proverbial bandwagon."

Though he smiled charmingly, Josie noted the tightness around his mouth. She couldn't help but feel a little chuffed at upstaging him.

"Thank you. But, I've *no* idea what you're on about. I thought maybe you might've gotten impatient and sent that stuff about me to the media after all. No? Wasn't you? Oh, well…someone else, then."

They regarded each other for a moment.

Adam watched mesmerized at Josie, and her interaction with Ho. To be just present to witness her walk among the mortals was enough for him to forget everything he'd done before. If he could live the rest of his life just watching her, he'd die a very happy man. Despite her hesitant and quiet nature, she carried with her a boldness that surprised even herself—and with such an eloquence to her words. He just hoped she didn't swear out like she normally did. Offending the enemy in the early stages was never a good idea.

"Margeaux would like to meet you before she dies."

"Who?" Josie blinked. "Oh, you mean my niece? Sorry, I don't think you'll harm her. You do want that code, don't you?"

Ho chuckled softly, his control returned. "I am sure you are changing the codes already. How you managed to organize it so quickly amazes me. But you will stop and hand it over regardless."

"Exactly what code are we talking about?" Josie spread her arms. "They are just hundreds of codes you could possibly mean. Unless we know exactly which one it is…" she shrugged dramatically, "for all we know, you could be asking for the codes to unlock the shit-tanks in the recycler vats."

Adam grimaced and took a small breath, held it.

With a tight-lipped smile, Ho cast his eyes to the floor. He seemed to be considering something for a moment then took a breath and sighed. Extending a hand, he beckoned someone from his right.

A young girl, reed-thin and awkwardly lanky, walked into view.

Josie cocked her head, her eyes widened to take in this new person.

The girl looked to be no older than thirteen or fourteen with the delicate softness of childhood still very visible across her small, compact face. She had a rich mane of black hair that matched the thick, highly arched eyebrows on her smooth round forehead. Her eyes, a sort of glassy hazel-green, were wide and large. The small but generously full mouth—pouting—was parted like a young child to reveal the tips of smooth white teeth.

Her manner was hesitant, a little scared, but otherwise she exuded a certain braveness about her—composed was the word that came to mind. Like a ballerina, primped and preened, awaiting the performance of her life with a calm sureness. Dressed in a severe, short-sleeved, knee-length, black dress; the kind only young girls seem conditioned to wear. On her legs, stockings in a brilliant white, and neat black shoes. She stood with her hands clasped before her—primed and ready, it would seem.

But what shocked Josie more was how close in resemblance this girl was to her. It unnerved her. Adam, from beside her, could be heard drawing in a sharp breath. Were it not for the fact that this girl had black hair, different colored eyes, a slightly mixed-race complexion and features, and was visibly shorter and much younger, Josie might as well have been looking at herself a dozen years ago.

"Hello, Josie," Margeaux called out, a little breathless—excited, awed. "It's nice to finally meet you."

Josie swallowed. *It's a trick,* she kept repeating to herself. Ho had found someone that looked close enough to her to pose as this so-called niece. *A clone!* She suddenly wanted very badly to speak with Aline. Though she was surprised—shocked—a skeptical frown formed between her brows. She barely registered the door engage, open, and John muttering something inaudible.

Beside her in two quick strides, John clutched her elbow and glared down at Ho.

"What is this?" he hissed. "Playing parlor tricks with us? You find some gullible girl to pose for you, dress her up to make her look like my wife, and then try to pass her off? What sort of fools do you think we are?"

"This is no trick. I take it you tested Margeaux's sample that I sent you? There is no mistaking that she is the real deal."

"It's true," Margeaux spoke up softly, her voice high and clear. "I did not want to believe it at first. Mr. Ho explained it all to me. I understand now, everything makes sense."

"Explain it to us, now." John could feel the pulse at Josie's elbow beat rapidly. The look he saw on her face when he arrived made his heart stop. She looked as if she'd seen a ghost, or was ready to face an executioner. The color had drained from her face, though she kept it tight with control, he could see the inner battle within. He squeezed her arm reassuringly and felt her relax slightly.

Ho smiled broadly, obviously pleased with the reaction he'd seen on Josie's face. "That would take too long. I can however transmit a detailed chart of how Margeaux has come to be."

"What happened to your parents, little girl?" John pitched his voice to sound mocking. He'd no sympathy for this girl, however innocent she may be. For the moment, she was a threat and would be treated like one.

"They're...dead. I do not know who my mother was. After my father died, the temple raised me."

"Temple?"

"Yes, sir," Margeaux replied earnestly. She stared wide-eyed at John, clearly realizing that she was indeed speaking with the world president. She looked enthralled. "In Hong Kong, the Buddhist Colony. That is where I am from, sir."

John inclined his head, his severe expression never once changed. She spoke honestly enough, if not a little rehearsed. He was about to say so and see her reaction when Josie interrupted from beside him.

"He's going to kill you." Josie finally managed to speak. It came out in a croak but she tried desperately to make it sound suspicious, nonplussed. "Doesn't that scare you?"

"I am a Buddhist. I accept what will happen because it is meant to happen so," Margeaux replied calmly and cast her eyes down. She took a breath and continued in a lower voice. "To be afraid will only prolong the act of dying. I look forward to reaching my enlightenment."

Josie blinked and looked as if she hadn't heard correctly. She glanced at John, the look said that clearly the girl was a little off in the head. John snorted beside her.

"You expect us to believe this? This is ridiculous! Be gone with your silly pranks." Angered, he made as if to callously dismiss Ho, he even opened his mouth to order, 'End transmission,' when Ho held up a hand.

With an air of great patience, John returned his attention to Ho—askance in manner.

"Ask your brother what we spoke of in Taiwan when we first met. That might jar his memory. Deliver the master code to me by midnight tonight at the encoded address I am sending you." Ho yanked Margeaux's hand in one swift move and raised it, palm out, for them to see. He held her tightly by the wrist. With his other hand, he swiped a gleaming blade across her hand—Margeaux gasped in shock and went rigid—he let her wrist go. Blood welled up from the gash in an instant and ran down her hand. "Or the next time, I run this blade across her throat."

The transmission ended abruptly as Josie gaped in horror.

~ * ~

I emptied my stomach, for the second time, into the sink.

When my retching finally eased and my breath levelled out, I slumped to the floor and pressed my forehead to the cool tiles. I wasn't sure what I felt, but sick to my stomach from what I'd just witnessed, I was.

The casual manner in which it'd been done, the quick shock on Margeaux's face, a face so closely resembling my own. And that gaping slash of flesh—Was that flash of white the bone? The brilliant red of blood...

I was in a bathroom in an adjoining room. Outside, the vague voices of John and Adam could be heard, their tone angry.

Weakly, I stood. Water ran down the sink as I stared bleakly at my reflection in the mirror. I'd seen quite a bit of what people could do to each other, the brutality of it and the end results. I, too, had done such damage—had to. But it was still a shock to see it, first hand, full-in-the-face, in brilliant living color.

I rinsed my mouth, splashed cold water on my face and then stood over the sink, hands braced on the porcelain sides.

Margeaux.

I'd convinced myself not to feel anything towards her—that she was an impostor. But seeing her as I did, I could no longer be sure. Her close resemblance to me aside, I couldn't help but see a little of my brother's daughter as well.

Though she'd been only a little over a year old when I last

saw her, she too, had those sparkling hazel-green eyes, set wide and large on a cherubic face. Her baby mouth pouted and parted just as Margeaux's had. Try as I might, I couldn't shake the image of young Fern out of my head.

Again, I told myself that Ho had copied—no, cloned—Margeaux from the old discs that he'd discovered. That this was all a big trick. It had to be!

And again, something inside me pitched and ached with a tug of longing, of wanting. A need to connect? To be part of a family...

John came into the small bathroom to find me still hunched over the sink, water running endlessly down the drain.

"Josie...?" he called out softly. His voice sounded tense, worried.

"I'm all right," I replied quickly.

I didn't trust myself to look at him just yet. I felt like crying—wailing—for no reason at all. Taking a deep breath, I raised my head, fussed with the sink, turned off the tap. With wet hands, I ran them through my hair then reached out for a towel.

"Josie," he said again.

I felt a hand take my shoulder and tug it gently until I was gathered into a warm chest. I didn't resist and pressed my face into his neck. He held me for a moment. It felt good. I let out a big sigh.

"I can't tell you not to feel." He spoke into my ear. His voice alone was enough to bolster my spirits and calm my confusion. "Whether this is all a trick or not, I can't say. But whatever it is, we will find out."

"Okay," I mumbled into his neck. "Did you see...?" I couldn't finish.

"Don't," he squeezed me tighter. "The man is clearly insane. Don't let his actions distract you from his goals. He means to destroy us by any means necessary. He doesn't care about anything else. Remember that when it comes time to fight him."

"Okay," I nodded as he pressed his lips to my own clammy neck. His simple way of putting things, so matter of fact, so clean, so calm, made me feel ten times better.

Almost.

John pulled away enough to look at me, brushing the hair

away from my face. "He's sent over a detailed log of the girl's family history. I've sent it directly to Aline for her to compare." He put his fingers gently to my mouth when I opened them. "Shh... The moment she finds anything, she'll let us know. But for now, let us concentrate on the more pressing matters."

I nodded. "She looks so much like—"

"I know." He cut me off and gave me a small smile. "Don't let that distract you either."

"You think it's a trick?"

"I think a lot of things. I'll believe it when I see it for myself."

I nodded again, feeling close to tears again. I pushed it away, forced it down, and managed a smile in return. "Okay. I won't be distracted." It didn't sound too convincing, even to myself.

"Come with me." John wrapped an arm around my shoulders and we headed out the room. "Adam seems to think Ho wants the master code for all the droids."

"What?"

"They spoke of it briefly in Taiwan—the possibility of a privately run automated armed forces."

We'd stopped just outside the bathroom door. From the corner of my eye, I could see Adam slumped in a chair, hunched over, hands to his head.

"I don't understand."

"The government—my government—runs all the automated armed forces as well as the domestic and service droids. We alone hold the controls for them. To put it into the hands of a privately run organization is madness. The temptations to abuse it would be too great. And yes, there is a master code for controlling the droids."

John ran a hand down my arm when he saw the shock that was obviously on my face. I disliked the droids mostly because they reminded me too much of creepy life-like dolls. But it was their plastic faces, waxy and pasty, their programmed polite manner, their unblinking soulless eyes—all lent to the half-hysteria I sometimes felt when I saw them...or was left alone in their company.

To me, *they* were the abominations. And as for the armed forces, they were nameless and faceless save for their gleaming square frontal viewfinders that were their eyes; wrought together with shiny pieces of molded body parts to resemble their human counterparts—ruthlessly metal and brutally accurate in their single-minded programmed drive to destroy. They were just like the science-fiction movies I used to watch—where the alien robots took over the world.

I must've gulped audibly for I received a soft kiss to the forehead.

"So Adam does have the codes."

John shook his head. "No, he does not." He watched me closely before he spoke again. "But Wellesley did."

"What?"

Eight

It was turning out to be a long day.

The fallout from Josie's fabricated past still buzzed through the media like an endless nightmare. More stories, even wilder than the last, popped up like warts from all corners of the world.

Some so wildly unbelievable that even Josie had to laugh out. Her personal favorite being that she was the spawn of a half-mutant alien being, raised on the research colony on the Mars space station. Josie much preferred that story to the one about her being a droid, programmed to pose as the presidents' wife since he was an alternative—the preferred term now for homosexual—and that he was impotent but needed an heir. So her droid-self would then pose to look as if she were pregnant, then later pretend to give birth, when supposedly, they were breeding his cloned spawn in large vats in a special underground laboratory.

Whatever the case, the media just lapped it up, spewed it out, and, as predicted, made Josie's life quite uncomfortable. Although, living sequestered deep inside the Citadel, the brunt of it was buffered and tamed for her benefit. In any case, she didn't care. It was what she'd agreed upon—conspired. Besides, her mind was on more pressing issues.

Loeb had been assigned the sole task of handling the media, which he did with aplomb. His boringly honest and bland features made good camera-ready respectability and sincerity. And he deserved a shit-load of awards for his superb acting abilities.

As agreed, Loeb arranged for Josie to release a statement. So at the appointed hour of four in the afternoon, a queasy-stomached

Josie faced a camera and prepared to read her brief statement.

She was made to dress simply in a tailored black pants-suit, which hugged close to her body to emphasis her toned form. The wrist holster for her krima, made purposely visible, as her sleeves ended just below the elbows. Josie was then instructed to sit and glower at the camera and speak as if offended.

In her prepared speech, Josie detailed her shock and offence at being the target of such ridiculous fabrications. Again, she briefly spoke of her history, deemed it to be the absolute truth and dared anyone to beg differently. She ended the six-minute statement by telling the world that she was just plain disappointed with them for believing in such nonsense. That there were far more serious matters that affected them daily, and efforts should be concentrated on these and not the frivolous lies that the media helps to spread and fester.

When she finished and the live camera-feed winked out, she slumped back into her chair and nearly got sick on her own lap. This president's wife business, she thought to herself, was nothing short of misery.

Before Loeb could offer her a glass of water, Josie launched herself out the chair and bolted out the door, nearly crashing into Aida, John's assistant, who let out a dignified squeak and yielded against a wall.

The press release was held in Josie's offices, or what was called her offices. A specially constructed room, attached to John's own offices, it was a mere box of a room with a faux window to show a view of the Swiss Alps. It held a desk with a small communications dock, and a chair. Josie herself had no idea what it was really used for other than to sit and pose for press and public relations photos and recordings. She rarely used it, preferring to loiter in John's offices next door whenever she ventured in the area. She was still a little clueless as to what her real duties as the wife of a president entailed.

When Josie rounded the corner she gasped a big sigh of relief and put the ordeal out of her mind. It was done—over with. Without knocking, she walked into John's office to find Simon there with him.

"Hey," she called out, a little out of breath.

John smiled encouragingly in return. He'd said it would've

been best for him not be present during her statement, preferring she concentrate on her speech and acting skills.

Simon turned looking a bit strained, nodded once to her, and continued his conversation with John. "They haven't so far—they've swept the entire place twice. All is as normal as it could be."

John rose from the desk he propped on, scrubbed a hand through his hair in annoyance.

As soon as they received the location for the exchange of the master code, Simon had his men sweep the entire area, in hopes they'd find something that would lead to Ho's location. While it was a predicted and expected move, Simon declared he didn't care. He'd preferred to show Ho what they did on purpose, while secretly doing something else, like trying to change the codes to the droids, which, in itself, was a tall order.

Ho had obviously known exactly how to play them. To change the master code for the droids took at least two days to complete—hence the run-around with the guessing game. It meant first shutting down every single droid, sector by sector, all across the world, then enter the code, delete the current program and commands, re-enter a new code against the old code, reboot and re-launch using the new code. And unlike the master code for the communications satellites and stations—it couldn't be done remotely. One had to go there physically, to the space station ST-Cy 15, better known as the Scrap Yard. This space station was specifically for the design and creation, manufacture and distribution of cybernetic technology.

If ever there was a mother ship, this was it.

Moorjani had only managed to catch an electronic shadow from Ho, which was indeed near Switzerland. The most she could gather, that Ho was somewhere in the region of France or Spain—close enough to hide under echoes and shadows. All this had meant nothing to Josie, whose limited knowledge of technical jargon of this future was pitifully non-existent.

"Could it be a trap?" she asked, snagging a glass of water from the bar. She sat down in a chair before John's desk and gulped it down. "The location, I mean."

"Possibly, but why set a trap when we have something he wants." Simon cocked his head to her, noticed her pale and clammy face. "You're not going to throw up, are you?"

"Nothing left to hurl." Josie gave him a smirk and tried to look casual. "I'm just glad it's done."

She knew it wasn't the press release that made her feel sick. It was the constant image of Margeaux's hand being sliced open that replayed in her head like a stuck record. Try as she might to shake it out of her mind, she couldn't. And each time, all she could see was the sudden slash of pink flesh gaping open, parting like a blinking eye, then the sudden rush of blood—that bright, fresh, red.

Understanding his wife, John watched as she struggled mentally. He knew too that aside from that image, it was the nagging thought that maybe this girl could indeed be her niece, and she was helpless to save her. He wondered for a moment how he would react if he were to see his own niece, Amelia, sliced open so. He couldn't. He would've gone blind with mad fury.

"So." Josie changed the subject feeling uncomfortable that John watched her, seeing through her. "What did I miss? Who *does* have the code?"

"The Governor of the space station," Simon said. "General Ayo Mwenye."

"Oh."

"And, no. He's not going to change it."

"Why?"

"Because, Josie." John decided he needed a drink—a very stiff one. He reached into the drinks cabinet and poured himself a tall measure of whiskey, took a sip, turned, and continued. "Before automated technology was made standard and world-wide, most of them were independently controlled. As in, each unit was programmed and controlled by the user. That still is the case, for personal-preference programming only, but the main control or mainframe exists on the Scrap Yard.

"About twenty-five years ago, a master code was developed to safe-guard the mainframe controls. Every new unit developed and distributed since is, naturally, under the control of the mainframe. Once a new unit is created, it's merely added on to the existing program. Of course, the code is needed for this as well. Older units can be upgraded, what have you, by logging onto the mainframe. Again, the code is used. But a total shutdown to change the code is borderline madness. First, you need to enter the code to access the kill-switch then every single unit would have to be shutdown throughout the world. That would take close to a day. Not to mention the chaos it would create when things that we depend on by the automatons are stopped—suddenly—without warning. By informing the public, we will also alert Ho. And, because this code is used so frequently for basic operations and for access within the mainframe, it is impractical to change it—at least, not at the drop of a hat. It takes time and preparation for something of this magnitude to be done."

"Oh. Fine." Josie sat up. "But what I don't get is why did Ho think Adam would have this code. Surely people must know that this Governor Mwen-whatever holds it."

Simon piped in from beside her. "Not really. It's not that common knowledge. Most people don't like to think that we control their droids."

"I wonder why?" Josie answered sarcastically. "But how did Lorcan get it, then?"

Because she had to be coached on her press release by Loeb, Josie had missed some key points in the subject. Simon filled her in.

According to Adam, he and Ho had idly discussed the possibility of a privately run cybernetics company. There were already many privately run companies, under the strict guidelines and controls of the government, who then took control and implemented these into their own system. There had been casual mention of how it worked. Adam had supplied basic knowledge he had on the subject. Ho seemed keenly interested but immediately changed course and concentrated on matters more relevant to Max Wellesley's cause. And never mentioned it again.

At some point, Ho must've acquired this code. John and Simon had a vague idea how. What caused Ho to think that Adam had stolen the code from him, they'd narrowed it down that it must've occurred when Ho vanished, soon after Lorcan disappeared and after Josie had come to be at the Citadel. Ho had been in Korea, and so was Lorcan. Lorcan had followed Adam—who he knew only at that time as Mr. Jones The Expert—in the hope that he'd lead him to Ho, which he did. However, Adam claimed he never went to Korea but knew that Lorcan was following Ho. And now Lorcan was dead along with whatever he apparently stole from Ho. It was sketchy, but the best answer they could supply.

"But." Josie had to stand and pace. "What I don't get is, why, if Ho had the code in the first place, could he not have gotten hold of it again—like how he did the first time? Why ask for Adam? And why the fuck didn't he make a copy? That's pretty dumb on his part, considering he's meant to be so smart with himself and all."

Simon rose to pace with her. "Adam was the likely choice. Ho thought he had it. You see the code is heavily guarded. The space station, that is. There probably was that one time that Ho could have gotten the code—when Mwenye went off-site to attend his mother's funeral. We've contacted him but he doesn't remember anything but the actual funeral. There are gaps in his memory. Suspicious? I would say yes. He had pegged it down to grief and thought nothing more of it."

"So, basically, Ho just couldn't be bothered to get the code the hard way but would rather—Oh, fuck!" Josie spun around to face Simon while John smiled with satisfaction that his wife caught on so quickly. "Ho had his mother killed just so he could go off-site!"

Simon nodded. "We had a look at how Mrs. Mwenye died. It took some doing, but it's very interesting. She was murdered, a shot to the head by a pulse gun. Made to look like a robbery, her home was ransacked, but nothing was taken."

"The little fucker!" Josie exclaimed. "So, why not just come right out and say that *that* was the code he wanted? Why the big guessing game?"

"God only knows how the mind of the insane work," Simon muttered. "But, I'm thinking that he also knows that to change it would take a lengthy process, and the longer he waited by keeping us guessing, the less chance we would have of actually changing it. To be honest, there is really no point in changing it. Once he has the code, he'll do so himself and we can't stop him. And, it's pretty obvious that he didn't know that Wellesley might have taken it from him. Just probably just assumed it was Adam since he discussed it with him once."

"So, this really had—*has*—nothing to do with Max in the first place."

"Doesn't look like it. I think Ho's been planning this on his own." Simon looked at John who'd just finished his whiskey. "I think I need to go to the Scrap Yard, personally. Once Ho gets the code, he'll be heading there."

John glanced at his friend and seemed to consider something. "Unless he means to hold it for ransom."

"There's that," Simon agreed.

"You're actually giving him the code?" Josie sounded horrified.

"What else can we do?" Simon levelled a look at Josie. "He appears to be holding all the cards for the moment."

"Well, what will he ransom it for?"

"Everyone wants to rule the world."

"What, so he'll turn all the droids against us?" Josie gasped out. This was really starting to sound like a really bad science-fiction movie. "And you're just going to let him? I don't buy that."

"What do you suggest then?" Simon clasped his hands before him and raised both his red brows. Blinking.

"Give him a fake code," Josie offered, flapping her arms out, she looked from Simon to John. "Stall *him* for a change."

"He'll know it's a fake," Simon snorted. "He'll use a scanner to verify."

"Can't we hold him off? Come up with some excuse?"

"No." Simon tucked his personal unit into his pocket, making ready to leave. "I'm sorry, Josie."

"There must be something we could do to stall him. We can't just give him the code." A little panic started to creep into her voice.

"Yes, we have to." John looked at her. "If we don't, he kills your niece."

"But we don't know for certain if she *is* my niece. There's no proof. Don't be distracted, you said."

John reached out and touched her arm, giving her a look. She made an involuntary noise, it sounded close to a whimper.

"Aline needs to speak with you." He cupped his hands to her face, wishing he could crawl inside her, take her place, take her hurt. Instead, he simply held her face and watched as those bright green eyes, those pools of vivid light, clouded over.

She lowered her eyes and nodded. "Let's go see your sister."

Nine

Aline Lancaster, after a quick and early dinner, kissed her children and instructed them to go into their rooms and be quiet. She told them that their Auntie Josie was coming with Uncle John, and they had some serious talking to do. They were old enough to listen to reason that she didn't fear they'd be interrupted.

August, eight, old enough to know that something serious was up, but young enough to pout and stomp his foot in annoyance. Amelia was only four and still listened with rapt attention to her mother. She obediently retreated to her room and primly shut the door to a crack like her mother usually did, trilling out "night-night" as she did so.

With a sigh, Aline joined her partner Rand in the living room. He was a tall, handsome man with exotic features. He gave her a bolstering squeeze then fussed with the coffee tray he'd laid out, knowing John would be prompt. He knew, too, that Josie would want something to eat, no doubt having put off or missed her chance to eat anything earlier. John could survive on nothing for days and would forget to remind her to eat. He knew Josie could not—would not forget—but would be too polite to remind John.

Rand eyed the sticky treacle tart pudding he'd made, thinking Josie would approve. Sweet things usually put people in a better mood.

John walked through the door, three minutes later, without knocking. He never did. An annoying habit that Rand still tried his best to get used to. After nearly a decade with the Lancasters, Rand supposed he could turn a blind eye to John's lack of manners. But then again, after nearly a decade, Rand reasoned that if the man hadn't clued in yet—president or not—John probably never would. And now, Josie seemed to be borrowing this annoying trait.

Josie followed two steps behind her husband, trying her best to look brave.

Rand greeted her first and kissed her warmly on the cheek. He gave her an extra squeeze on her shoulder. "All right?" he said as he tucked an arm through hers. "I've made something nice and sticky for you."

She grinned, despite herself. "Yum, I can smell it already. I'm so starved—I puked up my guts for the whole day."

"What's wrong?" Rand, his brow creasing, inspected her and held her chin up to see her face better.

She didn't resist, after all, he was very easy on the eyes. She even smiled for him.

Josie told Rand briefly of her day while Aline and John murmured their own greetings and shared silent looks between one another—a Lancaster trait.

Rand, a former professor and now a professional homemaker, had taught and specialized in the Techno-Generation of the early twenty-first century. He and Josie had much to talk about at the best of times. Sleekly handsome with a golden complexion to suggest a rich mélange of mix-raced ancestry, he exuded an aura of ethereal calmness that beckoned one to confide in him.

Josie didn't realize it, but she leaned heavily on his arm. He guided her to the couch and sat next to her with an elegant and regal air. If he purred like a contented cat, no one would've been surprised. Despite his dashing and charming personality that oozed seductive maleness, Rand still managed to pull off being a girl's best friend like a sexless eunuch.

"So," Aline said a little hesitantly. "You've got yourself a niece."

Josie looked up to her with a sigh. "Just tell me."

Margeaux Laperriere, daughter of Thomas 'Tucks' Laperriere, mother unknown, born in Hong Kong thirteen years ago. Her father had been listed as a musician, who died of a drug overdose when Margeaux was only three. It had been his wish that should anything happen to him, she be raised in the Buddhist

Colony. Her grandparents were Craig and Swan Laperriere, stage actors from the United Americas. It was her grandmother Swan that carried the original genetic traits. Swan, originally a Matsumoto, came from two generations of Matsumoto's, who came from a Gopnik, who came from a Sozanski, which was where it ended—about a hundred and forty-odd years ago. The highest concentration of DNA spikes and traits came from a Brandon Sozanski, the original DNA donor. His was the DNA that closely matched those of Josie's, which suggested that his parents, were, pretty much a direct descendant of Josie's brother.

Aline then went on to explain that certain females and males showed stronger spikes and traits that suggested where the linkages and direct descendents occurred, along with other technical and medical terms that only clotted Josie's brain.

Josie couldn't hear anything else. Her mind had raced backwards, trying to understand, to grasp where—who—had been the actual original. Was it Fern? Was it Conrad her nephew? Or did her brother have more children? It was possible.

"Stop." Josie held up a hand. "Just stop a minute. I need a minute."

John placed a hand over Aline's shoulder, gripped it. Absently she reached up and patted it like a mother would to a worried child.

"There is a big gap—a very sizable gap—from your time to when Brandon Sozanski offered up his DNA. He was military, joined at sixteen, just before the first onset of the urban and civil wars. It was mandatory then to submit a full DNA and medical history. It showed that he had one surviving parent, a mother named Zara who lived in Quebec. She's listed as a scientist. Brandon then married and had three children—all but one died. A daughter survived and had a child late in life, through a Gopnik. Her daughter then had two children with a Trey Matsumoto. Their son then had children with a Marisa Coolidge, who had Swan. Swan appears to be the only one that had children." Aline rose, pulled out a memory stick from her pocket and placed it before Josie. "Everything I've found and matched against Ho's information is in here. Of course, I'd also need to compare them with the actual samples in Iceland for a proper confirmation."

Rand leaned towards Josie. "These are just electronic matches, Josie."

"Meaning," Josie stared hard at the memory stick, "that they could've been tampered with?"

"We can't rule that out. But for now, they match." Aline started to pace the room. "I need to get to Iceland."

"So is she or isn't she my niece?"

"For now, she is." Aline tugged her lower lip in thought. "You'd have to be very clever to alter the electronic DNA files. They are countless fail-safes and passwords that you'd have to bypass in order to alter them. And even then, you'd have to have a detailed knowledge about DNA and genetics in order to make a fake one. But anything is possible if you knew how, and had the funds to do so."

"Could it not also be another relation? I mean, say cousins…I had one cousin on my father's side and two on my mother's. Could they be related to them instead?"

"It's a possibility, only that the spikes are very strong to indicate a more direct link."

"When are you leaving?" John asked quietly but watched at Josie. She looked extremely pale.

"Not right now—I can't," Aline said apologetically. "I've got a full plate and I cannot neglect my other patients. I've a few surgeries to perform as well, the trade minister's new kidneys, remember? The closest I can do it is in about two days. And even then, it will take me at least half a day to gather up all the samples and check them personally—Hontag-Sonnet is very strict on what you can or cannot do with their samples. And I want to be thorough."

"Do it then," Josie said in a surprisingly strong voice. "This memory stick, it comes with images?"

Aline nodded. "Some look alike. Facial characteristics and bone structure. They too can be altered, more easily than with the DNA strands."

"Josie." Rand reached for her hand. "Treat her for the time being as your niece. She may very well be and think of the opportunity that may have slipped by. Am I to understand that she is in considerable danger?"

Josie nodded, John grunted.

"That is an understatement," John compressed his mouth.

"But, yes. And Ho does not strike me as the kind of person to leave well enough alone once he's gotten what he wanted. She might end up dead, regardless."

"I don't want to look at this right now," Josie said with some force. She picked up the memory stick and was about to hand it back to Aline when John placed a hand over it.

"I do," he said as he looked Josie in the eye.

He looked angry, pissed off.

He was. If this was some massive trick on Ho's part, no way was he was going to let him get away with it. He would look at the data that Aline provided, and look at it with a fine-toothed comb.

~ * ~

Simon ended the transmission with Governor Ayo Mwenye. He had a headache, dead centre of his brain. What an idiot, he thought to himself as he replayed the conversation he had with Mwenye. It was more like a shouting match, Mwenye doing most of it.

Mwenye was simply being protective of what was his. And for good reason—reminding Simon of what his responsibility to the Scrap Yard was, and the catastrophic results of what could happen *when* the code goes into the wrong hands.

Simon saw no reason to disagree with him on that point; only it was *how* Mwenye decided to voice his displeasure that needed a little attitude adjustment.

"Give a person a little authority and it goes straight to their head," Simon muttered to himself. "Even if they've been doing it for the last fifteen years."

Personally, Simon thought Mwenye needed to leave the space station more often, maybe get a little fresh air—find a woman, or man, to divert his frustrations—whatever tickled his fancy.

But then again, his attitude also stemmed from the fact that Mwenye must've felt like an idiot by allowing someone to drug him, make him talk, and practically gift-wrap the code and hand it over. You couldn't blame the man for being a bit touchy.

Simon copied the master code onto a swipe-card with an embedded Lancaster insignia to mark its authenticity, did a clean-erase of the transmission, and logged off the secure communications link.

He pocketed the swipe-card into his breast pocket, patted it once, and called John.

"I have it."

"Any word from Ho?"

"Yes, and you're not going to like it."

John's image on the personal unit glowered back with a clamped mouth, waiting.

"He wants Josie to do the exchange. No one else."

"Not a chance. No deal." John said with a casual air.

"That's what he said—if you refused. And the girl gets dead." Simon considered something. "We've enough time to send a lookalike in her place."

"Ho will know the difference. We're at my house, come by and—"

"I'll do it." Josie's image peeked through into the small viewfinder.

"You will not." John looked annoyed and turned to face her. "I will not have you endangering yourself like this. And might I remind you *who* you are now?"

"Whoopie, the president's wife. Big fucking deal."

"There are some things that people in our position simply do not do?" John spoke with what appeared to be ultimate patience. "This being one of them."

Simon could see that an almighty hissing match would erupt between the two. He cleared his throat to remind them he was still there. It didn't work.

"Oh, like *you* haven't done things personally and put yourself in a position that endangered *your* life? Give me a break here. You do it practically all the time!" Josie had pushed her face into his and glared menacingly.

"I've been doing this a lot longer than you have. And, might I remind you, I have been trained in *other* things to know how to handle myself. Unlike you, who has only had the very basics in combat tactics."

"Ho will kill Margeaux if he doesn't see me there."

John snapped out a quick, snarling smile. "So it's *Margeaux* now. You've stopped calling her 'the girl.' You're making this personal."

"Isn't it?" Josie hissed, baring her teeth.

"Josie, she may very well be your niece. That does not mean you throw caution to the wind and jump through every hoop Ho offers. Use your head!"

Obviously affronted, Josie gaped back. "Don't speak to me like that? I'm not a stupid, fucking idiot, you know."

"Well, you're certainly behaving like one now." John had his mouth curled into a thin line; his teeth worked at his jaw. "You will not do this. Simon," his attention snapped back to his personal unit. "Get the lookalike and brief—"

"Simon," Josie interrupted. "Forget the lookalike. I'll do it," she rudely nudged John away when he tried to say something. "Only if you come with me. Tell Ho that is the deal—or I don't come and he can kill *the girl* as he pleases. Tell him that the *wife* of the president does not go out alone, or unaccompanied, in the middle of the night and that he should know better than to insist upon such a thing." She turned and glared at John.

He glared back.

Bad idea, Simon thought. But, it was better than using a decoy. He liked that Josie insisted he should be there to make sure things didn't go wrong. He'd every intention of being there from the very beginning anyway. Throwing Josie in the mix just made this very ticklish, but he wasn't about to argue with her.

Simon wasn't particularly afraid of women. He understood women perfectly well and, in general, got along with them harmoniously. But he knew that when a woman's eyes gleamed with pure malice like how Josie's did, like how his wife's sometimes did, to be very nervous and do everything they said. Without protest. Self-preservation came first. John still had much to learn about the ways of a woman, he thought with a sigh, and the intricacies of marriage. He needed to learn the art of compromise.

"I'll contact him," Simon replied to them. He noted that they didn't even bother to register him. *My God, what a fight they will have now.* "Josie, be ready in one hour. Let Mrs. Trudesson prep you personally, do you hear me?"

He ended transmission before she directed those glacial green eyes at him again.

~ * ~

Mrs. Trudesson was Simon's wife. I didn't know her first name, nor would she tell me. Nor was Trudesson Simon's last name. Mrs. Trudesson was such a cumbersome name, so I took to calling her Trudi instead. She didn't mind. And now, even John began calling her that.

Trudi was Asian or something very close to Asian. These days, everyone seemed to be a mix of something that it was hard to be sure of their true ethnicity. Even John, at the oddest moments, could look very Asian.

But at this very moment, he closely resembled a Neanderthal—right down to the brutish way he held his face.

Trudi was short, toned, blindingly quick in her movements, and an excellent cook. She made the most wickedly tasty pastries you could imagine. My personal favourite was her jellied fruit custard tarts, which she usually kept me in good supply with.

For a time, she used to be my housekeeper and body-assistant—my minder. Now, when the times called for it, she was just my body-assistant, the modern term for bodyguard.

It had been Trudi who initially taught me the basics in self-defense and combat. She still did, though John now insisted that I use one of the specialized trainers or sparring droids. But every chance Trudi got, she would still give me pointers. We were more good friends now than anything else.

"Men are just such pains in the ass sometimes," I grumbled fretfully under my breath.

After we broke transmission from Simon, John and I had another round of words, a few jabbing pokes into each other's chests and arms, and finally, the silent treatment.

Had I not been going with Simon, I knew that John would never have let me walk out of the house—let alone live—in the first place. That was one consolation because I was determined to go, one way or the other. I couldn't explain it, but I just had to see Margeaux, first-hand, for myself. Yes, I was making it personal. I had to make it so. It was practically clawing at my insides.

Trudi supervised my dressing. She tucked weapons discreetly about my person, some visible, other not. Some were traceable if we were scanned, others not.

She dressed me in combat gear—dark, close-fitting trousers

with discreet multi-function pockets and compartments. Also a body-hugging grey jersey over my body-shield; a weapons harness for the Snare Gun 3 across my mid-section; light-weight boots with steel-tipped points, heels, and ankle guards; a specially designed long black jacket that also functioned as a body-shield—it too came with many pockets and compartments. I had trouble remembering which pockets contained what.

And of course, my krima, firmly attached to my wrist holster. I felt like a pack-mule.

Simon was similarly attired, although, I suspect he didn't require the assistance of a dresser—and no doubt knew exactly what each of his pockets carried.

John purposely loitered in the background and watched with microscopic inspection, every step and process of my dressing. His eyes were all but glittering with intensity. Every once in a while, I would cast an aloof glance at him. He'd return it in the same manner.

"Ah, men," Trudi let out a humorous chuckle. "Don't you know they're still little boys—it's very hard to give it up. They just pretend they are grown ups. They don't know how to play fair and think everyone wants to play by their rules. And they think everybody wants to play like them." She cast a none-too-discreet stare at Simon who silently entered information into his personal unit. "Take The Mister, for instance."—Trudi's term for Simon—"He thinks he's a know-it-all. Thinks the entire world rotates around his reasoning. What an idiot."

"I'd like to rip John's face off right now. How dare he speak to me like that—like I'm some silly little kid that doesn't know any better." I muttered under my breath. I could feel John's glower burn the back of my neck, making it itch. "I need to know if this girl is my niece, you know what I mean?"

"Of course. Connection—bonding. The need to be a unit. You see, men don't get it. It's because they don't have a uterus."

"What?"

Trudi's comment brought me out of the prickly red haze I'd been in. I let out a howl of a laugh, which caused Simon to raise his head up and frown suspiciously. A quick glance at John told me he was burning a hole in the floor with his eyes, his lips were non-existent; the furrow between is brows deep enough to look like a ravine.

We were in Simon and Trudi's home. It was just after eight in the evening, their young daughter Yumi, already tucked into bed. Their home was similar to all the other houses in our sector. The presidential sector, where the special VIPs and close family members of the president resided. Ours, off to one corner, had the full magnificent view of the Doucet Falls. Aline and Rand were across from ours, and Simon and Trudi tucked away in another corner. Dotted nearby were a few other residences, one of them occupied by vice president Sarah Tretyakov and her family. Most of the other residences were vacant. At one point, I used to live in one of the vacant units.

John and I lived in a spartanly furnished house with sleek and sterile metal accents and masculine sharpness, a reflection of his bachelor days that I still hadn't had a chance to remedy—I was hopeless at home decorating anyway, not having inherited any of my mother's aesthetic sensibilities. Simon and Trudi's house was a home. It had the warm finishes of wood, soft colors, feminine touches, the smells of food and the scatter of toys, and the faint traces of clean and freshly laundered clothes. Aline's house, I noted, never smelled this way. It was homey, but sterile like disinfectant, like the clinic she worked in—and immaculately ordered.

"Nearly done?" Simon quirked up a red brow and looked at his wife.

"In a minute." Trudi waved him off like a fly. "Now Josie," she leaned and looked serious. "You follow Simon's lead, now, okay? And here," she gave me an elastic hair clasp, "tie the hair back in case of combat. The last thing you need is to be wasting time spitting out hair."

I nodded. Determined as I was at meeting this so-called niece of mine, I wasn't about to get myself killed in the process. "Don't worry. Going is the only foolish thing I'll be doing. Don't tell John that."

I made ready to turn and follow Simon, who, I noticed, reassuringly touched John's shoulder on the way out the door.

As I walked past, John spoke without raising his head. "Wait."

He said it so efficiently quiet, so calmly, that I froze. He snaked out a hand and grasped my arm—none too gently—and turned me to him.

With a purposely-placed scowl on my face, I looked up at him. His face, very close to mine, was bowed and staring me down. I could tell he tried desperately to compose some words without sounding angry.

"Come back safe," he finally said.

Softening instantly, I relaxed, leaned into his face. "I'm with Simon." I felt his breath warm my face as he let out a tight sigh. "I have to do this."

He nodded and managed a small, crooked smile. "Just...don't be a fucking hero."

I grinned easily and kissed the tip of his nose. So long as he managed to stoop low enough to use expletives, I knew his anger had gone, his mood changed. "You know, if we killed Ho, the problem would be solved."

"Josie," he warned.

"Just kidding." With a final nudge of foreheads, I turned and joined Simon in the foyer. A thought occurred to me suddenly. "By the way, Simon. Where the fuck are we meant to meet with Ho?"

"You're going to love this," he said casually as he raised his head up from his personal unit. "Your ex-boyfriend's house in North Yorkshire."

"What?"

Ten

Lorcan Wellesley, when he lived, resided in an old English country manor house in North Yorkshire. His mother, the dazzling and talented Terry Wellesley, had been an actress before she decided to enter a stasis pod and hide during the latter part of the first Lancaster regime. When she was resuscitated fifteen years later, she lived with Lorcan and his family until one day, the mentally scarred woman was pushed off the roof by her own grandson, Max.

The two-story house stood solidly square, homely. Welcoming, despite the fact that its owner had been dead for nearly eight months. Josie glanced across at the lawn, shrouded now in darkness and shadows. She remembered the big giant tree in the middle of the backyard, the brambles of hedges and flowering vines. And the endless stretches of grass and stepping-stones that curved and meandered throughout the gardens.

It had been a place that she enjoyed living in, a place where she'd recovered and recuperated. She loved this place, the quietness, the seclusion, and the romantic, wistful appeal of it. When you were in the gardens, it felt as if time had stood still, that the future she lived in now had never happened. And everywhere, the rich smell of flowering shrubs, cut grass, and fresh, clean country air.

They stood in the driveway, the gravel crunching beneath their feet, waiting. They were a few minutes early.

Simon himself had driven from the private landing strip, flanked by two outriders in unassuming vehicles. To ease the tension Josie felt, she settled it by bickering with him. Sensing she was on edge, he played along.

Josie had no clue exactly where they were, noticing only the endless winding country roads and lanes in a black night. When the familiar wrought-iron gate and gravel driveway neared, she grew silent. Something inside her tugged and dipped to settle uncomfortably in her stomach. It ached. In a strange way, it was like coming home.

Nearly a year had passed since she'd lived here, but it still gave her a warm sensation that made her smile wistfully. She rarely thought about the place anymore, refused to think about it. But here it was now, right before her eyes, still looking warm and welcoming. Homey.

A light was on over the large wooden front doors and more lights inside the house to indicate that someone still lived there, keeping the house alive. The curtains were still drawn open, letting the light spill out onto the stark gravel. It cast a warm yellow light that mingled with the surprisingly balmy air of the late summer evening with a comforting glow. The sweet scent of flowers filled the air. Josie inhaled deeply, remembering the smell with a smile.

"All right?" Simon murmured next to her. His brow crinkled with concern. He sensed her hesitation but refrained from giving her a bolstering hug. They both knew it would mortify them. Instead, he offered her a tight smile that came off looking like a grimace.

She nodded, shifting her shoulders and neck to ease some of the tension that built there. "Let's get this done. Quick, right? In and out?"

Nodding once, Simon strode up the wide steps and pressed the old fashioned doorbell. The door opened about five seconds later, it creaked with a familiar groan as the huge wooden door strained the ancient hinges. The face that peeked out looked terrified.

"Josie!" the face squeaked and its owner rushed forward.

Simon instantly whipped an arm out and barred the short and stout form of Mrs. Patel from moving any closer. She squeaked out again in surprise, craned back her thick neck to look up at him and took a frightened step backwards.

"Mrs. Patel." Josie grabbed Simon's arm, tugged it away. Simon's serious face tilted incredulously at Josie, but he stepped aside stiffly.

"You know this woman? This will be the cook?" Simon

barked. He snapped his head back to the cowering figure of Mrs. Patel, looking her up and down in a matter of nanoseconds. Deeming her safe enough, he relaxed a smidgen.

"Yes, she is. Now leave her alone. Can't you see she's scared out of her mind?" And that in itself was a feat. Josie recalled that nothing fazed the indomitable Mrs. Patel—or her meat cleaver, which she usually kept close at hand. Something horrible must be happening.

Of East Indian descent, Mrs. Patel spoke with the broadest London inner-city accent. Her lightly greying hair was bundled up in a thick wad behind her head while her thick hands clutched an ample bosom. The look of fear was very evident in the round, caramel-colored face.

"You're still here, I didn't know. I never bothered to—if I'd known... Are you all right?" Josie touched Mrs. Patel's arm.

"Oh, Josie!" Mrs. Patel all but wailed, bringing her hands to her cheeks, then dropping them down dramatically on her meaty thighs. "It's been such madness. I wish I could tell you more. There's so much to tell you. But that man," her voice lowered considerably even as her eyes swiveled to the side as if looking at him. "He's waiting for you in the living room."

"It's okay, it's okay."

"Josie, I need to speak with you. I'm just so happy you're all right. So glad you've found happiness after everything that's happened. Oh, Josie, I need to tell you—"

"Not now." Simon pushed forward and leaned down to the cook. "Where is he?"

"Oh." Looking frazzled, Mrs. Patel turned, gave Simon another fearful look before waddling inside.

Josie slapped a hand across Simon's arm. "You're such a fucking pig sometimes, you know that? Do you have to scare the living shit out of everyone?"

Simon returned a look of great patience and strode through the door, followed closely by Josie.

It hadn't changed at all. The couch was still in the same place, dead centre in the room. The large fireplace gaped before it, and a scatter of richly upholstered furniture were placed around the room in a semi-circle. Over the mantel, ornaments and images of the

Wellesley family. Shelves and small tables were neatly arranged throughout the room with more ornaments, lamps, and books. The smell of a recent fire hung in the air giving it a warm feel. A cozy feel…

Everything was still the same, except for the man standing callously before the fireplace.

"Who are you?" Simon asked coldly.

"Good evening, you must be Simon." The man inclined his head. He was neatly dressed in a black suit. A gleaming white shirt peeked out from under it; opened at the top to reveal a small flash of his chest. He looked to be about mid-thirties, tall and athletic, with soft, sable-colored hair that was tied at the back of his neck. His skin, lightly tanned to suggest a mixed-race heritage, his face square and strong like an old Grecian statue. He had elegantly shaped eyebrows over startlingly clear, amber eyes, a long straight nose and firm wide mouth over a proud and sculpted chin.

Simon didn't reply, but waited. His left arm dipped slightly behind him like an antenna to make sure Josie stood within reach. He'd known that upon entering the house, they were alone, save for this Patel woman. Yet, he still kept his awareness on alert, never once taking his eyes off the man. Simon sensed great danger exuding off this man before him.

"I am James. I represent Michael Ho." James didn't smile, nor did his expression change from the calm and slightly smirking manner with which he first greeted them. He titled his head to one side, registering Josie. "Madam Lancaster."

Josie didn't acknowledge. She simply stood where she was—safe—behind Simon and a solid brick wall at her back. With her hands clasped before her, she discreetly fingered the krima stick at her wrist.

"My instructions are to deal directly with you. Should you not cooperate, or prove not to be who you appear to be, I am to kill the cook and anyone who interferes."

"Leave her out of this. She has nothing to do with any of it." Josie spoke for the first time, steel in her voice. She flicked a glance to Mrs. Patel, who stood rooted in a corner, pressed up against a bookcase to their right, and staring wide-eyed at the man.

"That is the point. Innocence sometimes can be such a

burden."

Josie glowered at James, who stood aloof and composed. He looked dangerous—lethal. She'd seen that look many times on Simon.

"Madam Lancaster, I am to ask you a question which you will answer correctly," James continued with a slightly bored look.

"Go on, then." Riddles and guessing games seemed to be the norm in this particular situation. Josie made a face to suggest impatience.

"While you resided here, what was the preferred beverage of Mr. Ho?"

With a bold snort, Josie edged forward one step and stared menacingly at James.

"Rose hip tea." She said it deliberately, annunciating each word.

"Thank you." James inclined his head again.

"Where is the girl?"

"She is safe."

"Is she here?"

"She is safe." James gave her a curious look, almost like a wild beast sniffing the air to some appealing scent.

Simon stepped forward. "It was our understanding that the girl would be handed over to us in exchange for the code."

"That is still the understanding," James replied casually, his eyes still on Josie.

Josie pushed the feeling of discomfort aside, and boldly returned James' inspection of her.

James continued to keep his attention on Josie, seemingly mesmerized by her face. She narrowed her eyes, hoping they looked dark and suspicious—dangerous. She lowered her head next, jawline hardening as she deliberately studied him.

He twitched a corner of his mouth as if he wanted to smile but warred with some internal conflict that instead, he pursed his lips thoughtfully.

Josie judged him to be at least six-four, which meant he could cross the room in less than two seconds. Simon, no doubt, could match that time, or maybe beat it, if he didn't have to first push her to safety. To be courteous, she casually broke off the staring match and retreated a step back, pretending to lean against the wall behind her. She changed her stance and leaned more to her left, the quicker to dip her other hand to her chest holster.

Simon took note of the move without looking. He shifted as well, turning his body deliberately and placing his left foot forward.

James, seeing the moves, altered his own body to suit. He allowed himself a small smile now.

Like the pieces on a chessboard, each shifted and moved to gain a better angle of attack. James glanced at Simon, knowing who he was and how dangerous he could be. Simon, after all, was a legend. If it came to a fight, Simon would have to be dealt with first. The woman could wait. He'd been informed that she'd been trained and was skilled with the krima. He took note of her again, better to not underestimate her. She looked quick and agile. She did, after all, help bring down Uron Koh. The talk was that she rode upon Uron's back like a wild Arena-rider, stabbing him repeatedly with her krima until he was felled to the ground, where she then ripped his face open to expose his grinning skull. It was macabre, and it appealed to him greatly.

"Come now," Simon broke the silence. "We can do this all night and get nowhere. We have to be leaving shortly—my ward's husband awaits her return." It was said like a threat. Should harm come to Josie, the wrath of the president would be great. "Deliver us the girl."

James directed a cool glance at Mrs. Patel. "Bring her."

With another squeak, Mrs. Patel jumped and bolted out the room.

"Why this place?" Josie asked from behind Simon.

James smiled broadly, it changed his appearance—he looked like an angel. "For nostalgic reasons. It was Mr. Ho's idea. He thought to give you an edge, you see. You would be familiar with the place. In case you had to…run." He shrugged casually.

"How very considerate. Give him my thanks. But, I don't run much these days."

"And as a courtesy, I have come alone. There is no one else, but I assume you knew that already. Enough time was given to make sure you had a chance for a proper surveillance. Mr. Ho is not an unreasonable man, just one that is determined to get what he wants."

"Then there's no reason to kill anyone, is there? We have your code. Let's just do the exchange as planned."

James merely smiled. It was no longer the angelic look from earlier; a hint of wickedness could be seen. An involuntary shiver ran down Josie's spine. She looked suspiciously at him again.

From the other room the sound of shuffling of feet could be heard and a quick clop of hard shoes as they rapidly approached. Mrs. Patel, leading the way, came huffing into the room holding the hand of Margeaux.

She looked pale, disheveled, exhausted. Her small face was pinched tightly in a brave mold of determination. Her eyes were quick and darted across the room, taking in everything at once before they rested with a sort of shock on Josie.

Mrs. Patel brought her forward, protectively placing her hands on Margeaux's shoulders. Margeaux's left hand was tightly bandaged and she held it close to her body, favoring it.

"Don't be scared, child," Mrs. Patel gently whispered to her. "Don't be scared." She looked as if she too could wish the same. Had Mrs. Patel not had something important to tell Josie, she would've gladly thrown herself at this dangerous man with her meat cleaver. But Lorcan Wellesley's last words to her before disappearing to his death had been absolutely clear. Josie alone must be told and no one else. And Mrs. Patel had known Lorcan all his life to know that he didn't make such statements lightly. She gave Josie a meaningful look that was returned with a slight frown.

Margeaux was reedy, now that Josie saw her in the flesh. Thin and gangly with slightly oversized feet, like a child that grew too quickly. But she still wasn't as tall as Josie was at that same age. At least a full head shorter. Her skin was so pale Josie could nearly see the blue veins that ran beneath the surface.

"Margeaux," Josie simply said. She'd pushed off from the wall and stood erect, frowning at the girl. She wanted to ask so many questions, but knew now wasn't the time for lengthy conversations.

Unable to speak from surprise and shock, Margeaux merely stared back.

"The code, please." James brought Josie back to her senses.

Simon grunted next to her. "I have it. If you will allow me to remove it from my pocket."

Shifting his position again, James nodded. Simon dipped one hand gingerly into his jacket, brought out a metallic card and held it up before him.

"Now, how shall we to do this so we don't go killing each other in the process?" Simon smiled broadly.

James returned the smile. "First we must check to see that this is the correct code." He carefully pulled out a small rectangular device and held it up to Simon. "Insert the card. Let Madam Lancaster do it."

"Not a chance." Simon stepped forward to insert the card himself.

Both men watched the other as the device uttered a series of burbling noises and a final tone to suggest the scanning was complete.

Simon still had his hand on the card. With his left hand behind his back, he flicked a signal to Josie. She caught the signal without giving it away. With care, and no sudden movements, Josie sidled towards the entrance of the room, and stood next to Margeaux who watched her with reverence.

"Wait for me by the door," Simon said—their agreed signal. It also meant under no circumstances, unless given no other alternative, was she to engage in combat—and, to keep her back against the wall with weapons at the ready.

With delicate care, Simon removed his hand from the card and took one slow step backwards.

It was nothing but a blur. Simon's left hand snapped out, gripping James' extended wrist—the scanner juddered in it briefly. Simon whirled backwards in a spin, leading with his right hand and smashed his fist into James' neck—or what should've been his neck. James had already hurled himself back, felt the gush of air as Simon's fist swept over him. He snapped up like a spring and slammed a clawed fist into Simon's mid-section, missing as Simon curled his body inwards like a marionette that had suddenly snapped free of its strings.

Their hands still joined, Simon grunted, whipped a counter-punch, hitting James on the chest. It was like a dance, two stags locking horns until finally, reluctantly, their hands parted in a snap.

Simon did a sort of upward twirl and kicked James' shoulder

with a foot. James staggered, dipped down into a crouch, jabbed a leg at Simon, who jumped up and did a back flip, landing with his pulse gun already in his hand.

James shot up like an arrow, lashed out his open palm at a lamp and sent it flying through the air towards Simon. With an easy flick, the lamp was deflected away in a shower of sparks. Simon took aim, fired. But James had vanished. He swung around to Josie—still aware that she was behind him—unharmed.

With her back to the wall in the entrance hall, the thin form of Margeaux wedged behind her, nearly suffocating, Josie stood with her krima engaged and her Snare Gun in the other hand. The expression on her face was tight with readiness.

"Took you long enough—can we go now?" she said but waited until Simon reached her before peeling herself off Margeaux. She cast a quick look at the cloakroom door. "Mrs. Patel, you can come out now."

"Steady on," Simon muttered, not liking that James simply disappeared—he could be anywhere. When Mrs. Patel's lumbering form emerged, he grabbed her quickly. She squeaked as he brought her close to his side. "Stay close."

They moved to the front door. "Josie, behind me, now. Put the girl behind Patel."

Dragging Margeaux by her skinny arm, Josie did as she was told, instructing the girl to hold tight to Mrs. Patel. Then Josie angled her body so she could see behind them, never once disengaging the krima.

They pushed through the front doors. Simon caught the signal from the outriders who were outside the property watching. Too far away, but close enough to know if something was amiss.

"Status," he muttered.

Through the earpiece he wore, he got an all-clear. Leaving nothing to chance, they kept their formation until reaching their vehicle. He ordered Josie to get in first, then Margeaux and Mrs. Patel. With a final sweep of the area, he jumped in and engaged the engine.

"Wait, I can't leave my husband!" Mrs. Patel screeched out. "They'll kill him!"

Simon slammed on the brakes while Josie gaped at her.

"Is he in there?" Josie barked. "Where?"

Mrs. Patel shook her head vigorously. "No, they have him. I must stay here. They said he'll be returned to me in the morning—if everything went as planned. Please, I must stay here!"

"I'm not letting you stay here!" Josie looked horrified. "You're coming with us."

"Josie, we must hurry," Simon said tersely through his teeth.

"It's true. They have her husband." Margeaux spoke for the first time. Her voice sounded ragged and hoarse—like she'd been screaming the whole day.

Josie shuddered at the thought, remembering the blood...

"I saw a man being brought into the room I was in, before I came here. He looked very scared. He kept saying that they took him before he had his breakfast." Margeaux continued, she looked from Josie to Mrs. Patel. "He had grey hair, receding? Plump with a moustache?"

"Oh, my! Yes, yes!" Mrs. Patel groaned loudly. "Please, Josie. You must let me stay here."

Josie exchanged a look with Simon. What were the chances that they'd let Mr. Patel go free? Let alone live...

"Look, Mrs. Patel," Josie said. "Come with us. We'll leave someone here to wait for him. But you have to come with us, you'll be safe."

Simon was already driving away. He felt like a sitting duck and the back of his neck prickled with anxiety. He summoned the outriders to move into position. The moment they sped through the gates, two vehicles peeled out of nowhere and flanked them.

"I have to tell you something important, Josie," Mrs. Patel squeaked out, nearly incoherent with worry. She gave a longing look at the house, whimpered at the thought of her husband. "Before Mr. Wellesley went away—"

Josie patted her from the front seat. "Okay, not right now. Wait until we're airborne. Margeaux," she looked at the small form of the girl that cowered next to Mrs. Patel, "are you...all right?"

Margeaux nodded. She still hadn't taken her eyes off Josie. She appeared to be enthralled, fascinated, with the way Josie barked out directives and instructions with such casual ease—like she'd been doing it all her life.

"I am fine."

From the driver's seat, Simon made a noise and spoke into his communicator. "Are you sure?" He waited for the response. "Damn it to hell!"

"What?" Josie looked at Simon. "Are we being followed?"

"No." His mouth, a grim line, sent his sharp features jutting into angles of tenseness. "But they're tracking us. A low level signal."

"What?"

"Possibly to make sure we leave."

"Is it on the vehicle or…" Josie slid a suspicious glance to the two new passengers. "Elsewhere?"

"Remote tracking—they've locked onto our position," Simon explained. "And they're jamming us. I wonder why?"

"We've lost our communication?" Josie gasped. "Shit. How much farther until we get to the landing strip?"

"Another twenty kilometers. Hang on," Simon pushed a button that sent everyone slamming against their backrests. "Make that about eighteen kilometers."

~ * ~

John was beside himself with worry. He kept repeating to himself that Josie was in good hands. Still, it didn't make him feel any better, nor did it settle his nerves. He should've tied the silly woman to a post to prevent her from leaving.

When he heard that their communications had been jammed, he roared out a curse that had the two others in the communications room cringing in fear.

"Are the backups in position?" he bellowed out.

"Yes, sir. Ten-man unit—the shuttle is secure." One of Simon's trusted men replied.

His name was Todds, a solid and reliable communications expert who could be counted on to keep his cool—and his head. He was familiar with the president's temper, but that didn't mean he was petrified of him. Aside from the awe of simply being in his presence, it was the fear of being struck by a bolt of lightening that loosened Todds' bowels. The way the president looked now, if his fingers crackled blue with static, he wouldn't be surprised in the least.

John pushed off from the chair he'd been leaning on and

stalked the room. He was tempted to just go there himself. "Can the jammer be countered?"

"We're trying, sir," Todds responded in an even voice that belied his fear.

John glowered back. His brows knitted together tightly, mouth clamped into a thin line. "Try harder. Do we know why? Is there anything in the area that could pose a threat? Are they being followed?"

"No, sir."

Resigned that he'd have to be satisfied with that, John moved off into a corner to scowl.

"Sir, the jam is hiding a tracking signal."

"A what? Are you sure? How long, since their last position, before they reach the shuttle?"

"They are about twelve minutes away, providing that Simon hasn't punched it."

Simon would, John thought. He remained silent for a full minute, suffering from something close to sheer horror, that he could feel the blood draining from his face. Simon, he knew, would see to it that everything was under control—safe. He knew that.

But Josie...

Panic started to rise inside him. His Josie. He refused to think that something, this very minute, was being done to her. Harming her.

"Sir?"

Since they'd met, there had not been a moment that they were parted for any extended period of time. They'd grown to depend on each other. The bond between them was brutally strong that sometimes, it scared him. He knew that if harm came to her, it would destroy him. And he'd move mountains to prevent such a thing. Every bone in his body raged to be there with her.

"Sir?"

He needed to focus now, he told himself. This had been planned from the very beginning. Ho had done this purposely. To what reason, he'd surely find out. He had every intention of finding out.

John ordered himself to stay calm but keep his anger boiling. Anger would see him through this. And when Josie was safely home, he would hold her tightly and drown in his relief. Then he'd tie her up and lock her in their room.

"Simon will see to it that they return safely," John said calmly.

Todds looked relieved. He thought for a moment that the president was about to have a seizure. He knew how much the president cared for his wife, and she him. They were a team. He admired them, and was among a multitude of other men and women who were not only envious of their relationship, but enamoured enough with Madam Lancaster that they'd offer themselves up for a sacrifice if it meant saving her life.

"Yes, sir," Todd replied and redoubled his efforts to counter the jamming signal.

~ * ~

It was early dawn when we arrived back to the Citadel. I was exhausted but barely felt it save around the edges of my awareness, like a dull sensation in my joints. At a guess, I hadn't slept in close to twenty-four hours.

After our communications were knocked out, Simon drove like a bat out of hell and beat his own estimate by arriving at the landing strip in four minutes flat! I barely managed a few clipped words through tightly clenched teeth during the ordeal, my face felt stretched from the G-force. He'd pushed the vehicle until the speeds clipped just under the hypersonic mark. Any faster, and we'd have zoomed straight off the country and into the next continent. As it was, Simon had to go half-airborne so he wouldn't crash into trees or wreck the asphalt from the heat coming off the engine.

I had no chance to speak with Margeaux other than to give her short instructions, nor did I get a chance to look at her in any close detail. As we boarded the shuttle, already primed and ready for take-off, I was sent directly into a safety ejection pod—strapped in, secured, and sealed off from the rest of the passengers.

This pod, upon sudden altitude change, impact or manual override, was designed to immediately eject outwards, engage its own independent engine and transport me directly back to the Citadel. It was fully equipped with its own air supply, communications consoles and navigation equipment. Not that I was required to use these unless emergency manual operations were required. Ironically, to date, I'd never been given any flying lessons.

During my confinement, I sat with an utterly blank mind, gripping the straps of my harness as I listened desperately to any outside noises. There were none, save the loud ringing silence, interspersed with the reassuring mechanical beeps and buzzes that told me everything was still in working order.

Meanwhile, I was told later, Simon worked furiously with the on-board communications link, trying to emit a signal via a rogue network. He didn't having much luck. It was only as we approached Switzerland that the jamming signal lifted and we were finally able to contact the Citadel.

When we disembarked, scurried through the docking bay located on the other side of the mountain the Citadel rested on, I allow myself a sigh of relief.

I saw John—zeroed in on him. His face that was tight with strain went completely slack the moment he laid eyes on me. In a quick sprint, I launched myself at him. We clung onto each other for a moment, all else forgotten, oblivious of the people around us.

I leaned back and grinned foolishly. "Can't get rid of me that easily."

He allowed himself a weak smile. "Do I get points for trying?"

Simon approached us with Margeaux and Mrs. Patel in tow. Margeaux darted her quick eyes all around the docking bay anteroom while Mrs. Patel seemed to have drawn into herself. She wrung her hands with worry and sighed repeatedly.

"All right?" John asked Simon, who nodded with a shrug.

"Can't say I completely understand why they jammed us," he replied and drew his red brows together in thought. "Unless to ensure they got a head-start and to make sure we headed straight back here. Like a distraction, make us panic a little, while they got away unhindered."

"I wondered that, too." Unconsciously John gave my arm a squeeze. It felt possessive and greedy and I welcomed it. I ran a hand along his shoulder in reassurance.

Simon suddenly grinned and I caught him signal John with a nod. I frowned at them suspiciously. He turned and instructed

Margeaux and Mrs. Patel to follow him and they disappeared through the doors.

John looked at me with concern as we followed.

"I'm okay," I said. "Just need some breakfast and a big jug of coffee."

"She looks very young," he said quietly.

"She looks so tiny." I ran a hand through my hair. "I'll talk to her afterwards. Where's Simon taking them?"

"In some guest rooms. You'll remember them."

I'm sure he was smirking. By guest rooms, he meant the specially designed rooms for detainees. I was once a 'guest' in such a place when my presence here had been questionable. Watched all the time, restricted in where I'd been allowed to go, and fashioned with a security bracelet that I tried habitually to remove. That was a year ago.

"You think she's a threat?" I wasn't upset and understood the need to be cautious, but a small part of me was in turmoil. Defensive.

"I think they both are," he said flatly. "I'm sorry, Josie. I can't have two potentials roaming freely in the Citadel. Until they are proven otherwise..."

"I know, I know," I replied wearily, wondering, yet again, the strange sensations I felt.

Maybe Trudi was right. I needed to feel connected, to be a part of something, a sense of belonging. While blood didn't necessarily dictate family, right now, it meant a great deal. It was confirmation that I needed. I wanted it. If I just spent some time with her, maybe I'd know for sure. Would I feel it like a bolt of lightening?

"She must be really scared. She's been very brave," I said with a bit of concern. It popped out of my mouth before I realized what I said.

John gave me a strange look, making me slightly uncomfortable. "I want—would like it—when you speak with her, to be there."

I nodded and reached out to hold his hand as we walked. I was about to object, but then, thinking about it, I decided that he was right. And right now, I needed him more. Whatever it was that I felt,

I knew that if he were there, everything would be all right.

Eleven

He left her to wolf down a quick breakfast and take a shower. He even made the cereal and coffee. Crocker had been manually shut down and locked in her storage cupboard. In fact, all of the Citadel's droids were on manual shutdown as a precautionary measure. The reason given, technical issues with the latest download commands.

Governor Ayo Mwenye was at this precise moment rerouting the mainframe controls to manual override. Or so he begrudgingly claimed.

The nod from Simon confirmed that at the last minute, he'd managed to switch the master code with a fake. John expected Ho to summon him shortly once the deception was revealed. No doubt Ho would be in a roaring rage. John allowed himself a small chuckle.

Simon, aside from being the best at what he did, was nimble-fingered. It was Simon's idea to begin with, to make the switch, and the idea itself had been spawned by Josie's idle suggestion. They had needed the real code to pass the scan, since they didn't put it past Ho to use the same scanner he'd used when Mwenye gift-wrapped the code to him. Most code scanners kept a log of what they'd last scanned. So Simon had made sure, at whatever cost, he was the one to hand over the key-card personally.

"What are you grinning at?" Josie emerged from the bathroom with her hair still dripping with water. She looked freshly scrubbed and pink though shadows of exhaustion still smudged under her eyes.

John felt a slight stir in his stomach as she strode up to him.

The towel draped over her shoulders to catch the water from her hair did nothing to cover her bare body. He indulged himself with a lazy gaze along her long, lean body.

"I'm too tired." Josie warned him with a look when he grazed a hand against her breast. "What *are* you smirking at?"

"Private joke." He drew her in, nuzzling her neck and tossed the towel aside. He drew in her clean scent and nearly groaned.

"Really? What of?" Despite herself, she pressed in close and wrapped her arms around his waist.

"Did you really think we were going to just *give* the code to Ho?" He nibbled her ear.

"I don't get it?" Her voice went slightly slurred. "Oh, my God!" Pushing back suddenly, she gaped at him. "You gave him another code?"

John grinned broadly, showing even, straight teeth.

"You did not! But... How? It passed the scanner thing."

"Josie," he scooped her up into his arms and placed her onto the bed. "In a previous life, Simon was a great magician." He settled himself on top of her like a cocoon, trapping her.

"He switched it? How? When?" Josie had seen the entire exchange and then the ensuing fight. "There's just no way Simon could've made the switch."

"Josie. Be quiet." He covered his mouth over hers; stifling whatever else she was about to say.

He kissed her slowly, drinking her in. He was in no hurry. He needed to taste her, feel her, touch her. To reassure himself that she was still there. His. To squash the panic he'd felt, the sickness that his heart had felt when he thought something could've taken her away from him.

He felt her respond; the easy slide of her hands along his body, the soft sounds of pleasure as her body relaxed.

They took their time. Exploring each other like it was their first time, so when they finally joined, it was like a warm furry sigh. And at the final moment, when they lost all track of everything else, when the need for release empowered them and drove them blind, he nearly cried. He clung to her desperately, his anchor. He felt her release like a slow, rolling storm—heard her breath falter, then he emptied himself into oblivion.

They lay tangled, bodies and limbs, feeling loose and relaxed, and…together.

"I like how you welcome me home," Josie murmured thickly.

"You are so easily pleased," he spoke into her neck.

She giggled. "You make me sound like such a sl—"

"*Don't*…say that word." He shifted and nipped her neck. "You'll ruin the moment."

"Sorry," but she still giggled and turned under him so they lay side by side, facing each other. "So. I take it that Michael Ho won't be too pleased when he finds out."

John smiled lazily. "I don't care."

"Yes, you do." She poked his belly. "Thanks."

"You're welcome," he replied, then, frowned. "For what?"

"For allowing us to get Margeaux—and Mrs. Patel—out safely."

"Hmm," was all he said. He rolled onto his back and closed his eyes meditatively, the way only a man could do with such ease, accompanied by that certain satisfied look. "Mrs. Patel was certainly unexpected. And it's quite unfortunate about her husband." His words already started to slur. He made a soft, snuffling sort of noise, which meant sleep was near.

"You don't think they'll let him live either, do you?"

"The possibility of him being spared, now, is extremely thin."

"How long do you think it'll take before Ho finds out?"

"Depends on how quickly he wants to take over the world. No doubt that will be soon." John turned his head and looked at Josie. Her hair was tangled and her face screwed up in thought. "Ho strikes me as a man who does not like to be pushed around or outsmarted. He also strikes me as someone who will bide his time and wait for the right moment before he shows us his displeasure. Tell me more about this man James."

Josie blinked. She'd learned that John's mind tended to flit quickly from one thought to the next, especially when he was engrossed in his own thoughts. Or when he was upset…

"Tall, athletic—drop-dead gorgeous with a supermodel bod." She kept her face bland.

He stared at her for a moment, blinked, and then squinted when he realized she was teasing.

"So, you fancy this man, do you?" He clamped his lips together but said it casually.

"Well, he *is* good looking, in that scary sort of way."

"That's what you thought of me. And look where we ended up." He returned her blank look and received a snort.

"He's skilled, extremely skilled," she replied in a more serious tone. "He and Simon looked equally matched and, well, he just *disappeared*."

"That's nothing," John shrugged. "Distractions and foils to take your attention away. Ancient methods that never go out of style. You'll find he's no more a magician than Simon is."

"But, it means he's been trained like you guys. Do you think he could've been one of yours? Military? Special ops?"

"Possibly. But we are not the only ones who are trained this way, nor are we exclusive to the training of it. We just have better teachers." He sounded smug.

"Stop boasting." She rolled off the bed and headed back to the bathroom. "I bet I can take you on any time—and flatten you," she called over her shoulder and quirked a brow towards the shower. "I know all your weak spots. Wanna see?"

"Who's boasting, now?" John pounced off the bed with the grace of a cat—a very dangerous cat—and followed his wife into the shower. "I'll show you who's skilled."

He heard her squeal when he grabbed her rump and in a quick twirl, had her pressed against the shower stall, arms pinned above her head.

She made a curse, a howl of laughter, and then a sharp moan before he feasted on her.

~ * ~

Simon eased back into his seat, pushed the recline button, and tried to relax. He hated space travel. There was just too much of it...space, that is. Too much you couldn't see. And for a man who spent his entire life looking at things before they came, being ready, alert—space made him go blind with its nothingness.

He ordered his mind to empty, leveled out his breathing and tried to focus on...nothing. To anyone who looked at him, he appeared to be gazing placidly out the window. His heart rate dropped, his mind cleared, and he was able to re-focus on the matter of James.

James was definitely adept and trained. Quick, sure, and most definitely lethal—like him.

For his own curiosity, Simon ran a scan on him. So far, nothing. Not surprising. His records could've been wiped just as easily as if they'd been written in sand.

The man, however, didn't strike Simon as being strictly loyal to Ho, which meant that he was a Rogue. A hired gun. Not an assassin, though they weren't overly particular about their assignments. More like glorified operatives—which was why they usually tended to be so cocky with themselves. Money motivated people like James, nothing else. The petty squabbles and desires of the power-hunger meant little to them. The only loyalties they had were to themselves. When the going got tough, they got the hell going and moved onto to greener pastures.

In his career, Simon had come across a few of them and knew how to deal with them. They were best dealt with when they were dead. Only two had ever slipped through his fingers. The first, because he'd still been young and distracted by her guile, which he cursed himself shame-facedly for. The second because he took a hit from the Rogue in order to protect John.

And now, this James. The way he moved, his style of fighting that was like a rapid two-one beat. *Punch-punch, punch.* It was vaguely familiar. Familiar enough that it bothered Simon—like he'd forgotten something he should be remembering. Where had he seen that style before? He pushed the niggling thoughts away and let his mind refocus.

It bothered Simon too that James had gotten away. He would've been able to stop the Rogue, but it was either prolonging the fight, or fleeing quickly to protect Josie. And frankly, given that choice again, he would've done exactly the same. Josie was indelibly connected to John—the two were the same. To lose one, you lost the other. And he wasn't about to lose either of them.

Once the deception was discovered, Ho would go on the warpath. And, so would James. If it's one thing that a Rogue didn't like, was being out-smarted and miss out on getting their paycheck.

It was with this in mind that Simon made haste and boarded the Bullet to the Scrap Yard.

Smaller, compact, and stripped of all the usual amenities space travel had to offer, the Bullet was specifically designed for speed. It could reach a destination like the Scrap Yard—which was the closest space station beside the Agro Colony—in just under twelve hours as opposed to the thirty-six normal deep-space shuttles took.

Governor Ayo Mwenye had been warned of the possibility of an attack. He didn't take it well, but he wasn't in a position to argue.

Simon glanced briefly at his team. They were six of them, personally handpicked by him. They, like him, wore the stark black suits with the crimson trim on their collar to indicate they were his Elites. No other marks or insignias to indicate rank, the Elites were known the world over for their specialized skills.

Surrey was there. He'd proved himself, yet again, during the recent siege of the Citadel. Thick-necked, stoic and deftly musical, he sat with a bland look. No doubt, composing another masterpiece in his mind. His calm brown eyes, slightly Asian in appearance, seemingly lost to the classical notes that resonated through him. A gentle man and a polite man, Surrey was careful and always thoughtful with himself and others. Simon knew that if it meant protecting Josie, Surrey could be depended on to fight to the very last. He was smitten with her like a schoolboy.

Ox, a brute-faced black man born Mikah Watts, sat nearby like a giant in a child's chair. For a large man, he moved with grace and speed. His specialty with electronics earned him permanent placement with Deidre Moorjani. Simon recalled the hissy-fit she'd made when he took Ox from her. For such a tiny woman, Moorjani, the Citadel's Chief of Communications carried a truckload of temper and insults—not to mention the same amount of brute force that Ox had.

Minnows sat close to Ox. He was like his name, small and slightly built. While Ox was gifted with too much speech, his friend Minnows was quiet and shy. Pale, platinum-haired, nearly see-through blue eyes, Minnows was borderline albino. Simon knew his mother, Anya. He looked just like her. The youngest of the team,

Minnows had a tendency to second-guess himself, but he was nimble and quick with his krima. And the titanium chest plate he had to replace the crushed sternum and ribs when he was younger was a definite advantage in close combat.

Agnes, weapons expert. There wasn't a single weapon that didn't intimidate her, or one she couldn't rig up out of practically nothing. Long, lean and graceful, with golden hair, cut brutally straight over her neck and brows, Agnes could easily have been mistaken for a superstar. Her face was soft, delicately heart-shaped, with a gentle mouth and warm amber eyes. Her only fault was that she sometimes didn't know when to stop her lethal destruction, preferring to kill everything in sight and ask questions later. Her past was hazy, but Simon didn't care, so long as she did the job and proved her loyalty. Which she'd done countless times in the past.

Renna Djankovski, like Simon, came from a long line of body-assistants and special operatives. They'd both trained together and grew up with John. She once had an amazing crush on John, who'd been far too busy chasing the Italian minister of trade's daughter. Renna was a trusted friend and their history proved that. And like John, she rarely needed to speak or receive verbal direction.

She'd just had a baby, four months ago. Simon hoped her mind could stay focused on the job. He, too, sometimes caught himself drifting when he thought of his own daughter, Yumi. Renna was sturdily built, not stocky, but solid. Her raven-colored hair was tied severely back from her oval face. Quick brown eyes darted, taking in everything, her generous mouth permanently in a crooked purse. Sultry was what came to mind when you saw her, and her mixed-race complexion only added to her beauty.

The last to make up the team was Madds Ols, an unassuming, average-sized man. He, too, trained with Simon—a year younger. His father was now a trainer in hand-to-hand combat, Josie's other private instructor. Madds was *skilled,* very close to Simon in his abilities, a degree shy of being First Level. Simon was confidant, should anything happen, that Madds could replace him. Madds, like his former partner John, used his mind first—then his fists. And, he didn't stammer in the face of John's wrath, a definite plus considering Simon was personally grooming Madds to one day replace him.

While Simon and John were an unbeatable pair, circumstances prevented Simon from dragging his old friend into this particular fray. As much as John would've loved to join him, being world president had its drawbacks. Simon could recall a certain sullen mood on John's face when they last spoke. Though John would never purposely pout, there did seem to be a particular struggle on his face.

In any case, John needed to be with Josie and guard her while she was with Margeaux. Something niggled Simon about the girl. This man James had set the ball rolling in his head about deceptions and foils. Tricks…

He'd seen Josie's expression when Margeaux appeared. It was a look of longing. The fact that Margeaux looked a lot like Josie, only added to his unease. Like a beautifully wrapped gift that when opened, would reveal an ugliness like that of Pandora's Box.

Yes. John needed to keep Josie safe. Remind her that family ties, whether true or not, didn't necessarily mean they were innocent.

Just look at Adam, Simon mused to himself.

He hoped that Margeaux was genuine, really hoped it. Josie was smart and moderately tough, but she wasn't immune to being hurt the way only Margeaux could hurt her.

He sent a coded message to his wife, adding his concerns about Margeaux. He instructed her to keep her eyes open with Mrs. Patel, and told her that he missed her. Then he reminded her to read chapter five for him in the storybook Yumi liked. He'd promised to do it tonight, but now he couldn't. He felt a guilty tug in his heart and knew exactly how Josie felt about wanting a connection, a family. He wondered if he could picture a life without his.

He couldn't.

~ * ~

The room was just as Josie remembered it. She hadn't been there, had no reason to, in over a year. The room in question was a subtly guarded unit, specifically reserved for 'detainees'.

Basically, it was a single room that had a living area with a lone couch, a small kitchen with very basic amenities, and a bed. Connected to it, a small bathroom. It boasted a stingy little terrace that led out from the living area, fully enclosed by a fifteen-foot brick wall. A single wooden bench sat by itself atop a square patch of artificial grass and a lone scraggly bush.

In her time, detainees were given a set of three pairs of white pants, the same of shirts and underwear, and one pair of canvas shoes. The kitchen was stocked with two days worth of meals. The only beverages allowed were water, coffee, and tea. She noted that things hadn't improved much since she'd last been there.

Margeaux had been medically checked, cleaned, and fed. She sat now, a little wearily, on the edge of the bed, holding her bandaged left hand in her lap. A saline and antibiotic patch was stuck in the crook of her arm. The stark white of her new clothes did little for her pale complexion. She looked like an apparition.

Josie had asked John for ten minutes alone with Margeaux before he joined them. Reluctantly, he agreed. She knew he would've preferred her not to go in at all, but she remembered that he'd clamped his mouth considerably shut. It would've led to a massive argument if either one of them uttered another word. He knew full well that he couldn't always protect her, buffer her pain, even though he tried every chance he got. But, a useless point was just that. So, she noted that he'd kept his mouth shut and nodded instead, knowing she saw right through him. Instead of giving him a knock across the head and a choice expletive if he refused, she had the good grace to kiss him gently in thanks.

"Hey," Josie said.

Like John before her, when she'd stayed in this very room, she didn't bother to knock on the door, and instead just walked in. It had its advantages; it caught the person inside off-guard and wide open for observation. No wonder John did that, she thought.

Margeaux jerked her head up abruptly, startled. Her thin shoulders hunched in reflex, she made as if to stand. Jose indicated for her to sit.

"Hello...Josie," Margeaux replied cautiously, clearly uncertain whether or not to be so familiar with her. She stared at Josie for a moment. "I must give you my thanks for saving me. I am truly indebted to you."

Margeaux let out a small sigh, she sounded exhausted.

Josie made an uncomfortable shrug, more to ease the tension she felt. She wondered with a frown, once again, how differently people of this future spoke. With such proper formality and diction—

a primness. She decided to focus on that instead of the unexplained urge to rush forward and babble like a mother deprived of her children. Why she felt this way, she didn't know. She rolled her shoulders again.

Be calm, Josie ordered herself. *The girl is a complete stranger.* But the image of Fern kept merging in to replace Margeaux's face.

"It's Simon you should really thank," Josie said mildly. *My God, she looks so much like Fern! And the way Conrad tilts his head. Are mannerisms genetic as well?*

Margeaux blinked those large, glassy eyes as if recalling there'd indeed been another person present at her rescue. "Oh, yes. Will he be coming here soon? If not, please give him my thanks."

"Sure." Josie walked closer, pretending to give the room an interested look. "Hope this place is okay for you. It was all very last minute. We'll arrange for something a little more homey soon." Over John's dead body, it would.

"Oh, no. This is more than adequate. My room at the Buddhist Colony, the Serenity Gardens, was much smaller. I am quite accustomed to living simply. In fact, we are encouraged to seek comfort within our own selves rather than in material comforts."

"Oh." Josie leaned back against the kitchen counter and regarded her 'niece'. "How are you? You weren't mistreated," Josie winced and tried not to look at the hand, "too badly, I hope...by Michael Ho?"

Margeaux glanced uncaringly at her hand and shook her head easily. "He was quite well-mannered until..." her hand rose a fraction. "But that is unimportant, now. It was meant to be and the pain will be my reminder that human beings are far from perfection." She shrugged noncommittally and smiled. "I am here now."

Josie suppressed the urge to gape at Margeaux's response. Aside from that bothersome feeling of discomfort in the way she spoke, Josie also suspected that Margeaux didn't leave the farm too often. She seemed too absorbed with her religion, too sheltered. Boy, did the kid have a lot to learn! The discomfort was further increased when she compared herself to the girl. Considering the things she'd seen and done, been through, Josie felt like a haggard and grizzly old woman. A dusty old relic...

The doors engaged and opened, John entered. Only five minutes had passed. He looked impatient and gave Josie a quick, 'what of it?' glance. She returned it with a withering look, which thankfully, Margeaux didn't notice. Her eyes instead were transfixed on John.

He nodded politely, walking unthreateningly towards her. When he stood three feet away, he extended a hand—something he never did. Margeaux stared at it briefly in wonderment, snaked out a thin hand and shook it.

"Margeaux Laperriere," he said quietly, pronouncing her French name perfectly. "It is a pleasure to meet your acquaintance in person."

"Oh, no, sir. The pleasure is mine. I have heard so much about you. I cannot believe that I am actually here, meeting with the World President." Margeaux all but gushed, gazing wide-eyed at John's carefully chosen pose of bemusement.

"I see the physicians have tended to you." John pointedly looked at her hand, his tone changed to that of authority, cool and direct.

Josie watched the exchange with interest. While she would've preferred to talk with Margeaux herself, she felt a little relieved that he'd taken over. He always seemed to know what to say, how to say it, and the right time to say it. He even knew how to behave, pitch his voice, his manner. Right now he used his bold presence in the hopes of intimidating the girl. Staring down the poor girl like some imposing god of destruction.

"Oh, yes, sir. They have been most kind. I hardly feel any pain, now." Margeaux nearly blushed. She kept her head lowered and averted her eyes demurely.

"I trust that there will be no permanent damage. Should you need it, we can arrange for a follow-up corrective procedure. It would be most unbecoming for a young lady to be so marred."

Now it was Josie's turn to press her lips together into a thin line. What was he playing at? Trying to flatter the girl, now? Could she go any redder? It was bad enough that she seemed infatuated with him already. John behaved like a cat playing dispassionately with a scared little creature. If he had a tail, it would be gleefully twitching.

Ignoring his wife, purposely, which Josie knew he was doing, John idly walked past her and stared into the kitchen with mild interest.

"I will see to it that your nutritional needs are met as well. You are a vegan, no doubt, being Buddhist." He flicked a casual look at the girl as she nodded vigorously. "The facilities here are very meagre. These rooms were designed for another sort of guest." Despite his aloof air, he seemed unable to resist sliding a teasing sideways glance at Josie, who stood silently glowering at him.

"Thank you, sir. You are most kind."

"Not at all." He turned suddenly and stared down at Margeaux, tall and imposing.

Josie could recall a time he did that to her when they'd first met. It appeared to have the same effect on the girl, who seemed to cower within herself, her large eyes nearly popping out of her head.

"Margeaux." Josie pushed off from the counter and stood between them. "Tell me what Ho has told you about our…connection?"

Refocusing with determination, a slight frown knotting her brow, Margeaux titled her head up to Josie.

"Mr. Ho has told me that you were a pod-survivor. From quite some time ago." A faint look of awe mingled with distaste could be heard in her voice.

Taking note of the expression—a common reaction—Josie cleared her throat. "Yes. I am. Does that bother you?" *No point being delicate about it.* She felt John's fingers brush her arm. "I am considered an abomination, of sorts."

"It does bother me a little, and, it does not. But you are still human, I can see that." Margeaux considered something with a serious look. "It must have been quite a shock for you. To go to sleep in one century and arise in another."

"It was, yes."

"Mr. Ho has told me that I am a direct descendant of yours from my father's family. I never knew my mother. The monks told me that she was a transient singer and that she died soon after I was born. She was addicted to Cloud. So was my father; that was how he died as well. Mr. Ho also tells me that aside from the fact that I look very much like you, I look, also, like your first niece and nephew,

Fern and Conrad. Isn't genetics truly amazing? Generations can skip by before traits are repeated."

Josie had to control her breathing as a sudden ache constricted in her lungs at the mention of her young niece and nephew's names. She could scarcely hear anything else. She hadn't realized it, but to hear it aloud, somehow, made Margeaux's presence feel more real.

"Yes, you do. You look very much like them. Especially Fern. Did he show you any pictures of them?" Josie heard the slight hoarseness in her voice; she cleared it.

"No, he did not. I would like very much to see them, if I may."

No, you can't! Josie thought selfishly. It was there like a flash of temper. "Uhm...well, uhm. Of course..."

"It will take a little time to retrieve them." John spoke up from behind Josie, walking slowly to stand beside his wife. He nudged Josie backwards in a masterfully subtle way. "You must understand that they are not for everyone's eyes. Perhaps when you've had a short rest, we can arrange it."

"I understand, sir. Mr. Ho is trying to blackmail your wife with what he discovered. But, I am not tired."

John levelled his eyes at her, resorting to his bowed-head stance and inspected her.

Josie could see him considering something about Margeaux. He seemed to sense that her manner was quite determined. Josie saw it too. That she may be young, but knew how to draw out what she wanted with surprising force, using childish impertinence to mask it.

And her responses, despite her supposed trauma, seemed clear and direct—rehearsed.

"It will still take some time to retrieve them from their secure location," John said flatly so that there could be no mistaking the finality of it.

Margeaux nodded politely, paused, and turned to Josie. "Perhaps you could tell me a little about my ancestors?" Those glassy eyes batted once and stared expectantly up at her.

With a slight hesitation, Josie nodded. "Sure. Of course." She needed to pace. "Where shall I start?"

She started at the beginning. Margeaux sat listening with

rapt attention, never once interrupting, merely absorbing every word that came out of Josie's mouth.

John stood back and let Josie speak. His wife, tense at first, seemed to relax as she told her tale as briefly as she could. He realized now that this was what she needed to do, to say it out, and to join the dots with the lines to complete the circle.

And Margeaux, so closely resembling Josie, enraptured by her. Maybe, she too, needed confirmation. To have grown, not knowing her parents, being raised by monks—surely it must've been hard. She would've created her own circle within her small and sheltered world. And now, to discover that the last dot in the circle didn't end with her—or begin, depending on how you looked at it—but was in fact much, much larger and more detailed. Yes, she too needed this.

He watched them both. Watched how they interacted, hesitated, and familiarised themselves with one another. Openly staring when the other wasn't looking or aware, a stare that would vacuum in every single detail in a moment, and the polite smile that hid nervousness and gave them a chance to compose their thoughts. They danced around like mating birds, offering a chance to get close, then retreating quickly and slamming up the walls, re-grouping.

It was like watching war, too. The formalities that needed dealing with first, the exchange of offerings, the consideration of these offerings, and then the waiting as both parties opened their doors to see what came next. And if it didn't satisfy, war was declared.

They spent the next two hours with Margeaux. Josie still talked, having covered her entire life history as briefly as she could, as well as those of her brother, her parents, her uncles and aunts, and cousins. Margeaux asked short questions, but otherwise remained silent.

At some point, Josie ended up sitting on the bed with the girl. She looked relaxed and she even smiled, sometimes laughing at funny moments in her recollecting.

John had moved off, ambling casually to different parts of the room, never far and never taking his eyes off them. He consulted his personal unit once, responded with a frown, then, resumed his ambling, directing a portion of his thoughts elsewhere.

Simon was four hours away from the Scrap Yard. Moorjani's tracking of Ho turned up nothing. But an unidentified shuttle had just made an unscheduled launch from the north of Fiji. This was then, almost immediately, followed by two more unscheduled launches, one in Alaska and the other from Korea. All three were from neutral territories.

While unscheduled launches were unavoidable in these neutral zones, where the Lancaster government had no business meddling with in the first place, their final destination drew more than a raised eyebrow. The Bacchus Dome—the wildest entertainment and pleasure centre this side of the galaxy. And the Scrap Yard was just one stop away from it.

Most shuttles preferred to dock first at the Scrap Yard for refuelling and maintenance checks since the facilities there were far superior to that of the other nearby Agro Colony. With state-of-the-art droids in attendance to the superstore that offered electronic gadgetry and devices at wholesale prices, not many could resist its lure and would stop for a visit first.

And John would bet his last dollar that the three unscheduled's were heading straight there. And the chances that Ho was on board one of them, even greater.

~ * ~

I caught a look from John. It said 'hurry up.' I'd lost track of time completely. Having talked so much I became a little thirsty. Maybe it was a good idea if we took a short break.

Margeaux, however, looked ready to spend the rest of the day with us. She'd relaxed enough around us both, though she still looked to John with reverence. At least she no longer hesitated when she used my name.

Did I feel any different as well? I wasn't sure. I thought I'd know in a flash—expected it—if there was a real connection between us. Instead, what I felt was that she was just like me, in a sense.

I had also come to the Citadel alone and scared, uncertain. I definitely knew what that was like and felt sorry for her. Though she wore a brave face and relied heavily on her religion and beliefs to see her through this particular nightmare in her life, I could see, too, that she was still just a very young girl. A mere child that was curious, awkward, and open.

I saw something else too, that peculiar childlike tendency to want—and want it now. A tiny glint in the eye before being covered up with remembered politeness. The slight flush in the face before a temper tantrum, quickly shrugged off with an intake of breath, a toss of the head.

I could see, too, that she liked neatness and order. She fussed unconsciously at her shirt, brushing lint, straightening it and smoothing it in a slow, deliberate way. She fussed with her hair as well, to make sure it was still neatly in place, then turning her attention to the bed-sheets after I rose to yet again pace and stalk the room.

I caught John studying her with detail, absorbing her, like how he once observed me. He'd no doubt store, process, analyze, and then categorize each minute detail about her and bring it out for later use—with sub-headings and footnotes attached to each.

I was nearly finished with my tale, and exhausted, having gotten as far as waking up in New Zealand with the Aguilars. John saw a chance to give me a meaningful look when I stopped to think how best to carry on, without going into too much detail about how Madge had died. Out of pure selfishness, and also out of security reasons, I refused to speak of it with too much detail. Not only was it still very painful to talk about, but a part of me wished Madge's memory to be private, and mine alone.

"You must forgive my wife," John said. "They are some things that she cannot divulge. Tell me, Margeaux. Do you recall where it was that you were taken to with Ho?"

"Oh. No, sir." Margeaux frowned. She looked distracted and slightly annoyed to have been deprived of my story. "I do not. Only that it was a house, a modern one with lots of real wood. I was only ever allowed in three rooms—the communications room, the bedroom, and bathroom. I arrived blindfolded, but I remember that I had walked along a path from the vehicle I arrived in. It was a short walk, then, up a short flight of stairs and directly into a large room. I could hear the slight echo of my footsteps, from the wooden floors, so I knew it was fairly large and open. And then I was led straight into my room."

John inclined his head with an expression close to mild respect. "You are very observant and attuned to your surroundings."

"Meditation helps, sir."

"What do you remember of James?"

"He was the man that took me to the other house. He was very nice to me. In the shuttle ride over, he asked me if I needed anything for the pain." Margeaux raised her hand and looked at it.

"How long was the shuttle ride?"

Margeaux blinked, thinking for a moment. "I am not sure. I had to use the bathroom twice, I had a beverage and I meditated for about thirty minutes, which is my usual time. I think it took close to three hours."

John didn't reply, just stood watching her in thought. His face closed from any expression.

"You're very good," I said mildly to break the sudden awkward silence. "I usually fall fast asleep, if I meditate."

"Thank you. That is because you have too many thoughts that the mind cannot clear fast enough before sleep takes over from tiredness."

I nearly made a face at the remark. Instead, something foolish popped out of my mouth to cover my discomfort. "Do you do that chanting thing as well? While you meditate."

Margeaux looked at me as if I'd just uttered a blasphemous statement. Even John cut his eyes at me in exasperation.

Ignoring me, Margeaux simply asked, "Does everyone in your family have green eyes?"

"What? No, uh…" I blinked rapidly for a moment as my thoughts derailed. I tried to refocus on the question that hit me like a brick. "My, uh, my brother had. So did my mother but hers was lighter. My father's were blue."

"What about your brother's children?"

"Uh, Conrad had hazel, very light hazel. Fern's were just like yours, slightly green."

"Your eyes are very beautiful." Margeaux smiled, making her look much younger.

"Thanks." I felt flustered that I blinked. Then stood staring at her—my mind had gone completely blank.

It was time to go, John seemed impatient with it but he

sensed my sudden uncertainty. He made some excuse and we left, leaving her still on the edge of the bed as we'd found her.

"What's Cloud?" I asked immediately as the doors closed shut.

"A hallucinogen. Very, very addictive." He snorted suddenly. "I'm surprised she does not suffer from its affects. She must have been properly purged at birth."

"You don't like her, do you?" I said as we walked outside along a length of corridor.

"Why would you think that?" He looked annoyed and knitted his brows.

"You looked pissed off, that's why."

"I have no opinion of her," he said casually.

"Bullshit," I retorted with a bit of anger. "You always have opinions."

"Fine." Unclenching his teeth, he glowered at the path before him. "I think she thinks she's very smart. She knows what she wants and will find ways to get it. She won't stamp her foot nor will she make a scene—but get it, she will."

"What do you think she wants?" I asked fearfully.

"You."

"Me?" Surprised, I stopped walking. "What do you mean? Like, as in me as an aunt, a family?"

John stopped and stared at me for a moment. He looked tired and unhappy but he kept his glower in place. "*That* is what I have no opinion on at the moment." He reached out to cup my face. "But whatever it is, there is a selfishness about it. I know you've seen it in her—I saw you register it. Be careful."

I did see it, plain as day. What annoyed me was that he was so dispassionate about it, crudely so.

"You think she wants to harm me?" I frowned back at him. He didn't answer, merely stared at me. "You don't think, believe, she really could be my niece?" Even to my ears, it sounded petulant. I pulled away. "She's probably just scared, nervous. I am—I would be. She has to be...my niece. Just *look* at her."

"I have been. And I don't like what I see. If I am wrong, then you'll have my apologies."

"Your...*apologies*? I don't think I like that tone." In fact, it hurt me for him to say it. That he could say it so carelessly, and so calmly. Did he not realize the enormity of this? The wild possibility, that seemed to be narrowing every second, that this girl, could, indeed be my niece.

I must've recoiled because he averted his eyes as if I'd slapped his face. Collecting his thoughts, he reached out to take my hand. I pulled away, turned, and walked off, but not before I saw the hurt in his eyes as well.

Good, I thought with venom. *Hurts, doesn't it?*

Seething with my own hurt and fury, my walk broke into a run, which I did blindly in whatever direction I'd been facing. It was no surprise that I ended up in the communal gardens that I so liked, found so calming.

John could be cold and heartless without a second thought. It burned me that he *felt* nothing.

Yes, I did understand the need to be cautious, but uncaring was another matter. How could I not care? Or feel anything? How could *he* not?

Doesn't he understand what this means?

I slumped into my favourite bench that overlooked a side of the mountain. The view was breathtaking, but I was semi-blind to it. The scene before me was like in a fairy-tale world and the clouds fat and high in an impossibly blue sky.

I wondered—hoped—if John would follow so we could have a proper shouting match; one where he'd end up apologizing and groveling at my feet saying he was sorry and wrong. I even looked back to check. There was no sign of him, only a few stray people, some that I knew by name. They gave me a respectful distance. I did, however, note that some gave me a slightly suspicious look. The news reports and gossip mill must surely be working overtime. I could just bet that they'd then rush off and inform their friends that they'd just seen me running into the gardens looking upset. Tongues would wag and rumors would start—adding more fuel to the already raging fire that roared beyond the Citadel walls, wilder and more outrageous than the last. I could just see it now: 'Half-alien spawn seen to show emotions, maybe she is human after all', slotted next to a picture of me with extra large green eyes to resemble said bug-eyed alien.

Suppressing a snarl of anger, I crossed my arms over my chest and closed my eyes. *Clear your head,* I ordered myself. *Breathe.*

I must've sat there for some time, doing nothing more than breathing evenly—rewinding all the events that had taken place over the last twenty-four hours.

Mrs. Patel! I thought suddenly.

I'd completely forgotten about her. And her husband—I'd forgotten that, too. Had the operative that we planted at the estate reported back? I didn't know and made a note to ask John. Oops, no, I meant Simon. I forgot that I wasn't speaking to John at the moment. But Simon was on his way to the Scrap Yard. Shit. Trudi, then? She was, after all, *looking after* Mrs. Patel.

I should go and see her, I thought, and stood up suddenly. But Margeaux popped into my head again, which made me realize that she'd never left my head in the first place.

Without another thought, and deliberately disregarding John's warning that I wasn't to visit her alone, I marched back to Margeaux's room.

She'd moved to the kitchen when I walked in, just about to place a plate into the washer. The room smelled of tomatoes and vinaigrette, and a sharp pang of hunger bit into me. My mouth watered.

Margeaux looked up and blinked, a small smile spread across her face, so like a child when they first awake and sees someone they love before them. It was blindingly pure in its deliverance, I nearly faltered in my steps.

"You came back," she said and grinned from sheer pleasure.

"I was on my way to see Mrs. Patel," I lied. "Thought I'd just stop by to see if there's anything else you might've needed."

"Oh, no. I am quite fine. Thank you. Please thank Mrs. Patel for me. She was very kind to me—a complete stranger to her." Margeaux smoothed the side of her hair, then, tucked it daintily behind her ear. Her manner composed again.

"I will," I replied. "Mrs. Patel has always been like that. Doesn't matter who you are, she likes to take care of people. But only if she likes you." I smiled back and eased a hip onto the arm of the single couch.

Margeaux moved from behind the kitchen counter and stood before it, leaning back against it with her uninjured hand. Her feet were primly placed before her, close together, and a pensive look clouded her face.

"Am I really a guest? Or am I considered a prisoner?" She asked this so suddenly, calmly and direct, that it made me blink in surprise.

"You are..." I paused, searching for a more appropriate word.

"It is quite all right," she replied pleasantly. "I do no mind, either way. In fact, I understand that you need to be careful. It is a natural response. And I would prefer it that you were thorough in your investigations regarding my identity. It is in my interest as well."

Uncertain how to reply, I shrugged one shoulder and smiled. 'Sorry' just didn't seem like the right thing to say. I remembered the time last year, when I, too, was put in the same position. Only then, I *did* mind and I *was* a prisoner. And my past, I guarded like a secret treasure.

"You're very understanding," I ended up saying. "Very grown-up about it all. I do admire that."

"Thank you," she smiled again. "I am nearly fourteen. It is hard growing older, but I welcome the challenge. Do you think that, maybe, I may be allowed to leave?"

"Your room? Oh, of course." Could she? I wondered, not sure if John would allow such a thing. She wore no security bracelet like I did once, but to have her let loose in the Citadel would make him—and Simon—have a catatonic seizure. "But maybe, not just yet. I mean to say your presence here would first have to be properly explained. People will start wondering who you are. It's like a small town here and, well, we all know one another, sort of..." I was talking too quickly, and even to me, it sounded like a poor excuse.

"I understand. But I meant after everything with me has been sorted out. And, I meant, if I could leave the Citadel. I do not wish to stay here permanently. I already have a home."

"Oh," I stammered out. "Oh, well. I guess so. I see. You want to go back home."

She nodded, looking down at her feet.

"Of course, you do," I said more gently. *Of course, she does. How stupid of me not to think that.* Being kidnapped and dragged halfway across the world, like how I was. Of course she'd want to go back home. I knew exactly how she felt. Only she could, and I never can. "You must miss everyone at home."

"I do, very much." Her eyes were still downcast but they flew up quickly, bright and excited. "You could come, too. Meet everyone there. You will love it there. It is so peaceful and friendly, and all of the monks will simply adore you and—oh," her face went tragic.

I leaned forward with concern. "What is it?"

"I just realized how worried everyone would be." She pushed off from the counter and walked away, her back to me. Her thin shoulders heaved up and down quickly.

I hoped upon hope she wasn't about to cry.

"I'm sorry, Margeaux." I stood and walked closer. "We'll contact them as soon as possible, if it hasn't been done already. Simon is very efficient at what he does. In fact, I'm sure that they already know you're okay."

Would Simon have done that? I wondered. It shamed me to think that it hadn't even occurred to me that she'd miss her home—the only home she'd ever known—or that people there would miss her, worry about her.

I reached out to touch those thin shoulders, they jerked in reflex and she made a stifled sound. I snatched my hand away immediately. I felt horrible, like a big, bad bully.

"I'm sorry, Margeaux. Really, I am."

She nodded, her back still to me. "I understand." She shifted and turned to face me with a tear-stained face. Her eyes were red-rimmed and watery but she smiled bravely, like a grown-up. "Do you think it will be over soon, auntie?"

"It will be...very soon. We just have to be sure." My heart ached, my mind muddled with images of Fern and Conrad. That single word, *auntie*, seemed to unlock a multitude of emotions. "Once it's all sorted out, you can go back home. And I promise, I'll come with you."

"Really?"

I nodded back, not trusting myself to speak.

"And you? You believe me. You believe what Mr. Ho discovered, don't you?" She stared up at me looking small and scared.

"I think," I hesitated a moment. "I think that I'm starting to believe."

How could she *not* be my niece? She was Fern, she was Conrad—she was parts of them just as much as she was a part of me. However distant, however watered down, however many years it had been.

She was, essentially, family.

Twelve

The Scrap Yard was massive. Floating in space, a sprawling mega-structure of metal like a grotesque, giant insect with its six arms extended around it like rigid tentacles. At each of these arms housed a docking day that operated independently of the main body. Each docking bay was large enough to accommodate five large shuttles as well as externally dock one deep-space cruiser.

The arms attached to a central body that made up the entire lower half of the station. In times of imminent danger, this lower section—arms and all—could be disengaged from the upper half, which housed the living quarters of personnel, control and navigational sectors, and of course, the precious mainframe. The entire lower deck was designated for the production lines and distribution centers, commuter facilities, hospitality sectors, and also the wholesale distribution centers for consumers.

Like the lower levels, each docking bay could also, at a moments notice, eject itself away from the main body. In the one hundred and three years that the Scrap Yard had been in operation, it only had to perform a full separation once, when a massive fire erupted in one of the distribution centers. Docking Bay 3 was also ejected away and destroyed twelve years ago when terrorists tried to contaminate the station with a deadly virus. The new Dock 3 boasted a fully automated processing centre, complete with sophisticated scanning sensors for biohazards on shuttles deemed suspect.

Simon and his Elites disembarked in Dock 1, reserved for VIPs and military-class shuttles. After the standard security screens and processing, they were directed to the arrivals hall where

Governor Ayo Mwenye himself met them.

An express shuttle ride along the arm, and an elevator ride up later, found them in the inner sanctum of the Scrap Yard—Mwenye's office and headquarters.

Mwenye was a tall, strapping man, just past fifty. His rich, dark complexion was complimented by the sleek, military-styled midnight blue suit; trimmed in gold to suggest his rank and position. At his collar, a single gold dot on either side. Officially, he was the Governor, General Ayo Mwenye. Most people tended to forget his rank and just called him the Governor. He didn't mind either way, his authority here was still the law even though the people he ruled over were not strictly military, and more of the technologically inclined.

While seeing Simon and his team relaxed him in the sense that he understood the military mind, it also sent his hackles rising that the bright and shiny special Elites of the Lancaster Regime had descended upon *his* realm to take matters into their hands.

Simon so noted and logged Mwenye's ramrod stiff composure, and chose to ignore it. He'd use a different tactic with him, after all, Mwenye was military, and he didn't reach his position by dedication to service alone. In fact, aside from his strict authority, Mwenye was known for his dependability, his swift action, but most importantly, for his tech-savvy. No man with his qualities would allow personal affronts to get in the way of what needed to be done to save the station, and the world at large.

Simon would use that to his advantage and try to exploit it. And in any case, though Simon had no markings or insignias, he outranked Mwenye right out of the known solar system.

"Governor Mwenye." Simon offered a hand, pleased to find Mwenye's grip firm, but not overly. The man had control.

"Simon," Mwenye replied. He seemed slightly disconcerted by the fact that Simon had no official title, and looked like he wanted to add more. Instead he followed through with a stiff and curt nod, not even sure if to salute.

Just Simon, head of security, the president's right-hand-man, the head of every military, intelligence, and tactical deployment group you could think of—whether overt or covert. Simon was to be feared and respected, his authority paramount and his actions deadly.

Mwenye's manner suggested he was quite ashamed that he'd compromised the security of the station and all that it controlled. He'd received no reprimand and that, in itself, was worse than actually getting one. He could be seen swallowing his shame and pride as he prepared to put his precious station into the hands of this sharp-looking, red-haired man with no last name.

"Tell me," Simon spoke with an easy tone and dived straight into business. "How far have we progressed?"

This was not a social visit so Mwenye didn't bother to offer any refreshments. Instead, he paced his sleek office, which had an impressive array of electronic devices stacked on shelves behind thick glass. On display were items like the ever-popular game consoles to the very latest in medical prosthetics from the more popular brands that the Scrap Yard produced, each emblazoned with their individual company logos or branding. They were prototypes as well, yet to be introduced into the general market, their manufacturing components and functions shrouded in strict secrecy and under tight lock and key.

"We've managed to successfully re-route to manual over-ride without interruption to service. You understand that to change the code now is unnecessary, since one press of a button will effectively shut down every unit across the world in a matter of minutes. It's a temporary measure and the system will reboot in twelve hours, with everything returning to normal. During this time, however, it leaves us wide open to hackers, providing they knew we were so exposed." Mwenye paused briefly; he seemed somewhat relaxed now that they spoke of defense tactics.

He continued. "You say as well that they do not have the correct code, so I've implemented a security lock-down should any alternative code be entered. It should give us some time to work with, should they manage to break in. But regardless, I've created a massive web in which they must slog through in order to change commands over to them."

"How did you manage this? And the droids that have been manually shut down beforehand, while you re-routed, will it respond to them?"

"Yes. Manual shut down of the units does not mean off-line, unless you put a blaster shot into their circuits." Mwenye allowed himself a small smile. "We re-routed by downloading a new function command to each unit as well as the operational consoles throughout the Yard. If we are breached, they will most likely use the usual function commands to take control, then, use the code to access the data and controls of the units. The new function command we downloaded to the existing droids and consoles will respond to this as a threat, therefore, going into sleep mode for the twelve hours. But once the enemy realizes that the code is useless, and the consoles useless, they will try to hack into the system. However, for security measures, the Scrap Yard droids haven't been given this new command. It's easier to contain their potential threat here than it would be worldwide."

"Agreed," Simon nodded. "If they hack in, won't they be able to access this new function command?"

"It will take a while, but even a good hacker will find it a lengthy process. It's been embedded into a series of folders, which need to be opened in the correct sequence in order for the command to activate."

Simon nodded and suppressed the urge to shake his head in consternation. Codes upon codes, sequences, secrets... It was never-ending. "And only you have access to this sequence?"

"And my Number Two." Mwenye noted the look of suspicion on Simon's face. "In the event...they were to drug me again."

Quite, thought Simon. "What's done is done, Governor. Our job now is to deflect Ho's attempts to take control. Give me all you can spare in manpower, I'll discuss tactics later. It's a good plan. Let's hope it doesn't come to anything more than ejecting another docking bay. In the meantime, maintain full security alert, guard that sequence and watch your back. Who is your Number Two? I was not aware you had one."

"Jane."

"I beg your pardon?" Simon blinked.

Mwenye opened a small locked cabinet with a palm-print scan. He pulled out a small flat device, much like the *Slide* personal unit. He placed it onto his open palm and offered it to Simon, who merely looked at it.

"Meet, Jane," he said. "I made her myself using the shell of an old personal. It has droid circuitry but runs completely independent of any network. Meaning, she is not attached to the mainframe, nor is she registered to any network nor, too, is she detectable or traceable. But she can source anything you want and not leave a trail. They are a few out there, quite like this one, but I've made my own modifications. She is like a brain. Jane stores all my sensitive data; she holds many secrets." With an audible intake of air, Mwenye gave Simon a serious look. "I'll put her into your care," and handed it over. "Now, you and I are the only ones that know of Jane."

Simon drew his mouth into a grim line. "Then you've left me no choice but to guard her with my life."

~ * ~

Simon glanced, yet again, at Jane. She looked like any other personal unit. Smart, he thought, to disguise such a device in plain sight. Foolish, however, to depend on a machine to keep all your secrets.

He'd known they were devices like this, used mainly by criminals and terrorists. Tinkerers, the do-it-yourself buffs, the wannabe scientists and engineers were the ones who made and used these independently run droids and computers. The devices came in all shapes and sizes, from the said personal units to television sets, even innocuous toys for children or existing service droids.

Simon didn't peg Mwenye to be one of them, a tinkerer. Still, it took all types, and he *was* known for his technical abilities.

He wondered what the outcome would be if all droids ran independently. He didn't have a good feeling about it. Mwenye had assured him that Jane was completely safe. Once her 'off' switch was engaged—she was off. And, she was designed strictly for storage and information and limited communication functions.

Simon brought to mind some silly science-fiction movie Josie sometimes blathered on about, where robots took over the world, where their 'brains' developed like humans—giving them feelings and emotions. The sudden urge to fling Jane to the floor and smash her to pieces grabbed him. Instead, he thrust her back into his pocket with considerable force.

His own personal unit buzzed, causing him to uncharacteristically jump in shock.

Yanking it out he barked into it. "What?" Seeing John's surprised face, he relaxed.

"Things not going well?" John asked hesitantly.

"I thought you were…someone else." Simon ran a hand over his face in annoyance. He sat in his quarters, a small room assigned to him in a sort of hospitality suite that he shared with his team. The dinner he'd ordered lay nearby, barely eaten since he'd spent half the time talking with his team and organizing strategies. The other half spent staring suspiciously at Jane.

Frowning, John regarded his friend with amusement. It wasn't every day you caught Simon looking so frazzled. "How goes it?"

Simon filled him in, omitting the part about Jane but making sure John knew that there were things that needed discussing over more secure networks and means.

"And you? How is the girl?"

John snorted with something like mild discomfort. "I think I've upset Josie."

"What did you do now?" Simon sighed. John still had a lot to learn about the politics of marriage. He listened while his friend explained, trying to suppress a chuckle.

"John, John, John," he said wearily. "Go tell her you're sorry, that you didn't mean nothing by it. She'll understand you were being objective—eventually."

"But I think I've hurt her feelings. You didn't see the look she gave me." John's brow furrowed with guilt. "I understand her need to want a connection, a sense of belonging. I understand that. But I think she's going in blindly. And if it turns out to be all a hoax…she'll be devastated."

"Did you tell her that? Just like how you told me? No, of course you didn't. What was I thinking?"

John's response was a glower, then a resigned sigh. "She walked away before I could even open my mouth again. I think she's already decided that she's her niece."

"Shit," Simon replied, as Josie would've done.

"Exactly." John scratched his head in annoyance. "Aline's still not been able to free herself. I need her in Iceland to get confirmation. It just does not feel right."

148

"I know the feeling. There's something not quite right about this whole thing. It's been bothering me. If Ho wants to take over the world using the droids and, say, creating his own droid army, what will that achieve in the long run other than making us redundant?"

"It will make him the most powerful and feared man on earth. Do the power-hungry need a reason?" John pursed his lips in thought. "It might also be that he's got some new technology that he wants to embed into the droids."

"Mmm. But, why then, this whole elaborate scheme to get back the code? Even if he lost it, he could have simply come, blasted his way onto this station and just taken it by force. Why give us the upper hand by alerting us, practically telling us, what code he wanted? I don't get it."

"You think this is all smoke? He has something else planned?"

"I think a lot of things, but I'd rather not say just yet." Simon gave him a look to suggest that they'd already spoken too much over the networks. John covered a nod with a hand that ran over his cheek, as though to check for stubble.

"Keep in touch, old friend." Using the coded language they'd created, John indicated that they would next use their own rogue network to communicate—every two hours.

"You too, my dear friend. Now, go find your loved one and give her a kiss—from me." *Understood, stay close, be ready, be armed.*

Grinning, Simon signed off and pulled Jane out again.

~ * ~

For reasons she couldn't explain, Josie found herself ambling towards Adam's quarters. The conversation with Margeaux left her itching to talk to someone other than her husband. She didn't trust herself to be alone right now. Knowing that Adam had a more sympathetic ear, and more to compose her thoughts and feelings and stave off the ever-present urge to hit John, she turned the last corner and wandered towards Adam's secluded room.

John is merely being protective, a little voice inside her head kept nagging her. *In that cool and dispassionate way of his! And insulting. And cold. And uncaring. And—Damn him!*

And Margeaux. The thought of the girl rattled her, unnerved

her. She was convinced, now, more than ever, that she was indeed her niece. How could she not be?

She had to admit that Margeaux did have a way of making her uncomfortable. Though, exactly why, she didn't know. Was it the fact that she was a strange child that spoke as if she were years older? Or was it that she might be foolishly allowing herself into believing that Margeaux really was her niece, and just wanting it so badly that she'd gone blindly to it, and was just convincing herself that it was so? Or, was it that she was just disgusted by the fact that she was an ancient ancestor—a relic—come to this future, to meet her descendant? It sounded sick, even to her. And she couldn't forget that brief look of distaste on Margeaux's face when she discovered how old Josie really was.

In a normal world—life—these things didn't usually happen. But what part of her life was normal?

Yes, how could Margeaux not be related to her? She *was* her niece. Just *look* at her.

Josie felt it, knew it. It had to be so. It had been centuries, and any number of possibilities may have occurred. The chances were very great, especially when she didn't know for certain, the fate of her brother's family. That missing gap that connected everything together, that first century, still remained a mystery.

And who knew how many more relatives she had wandering around, unsuspectingly, in this future. After all, she did have cousins. The thought disturbed her to no end. She'd even asked John to trace back his own family tree, just to make sure she wasn't going to be marrying a relative of hers. To be sure, she'd even asked Simon, Trudi, and Rand to do the same for no other reason but to settle her mind. She'd thought for sure that Simon would laugh out and call her a silly fool, but he'd complied without a word and assured her he was no relation.

Josie let out a fretful sigh and continued walking with her head down, staring hard at the path before her.

By the time she'd cleared the security droid and reached Adam, it was very late in the afternoon and she was hungry, having missed lunch—again. She walked straight into his room, and froze.

Walking in unannounced had its drawbacks. He sat on his terrace, idly picking his nose and staring off into the distance. He rolled the extracted boogers meditatively between his fingers before flicking them over the rail.

To spare them both from mortification, Josie pretended to hook herself onto the doorframe and made enough noise and expletives to alert the dead.

"Ah, Josie," Adam called out cheerfully. "A pleasant surprise, as always."

"Hey," she replied, relieved to see he was composed and standing. She tried not to stare at his fingers. For an obsessive-compulsive, he didn't appear to have any qualms about touching his own boogers. For once, she was glad that he didn't like to touch other people.

"You look tired. Come sit down." He offered her a chair. "Everything all right?"

"Yeah, pretty much." With a sigh, she sat.

The late afternoon shadows streaked across the mountainside, the pine trees looked like majestic giants casting golden glints of light everywhere. It was a sheer drop down from the terrace, and only a lunatic would dare look down.

Adam chuckled, watching her closely with that blasted all-seeing Lancaster inspection. "You've come to pick my brain."

"Pick what? I have not," she answered with a start, still thinking of boogers. "Can't I come for a simple visit?"

"Josie," he steepled his fingers meditatively under his chin, "you've seen me three consecutive times so far. Normally I only see you every few days. What troubles you?"

She returned his inspection of her. After a moment, more like an internal consultation with herself, she cleared her throat.

"Adam," pausing to compose her thoughts. "I'm not really supposed to tell you, but as you were present yesterday when Ho, well...I'm sure you realize, and wondered, that I'm not really as *young* as I appear to be."

He nodded. "Yes. I did wonder. In fact, I've always wondered.
There's always been a sort of strange manner with you. Can you tell me? How old you really are?"

She smiled uncomfortably. "I'd rather no say, but *old*, comes to mind."

It was Adam's turn to nod but he didn't press her further. But his expression, a smug self-satisfied look, said that one day he'd find out. He sat considering something, his intricate brain seemingly working over it with detail.

When he spoke, it was as if he was clairvoyant. "You believe, then, that this Margeaux, could in fact be your long lost niece. And it bothers you because you want it to be so."

"Uhm, yes," she shifted in her seat with a small frown. "Is that so wrong? I mean, she could be—well, I'm certain she is. My niece. But..."

"But John is being careful—wary. He is quite right to be. I would advise it myself."

Annoyed, Josie glared back. "Am I so transparent?"

"Josie. It is only natural. You're human. And humans have feelings and wants. And we care."

"I *do* care—that's it. I *care*. And...he cares." She scrubbed a hand over her face, realization washing over her, and that nasty feeling of guilt at her behavior towards John. He cared enough, more than enough, to be able to see things with untainted eyes. To make himself see and think things out clearly, so she wouldn't have to see it or bear it, even feel it.

Of course, he cares. He was John. What an idiot she had been!

"And you thought John did not. He does. Especially for you."

Josie laughed easily. "I get it. He's being objective for me since I can't. I get it, I get it."

"But that's not all, is it?"

"No." She leaned back and stared out at the view, oblivious of Adam's tender gaze as he studied her. "All this talking and remembering of family is making me so homesick. I miss them. For me, it was just like yesterday when I last saw them. When, actually, they've been gone for a long, long time. And then, to see Margeaux, looking back at me, looking so much like my brother's children... It just brings it all back. It hurts, in here," she pressed a hand to her chest. "Really, really hurts. And—it's her. I know it's her. She's mine. I can't explain it. She *is* who she says she is. I know she is."

She wanted to cry, felt it very close to the surface, but she swallowed it down with force.

As if unable to bear seeing her so sad, Adam lowered his eyes. He would've touched her, pressed her to him and comforted her. But he couldn't. So he sat where he was, looked away.

"Josie," he said quietly, a little reluctantly. "Go to John. You need him—and he, you."

She smiled tightly and looked at him sadly. "I will. But...not yet. He's being so *John* about everything. And I might just end up hitting him."

Adam smiled back warmly and changed the subject. "Tell me, if you can. Has the girl been saved? And the code, it's been handed over?"

What did it matter if he knew? He was a part of this, after all.

"Yes," she replied, deciding to omit the part about the switch. "But you didn't hear that from me."

"Of course not," he winked conspiratorially. "So, it looks to me, that Ho wishes to take control of the droids. How very interesting. You know, until now, I never thought him to be much interested in things like that. He has only ever been interested in making money—nothing more. To him, money is power."

"Some would say that about you." Josie risked sounding cheeky and got a crafty smile in return. "You don't think he means to take over the world with the droids?"

He thought a moment. "I think he means to *hold* the droids as ransom. Whoever has ultimate control over them, has control of asking for whatever he wants."

"He could ask for the world, you mean?"

Adam laughed. "Yes, he could."

"Why droids? Why not something more in line with what he's good at, like making money?"

"Maybe he's got some new technology. There are many illegal forms of technology, that if one were allowed to use and implement, well..." he pursed his lips thoughtfully. "Furthermore, if he held the droids as ransom, to sell to the highest bidder, once the deal is done, he'd lose control over them to someone else. Not likely. No, he would not go that route. My bet is technology. Something that will bring money in repeatedly and with assured consistency."

"It must be that, then. Why then would he concentrate solely on droid technology?" Josie too pursed her lips in thought.

"There are many private individuals that would pay through their noses to be able to manufacture certain forms of technology. If someone who did not have scruples or were, say, not law-biding enough to care, then..." he shrugged nonplussed.

"And if one person controlled this technology, he could ask for whatever he wanted to produce whatever he was paid to produce. There'd be no limits, whatsoever. The world would be littered with scary stuff just ready to jump out and bite you in the ass."

"Very true," Adam nodded appreciatively. "And he could use the droids to keep the masses in line. Make sure a certain pecking order was established, so to speak."

Josie shuddered. "Don't droids ever make you feel, I don't know, uneasy?"

"Were you not yet born when droid technology came about?" Adam raised a brow, in hopes it would prompt her back to her secret past.

"Hmm? Uhm, not quite." She didn't bite, instead changed the subject. "What sort of technology is considered illegal?"

"There are many," Adam replied with a sigh. "For instance, there's the—"

"I thought I'd find you here." John spoke quietly from behind them.

Josie jumped in surprise, Adam merely twitched.

"What are *you* doing here?" she snapped irritably.

Leveling his eyes to her, John gave her a cool look with a hint of annoyance. "I could ask the same of you."

She squinted suspiciously up at him. "How long have you been standing there?"

"Long enough."

He watched her until she started to squirm. In fact, he'd only just arrived, catching the tail end of their speculations on Ho. What Adam said made sense. His reasoning was very close to what he himself had been speculating upon. The Scrap Yard was, in a sense, a world of its own. And with the droids under Ho's sole control, it could be guarded effectively while he made his demands from now until the end of days. Every cybernetic device known to man was manufactured there. With the sole claim to its production and distribution, Ho could make a literal killing. And, make whatever he wanted—for a price.

"Come with me," John spoke to Josie, reluctantly offering his hand. "Loeb says you need to respond to a question."

"What—why? I thought I was done with all that." Annoyed, she stood, ignoring the offered hand. She saw him take in a breath and withdraw his hand, tucking it neatly behind his back and lowering his head with a knitted brow. "Why can't he just make up a response like he usually does?"

Adam marveled at the subtle plays of marital war. He seemed mesmerized by it. He watched as Josie pointedly turned her body away from John, how John then feigned an uncaring lack of interest by turning his head away to take in the view instead. How Josie then noted it as a subtle snub and glowered, bristling with annoyance. She positioned herself into John's line of sight, puffing her chest out slightly but ignoring him with an aloof manner.

"He said that it was preferable that you responded in person, so he could formulate a proper response—knowing your true *feelings* on the matter." John spoke as if his teeth hurt.

Was there a double meaning in that statement? Josie huffed in annoyance.

"Fine," she said airily and brushed past him. "See you, Adam."

"Good evening to you, Josie. Come visit again." Adam rose and politely waved back.

With a scathing look at his brother, John turned and followed his wife.

They walked in silence through an empty corridor, both finding the smooth marble floor before them greatly appealing. The tension between them was thick with ice and practically crackling with static.

John stole a quick glance at her; her face set in a scowl, which sent his hackles rising impulsively.

She in turn risked a quick look at him under the guise of rolling her neck with impatience, and noted the line between his brows were deep like trenches and his lips non-existent.

The silence continued save the clomping of both their feet.

Unable to bear it any longer, it was Josie who broke first by mumbling something incoherent.

"Pardon me?" John replied coolly, pretending he was lost in his thoughts. Instead, he'd been racking his brain, trying to come up with the right thing to say without provoking anger.

"I said, *sorry*." She folded her arms across her chest and slowed her pace. "For earlier."

"Hmm," was all he said.

She snapped her head at him, then looked away, affronted. "Fine, then! I'm very, *very* sorry. Now can we just get back to normal?"

"Josie, there's no need to…apologize." He cringed. It was the very word that started this whole thing.

She caught the meaning and tried hard to suppress a smirk—and lost the battle. She ended up snorting a stifled laugh. "Adam was right."

"Was he now?" Sensing the mood had lightened, he cocked his head to her, giving her a faux suspicious glance. "About what?"

She hooked an arm through his—feeling better for doing it. He was warm and solid, like a reassuring rock. "That you were just trying to be objective, and protective. Because you care when I thought you were just being a cold-hearted pig. Thank you. I over-reacted."

"You had a lot on your mind. I should not have been so casual in my response."

"Yeah, yeah. I still shouldn't have over-reacted like I did. I didn't think past my own feelings. Shit," Josie groaned. "I sound like such a grown-up prat."

A small smile tugged at his mouth. He pulled her hand and brought it to his lips, kissing it gently.

"Sometimes," he said softly without looking at her, "I forget to remember that not everyone appreciates my bluntness."

"You're a shit, I know." Josie smiled broadly back at him. "I can be blunt, too."

They walked hand in hand, feeling light-hearted and at ease once more. The stifling cold weight had evaporated to nothingness. The shift in the earth had righted itself.

"Maybe," John muttered more to himself with a

contemplative pursing of lips. "I should allow Adam to have a set of books…to occupy him. Did you find he seemed a little odd? Like a bored animal in a zoo?"

"I caught him picking his nose and flicking the boogers outside. I thought for a moment he was going to eat it. Gross!"

John chuckled, glad that the world had righted itself once more, the gap in the land had closed. "He still does that?"

"Eww."

"I do love you," he said quietly, watching her from under his brow. "Maybe I should say it more often."

Caught unaware, she felt her face flush and tucked her lips in to bite back the broad grin that she knew would erupt. Her heart was all but melting away. She didn't trust herself to speak.

"I can see you do, too." He squeezed her hand, making her turn crimson. Leaning in, he kissed her lightly. "Even when you curse me 'til you're red in the face."

"When was I cursing at you?" she muttered knowing he meant earlier.

How could she reply to something—exactly what she most needed to hear—so perfectly said, at the perfect moment?

"You didn't say it out loud, but if looks could kill…"

"I was thinking of something else." She shrugged casually with a silly expression. "And now you've gone and distracted me by being so mushy. When did you become such a girl?"

Thirteen

The Citadel, the famous capital of the world, lay draped across the southern mountain slopes of Switzerland close to the Valais Alps. Just north of Italy, facing Lake Geneva in the west stood the massive, sprawling, super-structure city—self-sufficient and independent from the rest of the country and the world at large.

Roughly twenty miles long, and ten miles wide, the Citadel hugged the sides of a series of mountains. It stretched from mountain peak and then down into deep valleys and gorges. The Doucet Falls was the one main waterfall, renamed after the maiden name of Dane Lancaster's mother; it fuelled and supplied the entire Citadel with power.

The Citadel was a brilliant fusion of both modern and old architecture style. Sleek metal structures speared up the side of the mountain, meshing harmoniously with impressive stone columns and arches. Buildings stacked one on top the other, taking full advantage of the mountains many levels, crags, and plateaus—it was a marvel of modern innovation. And within the bordering walls were immense forests, complete with live animals, massive manmade arboretums, parks, nature trails, and even small farming communities for livestock and small-scale crops.

Housing the Lancaster governing body's offices and council buildings, including residential sectors, schools, and many institutions, the Citadel was also home to many entertainment facilities, sporting complexes, restaurants, bars, and shopping complexes. Intricate transportation facilities linked everything together like the weavings of a web, carrying special vehicles and trams. It even had special walkways and passages, underground tunnels.

With a population close to one hundred thousand, which were those that lived and worked within the Citadel walls, still yet another few thousand came daily. Whether as day-students to the three universities, or as consultants and specialized technicians to the various institutions, to media correspondents. Many were also granted special visa statuses as visitors, guests or tourists, and of course, the government officials that came and went on a daily basis.

Created by Dane Lancaster, nearly sixty-five years ago as the world's capital state, it was a reflection of his blatant tyrannical approach to rule. There were secret underground passages and escape routes, entire blocks of rooms and facilities as emergency shelters. With the changing times, it progressed, expanding and modifying.

Until twenty years ago, no one had been allowed into the Citadel unless specially invited. With the changing times, John's father Baird, added two more universities and special clinics and research facilities—he even opened the doors to the general public. While this was a positive move, it brought with it dangers far greater and more challenging than ever before. Security issues were tantamount. But the Citadel was still considered the safest place on earth, the most heavily guarded, and most private city imaginable. However, the recent siege shook its foundations—shattering its image of impenetrability. And it brought, too, a new level of boldness from outsiders, who seemed all the more willing to attempt anything to get within the Citadel walls, whether to wreak havoc or seek refuge.

Still, with a multitude of people continuing to come through its doors, threats were expected, and so its inhabitants adjusted. To protect their safe haven, people merely slotted in, fighting even harder to protect what was their home.

John and Josie lived in the southern sector, high up on the elevated plateaus of the mountainside. It was barred from the rest of the Citadel with an impressive series of security doors and checkpoints. Below them housed the governmental cabinet offices, affiliated annexes, and community areas. Through the special express elevators that traveled along on special grids, including the secret private passageways that Josie kept discovering daily, one could get anywhere in a matter of minutes.

Josie's meeting with Loeb lasted a good forty-five minutes. Most of it was in argument, which Loeb did most of the listening with a polite and professional cool. He nodded sagely to every scathing remark she'd made regarding the media houses, and where they could shove it.

She was fretful again, John noted. Knowing her mind, he reasoned that she'd moved forward, their recent disagreement put aside. However, the situation no doubt was duly noted and tagged with care, categorized under things she should remember not to do that would offend her husband. Marriage appeared to be hard work for everyone concerned. At least, that was one thing they could agree on wholeheartedly.

What troubled her now was minor, but he knew it covered the fact that Margeaux still loomed in her thoughts. And Loeb's news that the media demanded to know where exactly she came from was like an annoying thorn in the side. It was expected, she'd been warned, but it was annoying all the same. Then the additional interview requests that came barraging into the communications network every second. Even though Josie didn't offer interviews, still, they asked boldly.

Place of birth aside, and the speculations that she could be from the Americas, due to her accent, they wanted to know if she had any relatives. Considering that was already a touchy subject, Josie seethed with feeling and nearly bit off Loeb's poor, unassuming head.

"Tell them that the whole fucking point of being 'deep-cover' is to keep your private life private," she roared back. "What kind of stupid-assed question is that? You want my response? Read my lips: Fuck off!" And with that she turned on her heels and marched out of the office.

Loeb cast a quick glance to John where their eyes met in the age-old manner of men in sympathy with one another. John patted Loeb's shoulder and followed his wife, knowing she'd now head straight home, straight to the kitchen and stand glowering at the fridge expecting something edible to materialize on demand.

When he arrived home momentarily via the special elevator

connected to his office, he was quite surprised not to find her there. He ordered a scan of the rooms, discovered she was nowhere to be found. She wasn't home.

Strange, he thought. He would've sworn she was. The last time she went missing, it had been on purpose because she'd been juvenile enough to draw a moustache on Crocker, just to be spiteful. He'd eventually found her lurking in Aline's house, stuffing her face with some sticky pastry, hoping his sister would protect her from his annoyance.

He called Aline's home, spoke briefly with Rand and exchanged pleasantries. She wasn't there. She wouldn't go back to Adam, he thought to himself. Mrs. Trudesson? he wondered. No, she wouldn't disrupt their daughter's routine at this time of the evening. Yumi was in pre-training, and after dinner, would learn the art of meditation with her mother.

To be certain, John opened Crocker's cabinet to check. The droid was still on shutdown mode and stood docilely in the darkness, moustache-free.

He patted her shoulder affectionately and turned away, brow furrowed in thought.

Margeaux, he thought in a flash.

Damn her.

Josie knew he didn't want her to visit Margeaux alone. He stormed out in haste, practically running the distance to the elevators that would take him to the detainees' quarters.

A few, impatient minutes later, John strode out the elevator and glowered at the automated guard stationed there, who nodded, and a green light blinked in his chest. He'd have asked the guard if Josie had come through, but instead, with an irritable push, he engaged the door and marched into Margeaux's room.

A single light was on by the bedside table. Margeaux lay dozing, but not quite asleep. She jerked in surprise and scrambled up.

No sign of Josie.

John felt an odd sensation run through him—something very close to fear. For a moment, he forgot what it was he was doing in the room.

"President Lancaster," Margeaux gaped.

"I'm sorry," he nearly stammered in distraction. "I thought

my wife was here. My mistake." He turned to leave.

"Wait, sir," Margeaux called out. She hopped off the bed and walked a few steps closer. "Thank you for the new meals I received."

Frowning, John flicked a glance at the kitchen, remembering his offer to change it. He nodded haltingly. "I trust it is satisfactory."

"Yes, sir." Margeaux tilted her head and studied him. "You do not like me." It wasn't a question and was delivered with a precise stab of accusation.

Turning to fully face her, John slowly rotated his head to level his eyes on the girl, a deadly look on his face. A movement like that would've normally frozen the hearts of the more imposing enemies he'd faced. But this girl merely stood there staring up at him innocently. No, wickedly. The cocky tilt of her head still in place.

"It is not that I do not like you," John replied carefully, soft and quiet, lacing his tone with the practiced acidity and chill he'd all but mastered. He saw her hesitate briefly, an uncertain twitch near her large, glassy eyes—looking so closely like Josie it was distracting. "It is that I do not know you."

"It must be quite hard for you to accept that I am Josie's niece," she answered boldly.

Is that a smug look on her face? "Until it is proven, you will remain a stranger."

"I do not fear you," Margeaux said flatly.

John winged up a brow. "You should."

Margeaux smiled like a young child, sweetly. "Your threats will not distract me as you hope, Uncle." It was clear she said the word purposely to watch his reaction.

He gave her none.

"You, however, fear me," she continued. "Why? I mean you no harm. But it is understandable to fear me. I am, as you say, a stranger."

"Have you not learned, child," John kept the same chilly tone, soft as you would talk to a sleeping baby. "That your religion does not condone boastful statements, nor does it allow for deceptions. Now you have lead me to believe that you are not who you say you are."

"I am *not* deceiving anyone. I am who I say I am." She sounded slightly petulant.

John noted another small twitch near her eyes. A nervous tic? A lapse in her control? "And, you will also learn to welcome fear like an old friend. Without fear, you are no longer human. Do not be ashamed of it. Your comments alone tell me that you fear, very much. So do not try to convince me otherwise."

Of what does she fear? he thought. That her mystery would be solved and proved she wasn't a blood relative after all? He noted and filed her manner and behavior for later use. *Why is she playing this particular game? Does she think we suspect something? I wonder...*

"Stop talking to me in riddles." Her leg shifted slightly and she scoffed.

Was that a tantrum wanting to erupt? "Riddles? You have a lot to learn about life, child." With a look of distaste, John glowered at her.

"You're trying to imply that I'm not a human. I'll have you know that I fear a great many things, but my religion, as you stated, teaches me to appreciate my fear. In the end, there really is nothing to fear, but fear itself."

"Nicely put," John replied, still studying her with care. "Nicely repeated like a verse you learn at school…you speak with no emotion or experience. Do not try to speak beyond your years."

"I can only speak about what I've been taught." Margeaux stood straighter, puffing out her chest with pride. "Do you mock my religion?"

"I do not mock religion—only hypocrites. Which you are."

"How dare, you!" Margeaux flashed true anger, her face looked pinched. "You know nothing about me, yet you dare call me a hypocrite? Why, because I recite my religion like a textbook verse?"

"That is exactly why." John replied with a cold expression. "I know *nothing* about you."

"So that's it, then." Margeaux looked satisfied. "You think I'm not her niece."

"You may have managed to deceive my wife, but you will not with me."

"I have not deceived her. I am her niece."

"I did not mean your blood-link."

"I don't understand," she nearly pouted.

Yes, petulant, he thought again. She appeared to be selfish and mean-spirited, eager and impatient, vindictive and spiteful. But most importantly, she was wickedly sly and coy. What would all that be without being bold and having a bit of misplaced pride? The question was... Why? And to what purpose?

"Your petulance is annoying, child." Josie flashed into his mind with a renewed urgency. He turned to go and left her standing, scowling at his back.

John was impatient to leave the room. He'd question the girl later when his mind cleared. He'd let her sleep off her petulance and tackle her in the morning. Right now, his missing wife was all he could focus on.

But thoughts of Margeaux tickled his mind again. *What was that all about? Was she growing weary of her supposed incarceration?*

Or was the child in her unable to stand quiet any longer? Margeaux's behavior disturbed him, but he shrugged it away yet again, refocusing his thoughts back to Josie.

He strode back to the elevator, cursed himself for the delay, and the bitter taste Margeaux left in his mouth. He'd tried earlier to reach Josie by her personal unit. No answer. She'd probably forgot to have it on her or left it someplace.

And again, Margeaux's irksome manner irritated him and infiltrated back into his thoughts. It scared him, too. She meant to harm Josie in some way. That bit was clear, even if she didn't say it out. He had to find Josie. He had a very bad feeling creeping up his spine.

He called Deidre Moorjani, who was still in her office as usual, and asked her to run a security scan for his wife with her exact location. To ease his mind, he ventured back to Adam's via the communal gardens she frequented, even though he knew she never went there in the evenings. But she left the office in a boiling rage, maybe she needed some fresh air to cool off.

When a quick scan of the gardens proved she wasn't there, John continued on briskly, not even breaking his stride, and headed for Adam's room.

He found his brother, fully dressed, slowly—painstakingly

slow—eating his evening meal. Adam appeared distressingly like a man who spent too much time alone, a look of mild surprise on his face, fork midway to his mouth. He looked slightly guilty, like a child caught with his hand in the cookie jar.

"John?"

"Made a wrong turn, sorry." He turned to go, feeling foolish and a little disturbed by his brother's appearance.

I don't care about him anymore, John reminded himself.

But the image of his brother eating alone tugged a spot in his heart that he thought he'd closed—severed. He could've sworn Adam also talked to himself...or to an imaginary dinner guest.

"Oh, dear. You've gone and lost her?" Real concern showed on Adam's face. "You really must learn to speak to her with more kindness."

It annoyed John that Adam could read him like a book.

"What would you know of kindness?" John snapped. "Good evening, to you." He turned and left, leaving Adam, with his fork still mid-way to his mouth, frowning with worry.

Where *was* she? John tried her personal unit again. No answer. She wouldn't stray far, not these days. In fact, she never strayed far, and more often than not, would inform him of her whereabouts. No matter how angry she was, or how upset, eventually, she'd inform him or return. And to be perfectly honest, she was more upset with Loeb than with him. This didn't feel right.

He found himself zigzagging through the back alleys and hidden passages that he preferred to use. Without realizing it until he noted the direction sign on the elevator he found himself in, he was headed down to the sub-levels. When he'd reached the primary sub-level, the communications hub, he tagged Moorjani again. Still nothing.

Letting himself into Simon's office, he locked the door. The cool darkness that Simon preferred to keep it was a comfort. The room was large with a massive screen on one wall. Before it, on the other side, a large table console that was sleek, impressive, and designed strictly for business. A pilot-styled cockpit chair sat behind it, John climbed in and engaged the armrest controls, opening the rogue network link-up.

"Simon."

"Something's wrong." Simon quick eyes took note of John's tight expression. John's eyes were slightly wider than normal, the lines around his mouth rigid. "What is it?"

"She's missing."

"Josie..." Simon's mouth drew into a tight line. "How long?" he continued.

From the massive screen before John, he could see Simon sitting up from a small narrow cot. "Close to two hours, now."

"Moorjani?"

"Nothing." John's voice quivered slightly, hardly noticeable, but Simon caught it immediately.

"John, steady on." Simon saw the first glimmer of panic in his friend's eyes.

"My next check will be the exits. This feels bad, Simon."

"I know. I feel it, too. I don't like it that they are two outsiders in there. And now, Josie..." Simon shook his head. "Lock them down good."

"Already done," John waved an impatient hand. Then, as if to keep his mind on other things, told his friend about his encounter with Margeaux, of Adam's thoughts about the droids, and how he and Josie had made peace.

"Damn it, Simon. If she's been taken..." he couldn't finish so instead, slammed a fist on the table. "How *can* she be taken? This place is watched more closely than anywhere else in the world! Every single guard and security droid knows *who* she is—she can't have just walked out of here without raising an alarm."

"I know. Listen, those three unscheduled's, only one docked here—about ten minutes ago. It arrived ahead of time. There is nothing unusual about it, a private wedding party on their way to Bacchus. The other two seem to be heading directly there without detouring. We're on full alert, and no sign or movement from Ho. I don't understand. This does not feel right."

Simon scrubbed a hand over his brow, then told John about Jane. When John reacted with a slight note of distaste, he nodded in agreement. "My thoughts exactly."

"Sir," Moorjani's voice interrupted from the door intercom.

John disengaged the locks immediately. For Moorjani to come in person meant it was serious. Something greasy slithered about his stomach that he instinctively tightened the muscles there.

Deidre Moorjani, a short, tiny woman with a thick mop of black hair that tended to flop into her face, came marching into the room—imposing and commanding despite her size.

"Something weird is going on." Deidre propped on one leg and stood beside John with a fist to her hip, saw Simon on the large screen, nodded. "I've tracked your wife since she left your offices and entered Elevator 2, which would've taken her straight to up your residence. Somehow, the elevator was re-routed—it took her down to the courtyard in South Sector A. The last image of her is sitting on the chair inside the elevator, getting up, and leaving. After that, there is no trace of her."

John's mouth clamped down tightly, his teeth nearly cracking as he ground them hard.

"The exits?" Simon spoke up. He'd apparently rested his personal unit on a table since he could now be seen pacing the small confines of his room.

"Normal. No sign of her there or unusual activities. I'm running retinal scans to make sure the ins match with the outs at the checkpoints. I need to crosscheck them with visa's issued as well. That will take a little time."

"This does not leave this office, understood?" John managed to speak at last. He sounded hoarse. "How much longer before you complete the scan?"

"Not for another hour or so, possibly longer." Moorjani took note of John's distress and lowered her tone slightly. "We've had close to thirty thousand visitors today—ever since news of Josie's past came out. People just got curious. And security have been getting stressed over it."

"Thank you, Moorjani." John waited until she had left, then slumped into the chair. "My God, Simon," he groaned in pain. "They've *taken* her. Right from under my nose. It's him, I know it is. I will kill Ho for this!"

"Steady, John, steady." Simon could see the anguish on John's face, and matched it with one of his own. "We'll get her back. They're bold enough to take her where she's most protected. They're smart and savvy, but they'll make a slip, and we'll get them then. I don't think they'll harm her—not yet. If she keeps her head, she'll find a way to foil them or contact us. Trust her, John. And remember, we've taught her well in such a short time. She'll not forget what to do and she'll hold her own. I have every confidence in her. She did well during the exchange."

"But for how long? You know what she's like. She'll do something...stupid."

Simon took a breath with effort, keeping his face positive for his friend's sake. "John," he said calmly. "Give her some credit, all right? She'll keep her head."

John nodded weakly, nearly frozen with agonizing pain. His lungs were tight while his heart raced wildly, his mind clotted. Josie was all he could think of. The panic ate great big chunks out of him. *Let her be unharmed, please...please.*

"John, get a grip!" Simon barked. "Where is that anger you're so fond of? Use it! John, do you hear me? Don't be a fuck-head!"

"I hear you," he growled back low. "I just...need a moment."

It was there—the anger, the boiling rage—slowly clawing its way up, ripping and tearing at the panic. And so was an icy, cold calmness. He was going to get back what was his, and be damned with anyone who stood in his way.

~ * ~

When it first hit me, I barely felt it. Now, since whatever *it* was had worn off, the side of my neck throbbed like a toothache gone wrong. And my temper, which was all but boiling before, hadn't improved in the least.

I barely remembered what happened, only that someone had been holding my hand and leading me along. The man, as I judged him to be male even though his hair was long, had touched my face—then he sprayed something cool in my eyes. It wasn't painful, only annoying. I must've made a noise and tried to push him away since he told me to hush. After that, I don't recall much other than walking, movement, and darkness. What I did remember, was that I'd been very agreeable and followed along happily, as if I were a sheep being led to pasture and doing so was the most pleasurable thing on earth to do.

The fuzz was starting to wear off, and with it, the realization that something was terribly wrong. I lay on something narrow but soft. My left side was blocked so my movements were restricted. A male voice could be heard talking nearby. With a sudden jolt, I sprang upright and looked about wildly.

It was a room, a living room, small, neat and very...hotelish. I was on a couch, which explained why I couldn't move my left arm much. A smell of something floral mingled with disinfectant, and clean laundry filled my nostrils.

"Good morning," the voice called behind me.

I flung off the couch, spun, grabbing uselessly at my wrist. My krima was gone! Without looking to confirm, I kept my eyes riveted on James.

He stood propped against a wall that opened into another room, and watched me with a curious expression.

Instinctively, I put a hand to my neck and rubbed it. "You fucking drugged me."

His dark brown brows winged up in mild surprise, then, he tucked his hands into his pockets. "They did tell me that your language skills were a bit lacking."

"Where am I?" I risked looking around quickly to make sure no one else was in the room. I reasoned that he must've been talking to someone over a personal unit. My eyes felt slightly sticky and itchy. I blinked a few times to clear them.

"You are safe. And properly hidden." He shrugged mildly and shifted to another leg. "The eye-dye will irritate you for a little while. Use this to clear it." He pulled out a small bottle, presenting it to me carefully before tossing it my way.

I let it fall onto the couch without bothering to catch it—just in case it exploded on contact. Deeming it to be non-threatening, I picked it up, inspected it.

It looked like eye-drop solution. I glanced up at James' amused face. He looked like one of those dashing leading men in an adventure movie, his bronzed skin only adding to the effect. And the smug look he had right now had me wondering what he'd been up to while I lay unconscious on the couch. A brief internal consultation with myself assured me that I was still virtuous. But my skin still crawled at the thought that he would've had ample time and free reign in touching me wherever he pleased.

"Don't worry, it's just a mild saline solution. I won't let you burn your eyes out. They are too beautiful to ruin."

"Why've you taken me? What does Ho want with me? You *do* work for him, don't you?"

He inclined his head in a small nod. "For now, I do, contractually speaking. And as for the why, I'd rather not say." He made a tiny frown; his amber eyes appeared to cloud slightly with displeasure.

"You're what they call a Rogue, aren't you?"

James smiled pleasantly showing brilliant white teeth. "I see I've made an impression on you—enough for you to seek out my profession. I am touched."

"I didn't seek, I took an obvious guess," I replied testily.

It was John who'd told me, and that made me think what his reaction would be like when he found I was missing. I squashed down that thought and tried to focus on James. "So, if I were to offer you money, would you work for me instead? Then you'd be paid to get me the hell out of here."

"It's not that simple, I'm afraid." James shrugged good-naturedly and pushed off from the wall. "I have no quarrel with you and wish you nothing but the best. But...a contract is a contract, until it is completed. Perhaps afterwards?"

"Pity. Now I have to miss my favorite game show and be inconvenienced by all this." I shifted slightly in case of attack. He saw my movement and held up a hand.

"How is your niece?" he asked, slowly walking towards a drinks cabinet. He pulled out a bottle of wine, looked over to me in offering. I didn't respond, but he poured out two glasses anyway.

Was that a bit of affection in his voice? I wondered. Did he have a soft spot for the girl?

"She's fine." And on impulse, "She spoke kindly of you. Hurting children not your cup of tea?"

"Even Rogue's have certain standards to maintain. Assassins, not so much." He extended a hand to me with the glass of wine. "Furthermore, the welfare of children do not interest me. But if a person is mistreated for no apparent reason but to prove a point...that is, well, distasteful."

I took the glass cautiously, watching his every move, cringing slightly as the tips of his fingers brushed mine. I didn't drink even though I desperately wanted it. My heart thudded frightfully despite my composed face and steady hands. But my knees needed a little bolstering from a good swig of wine before they betrayed me.

I stared up at James' face. He, too, studied me. His eyes crawled all over my face and body. We were feet apart, and with effort, I tried to look offended.

"Yet you were ready to kill Mrs. Patel if we didn't do as you said." I reminded him.

James chuckled softly. "Have you never heard of a bluff? Patel was never part of it unless she interfered. Once she understood this, she was most cooperative. Contracts with Rogues are very precise and detailed. We don't randomly kill people and chalk it up at the end of the bill as incidental costs. If we foresee potential obstacles, we incur that into our cost beforehand. No questions asked, or the deal is canceled."

"How very considerate and most insightful. And what about women? Do you have any qualms about hurting them?"

"Depends on the woman," he sipped casually. "And if I've been contracted to hurt them. It's the same with men. We don't discriminate."

"And what is your contract with me?" I backed away, stood at an angle, my left side to him. I desperately wanted my krima back but the wine glass would have to suffice for now—should it come to that.

He sighed wearily. "To deliver you whole. Do not try to resist or escape, you cannot win. I am much stronger and faster. And," he glanced at the wine glass, "it is wasteful not to drink the wine."

"Whole?" I snapped out a little surprised.

"Whole." He smiled again, very pleasantly, as if we stood chatting about the weather. "You see, Madam Lancaster. I wish you no harm. I am not a brutal man—in the sense that you may be thinking. In fact, it would cause me great distress if something terrible were to happen to you. I do so admire you. But, I have a job to perform. Let us make this easy for both of us. Do not resist." He gave me a 'cheers' with the glass and took another sip, his yellow eyes still watching me.

It did cross my mind that he might attempt to pounce on me and rape me senseless, and it rattled me slightly. Professional Rogue or not, he gave me the creeps. There was something in his eyes that glittered a little too much with malice. What kind of malice, was yet to be determined.

Getting out of here with my life intact—any way possible—however, was the most pressing issue at the moment. But the exit meant that I'd have to tackle this large obstacle and I'd seen how he moved and fought—disappeared—that it had me rooted to the spot.

With nothing else to do for the moment, but be submissive, I took a sip. It was a dry chardonnay, smooth and soothing, and like he said, wasteful not to drink. I wanted to gulp it down but resisted.

"How much longer before I am delivered whole?"

"A few more hours," he replied easily. "Mr. Ho will come for you himself."

"Ooo, I'm so happy. And then what?"

"Couldn't say. He's very secretive and it's none of my business. That was a nice trick you pulled with the code, by the way." Smirking with a shrug, James strolled about the room.

"Haven't a clue what you mean." *Fuck!*

He smiled broadly. "Josie. May I call you that? You forget who I am. I didn't actually see the switch, but it occurred to me that Simon would try it. I certainly would have. So I scanned the code again to be certain."

"You haven't told Ho, have you?" I squinted at him and watched his behavior. Odd, I thought.

"He wanted a code, I gave him a code. He did not specify what code. I was to verify its validity and deliver it. I did both. Breakfast? I know it is too early but I've just ordered some before you woke. It's been a long night, won't you say? And I'm starved."

"I wouldn't know," I answered with sarcasm but studied him with interest. "Why didn't you tell Ho about the switch? Isn't that a little unprofessional?"

He shrugged. "Because it appeared to me that the code was

not the most important thing he desired," he tapped his head and gave me a wink. "He wanted you more."

"What? Why?" Despite my wariness, I walked closer to him. All I could think of was when Ho used to look at me with a creepy, oily look. I nearly shuddered.

"Couldn't say." James gave me a worried look that looked nearly genuine. "I'm sorry."

"Don't you even ask when you have a contract to do?"

"No." He sipped more wine and shrugged, yet again. "Unless I need to know, that is. And in this case, I didn't need to know anything past my deliverance of you to him."

"You could be a dear and ask," I smiled forcibly with politeness.

"I only ask questions when it is necessary. Haven't you been paying attention to anything I've been saying?" He looked mildly hurt.

"I could pay you more than what Ho is offering you."

"That would not be ethical."

I snorted out a laugh. "Kidnapping and god-knows-what else and you're worried about ethics."

"As I said before, even Rogues have certain standards we follow."

"Shit. Fine. What is the time anyway?"

"Just after three in the morning—your time. About one here."

"What? Where the fuck, are we?"

James quirked a brow at me and gave me a strange look. "Iceland."

Fourteen

John, nearly dead and numb with worry and exhaustion, had been up for a straight forty-eight hours. Every bone in his body ached, protested, and begged for rest and sleep. The old injury at his hip quaked with pain. It had long since healed, but it still throbbed once in a while. He rubbed at it thoughtfully.

He sat in the conservatory that connected to his offices. His favorite time of the day, dawn, had come and gone but he barely noticed. He'd forced himself earlier to drink a nutrition shake because some small part of his brain that still functioned normally, had told him he needed sustenance. It sat greasily in his stomach.

The raging anger that he'd been afflicted with had long since passed, though it still simmered and bubbled below the surface. Icy fear and worry alternated like shock waves through his body. He told himself that he needed to sleep, but sleep wouldn't come. He forced himself to clear his mind, and all he saw was Josie, imagining her hurt, bloodied, in pain—helpless.

Moorjani had shown him a recording of someone looking very much like Josie walking right out the main entrances. Her eye color was different and she wore a garish lip color and had long blonde hair. Her face was blank, a pliable look, and she matched no one in the visitor's databank.

How such an obvious error by security had been overlooked sent John spinning into another fit of fury. He vaguely remembered throwing something, it made a horrendous crash that sent people scattering in all directions. For the life of him, he couldn't remember what it was that he threw.

But it had been Josie's escort that caused John to roar. A confirmation with Simon proved that it was the infamous James, cockily staring right up at the overhead surveillance orbs.

"He is dead!" John had raged. That much he remembered clearly.

He committed James' face to memory, his movements, his posture. Despite himself, John laughed. Josie was right, he was drop-dead gorgeous. And with that thought, John groaned in agony. The image of James touching his wife speared through his heart—disgusted him—and made him blind with fury.

With effort, he shook the image out of his head.

Calm yourself, he ordered. *Josie can take care of herself. She will fight tooth and nail to free herself from danger. She will know what to do...or die trying.* He shook that thought out as well. *Stop it! Calm yourself. Step to one side,* he instructed himself. *Do it, now! Step to one side.*

He stood shakily up. "Step to one side, John," he muttered.

Calm did return. He could feel it creeping, like a soothing balm, through his body, his mind, and into his limbs. His breathing leveled, his heart beat evenly. His mind cleared. He re-focused.

Find Josie.

Think...

Why would Ho want her? Josie disliked him, thought him to be a pervert. Did Ho want her so he could do vile and disgusting things to her? Keep her like a trophy?

No. He had looked into Ho's eyes; whatever he chose to portray was just that, a façade. The man was made of steel. And his objectives were clear and direct even though his methods were abstract. His core was cold and hard but he was eager in his wants—impatient with it. That was one fault, one weakness.

Did Ho think that she knew something, then? Some secret she'd learned of while living with Wellesley? Maybe a secret of Max's?

Or even a secret of mine?

John knew Josie would never divulge anything about himself or the Citadel, not even to save her own life. He considered this, noted it as a possibility.

Ho wasn't stupid. He may be impatient with wanting

something, but he'd planned long and hard for this. A whole year had passed since he last showed his face. It was like an orchestral maneuver, everything slotting into place with such exacting precision and timing.

First it had been the opening with the business of the code, drawing out Adam. Ho had coated it vaguely to ensure that there would be uncertainty with what the code was for. Then, he struck with the revelation of Josie's past, the discovery of the old discs and the blackmail threat—linking the first with the second.

Introducing the girl came next, bringing emotions into it, confusing things further. Then, declaring exactly what it was he wanted, and tying the first threat into a double threat, linking the first two with the third—leaving them absolutely no choice but to do his bidding.

Next came the exchange, the code for the girl.

The codes were switched, but still not discovered, or if it was—ignored. So, assuming that everything went as planned, the next logical step would be to go directly to the space station and take control, by force, if necessary. If the plan all along had been to take control of the droids, why then had he not turned up on the station?

A distraction, then? To lead Simon and his team away, to make them look elsewhere. That made very good sense, if the intention all along was to take Josie. So, why steal the code in the first place? Did he just pretend to lose it just to throw everyone off-track? Or to make it look convincing...

No, John remembered Ho's face. He lost the code. That was real, the sheer anger in his face, his voice. That was no trick. Ho was convinced that Adam had taken the code.

And the girl? The unexpected Mrs. Patel? John dismissed Patel instantly—innocent bystander. The girl, what did this girl have to do with it other than the obvious? Why the generous offer of giving the girl to Josie, when the intent was to take her?

Distractions. John scowled coldly at the early morning shadows that played across the cobbled floor of his conservatory. A fat koi sloshed lazily in the pond nearby, begging for food.

Ho had hired a Rogue, an extremely skilled one. One who walked right through the main gates and walked right back out with his wife. Josie had no doubt been drugged and made pliable, since there was no way she'd willingly leave with him—especially in the temper she'd been in before she went missing.

John thought of something else. The exchange. Ho had wanted to take Josie from then, which was why he asked for her specifically. The code was never the main objective—merely a distraction to draw them out. That was it. And the Rogue was hired specifically to get Josie, nothing more. This would explain why, instead of continuing to fight until a death, and therefore risk injury to Josie, the Rogue disappeared and entered the Citadel with the sole purpose of taking her when he should've been with Ho. And, it would also explain why no one had turned up at the space station.

The plan, however, to take Josie at the exchange was foiled, so the next move was to remove Simon—it had been Ho's backup plan all along. With Simon away, the Rogue could be assured to get in and out, knowing Simon would've pursued the Rogue to the very end. That much was true. Now, Simon was off-planet and his hands were tied. It didn't matter if Simon's Elites were on hand; the Rogue probably considered them inferior because he would've preferred to fight with Simon himself. Rogues, if anything, were notorious for thinking themselves superior than everyone else. Simon was the best at what he did, and the Rogue would've known that.

But why not take back the girl? John rubbed thoughtfully at his chin. *She'd served her purpose.*

This thought led John to believe that Margeaux wasn't quite who she appeared to be. Unless, it was the intention to have her planted inside the Citadel all along. Why? Surely, Ho would expect the girl's background to be checked and double-checked. Ho even went to the exacting trouble of tracing her ancestors, a most generous gesture.

Thorough.

It could mean too that the girl was, indeed, the real thing and by wasting time checking, they'd missed the whole point.

Margeaux. He needed to see her again. Without realizing it, he'd already walked to the elevators. Blinking with distraction, he ordered it to take him to the detainees' quarters.

By leaving the girl here, he thought again, *she would be safe. Out of harm's way. Protected.*

Why would it matter to Ho if the girl was or was not?

Clearly, her purpose had been served; she could be discarded away without a second thought.

But, if she mattered, then...

Yes, the girl mattered—she still has more to do. Her function here is not done.

This would explain why she'd been handed over so easily?

And what exactly would her function here be for?

With Josie gone, that left him. It was a logical conclusion. People had wanted him dead since before he was even born. This threat was nothing new to him. Did Ho have intentions of becoming world president? Why should he, if and when, the intention was to take the Scrap Yard? He could be king of the world after that. Why waste time being a mere president?

John found her meditating on the terrace. She sat crossed-legged on the tiny patch of artificial grass, her body thin, pale, and small. A year ago, he'd come across another thin and pale girl, in this very room. Josie. With her, it had been a completely different matter—the only similarity the two shared was the mystery of their identity.

For Josie, it had been affection and curiosity that drew him to her like a magnet. In Margeaux's case, it was danger and threat, and it repelled him. He felt his chest constrict with the sudden urge to lash out and hit her. He discreetly took a calming breath.

John watched her, sitting serenely, the early morning light glancing off her milky skin. The long black of her hair fell well past her waist and contrasted sharply against the white of her clothing. Margeaux appeared to be the embodiment of innocence and youth. It turned his already raw stomach. All he saw were lies and deceptions.

As if sensing his presence, she turned and locked those glassy, pale green eyes at him.

"Good morning, Uncle," she said.

"I am not your uncle," he replied without emotion. He tried to unnerve her with his calculating stare by never once taking his eyes off hers.

She stared back with a small squint, then, stood in one fluid motion. "You look tired. Are you unwell?" Her voice dripped with concern.

He continued to watch her. She seemed outwardly oblivious

to the attention. But for the briefest moment, something passed across her eyes—a flicker—a shift so minute that she made a half-blink to hide it. It was a calculating and cunning glimmer. She twitched the corners of her mouth in a small smile, amused at some secret only she knew.

With inspiration, John boldly tried something. "Ho has been captured."

Her body jerked slightly—a tiny twitch in the shoulders. Her eyes widened in surprise, followed by a small uncertain frown, a quick knit of the brows and a slight wavering of her eyes. Then it was gone.

It made John's heart soar with glee. *Yes, they are connected. That was not a grateful look.*

"Oh." Lowering her lashes, she linked her hands before her like an obedient child. "That is good news, then."

"He is dead."

Her eyes flew up in shock. Her lips parted into an O.

"I—oh. I am sorry to hear this." She shifted slightly, a small inward movement. Then, in a matter of seconds, her face was in control again. "It saddens me to hear of a life being taken."

"Even if he was cold and heartless? That he inflicted great pain without a second thought?"

"Yes. We must show compassion to all. Good and evil alike."

"Tell me, how is your hand?"

She glanced down, the first sign of discomfort—agitation—showed by a crinkling of her smooth forehead. "It is healing well. I have to get the bandage changed today." She looked back up to John, her eyes glittery with concealed anger. "How did he die?" her voice pitched to sound brave but it came out sharp and accusatory.

"I killed him," he replied calmly, slightly bored.

"Oh." She nearly jumped. "You... How? When?"

"Earlier this morning. You understand that he had to suffer a bit before he died." John delivered it as casually as if it were an afterthought.

"Oh...Why?" Margeaux's brow creased, not with horror, but hatred. The high pitch of her normal voice grew lower, nearly guttural with anger.

"He'd been very tricky. Kidnapping my wife, for one." *No reaction,* he noted as he continued to watch the girl. "She was hurt, quite badly, trying to escape."

Still no reaction.

"I don't believe you could kill him. He's very strong and skilled," she persisted. "How did you kill him?"

He waited a beat, watching her. "With my hands. It was personal, you see."

Involuntarily, she flicked her eyes to his hands. He'd mimicked her by clasping them before him, and could see her beginning to squirm under his close inspection. She unclasped her own hands, placed them at her sides, one fist balled tightly.

"That is quite...barbaric," she said breathlessly, tightly controlled, purposely looking away to portray someone deeply offended. "You...you, disgust me. You are the world president, you should...know better than to do...such a thing."

John merely shrugged. "You seem quite concerned with how Ho met his end than how my wife is—your *aunt.* Ho was quite violent with her. He met an appropriate death." He knew he sounded convincing as he kept an image of a helpless Josie in his head, right next to one of how Ho would look when he did, eventually, get his hands on him.

"Did you have to kill him?" she all but snarled.

"Would you rather he lived and gloated over his evils?" he countered quickly. "Don't insult my judgment in this matter. He has been dealt with. Why should you care? I do not. And your aunt certainly does not."

"He was..." she fought to control her voice. "He was still a person."

"An evil one," John replied mildly.

With a quick intake of air, Margeaux carelessly tossed her hair with a flick of the head, lowered it, and idly brushed away at something on her sleeve.

"How is my aunt?" she asked quietly, her voice under control, pitched now to sound saddened and concerned.

For an answer, she got John's quick hand to her arm, yanking her abruptly up to her toes and his murderous face close to hers. She let out a shrill, childish squeak. Real panic washed over her face in a flash, her eyes wide and almost bulging.

"Who is your father? Don't lie to me."

"What are you do— Let go of me!"

He shook her once, quick, fast, and rough.

"He is…he is, dead! I told you that already." She started to struggle, caught the icy look on John's face and stopped immediately. "I told you, he's dead. What're you doing, let me go, please."

"I know he is," he hissed out quietly. "Tell me something I don't know."

"I said he's dead! He was a drug addict—he died," she screamed out suddenly like a banshee—high and wild, with child-like rage and emotion. "He's dead-dead-dead! Can't you hear me? He's dead! Let go of me!"

Still gripping her skinny arm, John watched as she flailed about, shaking her head, kicking, thrashing, and having an almighty tantrum. She even grunted, a nasal sound.

"How did he die?" he snarled, baring his teeth in a nasty smile. "Tell me, I want to know." He shook her again, causing her head to jerk back and forth sharply. It pleased him to see her agitated further. A wicked part of him wanted her to snap into two, like a doll. "Tell me, girl! How?"

"I already told you how! He's dead. Stop shaking me—*please!*"

"How?"

"Drugs…overdose…" her teeth clacked together, her voice shook and vibrated in her throat. She made a noise—*nnnn*—in an effort to speak. "I…*told* you!"

"*How?*"

She screeched out and grunted like a wild animal in unabashed fury. Any control she had, left her.

"Because you killed him! You bastard! You killed him—you killed him. You *killed* him!" She shrieked wildly, hitting him with her free arm and jerking violently in his grip. Her head flung from side to side in rage, hair whipping about her face, that it lashed stinging pricks against John's furious face.

"That's right," he hissed, and with a disgusted looked, flung

Margeaux to the ground.

She made a high-pitched screech as her small rump hit the artificial grass with a satisfying thud. And then, absolute silence as she glared up at him in stupefied fury.

They regarded one another for a moment, both with hatred and disgust contorting their faces.

"She is *still* my aunt," Margeaux spat out in a growl. "And she believes me!"

"So you keep saying. But my wife's niece died a long time ago. You are no one but a girl who shares a trace element of her DNA. That alone does not make you family. You," he paused for effect, "are nothing."

He turned, and without fear of exposing his back to her, left.

It was the casual flicking of lint that shouted out to him. The hand, the long graceful fingers, poised elegantly like a ballet move, lightly brushing her arm—smoothing the sleeve with such intricate care.

Why had he not noticed it before? She was forever doing that! Just like someone else…just like *him*. The same manner, the same expression, the same way it was used to compose themselves. It was then, that everything started to make sense. It made perfect sense, and it made him sick.

It horrified him.

It meant that Michael Ho was her father.

And Josie's nephew!

~ * ~

"You have got to be joking?" Simon literally goggled back at John.

Behind his friend, John could see a tiny square of unfathomable black space dotted with stars. For privacy, Simon had ventured to a quiet corner in one of the Scrap Yard's observation bubbles.

"I wish I were." John rubbed a restless hand over his mouth, his horror and anger were managed now to the point it gave him a mild, nauseating headache. "It didn't take her long to admit. She's good, but still a child who allows her emotions control her."

"I wish I were there to have seen it. Did you make her pee like that terrorist back in Rio?"

"I wanted to wring her skinny little neck and pull it off and—" John compressed his mouth in disgust, more of himself. It had come very close. This girl had nearly caused him to sink so low that torture and murder spoke out to him like a seduction. "You need to come back."

"That, I will. But I'll leave my team here. It doesn't smell right—still. I'll come back with just Surrey, leave Madds in charge here. Have you spoken with Aline?"

"Aline? Ah, right. No, not as yet. I'll have her head straight to Iceland without delay. She'll just have to reschedule her appointments. I want another crack at the girl. She knows more. She thinks it's over, so she'll let her guard down slightly. But she'll try to be all submissive and sorry and attempt to use that to her advantage."

"John," Simon, seeing the strain on his friend's face, dropped his tone a notch. "She will be all right. The Rogue's objective is to deliver her to Ho. He won't harm her unless she tries to run. I don't think she'll attempt that knowing how skilled he is."

"She can be very impulsive, and we don't know yet if she's with Ho now or not," John reminded him, then, pictured that cocky, smug look from the surveillance footage—the way James possessively held his wife's hand. "Damn it! *Where* have they taken her?"

~ * ~

Having consumed a full breakfast of eggs, sausages, *and* pancakes, drowning with syrup and butter, washed down with three cups of coffee—witnessed with mild interest by James—Josie felt much better.

She ate with the aloof and regal air expected of a woman in her current standing—she'd been practicing—and the gruff, single-mindedness of a combat soldier.

"You've a healthy appetite," James commented, enthralled.

"So I've been told. I missed my dinner," she replied pointedly, glaring back. "I was hungry."

She pushed away her plate with finality, wiped her mouth with obvious satisfaction, and sighed. "Where is my krima? I want it back. I promise not to use it—on you, that is. It was a gift, you see. I'd hate to lose it."

"It is safe."

"Where is it?"

"It is safe."

"Why are we in Iceland?"

"I'm not at liberty to say." James finished his coffee, unable to mask the discomfort he felt. He didn't like Ho, his objectives or his methods. "But I have a feeling that it's not going to be very pleasant. It's good you've eaten well. Discomfort is always best faced when you have a full stomach."

"You have a conscience? I'm amazed." Josie gaped purposely.

He knew she was uneasy and scared, but obviously recognized that he meant her no harm—for the moment.

"But, I take it that the money was just too good to refuse, so fuck the conscience, right?" she continued.

"True."

She is just a woman, he reminded himself. Like any other, like so many others. An assignment—a contract. And when the job is complete, he'd move on to the next. So, why then did he feel that he had to warn her? To help her. Was it because of whom she was married to? And why did he feel so disgusted with Ho? Why was his conscience distracting him? Nagging him like a wife.

He found her studying him. She was attractive, not overly. It was more her uncaring manner regarding her beauty that made her more alluring. It triggered a spark within him—one he thought he'd managed, controlled. She distracted him. Her vibrant green eyes were the first thing you saw, then her mouth—soft, full, and delicate. What came out of it was another matter.

"They say you are very dangerous," he asked conversationally.

"They say a lot of things about me. You'd have to be more specific."

Whipcord response in the face of danger. He nearly groaned with appreciation. "You saved your husband by stepping before a flying disc. Took a full blast from an explosive and helped bring down Uron Koh."

"Oh...*that*," she shrugged. "All in a days work. Are you getting scared?"

"Is it true you jumped onto his back and rode him like a horse, and then led him straight into a wall?"

Josie rolled her eyes with an uncaring manner. "Somewhat true. I had no reins, so, it was a bit difficult to steer him." She let out a stupid laugh. "Would you like me to demonstrate on you?"

He sat considering something, ignoring her remark. She would fight to protect those she cared about, the most honorable way to fight, to live. Somewhere along the line, he'd lost his honor. For some reason, she reawakened it. Why? Surely, not because of her husband...

Why should that matter? This is merely a job, an assignment, he reminded himself.

"Be wary of Ho," he said quietly before he could stop himself. "He cares only for himself. Once he's done with you, you'll be discarded. He'll go back for the girl—not yet, but eventually. He cares a great deal for her, yet he can hurt her without a second thought. He did not say so, but it shows in his manner, how he speaks to her. Do not trust her even though she is young. She has been...influenced. They are both evil."

Josie's brows flew up high. James saw her swallow, as if an unpleasant taste seeped into her mouth, bitter like bile.

"I thought you liked the girl?"

"Admiration for her courage is one thing. That does not mean she isn't evil."

"What do you mean?" she snapped. "Why are you telling me this?"

Obviously alarmed, she pushed back from the table.

James sat between her and the only possible exit. All the drapes were drawn over the windows making them too difficult to flee out of at a moment's notice. On top of that, she didn't even know how high up they were.

"Are you telling me that the girl means to harm me as well? As in, after Ho's done with me, I get to go back? Or did you mean that she's a threat? As in, now."

John filled her thoughts immediately, knowing he would be out of his mind with worry for her. He'd automatically turn to Margeaux for answers. He could handle himself but if he were distracted... If he used discretion because of her possible connection to Margeaux, he might tread too carefully. And that might be a mistake.

Josie stopped herself from thinking the worst.

Seeing her inward battle, James shook his head. "He is not the target. At least, not yet, I think."

"Just fucking tell me. What does Ho want?" Josie demanded, standing up now.

"Your blood."

"My…blood?"

~ * ~

The first explosion took out the security post in Docking Bay 4—completely. The second took out a section of the main control room on the lower levels. By the time the alarms sounded, the control room was commandeered by a small group of mercenary-styled individuals. It simultaneously coincided with the lock-down of all the docking bay doors that led to the main body of the Scrap Yard. Whoever remained inside, were trapped.

Before the first alarm pulse could end, Simon was at a dead run heading straight for Governor Ayo Mwenye's headquarters. He'd only just come from him, having briefed the Governor of his impending departure and whom he planned to leave behind. Mwenye had insisted that Simon hold onto Jane until this whole 'nasty business' was over.

He found Mwenye, braced over his desk and barking into his communications dock, demanding to know what was happening. There was no response.

"Forget that!" Simon ordered. "You—with me—now. They'll come straight here for you once they know the code doesn't work." He took out his personal unit and summoned Madds. "Get to the mainframe, now."

"Already here. Secure. Team's in place."

"Excellent." Simon cocked his head to Mwenye. "Governor? With me—*now*."

As agreed, they went directly to the upper level safe zones, which were a series of chambers that lined the entire topmost part of the Scrap Yard. Each, once separated and ejected, became ten large, self-contained shuttles that could safely evacuate close to fifty to seventy personnel. It was in one of these, reserved for the Governor and other senior personnel, that Simon and Mwenye were to take refuge.

Renna, already there with six of Mwenye's specially trained Space Junkies, a term loosely used to describe the hardcore space militia who lived, breathed, and died for the love of space, and all else they swore an oath to protect. They were brutal, ruthless, and single-minded in their purpose to defend the station. Dotted throughout the station were hundreds more of them, mixed in with the specifically programmed security droids that ringed the docking bays, manufacturing and production sectors, and, of course, the mainframe.

Ox, because of his technical abilities, remained stationed in the mainframe. It was a large room, no-nonsense in its purpose, with a multitude of computers and electronics. A skeleton staff of fifteen rather scared-looking technicians and specialists manned the equipment and consoles. They nervously cast their attention to Ox, as if hoping he'd give them some sort of direction that would save their lives. Several Space Junkies, with varying grades of weaponry, and security droids gleaming in their sinister metal frames were also on hand.

And Ox, sat idly with a chin propped on his hand—waiting.

Fifteen

Aline Lancaster never had any cause to visit the Hontag-Sonnet Research and Archives Facility in Iceland. Because of who she was, and the position she held, her name had been automatically added to its meagerly short list of specially approved physicians and scientists who were allowed access to its facilities. She even had a seat reserved as a member of its 56-strong board of directors, and shared views, approved and passed mandates, directives, and whatever else was required of her. She even attended the annual Hontag-Sonnet Charity Dinner and Benefit Ball along with thousands of other members, affiliates, and specially invited guests across the globe.

Each year, she was required to renew her membership and update her pass-code, which allowed her to access its facilities, archives, and many services. And each year, she complied diligently.

To be associated with Hontag-Sonnet was like being associated with the god of medicine and science. They were the worldwide, independently run medical association with a history and tradition of one hundred and ninety-six years. They had many fingers and arms—and even legs—that infiltrated into many pies from private sectors, corporate groups, the military, and governmental organizations.

To prove her allegiance, and as a mark of pride to her profession, she wore the platinum signet ring with the double-helix emblem inlaid with emeralds to signify life.

Flanked by two body-assistants—one hers, the other because she was the president's sister—she disembarked from her shuttle.

Aline, still mildly annoyed with Dr. Shui, rolled her shoulders to brush away the tension. She'd left Shui in charge at her clinic, but their disagreement over her new biohazard emergency treatment procedures that they'd been working on for the last three months still irritated her.

Aline wasn't a weak woman. She'd inherited the bold and forthright manner from her mother, and the shrewd and calculating nature of her father. Like the rest of the Lancasters, she was a force to be reckoned with. Her position and upbringing had assured her the finest in physical and mental training and was ranked as a Second Level in the Bushi Code. Had she not answered to a different calling, she would surely have been president, or at the very least, vice president. But politics had never interested her, saving lives did. Unfortunately, the two seemed indelibly linked.

Not much passed her canny eyes, and not much dared. So, in order to surprise her completely, one had to be bold enough to walk right up to her and knock her over the head.

The sniveling, wiry-looking man that approached her now in the Hontag-Sonnet VIP docking bay, did just that—surprise her. Though he didn't knock her over the head, he casually offered his hand in greeting, which from upbringing and custom, she declined to accept.

Realizing his mistake, he then, in an embarrassed gesture of placing both hands to his chest, mumbled some apology and bowed his head in a comical gesture of subservience.

In a movement, too fast to see, he flung his arms out. A shield-penetrating, barbed explosive dart, commonly known as the prick-stick, shot out from each sleeve and struck the two body-assistants standing at either side of Aline. Two seconds later, a dull, punching sound could be heard as the explosives injected into their chests and detonated. No blood, no mess, just swift death as the missile mangled their chest cavities to a pulp.

They fell to the floor like crumpled rugs followed by a feint scent of burning flesh—the looks of surprise still etched clearly on their faces.

Aline had just enough time to blink with confusion. Reflex and conditioning had instinctively sent her muscles limber but on alert, ready. Another man quickly joined the wiry man and they flanked her immediately. The newcomer gripped her arm and stuck something cold and metallic to her side. The body-shield she wore crackled and hissed as its protective bubble was penetrated and neutralized.

She fell into step with them, not so much as a moment's hesitation hindered her movements. She knew when she was outnumbered and out-skilled. Feeling only mild regret—it wasn't the time for prolonged sentiment—for her fallen body-assistants, she allowed herself just one final look behind.

With swift efficiency, two more individuals materialized and were already carting her assistants back into the shuttle. Around the shuttle, more darkly dressed individuals; they crawled around like ants. Just before Aline turned her head away, she caught the blue-white muzzle-flash of an assault weapon discharging in the cockpit.

Shit, she thought, borrowing an expression from Josie. Under the circumstances, that particular invective seemed appropriate.

Not much scared Aline, she had a core like steel and nerves to match. But what did rattle her was the thought that she may never see her children again. With that in mind, a wicked gleam alighted her eyes as she allowed the men to lead her to the reception hall of the facility.

It had been a very long time since she'd been in an all-out combat. Nearly six years. And like a true Lancaster, she decided that she was quite looking forward to it.

She knew all there was to know about saving lives. And she knew how to take them.

~ * ~

Josie was made to wear the long blonde wig again, but instead of being sprayed once more with eye-dye, James thrust a pair of sunglasses on her face. It blocked her vision out completely. To keep her secured, he tied her thumbs with a hair-thin cord that ran the length of her body down to her ankles. To run wasn't an option for her. Then, in a gesture that she didn't understand, he gently—almost lovingly—placed a long overcoat on her shoulders, smoothing it into place with hands that lingered a fraction longer than was necessary. It smelled of him, faint traces of a sweet cologne mixed with maleness. She cringed, swallowing hard to calm her disgust.

"What now?" Testing the give on the cord, Josie shifted and moved her arms. The thin cord was razor sharp, her thumbs would be severed with any sudden movement.

"Five minutes," James replied close to her right ear. "He's very prompt."

"Can I, at least, not look at him when he comes?"

"I'm sorry, no. It is his wish that we remove you as quickly and as quietly as possible." James stood impassively beside her. "Timing is everything."

"Stop looking at me." Even though she was sightless, she could feel his stare, creeping all over her body.

"You are beautiful and I will look where I want. I may not have a chance afterwards," he said simply. Then, as if on impulse, he touched her wigged hair.

Josie sucked in a breath and flinched in reflex. "Stop that," and sidled away.

"Your husband is a lucky man." Unfazed, he tucked his hands into his pockets but looked away.

The locks on the door disengaged, she heard it open and cocked her head, feeling her stomach drop. Josie tried to calm the sudden panic she felt. Resistance seemed useless at this point. She cursed herself that she should've, at least, tried to fight or escape earlier. She knew it was *him*. The presence of Michael Ho all but sucked the air out of her lungs.

"Josie, my dear," Ho crooned. "Such a pleasure it is to see you again."

"I could say the same, but..." Glad to hear her voice was steady, she concentrated hard on her breathing. *Remain calm,* she ordered herself.

"I am sorry for your discomfort, but you understand the need for security and to ensure your safety. Your face is quite well recognized the world over."

She heard him approach and willed herself not to recoil in revulsion.

"Are we ready?" Ho directed this to James. "Ah, good. Shall we go?"

James took Josie by the arm, a firm grasp, and led her out.

They left the room, flanked by one more man, who stood close to Ho. They walked to an elevator that took them up to the roof of the hotel.

She couldn't see, but she could sense a few more people around her as they disembarked and walked through a sort of reception hall. Someone muttered to another as a door slid open with a gentle hiss.

A sudden blast of cold air hit Josie and made her flinch. James' hand stayed firm as a warning for her to remain calm. They walked a short distance then ascended steps, which Josie guessed to be of a shuttle, a small shuttle by the sound of it.

Once everyone was inside, James removed her restraints with a quick snick of his knife, took the sunglasses off and was about to go for her wig when Josie snapped out a hand and blocked him.

"Temper, temper," he warned with that cocky smirk.

"I'm quite capable of doing it myself," she hissed back with anger.

She didn't miss the casual, yet deliberate, hand that passed over her waist and lingered there when he removed the thumb restraints. Wrenching the wig off, she flung it to the floor.

"Your charm must be wearing off, James." Ho, already seated, made himself comfortable with a glass of amber liquid in his hand, watched her.

She snapped her head to Ho, then glanced around rapidly to check her surroundings. Besides James, there were two others. One sat close to Ho, the other stood at the rear of the shuttle looking burly and solid.

"Where are we going?" she barked out.

The shuttle was already thrusting its engines with a whine. Small vibrations could be felt underfoot.

"Somewhere more comfortable. But please," Ho indicated to a seat, "sit and relax. The flight is short, but we may as well enjoy it. Something to drink?"

"A vat of the devil's piss will do just fine, thanks."

Ho beamed out a smile, it creased his eyes to slits. He still smelled the same, a mixture of something thick and overpowering like old ladies' talcum powder, and flowers—funeral flowers—sweet and heavy. In the small confines of the shuttle, it was overpowering. Josie felt like throwing up.

"Your vocabulary is, still, most colorful," he replied.

"So I keep hearing." She sat, as far away as possible from Ho. For now, she would gladly take her chances with James, who loitered nearby.

"How is Margeaux?" Ho lifted a black brow elegantly.

"Fine. But not for long," she added with a shrug. "She'll be the first person my husband skewers with a club to find out where I am." With a regretful pang, she thought of Margeaux.

"That will get him nowhere," he took a sip, "as he will soon find out. She knows nothing."

"My husband will find ways to get answers." She shrugged. "Iceland...why here?"

Ho cast a slow, amused glance to James. "You told her?"

James shrugged. "She would not shut up."

"Yes, she is quite annoying." Ho turned his head to the man standing at the rear. "Go to the cockpit."

The large man obediently complied, lumbering by them placidly. The other man, who sat behind Ho, glanced out the window with a bored look. He was Asian as well, with sharp, high cheekbones, scowling features and a thin mouth. His hair was spiked like a porcupine; the tips dyed red and purple.

"You tell me why, Josie." Ho smiled across to her with a wicked gleam playing across his eyes. "I hear that you have a very...intriguing mind."

"You seem to hear a lot about me. I wonder where you're getting all of it from."

"I have my ways."

"I bet you do." Josie gave him what she hoped was a scathing look. "Iceland," she continued. "The only thing I can think of is that this is where all the DNA is stored. But you knew that already, didn't you?"

"Very good," Ho grinned, showing small teeth.

"Afraid the truth will be revealed, are you?" she asked boldly. "That Margeaux isn't related to me at all, so you've come to destroy all the evidence?"

"Oh, no. She is who she says she is."

"So what do you want *me* for? You've got your fucking

code. Deal's done."

"Not quite."

"Listen, just admit you've tampered with the electronic DNA samples. You succeeded in messing with my head. Bravo." Something in her—a hope, a need—deflated.

"Josie, my dear. I have done many things, but the only thing that I have tampered with, is the true identity of Margeaux's father. And her face."

She squinted at him for a moment. "What do you mean? You altered—surgically—Margeaux's face? To make her look like me, like my real niece?"

Ho said nothing, took another sip, and sighed with satisfaction.

"You fucking bastard," Josie said quietly, slowly. "So you did fool me."

Rampant hate bubbled very close to the surface, Josie wanted to see him dead—beaten to a bloody pulp, preferably. She felt...betrayed, and foolish for falling headfirst into the trick.

"Just tweaked a little bit of her face, to make it fit."

"So what *did* she look like?" She started to feel sick, and somewhere, deep down—rage.

"Margeaux is Asian, part Asian." Ho smiled with uncontained glee. "Like her father."

"I take it that Thomas Laperriere is not her father?"

"Oh, he is. But he is not dead."

"Really? Do tell." Josie had a feeling she wasn't going to like the answer. Watching Ho now, as she did, she had the distinct feeling that he'd rehearsed this moment many times, hoping to inflect the right amount of suspense and drama in his voice and manner.

"Oh, my dear, Josie. Surely you must have guessed by now."

"Oh, no, really. I have not."

"Josie. *I* am Thomas Laperriere." Ho seemed to wait a beat to watch her reaction.

She gave him none.

Josie stared back at him, keeping her features as bland as she could possibly keep them. Inside, however, something screamed out in horror. She'd guessed it in her gut, the way the conversation was going, but her mind was only just catching up.

"You don't really expect me to believe that, do you?" she replied, trying her best to sound nonplussed.

For an answer, Ho merely smiled his usual pasty smile.

"You can't seriously expect me to believe that *you* are her father."

James made a strange noise, something very close to one clearing his throat—but not quite. If he were a cursing man, it would've sounded a lot like 'fuck me', but Josie couldn't be sure. But it did make her hesitate before she could formulate her thoughts. She remembered what James had said about Ho and his manner towards Margeaux.

He cares for her greatly, he'd said.

"Understand that this is three hundred years later," Ho replied with an icy coldness in his voice. "A lot can happen."

"Do tell."

"It would simply take too long." Ho shifted slightly in his seat. His glass was empty and obvious control had him quelling the urge for another. But the sheer joy in playing with Josie had him desperately flicking his glance at the drinks tray for a celebratory drink.

"If Margeaux is your daughter, as you're leading me to believe," she bit down the temptation to shout and found comfort in gripping the arms of her seat. "Then you're a bigger and sicker fucker than I've given you credit for."

Ho smiled back. "How so?"

"You cut her."

He laughed, long and loud, which sent shivers running up and down her spine. "It was *her* idea. I merely followed her lead."

Josie didn't know what to do now, of what she was hearing. Uncertain, unconscious of her own behavior, she glanced up at James as if for support. He stood impassively with a bland look directed at Ho. Whatever thoughts he had, he kept them to himself.

Josie got up suddenly, anger spearing through her.

"Tell me," leveling her eyes at Ho. "*What* is it that you want from me?"

"I need you, what you carry." Ho brushed his suit smooth, composing himself. "But do not worry. It won't be too painful so long as you comply peacefully. I'll be happy with just taking some your blood."

"For what?"

"For the code."

"What?" Complete bafflement washed over her face. It was like a jigsaw puzzle made by schizophrenics, getting weirder and more confusing by the minute. "You already *have* the code."

Sighing and losing a bit of patience, Ho frowned slightly. "Josie, my dear. Your DNA strand makes up part—it may be quite a small part, but a part all the same—of a certain code. This code is a key, a master key that unlocks a program. I want this program."

"*What the fuck*, are you talking about? You already *have* my DNA. How else could you have found out that I'm Margeaux's—*your*—ah, fuck!" She sat heavily.

Impossible, she thought. Just freaking impossible! There was absolutely *no way* she could be related to this man!

"If I still had your DNA, do you really think you would be here now?" Ho made an unpleasant face. "But it is more complicated than that. I need a somewhat live specimen. The instructions were quite precise on that. By live, I mean the right temperature. I can't quite get the right temp with a *hair* sample, now can I? And it is *blood* that is needed, not a strand of hair, a gob of saliva or clipping off a fingernail. Blood."

Josie knew she had to get away the moment she had a clear chance—she had to escape. She had no intention of taking her chances with a man like Ho, a clearly deranged monster. This was too Frankenstein meets Dracula. Too mad-scientist! Her chest felt tight with anxiety, the tips of her fingers tingled with cold numbness.

She ordered her mind to calm down, to think rationally.

Don't be distracted, John's voice echoed back to her. *Don't be distracted.*

If they were in Iceland, the only thing she could think of was that they were heading straight to the DNA bank to get these live specimens. Ho wasn't there to tamper with anything, just seeking specific samples that made up a key. That still didn't explain why her blood was needed.

"So how did you lose my DNA? Don't you keep copies? Could you not have used that instead?" Trying her best to sound sarcastic as she possibly could, Josie made a casual toss of her head. But even she could hear the edge of fear lacing her words.

Ho sighed with impatience. "I had but one strand of your hair. Wellesley's cleaning droids were very thorough in their rounds. Of course, my specialists used every piece of that hair for their research. They were very precise in their investigations. However, they simply tossed it away once it was complete. But as I've said before, I need a *live* specimen. Really, don't be so dense. You are obviously not as astute as I thought you to be." He shook his head a fraction, then he actually tisked with annoyance.

"How very unprofessional of them," she snapped back. "That must've pissed you off."

"Quite. They have been dealt with accordingly." Ho, with irritation, leaned forward to a drinks tray panel and helped himself.

"Blood, you say," Josie mused, trying to sound conversational. "I heard you the first time, by the way. But then, why take me? You could've just as easily gotten a blood sample from me, the same way you had me kidnapped. You had ample time to take it while I was out cold, then, toss me. Why drag me out here and stir up an almighty ants nest?"

Ho grinned. "This way is more entertaining, don't you think? And it shows that I can—*take you,* that is. Right from under the nose of your husband. It is a very satisfying feeling."

"I'll bet. It's all about who's got the bigger balls, right?" She snorted and shifted in her seat. She felt queasy.

"Did you not feel it, Josie? That first time we met?" His voiced sounded enthralled.

Josie blinked in confusion. Her mind still reeled from the impossible realization that Ho, this man before her, was in fact, her...nephew. She felt truly sick.

"The connection," he continued, seeing her ignorance.

"I felt nothing but revulsion. I thought you were a fucking pervert." She all but spat it out. "I still do."

"I felt it—loud and clear as a bell tolling. The first moment I saw you, something about you spoke out to me. I thought at first it was just ordinary curiosity—you were quite an unusual woman. I did not believe Wellesley at all. You were no more an amnesiac than James there is a homemaker. So I did my own checking. It took a great deal of time, but eventually, I managed it. It helped that I knew where to look—I'd been looking for a very long time. And when I found the connection, well, you can just imagine my surprise. And luck. You see, your face, it was familiar to me. Certain parts, bone structure, facial expression, I had seen before. But your eyes, especially your eyes, the shape, size, coloring."

Surprise was an understatement. Josie stared hard at Ho. A part of her mind absorbed every single detail on his face, trying desperately to find some small mark of resemblance. She found none. What could he possibly have seen in her that caused him to think she was part of him?

She wanted to shriek her head off in hysteria, but instead remained silent, her mouth clamped tightly together.

"You see, for a number of years, I have been doing a specific type of research on my own. Well before Margeaux was even born, I have been keenly interested in a certain family member of mine—sorry, of ours. A one, Dr. Zara Sozanski. You may be familiar with her name. She was the mother of young Brandon Sozanski, the one whose DNA strand started this whole, intriguing mystery. Zara was a very talented and brilliant scientist. She specialized in cell regeneration and fusion."

"I still don't know why this has anything to do with me. You're talking ancient history here, and in my case…well…"

Smiling—practically beaming—Ho took a small sip of his drink. "Dr. Sozanski created this code, using the DNA strands of her family. It was an old-school method, tried many times before, but she trusted that it was confusing enough that people would become frustrated. You see she took samples of her son, his children, and her granddaughter. She also took a sample from herself. Once the code was created, she used it to lock a program that hid her entire research into fusion technology. The program was carefully scattered into the worldwide cyberspace platform. Your DNA will be the closest to her own DNA."

"Closest? Hello? Have you not been listening to yourself? Ancient history, remember? We're talking at least two hundred years close!" Josie leaned forward in her seat, practically goggling at him. "And, she's not even my direct descendant. How, then, can her DNA and mine, be similar enough to complete the code? Surely, there'd be gaps. Very *large* gaps."

"Oh, of course. The gaps will be filled in by my own brand of electronically generated genetic cloning, created through a run of possibilities via a computer program that I formulated."

"So why the fuck couldn't you have done that in the first place? And why not make up a batch of her son's DNA? He is, after all, much closer to her than I am."

"As I said, this way is far more entertaining. And, it will give us a chance to get acquainted—for however short a time that may be. But no, your DNA will be close enough for the program to decipher how best to clone the missing pieces. And then an actual clone DNA must be made on the spot—with your blood, of course, as the base. I cannot use Brandon's sample since it is limited, nor can I use my own DNA because I am a few generations too far, and my Asian heritage will be a hindrance. Yours would be like a pure source."

"Just drain me like a stuck pig, why don't you."

Ho chuckled, sounding pleased.

"Whatever. Sounds like absolute bullshit to me. Just kill me now and get it over with then, cause I know you're gonna once you get the blood out of me." She nearly rolled her eyes in frustration. "And, if you think that you and I are going to be doing any serious bonding, you got some big fucking expectations." For emphasis, she pulled the lapels of the overcoat James had given her, tugging them until they closed with a snap around her chest, protecting her from the evil before her.

Josie was more than disgusted, more than horrified. She wasn't quite sure what it was she felt, but ashamed came pretty close. How could she have allowed herself to fall for all of this in the first place? Was she that gullible? Was she that hard up for wanting a connection, a family? Was she so needy? She wanted to curl up and cry.

John had been right all along. He'd seen right through Margeaux. Didn't he tell her not to be distracted? And what had she done? Done the very thing John had warned her not to do.

John, she thought with a painful tug of her heart. He was probably going absolutely berserk with worry. And if—no, when— he found her, she had every faith in the fact that Ho would be beyond very dead. He would find her—nothing could stop him. But *when* would that be? And would he get to her before she was dead.

"I am not a very sentimental man," Ho said as he watched her over the rim of his glass. "But to be honest, it does sadden me to know that your time here is limited. Such a pity since you've come all this way. And yes, I will have to kill you. Keeping you alive could pose more problems for me than I care to deal with at the moment. Alas, everyone must die, sooner or later. And is it not better to spend what time you have left with family?"

Josie returned his stare coldly. "Go to fucking hell."

~ * ~

"What do you mean? She left when?" John said impatiently.

Rand knew nothing of Josie's disappearance. John, thinking it prudent not to mention it, tried to keep his face neutral. The less people know, the better. That Rand was fond of Josie, and practically family, was beside the point. He would understand the situation, John reasoned to himself.

"She left early this morning. She made an appointment early yesterday to meet with Dr. Maines at the Hontag-Sonnet facility." Rand creased his brow. "Is there something wrong? Aline had a free couple of days so she thought it best to make haste and get to Iceland."

"No." John rubbed a hand across his mouth. "No. All is well, for now. Thank you, Rand. I'll contact her later." He turned to go, feeling traitorous that he didn't tell Rand about Josie.

Rand wasn't stupid. John knew well enough that Rand was aware of the intricate, and sometimes, dangerous lives the Lancasters led. He'd been a part of their family for close to a decade and knew when not to press things. But he still felt the hot flush of shame flood his face that he didn't inform her about Josie's disappearance.

John didn't miss the sudden worried expression that came over his brother-in-law. Squashing back down the guilt, he walked on. They talked about him, his sister and Rand, about how pointless it was to barrage him with questions or demand answers. They thought he didn't hear, but he did. At the best of times, John could hear his sister now, he could be cold and seemingly uncaring when his mind focused on something. And Rand would counter that he knew what was at John's core, that he cared deeply about what mattered the most to him and his family.

Good old Rand. Somehow this thought didn't make him feel any better.

John, too preoccupied with Josie to give his sister another thought, already filed it away in his head to contact her when he had a chance.

He found himself marching straight to Margeaux's quarters.

That little girl is going to have a really bad day, he said to himself with a wicked smile.

He found her, just as he'd left her earlier, angry, scowling, and defiant in that petulant manner. Before she could utter a single word, he strode up and stared down at her.

"Tell me everything, from the very beginning, and tell me no lies. Trust me, I'll know." He yanked her roughly by the arm, dragged her to the single couch and flung her onto it. She let out a squeak of indignation but remained silent.

He would've hit her, a good, solid, open-handed slap across that wicked face of hers. But he didn't. Instead, he stood towering over her looking as menacing as he possibly could.

"I'm waiting."

"You killed my father. I have nothing to say to you." Margeaux folded her arms across her chest and looked away. Her high-pitched, childlike voice was no longer. Instead, it was hard with a brittle edge to it—like an adult.

"Unfortunately, before I killed him, he lacked the common decency to tell me what this whole business was about."

"How very rude of him, and unfortunate for you." Margeaux continued to look away. "Father never told me exactly what it was he hoped to achieve. What will happen to me now?"

Her words held a small hint of truth. But not enough.

"You will be dealt with accordingly. It depends, of course, on how you choose to behave." John kept his voice low, his face cold and blank.

Margeaux slowly slid her glassy eyes up to him. "What do you mean?"

"You have never come across as a stupid girl. You tell me."

"What does it matter what I tell you? It's over. He should

never have taken her so quickly. But he would never listen to me. He lacks...lacked foresight. I told him going there was a bad idea."

"Did you, now? And tell me, why did you think that?" Controlling himself, lest he shake the girl repeatedly until she confessed, John casually took a step back and cocked his head slightly.

"It would have been too heavily guarded. And, see, I was right. He should have listened." She cast her eyes downward, and for the first time, genuine regret and sadness swam across her face.

"And what was the purpose of attacking the space station?"

The last time he'd spoken to Simon, an hour ago, the Scrap Yard was under attack. John felt as if he'd split into two, the need to be with Josie versus the need to help Simon. He felt absolutely helpless where he was now. He was determined more than ever to break this girl before him.

"Didn't he tell you?" With a small curl of her mouth she looked up to him, the slyness returned.

"He was a little busy trying to stay alive."

"For the cloning, silly."

"Indeed?" John winged up a brow. "And what was the purpose of this cloning? We do not perform nor indulge in cloning on the space station. It is forbidden."

"Sorry, did I say cloning? I had meant to say cell-fusion by way of cloning of cells and manipulation. You have the facilities there to merge machine with man. Need I say any more?"

"That is strictly for the prosthetics." John clamped his mouth into a tight line. "And it is stringently controlled and monitored."

So, Ho planned to use the Scrap Yard to produce...abominations. How very interesting. It had been tried before, many times over, the results hideous and outright barbaric. But it was true; the Scrap Yard did have the facilities. The production of tissue-friendly prosthetics required specific conditions in which the recipients of these prosthetics supplied their own tissue samples that could be cloned for re-growth, making the final attachment of the prosthetic 'clean' and rejection-free—fusing man with machine. Fusion.

But why? Unless it was to create half-humans. Cyborgs!

Did this mean that Josie was at the Scrap Yard? He must

inform Simon at once.

"And your purpose here? What was it, to distract us?"

Margeaux shrugged. "Yes. And to get a sample from her. But she was never alone long enough for me to do that. *You* were always around—except for that one time, but that was too soon to do anything. I wasn't ready." She cast him an accusatory look and scowled. "Did he manage to get it? You said Father hurt her, badly. Did he get it, then?"

"I know of no samples, nor the purpose of why he wanted it. Do enlighten me." John, impatient with the game, itched to wrap his hands around Margeaux's skinny neck, forcing her to tell him. Patience, he told himself.

"Why should I, then?" Margeaux smiled now, wickedly. "You don't look to be a stupid man. You tell me."

John tightened his hands into fists behind his back. No, he wasn't stupid and he could guess. He half-lowered his lids, watching her impassively as he thought. Ho wanted a sample of Josie. But why? And to what purpose? Why were her cells important enough, other than the obvious fact that she was the president's wife? John couldn't understand it.

"Tell me, why did *you* have to acquire the sample? And how were you going to get it back to him? Through James, the Rogue?"

"Of course not. I was going to convince her to take me out of the Citadel. I had two days to do so before James was to come and do it himself. *That* was the plan. Timing was everything. The moment you learned of my identity, it was automatic that you go to the source to confirm. We made the first move, so we watched and waited until you made yours." Margeaux leaned back into the couch and tossed her head. "But, James played his hand too quickly—because he did not know the real reason. He is, after all, just a paid contractor, and stupid." She snorted then frowned. "Or, the timing hastened. So Father had to act quickly. I told him that this would be to be the riskiest part. I *told* him to wait at the source until I got it."

John stared at her, unsure how to answer.

"What? You don't believe me? That I could have taken the sample from her? I am very skilled."

At this, he laughed, cold and icy. "Skilled, you say? I have seen children, younger than you, take down a grown man twice my size without ever having moved an inch from where they stood. Do tell, what your skill is?"

"Persuasion," Margeaux retorted with anger. "I've spent all my life being trained for this moment."

"Well, it looks to me, you have failed. You have not persuaded me, or my wife, into anything. Your temper and pride get in the way. Did your teachers not tell you that? Or were they simply too intimidated because they were paid by Ho?"

"She believed me, because I spoke the truth to her. She came, afterwards. You didn't know that, did you?" She curled her mouth into a nasty smile. "She went behind your back and came to see me again. How do I know she went behind your back? Because, I do. You never liked me—it was plain to see. I know you told her not to see me alone. I would have done the same thing, if I were you. She was coming around, I needed one more session with her, and she would have done anything I asked."

"Session?" John hissed out. The thought that this girl could categorize his wife into such cold and scientific terms riled him. He was left stunned into silence, reeling in his rage.

Stay calm, he ordered himself.

"Yes," Margeaux smiled innocently. "Your wife is very trusting. Naively so, any child could see that. A few well placed tears, a little tonal alteration in my speech, were all that I needed to finally convince her that I was her niece."

"Well, you have failed all the same." Keeping the charade going, John forced himself to shrug. "No sample was obtained and your father is dead. The plan, too, has failed."

"Where was Father when you killed him?" she squinted up at him, the hate barely masked with the smile. "I want to know."

"It is unimportant."

Margeaux's eyes turned glacial. She seemed to sense that he wouldn't utter another word about her father.

"I hope she dies," she whispered coldly, unblinking.

That statement alone would have ensured Margeaux's own death, however, John remained resolutely calm. Right now, this girl was still very important to him.

He leaned in a fraction closer and whispered back. "You'll be dead before that happens."

She scoffed softly—like an adult—and leaned back with a 'just try it' expression on her face.

Shifting gears, John asked her another question. "What was the purpose of training you in the art of persuasion? You could not have possibly known of my wife's existence, nor could your father. It was only chance that she was discovered."

"Father was a visionary. By training me this way, the possibilities and the opportunities that lay before us were limitless. I could be used to convince any number of people into parting with their monies. When he found my dear aunt, it was my idea to change my appearance to look like her. Seal the deal, so to speak." Margeaux smiled wickedly. "It worked. I saw the confusion and the want in her eyes when she first saw me. She was ripe for the picking, so to speak."

John continued to look at the girl dispassionately, willing himself not to react violently. This child before him, this cold and wicked child—how dare she speak of Josie like this!

I must remain calm, he ordered himself.

Margeaux smoothed the front of her shirt and tossed her head casually. "So, what then, is to become of me? Am I to be sent to prison? Tortured? Executed?"

"No, not yet." The returning calm brought everything together so it made a little sense. Pieces began falling into place. "When my wife recovers, I will let her decide what is to become of you. Consider that a generous offer, she can be very lenient. Personally, I would have thrown you into the recycling shredder and watched while I had my tea."

"You can't keep me here like this," Margeaux spat out. "I do have rights as a minor."

"Watch me. You forget who I am. I can do anything I please, and I say you have absolutely no rights, whatsoever. And I am not done with you, yet."

"I demand a trial! I have a right to one!" Margeaux stood, her fist balled at her sides. "Look at me when I speak to you! You can't keep me here. I demand a trial!"

John turned and left, ignoring her rant. A new urgency pulsed through him like electricity.

Iceland!

...go to the source, she'd said.

How could he not have seen that? Why Iceland, that was another matter, but not as pressing as the need to get there, and get there fast.

Aline. Timing was everything. They needed Aline to get them into the DNA banks. Ho may be smart, but maybe not smart enough to break through the security barriers that guarded these precious remnants of people who once lived or were alive still. Generations of information stored and compiled over the years. Information more sacred than life itself—it was history, a story of civilization. Not anyone could just walk in and access them. He needed Aline's pass-code to get in.

Surely Ho was there, with Josie and Aline. Orchestral maneuvers and precision timing, it was all about timing. All the tricks, deceptions and distractions, were set up to take away from the fact that Ho was after the samples. The Scrap Yard was secondary. Without the samples, the facilities at the space station were useless.

Damn it, that's it!

Ho planned on creating some hideous half-man, half-machine creature. John had no doubts that Ho would also subject himself to this creation—cyborging himself. A man like Ho, he wouldn't waste his time making an army of these creatures and selling them off to the highest bidder, not when he could make himself invincible.

But it still left the question of why Josie was needed in the first place. Why was she needed? If Ho was related to her, they shared DNA. The Iceland facility stored countless DNA samples of countless people. *Whose* samples did Ho want besides Josie's? As confusing as it was, there seemed no point in wasting time thinking about it now.

As John marched briskly away, he asked himself again.

What possible motive would Ho have that he needed her DNA?

Sixteen

The Scrap Yard was under heavy assault by Ho's so-called army. They showed no discrimination as to who or what they destroyed, so long as the objective to take over the control room was accomplished. Already, they'd managed to sabotage the launching sequences for the escape pods. People were stranded—trapped on a floating mass of metal in the middle of space. And, they were locked in.

Simon had his hands full and the last thing he needed to hear was that Josie *and* Aline might be in serious danger in Iceland.

Though the conversation with John had been brief, and somewhat strained, he got the gist of it. Details, at the moment, weren't important. And now he had John to worry about on top of everything else. There'd be no stopping John and his single-minded purpose of saving Josie. Simon had to let go and accept the fact that John was still very skilled, and would know how to handle himself. However, being discreet, for now, was a secondary matter.

Simon turned to Governor Mwenye after juggling a call from both Ox and Madds.

"They've managed to get through the first of the stop-check doors. Practically all of your security droids are down—and quite a number of Junkies. The other two doors will not stand a chance now. Stay here with Renna. Do not move from this place. Understood? If the area is breached, use your magic and find a way to launch and get the hell out of here."

"I'm not an idiot," Mwenye retorted with a bit of anger. "Where are you going? I should at least help in some way. The station is still my responsibility!"

"You can help by staying here," Simon snapped back with the full force of lethal authority in his voice. "Renna," he turned to her quickly.

Simon's look alone told her that under no circumstances was the Governor to leave her sight. She gave him a quick nod then casually resumed her weapons check.

"Where are you going?" Mwenye repeated. "Might I remind you of what you carry on your person?"

Simon turned slowly to face the Governor, stepping closer so only he alone could hear. His eyes glowed with an icy blue menace that would've turned a lesser person into a puddle of water.

"Might I remind *you* that I am insignificant compared to you and what's in your head? The moment they find out that the mainframe has been rigged with that shut down sequence, the first person they will seek out is you. I need to get to the mainframe—now. Understood?"

Mwenye glared back but nodded tightly. He looked helpless. Useless. Like a man used to delivering authority, issuing commands, taking responsibility—and was suddenly stripped of it all.

"Understood." Mwenye balled his fists at his sides and took a breath.

Simon left Mwenye where he stood and headed out of the launch chamber. He needed to bypass the lockdown of the exit doors. It would be virtually impossible. The doors were thick, solid metal and reinforced to withstand the blasts and shock waves of high velocity ejection. The only possible route for escape was the underground cable ducts. He'd once saved himself by traveling for two miles along an underground cable duct; very similar to the one he was about to jump down into. It took him nearly a day then, but that was another time, another place.

A basic fault in most building designs, people never thought to secure these ducts; thinking no one in their right mind would ever dream of crawling over several thousand volts of electrical cables, on your belly, in a cavity no higher than two feet. Sliding over the warm cables, the smell of hot plastic casing with undertones of rubber and copper filled the senses. Sweat, oily and slick, rolled off the body and slipped through hands, making it hard to pull yourself forward. It would leave you to wonder when a stray bead of sweat would drop through a small opening and ignite—causing you to fry to nothing but dust.

Simon, normally right in the head, and in his logic, it took a sane man to do insane things and be able to appreciate it at the end—if you made it to the end. And he considered himself to be very sane, compared with the lunatics that ran loose all around this space station. With that thought, he jumped into the narrow opening and into the dim cocoon of the launching chambers underbelly, and began his horizontal crawl.

Using his keen sense of direction to get him—slowly—past the main doors, he reached the reception area and encountered a split that parted four ways. He took the right, which would direct him to the outer doors, and hopefully, he'd be able to surface somewhere just before them.

It wasn't a long crawl, not like the two-mile trek he'd once done. It took a mere forty-five minutes, but it was long enough and minutes now were precious. Judging the distance, he leaned up and felt his way along the 'roof' of his cocooned existence. Pushing and prodding until finally, one section gave in slightly. He pushed harder. A thin, bright stream of light shot through the dimness. Spying through the crevice, all was clear. He brought himself all the way up and found he was just past the doors as he reckoned, in a quiet corner near a vending machine.

Using the solid square bulk of the vending machine to hide himself, he slithered out quietly and crouched. In the distance, along the corridors, he could hear voices. They sounded agitated. Simon guessed there were at least seven people, three with distinct voices and tones that stood apart from the others, causing him to wonder if they were disagreeing about who was in charge.

Emerging from his hiding place, he edged along the wall until he came to the end and risked a look. There were eight, two were women, and armed to the teeth. It appeared that they'd been stationed to guard the launch chambers from anyone who tried to get in or out. By the looks of it, they still didn't realize that the Governor was within one of these chambers.

Simon calculated his odds. He could, if he wanted, fight all of them and get out of it alive, if not a little banged up. But it would draw attention—where there were eight, there surely would be more. The Scrap Yard was immense, and in order the take control of it, you needed a very big army. And big armies were very difficult to get your way around once you got their attention.

Stealth was the best option. But how was he going to get past without alerting them? There was no choice; he had to just barrel through and hope no more lurked around the corner. Taking a breath, he swiftly strode out from his hiding place and boldly greeted the group.

Before they could even register his presence, Simon snapped his arms out and slammed them into two unsuspecting throats. He heard the dull crunch as their Adam's apples broke; it gave him a satisfied feeling. Quickly, Simon grabbed one gagging man at his right and brought him before him, using the dying body as a shield. With a shift he kicked out, bringing down another man with a deadly blow to his chest that crushed the ribs into his heart. The man was dead before he even fell to the floor.

Without missing a beat, Simon spun with the body, dancing. Arching his left arm he grappled the ear of a woman, who barely had time to let out a startled yelp before he wrapped his arm around her head. He brought her head into the crook of his arm, gave it a sharp jerk, and snapped her neck.

And then confusion broke out.

Four were dead in surprised silence. The other four finally snapped out of their stupefied shock and hauled up weapons to take aim. Simon threw the body he held, knocked down one man, causing him to squeeze the trigger of the assault weapon, it sprayed the area with bullets. The bullets hissed by Simon's ear, who merely dipped low and kicked at someone's knees, bringing them down in a roar of pain.

The first man down now scrambled to get up, shoving the dead body away from him. By this time, Simon—forever moving with fluidity—had already flipped sideways, and in a graceful move like a courting heron, rose to grasp the weapon from the other woman. Without a single struggle, he used her natural movement to point the gun to him, to his advantage. Simon merely pulled her forward, twisted her up and over his shoulder. She landed with a crash atop the second man he'd knocked down. Before she could even land, Simon's leg already jack-knifed out to kick the head of the last man standing, who was in an animated struggle to pinpoint the exact location of his target without getting his friends killed in the process. The kick took in him in the eye, he hollered out in surprise.

The first man stood now, taking aim again with his weapon. Simon whipped out his arm to knock it away but the woman was already up and pouncing onto his back, wrapping brawny arms about his neck. He struck out with his elbow and felt it smash into her in the ribs—she grunted in pain. He spun, backing the first man and lashed out with his leg, it connected to something solid. Simon kept spinning, saw the man buckle over his thighs, then caught movement at his side as the second man struggled with his weapon.

He had to shake off the woman so he jumped forward, curled, rolling in midair and landed, with a thud, on his—her—shoulders. He continued the roll, feeling her grip slacken around his neck as she took most of the impact. She made an angry growl, he moved quickly now, ripping her arms away. He reared up and twisted, rammed her with a backhanded blow to the face. Instinctively, he hauled her up before him when the second man started shooting from his gun. He used a Snare Gun 3 and the quick, three-rounds per shot, hissed out like a spitting cat. The woman screamed out as the barbed bullets dug into her back, a second later, they exploded like firecrackers and she jerked rigid before dying.

Simon yanked out the knife he kept behind his back, tucked neatly in his belt. He threw it from his reclined position, the dead woman still on top of him; her burning flesh filled the air with stench. The knife found its mark, dead centre in the man's neck. He gagged and choked, dropping the gun as he fell to his knees. Simon was up, hopped lightly over the woman, and in two quick paces, removed the knife, spun, and sent it flying back out to the first man. It struck him in his chest. The man stood grimacing for a moment, a look of surprise on his face. Simon walked up to him, held the knife a moment, locking eyes with him before twisting it once, and then pushed the man off the blade.

Simon was in no hurry to dispatch the last man, who, still on his back, held his eye and mewled like a cat. He grabbed a handful of the man's hair; a shocked brown eye stared back at Simon in horror—the other eye rapidly swelling itself shut. With a neat thrust, Simon drove the knife up under the man's chin, twisted it, then drew it out in a spray of blood. The last words uttered before the man died was something that sounded very close to 'oh'.

Eight down and no more appeared to be materializing out of the woodworks. Simon allowed himself a moment to collect himself, listening intently for any sounds while he calmly wiped the blood from the knife along his sleeve. Surely the gunfire would've attracted the attentions of others.

Without wasting any more time wondering if an army was about to appear from around the corner, he quickly moved away, following the corridor to the elevators and stairs. He chose the stairs, two-stepped it down towards the mainframe level on Level 5, Deck 2. He pulled out his communicator and contacted Renna, informing her that he was out.

Agnes, stationed at Level 6 on Deck 3, where he was now, was just one flight of stairs down. She'd been posted there to secure the launch chambers, but the sight of the eight men he'd just removed meant that she was either dead or keeping low. There would have been no way Agnes would've let them through had she been able to. He tried to tag her, no response.

When he engaged the doors on Level 6, nothing but smoke and confusion greeted him—and the unmistakable stench of death. He dipped low instinctively, crouching and squinting through the smoke.

Level 6 was a circular room with several exits, ringed by a corridor that branched off into various smaller auxiliary rooms and elevators. From the corridor were three exits, two to access the levels below, and one to access the launch chambers that Simon had just come from. The room itself was a sort of command centre with equipment and machines that controlled the launching sequences of the chambers.

A voice farther away could be heard, off to one side, speaking low. The dull shadow of someone's head could be seen, partly hidden by the upturned shelving units and desks. Parts of machinery lay strewn across the floor, mingled with bodies and droids—ripped and torn. The carnage before Simon was unmistakably the work of Agnes.

He found her, sitting propped against a wall that faced the opening to one of the elevators, an array of heavy weapons before her. She snapped her head to him, her hand already aiming a pulse gun in his direction. Blood ran freely down the side of her head, matting her golden locks to her scalp. The front of her shirt was sticky with blood, glittering dark against the black of her uniform like macabre sequins. A small metallic object protruded from the top of her thigh, which was wrapped tightly with a cord.

"Took you long enough to get here," Agnes accused Simon. Her voice, steady and calm. With her free hand, she tapped the earpiece communicator. "It's gone dead—must've been the last explosion that did it."

"All right, Aggs? Lower your gun, girl." Simon glanced about, taking in the wreckage, turned to her and raised a questioning eyebrow.

She smiled and nodded. "Sorry. But I tried to make sure that I didn't hit any of the important-looking controls. We should still be able to perform emergency-eject."

"Where're the others?"

"I've two Junkies manning one elevator," she cocked her head to the right. "The others are somewhere in there," she indicated mildly to the mangle of bodies and droids before them. "A few of them got away—did you find them? They'd be the scared-looking ones." She grinned and then grunted to chase away the obvious pain she was in.

Simon nodded. "How long has it been?"

He crouched down and tilted her head to inspect her head wound. Bits of metal and debris tangled together with her hair. The injury itself looked rather deep but the blood seemed to be washing away most of the debris. He pulled out his skin-sealer and sprayed the wound. She flinched as the stinging antiseptic solution worked its way into the wound, dried, and sealed itself.

"About thirty minutes or so. I'm fine. It's the leg that's bothering me. I can barely walk. I think the shard has touched bone."

"Hmm." Simon peered at it. "Best to leave it be, it's holding in the blood for now."

"I can manage things here. You need to get to the mainframe and help Ox and Madds. Just before I lost communications, unfriendlies had gotten through the secondary doors. Heavy casualties, droids and humans alike."

"I was just on my way." Simon dug out a spare communicator and tossed it to Agnes. "That works on channel five."

Agnes nodded and affixed it to her ear making small adjustments that caused her to twist her mouth with effort. "Thanks. These guys, some are professional mercs. The others, I'm not so sure they even know how to handle a gun. It was like cutting through butter with a hot knife…"

"Like the ones you left me to deal with. I know what you mean. I think Ho's main interest is brute force."

"Well, he's doing just that. Any word from Minnows?"

"Not yet."

Minnows' role had been to 'float' around. His small stature and frame made him ideal to flit from one area to the next, unseen. He was quick, nimble, and knew the art of disappearing.

At that very moment, Minnows was engaged in a hand-to-hand combat with three mercenaries, hell-bent on getting through the last of the security doors that led to the mainframe.

Within, Ox, now joined by Madds and a few more Space Junkies, grit their teeth, preparing to defend the mainframe with their lives.

~ * ~

Aline Lancaster stared impassively down her nose at the small, wiry man. He stood an inch taller, but somehow, from her birthright and breeding, she managed to appear regal and superior to all those around her. If he appeared nervous from it, which he wasn't, he didn't show it. He was a Rogue and his job was to acquire Aline Lancaster and escort her to the reception hall and wait. How he did so and what he did to get her there, according to his detailed contract, was of no consequence.

The reception hall of the Hontag-Sonnet Research and Archives Facility was immense. Spartanly furnished, glossy and sleek with marbled floors, granite finishes and metallic accents along walls and furnishings, it had been designed to look like an underground cave made of ice. Small water fountains spilled over with lush ferns and plants, special lighting effects that were tucked in strategically, to create mood. The walls, too, were slick with sheets of waterfalls. The water collected at the base where fat koi swam lazily through a mesh of water plants and under miniature wooden bridges. A feint chill frosted the air and a suggestive sound-clip of ice crackling and creaking completed the entire atmosphere of a wintry fantasyland.

It was a far cry from the no-nonsense, industrially-stark docking bays a mile away. The transport from there had been incident-free. Aline didn't dare risk drawing attention to her escorts before she knew the full extent of her situation. She decided to attempt open combat in a more secure environment. As it stood, the entire docking bay seemed to have been overpowered by Rogues, mercenaries, and hired assassins alike.

Having cleared the two security droids at the entrance to the reception hall with her iris, DNA scan, and pass-code entry, they had proceeded along the immense stretch of the hall to the first checkpoint.

Her two escorts, posing as her body-assistants, were required to offer their wrists to be scanned. When the light pinged green and they were given the all clear, Aline could only raise an impressed brow. How they'd managed to steal the identities of her real body-assistants was quite a feat. Ho must have planned for this a very long time—which meant that his deadly fingers reached far and wide. She decided it was best if she chose not to put her trust into anyone at this facility for the time being.

So now she stood, in a roomy hospitality room, staring down at the wiry man before her. They'd cleared all three stop-checks without incident. Her appointment with Dr. Maines was scheduled on the log so she was breezed directly through. Aline and her escorts were even offered refreshments. She had declined politely.

"May I ask what is required of me once Dr. Maines arrives?" Aline asked casually.

She'd already estimated the size and weight of both her escorts. The other man, taller and stockier, tended to favor his left side, suggesting that he had a store of weapons on that side. It meant, too, he was right-handed. The wiry man was quick and fast. He had to be dealt with first—he appeared to be cunning, therefore, full of tricks.

"You will continue with your scheduled appointment with

him," the wiry man replied with a coy smile.

He had a shifty, edgy demeanor; whether it was purposely, Aline wasn't sure. *Like a cheeky, little monkey.*

"But you must insist we wait until your associates arrive," he continued.

"Ho?" Aline asked with a slightly bored tone.

"Mr. Ho will be along shortly with a few others. It is his wish that you simply receive him graciously. And please, do not try to alert anyone's attention. It could prove to be rather fatal for a certain individual that accompanies him. After that, your role here is done."

If Ho meant to come here directly, it indicated that he wanted something that was here. The DNA samples. Now, why would Ho need samples—the actual living tissues? Was this all connected to Josie and her history? The possibility of that was great. It also meant that Aline's main purpose here was to get them in. After that, she was dispensable. And that usually meant dead.

Hontag-Sonnet's security was practically foolproof. They took no chances and took no invitations or requests unless specifically approved or accompanied by approved personnel or individuals—like her. And who better, of all the people in the world, to okay Ho than Dr. Aline Lancaster? Sister to the world president himself, acclaimed physician, and a prominent member of Hontag-Sonnet. She felt used.

A surge of anger speared through her. She took a calming breath to steady herself lest she dispatch these two on the spot in a blind haze of rage. No, she ordered herself. Let it play out. That would be the safest way.

She stole a brief glance at the visible security camera overhead and wondered. If Ho needed her to get in, the chances that he had no one on the inside were great. Help might not be too far away. She needed to find a way to alert the security—as discreetly as possible.

Dr. Caleb Maines pushed through the doors to the hospitality room to find a severe looking, dark-haired woman scowling at her body-assistant. A look of panic shot through him. He seemed to quake in the presence of *the* Aline Lancaster. *The Dr.* Aline Lancaster. Maines was in charge of the Archival Facility, but right now, looked as if that honor was a curse and would gladly trade a Petri dish with tissue samples any day than to exchange small talk with celebrities.

Clearing his throat he greeted his guest, forcibly tucking his hands at his side as he'd been instructed to do. No touching, under any circumstances.

"Madam Lancaster—I mean, *Dr.* Lancaster. A pleasure."

Aline inclined her head and all but, regretfully, dismissed Dr. Maines as a feeble science-tech—and, therefore, useless in her current predicament.

"Dr. Maines." Aline had to repress a sigh. She imagined a thin trickle of sweat running down his spine, his elbow twitched at his side as if wanting to staunch it.

"I trust your travel here was pleasant? Did you require any refreshments?"

"No."

Dr. Maines cleared his throat again. He looked petrified and uncomfortable at the same time, like he'd drawn the short straw to get the difficult ones.

Aline suppressed another sigh. The rumors of her manner, bold, direct, and frightfully severe seemed to have reached as far as Iceland.

"Oh—well, ahh... Shall we then proceed to the reason for your visit? You had mentioned you wished to access some, some, ah, samples?" Maines stammered.

Exchanging a tight look with the wiry man, Aline pursed her lips. "Yes, but, if I may request that we wait until my associates arrive. Could you please inform security?"

Dr. Maines' eyes practically bulged; his lips trembled slightly. He clearly didn't know what to do.

"A-Associates? There are—there will be *m-more* of you?" He blinked rapidly. "Oh, well—of course. If you will give me a moment while I contact security. H-how many associates, did you say? And, ah, the, the names?"

Deliberately, Aline looked at her cheeky escort. "My assistant will tell you, won't you?"

With an apologetic look, the wiry man made a great show of fumbling and rummaging into his jacket where he extracted a personal unit and read off from a list.

"Four individuals, two are body-assistants by the names of James and Lee. I will transmit their ID codes in a moment. The associates are Michael Ho, civilian and industrialist, and Madam Lancaster—the president's wife. I believe she will be cleared without question."

"Oh…" Dr. Maines all but withered on the spot.

Seventeen

When I saw Aline, she looked ready to kill someone with her bare hands. I'd seen her upset before, even a little angry, but this went beyond that. And I saw a little fear and knew it was the fear that drove her to want to rip somebody's face off. Suddenly, I felt as if everything was my entire fault. In a strange sense, it was.

She nodded to me casually, glowered at Ho, and simply dismissed the presence of James and Ho's body-assistant, Lee. The nervous Dr. Maines, who introduced himself to us, looked nearly white with agitation. With effort, he puffed himself up and directed us to follow him to the elevators that would take us to the underground archives.

Ho made some indication to a skinny man—who Aline glanced at with distaste—and his companion to remain behind, then joined us into the elevator.

"How is John?" Aline asked me mildly.

"Pissed off," I smiled back tightly. "I missed supper last night."

Aline arched her eyebrows, understanding my meaning. "I'm sure he is."

Ho curled a hand around my arm, squeezing it to remind me to remain silent. He'd been reminding me ever since we disembarked the shuttle and made the trip to the reception hall. Not wanting to disappoint him, I opened my mouth to continue.

"Well, you know how John can be."

"That I do. But I'm sure he'll make it up to you." Aline glanced up at the security monitors in the elevator. "The first chance he gets."

I didn't miss the double meaning in her words. We both knew that once it was discovered that we were in Iceland, John would come. The only question was how would he know where we were? And when he did find out, how long would it be before he came. I was glad too, that Aline was here. Her presence bolstered my confidence and hope, which had rapidly deteriorated during the shuttle ride over.

The elevator doors opened and Dr. Maines practically tumbled out before us, scurrying and fumbling along the corridor as we cleared yet another security checkpoint. This was the last one, so he muttered as if to himself, before the entrance to the Archives Room, and from there, a stern-faced security guard escorted us into a decontamination chamber. A light spray of disinfectant washed over us, followed by a blast of wind that seemed to exfoliate every pore on the skin. And then we were clear.

The Archives Room was huge. And cold. Gigantic vaults were everywhere, stacked one on top the other, like a mammoth beehive. From floor to ceiling, they lined the entire length of one wall. I could barely see the end of it from where we stood.

Before us were small glass-partitioned rooms sectioned off like cubicles with various scientific equipment and utensils that outnumbered actual furniture. A lone technician could be seen in one cubicle, engrossed at the moment with something interesting under his microscope. He merely raised his head, did a double take and then, quickly ducked his head back to his work.

"These are the research cubicles," Dr. Maines explained helpfully, seemingly more at ease now that we were in the labs. "I have reserved a room for you, Dr. Lancaster, that is more private and secure for what you require. I'm sure you realize that these samples cannot be contaminated or tampered in any way. And you are aware that no part, not even a micro-syringe sample can be taken unless a family member or their representative has granted specific permission to you, and this facility. All pertinent information is logged and attached to each sample, should you need to know details. Log in and enter your name at the console, it will allow you temporary access to all corresponding electronic data. Once you are done, log out, it will automatically shut down and erase what you have viewed. If you require the use of—"

"Thank you, Dr. Maines," Aline interrupted and inclined her head. "But I'm not sure what it is my associates will require."

She turned to face Dr. Maines, looking at him directly. Then, she appeared to look somewhere behind him, pausing thoughtfully as her eyes went skyward. I discreetly glanced over to where she looked, wondering if she saw something that could help us. I only saw a security camera. If I didn't know any better, Aline seemed to be making some sort of signal to the camera.

I saw Dr. Maines make an audible gulp. "I'm sorry, I-I do not understand. You requested to see a few samples and do a background—"

"Dr. Maines," Michael Ho spoke up for the first time. "We are here at *my* request. Unfortunately, these ladies are my captives and have performed their functions quite well. Might I ask that you escort me to these particular samples that *I* require? I have a list."

Dr. Maines merely stood blinking rapidly, obviously trying to process the situation. From the corner of my eye, I took note that Lee had the other technician in some sort of stranglehold, and James had moved toward the main doors. He fiddled with the control panels, his back to us.

"I'm sorry...I-I don't understand." Dr. Maines stammered and looked from Ho to Aline. He saw his associate being dropped to the floor like a rag doll and gaped. "Sir, the security cams—this place will be overrun with guards. You can't succeed in whatever it is you want. Did you just kill...?" Horror spread across Dr. Maines' face, his voice clipped up a few octaves higher.

"That is not a concern to me. Please," Ho inclined his head to the direction of the vaults. "Time is precious. The samples?"

"Do as he says, Dr. Maines," Aline prompted. "All will be well. This is no fault of yours."

Dr. Maines nearly squeaked but obediently led Ho to the vaults in a sort of staggering shuffle. By now, Ho had pulled out a small weapon, a krima stick, standard size. It wasn't engaged, but he jabbed the blunt end at Dr. Maines' back who uttered another strained squeak as he led the way.

James had returned, along with Lee, and they both stood at either side of Aline and me.

"Do not try anything foolish," James informed us.

"You can't get away with this, you do know that?" I snapped. "There's cameras all over this fucking place. *He* just killed that man—right before everyone's eyes. This place will be full of security in no time!"

"Josie," Aline cautioned me. "It's obvious they'll use us as hostages to get out. Calm down."

"Fuck that!" I retorted. "Do you even know what he's planning on doing? He wants my blood, my DNA, for some goddamned master code that unlocks some freak of nature!"

In as few words, and most of them tagged with expletives, I explained to Aline what Ho's intentions were. And, who Ho really was. I watched as Aline's face contorted in what was first surprise, then disgust. I could even sense some of that disgust being directed at me.

"Until I met you, my world was very sane." Aline shook her head and seemed to consider something. "It's never a dull moment with you."

"I try to please," I smirked with as much sarcasm as I could muster.

"Tell me, Lee, is it?" Aline turned to face Ho's body-assistant. "How does Ho plan on getting us out of here?"

"He plans on staying here for as long as it takes," Lee replied. He had a voice that sounded as if he'd just finished eating something thick and sticky. "Come," he flicked his porcupine-like head to me and pointed to a room.

I glanced at it and saw a reclining chair, an array of surgical equipment, vials and bottles and odd-looking machinery.

"No," I replied.

James sighed from beside me. "Look, Josie. Make this as easy as it can be for yourself. Go, let Dr. Lancaster take your blood, and relax."

James came around and took my arm, forcing me to walk towards the room. "It is better if she does it. Ho will simply cut you like hung meat to get what he wants."

"Then he'll have to fucking cut me." I jerked out of his grip and dug my heels into the floor.

Aline made to move, but Lee's swift arm caught her in the

chest. She gasped out a breath and staggered backwards. Quick to recover, she spun and jabbed him with a roundhouse punch, clipping his side. He bucked back, twisted and sailed through the air, up and over Aline's head, grabbed a fistful of her hair and brought her down with him to the floor.

It all happened so fast—I barely registered it. One moment they stood and grappled with each other, the next, they were on the floor and Lee had twisted her arm high up behind her back. Aline lay, face red with fury, but pliant.

Without thinking twice, without even thinking why, I turned and ran. My reasoning? If they wanted my blood, they'd have to catch me first. But where would I run to—in circles?

But run I did, through the maze of glass cubicles, up and over desks and shelving, down the length of floor-space between the vaults, ducking through narrow openings that held precious samples of a generation of peoples.

This was madness, I thought. But I couldn't stop myself. I was in panic. Even my reasoning had become blurred and furry with fear.

James hollered out at me, so did Aline. I couldn't be sure of what exactly. I found a small enough crevice between a shelving unit and some sort of machine and wedged myself into the space. Then bit my lips and willed my breath to level out.

I heard a crash and Aline's voice growling in anger. I slammed a hand over my mouth to stop myself from calling out. I should help Aline, I thought. I knew how to fight, for Christ sakes! But instead, I hid.

Another yell—Aline's. Another crash. James called out to me—he was much closer. I bunched myself into a tighter ball, and then I felt it. I nearly stopped breathing altogether when I realized what it was.

Through the fabric of the long overcoat that James had placed over my shoulders, I felt my krima in one of its side pockets.

I dug frantically for it, pulled it out, and simply stared at it.

What...*what* was it doing in the pocket? Did James forget it there and mistakenly given me his coat? Or did he do it on purpose? Knowing I'd find it. Why?

I thought rapidly. He'd been helpful, somewhat, throughout

this entire ordeal. But why? He was a Rogue, and wasn't paid to have a conscience. Why would he want to help?

I pushed these questions away and tucked my krima into its proper place, in my wrist holster. No one would see it, no one—but James—would know, covered up as it was with the long sleeves of the overcoat. And no one would expect me to have it.

It was a poor excuse, but I didn't need to hide any more. I didn't need to run. I had a—not an ace—but a krima up my sleeve. And I planned to use it on Ho.

With a forceful grunt, I pushed out of my hiding place and stood waiting for James.

I saw him turn a corner from one of the glass cubicles. His eyes met mine, and for a second, I thought he could read my thoughts. He paused, just for a moment, then walked towards me to take my arm.

Did I imagine a small wink? I couldn't be sure, but allowed him to escort me back to Aline. She sat on the floor with a bloody nose, but otherwise fine. A weapon was pointed at her head and Lee looked ready to kill her on the spot.

~ * ~

Deidre Moorjani was a thorough woman. If something bothered her, she followed through until it exhausted her or the channels by which she followed them were exhausted. Josie's disappearance bothered her—greatly. She liked Josie. They'd fought side by side once during the recent siege of the Citadel.

The Rogue intrigued her as well. Why would someone who'd risked sneaking into the Citadel, then boldly offer his face up for the surveillance cameras? It didn't make sense. Unless…he wanted to be caught. Rogue's were known to have a superiority complex, but this was ridiculous. Even the best of them wouldn't risk blatant exposure like this.

She'd dropped his image into the image bank and acquired surveillance footage from all across Europe from the last twenty-four hours. It was madness and would take endless time, even with all her ten computers working non-stop. So when, nearly a day later, her computer pinged her, she broke out into a broad smile.

The Rogue had been tagged twice. At a service docking bay for private shuttles, again, bolding looking up at the cameras. Then, there he was again, at the front desk of a hotel in Iceland.

What intrigued Moorjani more was that Iceland was also the destination of Aline Lancaster's private shuttle. She didn't know the specifics of why Dr. Lancaster had gone to Iceland. Nor would she dream of asking, but something niggled at Moorjani's brain. To settle her thorough mind, she dropped Aline's image into the image bank, specifying that it target Iceland.

It didn't surprise Moorjani in the least that in less than five minutes, the computer pinged with several images of Aline being escorted by two unfamiliar men who appeared to be posing as her body-assistants. The images of Aline were bold, direct, and with purpose. No one could question the expression on her face. Aline needed help and needed it fast.

And who else should Moorjani see, but Josie.

Moorjani bolted out of her office and headed straight for John Lancaster.

She found him grim-faced, about to board a shuttle. Dressed in no-nonsense black and looking militant, John was just testing the grip of a weapon when Moorjani grabbed his attention. She looked about him and guessed immediately that he knew.

"Iceland," she said. "Got them all there. I have it on surveillance—everything. They're not hiding anymore."

"And that's where you'll find me," he replied quietly. "Simon needs you here. So do I."

Moorjani nodded. "I take it this is under the radar?" She looked at the small team, Simon's Elites. "*Way* under the radar."

"Inform Loeb, no one else." John affixed his communicator to his ear and nodded to the pilot.

"The Vice President?"

"Not even her. This goes bad, she can deny with honesty."

"I'll patch through the surveillance feed to you. Bring them back, sir." Moorjani looked as though she wanted in on the action. Her hand gripped the side of the shuttle door, more to restrain herself from jumping in.

"Maybe next time, Moorjani." John caught her expression then nodded to the pilot again. "I intend to see you later, make sure they keep this bay door open." He gave her a scary smile that made her glad she wasn't the one he planned on killing.

"How did you find out?"

"I beat it out of the girl," he continued to smile coldly.

The shuttle door slammed shut and within five minutes, they were off.

~ * ~

John allowed himself to relax. The knot in his stomach had ached and ached since he learned of Josie's whereabouts. It had taken every bit of control he had to get him through the last few hours while he organized his ad-hoc team, sans Simon. Mapping out a plan and then leaving the Citadel as quietly as possible had been a feat in itself as well. Usually Simon handled these matters—and he handled them like the magician he was.

Now that they were on their way, the knot seemed to ease. He willed himself not to bark at the pilot to go faster. They were on stream; they had the element of surprise. Ho wouldn't expect such a swift response.

And he knew that so long as they were all still in Iceland, Josie was still alive.

He didn't know who he wanted dead first. Ho or James. He informed his team to use extreme force. They weren't going to make a scene—this was a quick extraction. But they were going to use whatever force necessary to get it done. Quietly, but effectively.

Simon had picked his team well to take to the Scrap Yard but he'd left enough behind, more than enough, for John. Five were with him now. Two, he'd worked with countless times before and were seasoned veterans, the pug-faced McLinney and the dour Kakuta. The other three, Panna, Abrahms and Mamud, he'd picked for their no-nonsense fighting skills. In another life, those three could've been Rogues themselves...

I should have told Rand. John reprimanded himself, once again, and felt the hot rush of guilt on his face. *Too late, now.*

He didn't want to risk opening a communications channel with his brother-in-law now. Rand would understand.

He's one of us, he always understands.

Eighteen

Minnows back-flipped like a gymnast, his full-length krima blazed an amber trail beside him like a Ferris wheel. The last mercenary he killed seemed to have cloned himself and two more popped up beside him. One, a woman wielding a massive gun that looked like the grandmother of pulse guns.

While most pulse guns used compressed air that shot out like bullets, taking only one point five seconds to recalibrate and reload, larger ones tended to take longer and usually sucked the surrounding air like a vacuum. When the first tugging sensation tweaked his ears as the air around them compressed rapidly, Minnows was already airborne and flipping away in different directions like a rubber ball.

He heard the woman belch out in annoyance. The other mercenary preferred heat-seeking bullets and fired a quick burst in Minnows' general direction. Since the bullets hadn't had time to lock onto a target, they went wild and scattered every which way— seeking out any heat source. The woman yelled out at the man to stop.

Skipping and flitting across the walls and fallen furniture, over the bodies of dead men and machines, Minnows gauged his time with care. If he stopped too long, the heat-seeking gun could tag him and that would be the end of that. But, he also needed to get close enough to attack. He knew, too, that more mercenaries would come in their effort to get to the mainframe.

So, when in doubt, make a big impression. He whipped out a small contact explosive from his belt, launched off into a series of flips that brought him feet away from his targets, threw the explosive, and bounded away.

It wasn't a big bang, but big enough. It knocked off the entire booted-foot of the man with the heat-seeking gun. He fell to his knees, roaring in pain. The woman shot wildly about, the air around them went thin and tight, making everyone's ears pop from the pressure.

Minnows had already bounced away, practically running up the side of a wall, where he launched himself off and neatly lopped the head of the man with his krima as he passed over. Then he dropped behind the woman—she spun, shot blind. Minnows arched backwards, snapping out an arm to absorb the fall. He pushed up like a spring and brought the krima sailing down over her arm. It sliced it from the elbow, caught the metal of the pulse gun where it crackled and sent showers of hot sparks everywhere. Minnows pulled back quickly so as not to get any stray beams his way, spun low and finished the job with a backwards jab to her liver. She jerked and screamed, falling to the floor. Minnows felt mild regret, he didn't like killing, but it was necessary.

A noise behind Minnows had him scampering up and somersaulting away. He landed, took a quick look, and found it was only Simon.

"Good job," Simon said, glancing about him. "You did all of this?"

Bodies were all over the place, mostly human. A Space Junkie, still alive, a few feet away, propped up against a wall. She breathed heavily and the life seemed to be draining from her body. Nearby, the bottom-half of a security droid made hissing noises under the body of a man, its metallic limb flexed in spasms.

"I had help." Minnows looked regretfully at the dying Space Junkie. His words, always quiet and carefully spoken, never rushed. "She won't make it, but she helped. Her name is Petroski." He hopped over the carnage to squat beside her. "I will stay here, until she goes."

"Minnows…" Simon said, but didn't finish. There's no time for that, was what he wanted to say. Instead, he tagged Ox to inform him that they were outside, who then informed Simon that their scanners detected another wave of men coming in—fast.

"Minnows," Simon ordered with haste. "Grab the Junkie and

let's move it!"

The massive doors to the mainframe hissed and opened; Simon and Minnows flung themselves in. A second later, the doors slammed shut.

"What am I missing out there?" Ox bellowed out. "Smells like a blood-fest!" But he grabbed Minnows and gave him a full inspection. Most of the blood on Minnows wasn't his.

Taking note of Minnows' grim face, Simon reasoned that Petroski had died. He patted his shoulder roughly as he pushed past and strode up to Madds.

"Talk to me."

"It's like when we had the siege." Madds hovered over a console. "They're popping up all over the place. And some Space Junkies are among them."

"What do you mean? They've crossed over?"

"I think they've been over a long time—or are impostors to begin with. How else can all these mercs be popping up without detection?"

A serious-faced Space Junkie, Russell, spoke up. "Not all of us, sir. I think mostly the newer recruits—they don't train them like they used to. I've also gotten reports that two unidentified shuttles have docked here within the last three weeks—consecutively. It was listed as a cargo shuttle for parts but no one can confirm it. That's how they must've gotten in."

"Who's in charge of docking?"

"Each dock has its own, but the one in charge of everything is Becks. He's missing at the moment."

"How convenient." Simon made a face. "What else?"

Madds pushed up from over the console. "They've taken over Production—it's at a standstill. All the techs are under guard. Distribution as well. Not much casualties, they seem to be targeting mainly security. I've also just gotten reports that the communal areas are under attack. They've managed to herd everyone into the dining halls. All docking bays, except Dock 4, are locked off. We can assume that that is where they're coming in from."

"So they have an external ship feeding in more men?"

"There's nothing on the scanners to indicate that. But then, they could be manipulating our feed as well."

A dull explosion could be heard from beyond the doors. The room shook.

"Ox," Simon grabbed the large man's shoulder. "Is there a way to override their command and shut down Dock 4? I'd prefer to eject it out, personally."

"I've been trying, but its taking time," Ox replied. "They're running a scrambler that's making it very hard to pinpoint things."

"Use your magic." Simon looked at Madds. "Any news on Surrey? Did he make it?"

"No, nothing," Madds replied quietly.

"Sir," Russell stepped forward again, his earnest grey eyes looked serious. "We can activate the latest batch of security droids from here. They're offline and haven't been programmed yet, but we could so do now."

"How long will that take?"

"About fifteen minutes." A scared technician came forward. "Thirty, for the full program. But we could eliminate all the congeniality prog—"

"Do it," Simon snapped out. "How many do you have?"

"Close to five thousand, sir. Already primed and ready for service, just need the commands to activate." Russell replied. "But we'll need the code sequence unlocked to do so. I understand it's under lockdown right now?"

Simon nodded, fingering Jane in his pocket. "That'll do. I'll handle the sequence code. But in the meantime, we've got a big problem at our door. Any suggestions?"

A second dull explosion rumbled beyond the doors. It wasn't looking too good from where Simon stood. Another few blasts, and the integrity of the doors would be questionable. By the looks of it, they still wanted in into the mainframe—badly.

~ * ~

"Josie," Michael Ho shook his head with resignation. "You never fail to intrigue me. *What* could you possibly hope to achieve by running?" He raised his arms and made a slow, wide circle. "You have nowhere to go, you silly girl."

"I needed to clear my head," Josie replied with a shrug. "I get claustrophobic. Running helps."

Ho chuckled. He seemed happy, relaxed, and completely at

ease with himself. He didn't seem to care if an army stood outside trying to get in to stop him.

"I am *so* close," he muttered quietly to himself.

"Pardon?" Josie raised a brow. "Didn't quite catch that?"

Ho, seemingly unable to contain himself, beamed out into a smile. "Everything is running smoothly, according to plan. The attack on the space station is right on schedule. It is unfortunate that we couldn't shut down the surveillance cameras here, but," he shrugged, "no matter. Like your precious Citadel, there are too many fail-safes in place should anyone hack into the system. It is too much of a bother and too time-consuming. Any attack within Hontag-Sonnet is manageable, and should any outside interference come, then my men at the docking bays can take care of it. Timing is everything. And so far, everything is running smoothly—just as I had planned."

Ho pointed impatiently to Aline and Dr. Maines. "Dr. Lancaster, would you be so kind and acquire a blood sample from Josie? Dr. Maines, as you are still with us, you can be of use. The samples, please prepare and arrange them in *this* order." Ho handed him a list with directions. "And do not forget to bring the samples to body temperature, understood? Thank you."

From somewhere far and distant, vaguely audible through the thick doors, an alarm sounded. Ho cocked his head to the noise and a smile spread across his face.

"Give me your arm, Josie. Let's do what he says." Aline spoke quietly as she hefted the pressure syringe given to her. Their eyes locked. She lowered her voice so only Josie could here. "Why did you run, other than obvious panic? And why did you let yourself get caught? What's gotten into you? You could've stayed hidden and delayed things. I could've handled this lot."

Aline seemed to take note in the change of Josie's behavior.

Josie, still scared, but the panic gone, shrugged. She didn't answer but begrudgingly, offered her right arm, biting back a curse as the needle shot through the skin and sucked out three, fat inches of her blood. She watched mesmerized as the bright red fluid filled the syringe.

Her blood. Her blood, that also ran through the veins of Michael Ho. It sickened her, but it still managed to amaze her. She wondered, again, whose gene it was that caused madness. Was it part hers? Or was it from someone else? The way she felt now, she would've sworn it was hers that spawned insanity.

For a moment, she pictured what it would feel like to kill Ho. To sink her krima into that pasty face of his, rip it apart...

He spoke again, practically chattering like an animated scientist, a mad scientist. His cool, self-assured composure appeared to be deteriorating fast. He sounded a little breathless as well.

"...You will place them into these vials—understood?" he directed Dr. Maines, then, beckoned Aline to stand next to him. "And you, you will insert them into this unit, in the exact order that Dr. Maines gives you. Understood?"

Dr. Maines shook with nerves. Despite the chilly atmosphere, beads of sweat swelled up along his brow and upper lip. His trembling hands caused the vials to clatter, earning him a stern look from Ho.

"I will input the data once its been scanned—do not break the order, not even for a moment or we have to start all over again." Ho settled himself behind a small computer, a thin roll out platform that projected a hologram image, tapped instructions onto the digital keys that appeared before him. "Lee, open network."

Lee was at another unit, similar to Ho's, whose unit now projected a screen between them with a 3-D ghost frame of a DNA strand. It rotated slowly like a red and white barbershop signpost.

"Now, let us begin. On my mark."

Curiosity had both Aline and Josie dismissing any plans for attack.

On Ho's mark, Dr. Maines diligently prepared a sample. Carefully removing the frozen blood sample from its vacuum-sealed cylinder. He did so painstakingly slow as his hands trembled and sweat dripped into his eyes. He could be seen blinking rapidly, sometimes dashing the back of his hand across his brow. Once he brought the blood sample to the required temperature, Maines handed the first vial to Aline, who carefully inserted it neatly into a slot on a device that looked like a futuristic slide projection machine.

Ho's computer made a humming noise as it accepted the sample, processed, and sorted it through. Everyone waited. The computer made another noise, much like tiny a ping, and on the holographic projection, a small portion of the ghost strand filled.

Ho laughed with pleasure. His eyes glittery with uncontained joy.

"It is working," he whispered to himself. "Remove the first sample," he instructed again, then, indicated for the next sample to be prepared and inserted.

And so it went, slowly. With each new sample, another portion of the ghost strand filled up. There were five in all, Brandon Sozanski's being the first, followed by each of his three children, then his granddaughter. The last vial, the sixth, contained Josie's blood. It would make up a large portion of the remaining missing pieces that were those of Dr. Zara Sozanski's and another small portion that had been listed as a wild card gene.

According to Ho's reckoning, Josie's DNA would be enough to work with as it was the closest match to those of Sozanski's. His computer program could then run a probability and create a dummy DNA, which they could clone physically using Josie's remaining blood as a starter. But without the base samples as a guideline, those of Brandon and his offspring, it was useless. For the wild card DNA, Ho would have to run another probability scan and wait until the computer slowly pieced it together. According to Ho, the wild card was only a miniscule portion of the code, though by physical appearances, it looked big—nearly two inches according to the projected image.

Ho didn't seem too worried about getting it replicated because it was basically, one gene. It didn't matter if the DNA required contained no trace of their family genetics. The computer could run a general probability, extracting out what it needed by pretending to clone the required gene.

Reluctantly, Aline inserted Josie's DNA into the machine. Ho waited, drumming his fingers, while the computer processed it, pulling out the strands it needed and working out how best to replicate the remaining gene traits needed. When the computer pinged and accepted it, no one expected to see the majority of the missing pieces on the DNA strand to fill up, leaving just a small portion blank—a very *small* portion.

Ho paused in mid-motion with a frown, staring at the

projection. He tapped in some instructions on his console. Nothing changed on the image. He cast a curious glance to Josie, who stood with a raised brow staring at the ghost strand. Lee looked to Ho for direction, clearly confused. James stood directly behind Josie—expressionless.

Aline made a noise in her throat that brought Ho out of his thoughts.

"What did you do?" Ho demanded.

"Nothing," Aline replied. "But it looks to me that the last sample is a positive match for the majority of this key. I find this very strange, considering…"

"What're you saying?" Josie made a move forward but was stopped by James who held her arm. "Why is mine taking up so much of the key? I thought you said it would only make up a small bit and the computer would have to generate the rest of it."

Ho tapped at the console again, shaking his head slowly.

"Aline?" Josie called out breathlessly. "What's going on?"

"I don't know. But whoever this Dr. Zara Sozanski was, she seems to have obtained *your* DNA. How old did you say this key was?"

"About one-forty-odd years or so," Josie replied. She yanked her arm out of James' grip and strode up to Ho. "Is that about right? A hundred-forty years?"

Ho nodded without registering how close Josie was to him. His mind seemed preoccupied, flitting through a multitude of possibilities. He engaged the program to fill in the blank mystery gene. It would take a moment, and another for Maines to replicate using the formula that the computer calculated. Ho pushed back using the time as if to sort through his thoughts with a frown.

Sensing danger, Lee stepped before Josie, blocking her from Ho.

"Talk to me, Ho," Josie demanded. "How is this possible? How come you didn't have to make a new DNA sample, like you said you had to? How come mine was accepted—just like that?" Josie snapped her fingers for effect.

"By a guess," Ho said as the computer made another noise. It had created the dummy sample for the wild card, too quickly. Ho frowned then gave Dr. Maines the information for him to create

234

physically. "It would appear that Dr. Sozanski obtained a sample of your DNA. I do not know how, since at the time she created this, you were unavailable. That is the best explanation to this."

Aline raised her hand for attention. "Unless she had a sample from before. She may have been aware of your existence, Josie. She may have heard of you through her family. Maybe she sought out some remnants of you—tracked you down—and used your DNA as *the* wild card to ensure that no one but her could access the data she hid. Then made it out that the other sample was the wild card to mislead people...when actually, hers is the wild card since her DNA was never taken or stored here because these facilities didn't exist then. Hiding keys in DNA strands were quite common in those days. By using yours, she had insurance."

"It would be very slim—Josie's remnants. Skin, hair...time would have degraded them quite a bit. But, anything is possible." Ho tapped his chin in thought, one eye trained on Dr. Maines who fumbled with his cloned DNA sample. "And she would have heard about Josie through her family—people talked about it—not that anyone believed. That is how I have come to know of it. But I never suspected..."

"But she would have needed actual blood, not so?" Aline rounded on Ho. "Unless she cloned it from hair or skin samples..."

"Mmm," Ho muttered. "But that takes time and know-how. Actual blood is easiest."

"She was a brilliant geneticist, who specialized in cloning, fusion. She would have known what to do." Aline merely pursed her lips thoughtfully.

Josie looked from Aline to Ho. Her mind swirled in confusion. Did this mean that people *knew* about her? That her family *knew*? And did nothing to wake her up? All those years...all those long years...

"No, impossible." Josie shook her head. "Run it again."

"I have. Nothing changes." Ho hissed with impatience. "You clumsy fool! How long does it take to clone a DNA strand?" He drummed his fingers on the table, further agitating Maines.

Josie ran her hands through her hair, held them there and squeezed the hair between her fingers, hoping the sharp pain would bring her out of the sudden icy haze she felt. It didn't.

Finally, the rattled looking Dr. Maines offered another vial. "T-This should do it."

A grim-faced Aline took the vial and inserted it carefully into the slot. The computer made a strained noise. Everyone's eyes were glued to the projection. Waiting.

A few more minutes and it would be complete. Ho's lifelong wish was but moments away; he gripped the side of the table with anticipation. For the time being, the question of why Josie's DNA was so prominent seemed of no consequence to him.

"Aline?" Josie tore her gaze away and looked helplessly at her. "Can that happen? What you said, what he said? Can it?"

Aline nodded. "If the sample is good enough. Yes. But she still would have needed a blood sample, considering that her instructions were so exacting. And, yes, she could've cloned it. But she'd still have needed to get to you to obtain either of these things."

"So...so she would've had to...I mean. She found me, then? And just left me..."

Josie stood frozen, unable to think, feeling dizzy. Aline instinctively moved to her and gripped her shoulders, muttering something soothing.

The computer pinged, causing everyone to jump. The program was complete—all the pieces were in place.

Ho pounced to Lee's console and stared in fascination as the key, the full DNA strand, rotated and then dissolved into a multitude of tiny particles, turning the projected screen blank. The computer made another sound, and then the screen re-filled with colors and opened up a channel—a long, lost channel—buried for over a century on the cyberspace network.

Numbers and letters and diagrams flitted by the projected screen as information downloaded rapidly. Ho was ecstatic. He clutched the sides of the table, laughing uncontrollably.

"It is here. It is all here. At long last, I have it!" Ho clapped his hands. "I have it, at last!"

Without thinking, without even considering the outcome, Josie reacted. She swung out impulsively, forgetting she even had her krima tucked away at her wrist. Her fist struck Ho on the side of his head. The suddenness of the attack caught him off-guard, he staggered sideways in shock, blinking rapidly.

Lee's response was swift, catching Josie solidly in the face. She jerked back, fell onto James. Aline dipped low in reflex and shot out a leg that took Lee in the gut. Lee made a guttural grunt as he buckled; a mean glare glinted across his eyes. They eyed each other. Round two, it said.

Ho had collected himself enough to extract a knife from his jacket, he took aim at whoever was nearest—Aline. He let it fly; it nicked her arm, just as she turned to dodge it, before clattering to the floor.

Josie made to retrieve the knife but James had her arms pinned, hissing a warning in her ear. She struggled wildly and blindly struck out at him.

Aline had already leaped through the air, as did Lee. They collided in mid-air like two rutting stags locking horns. Crashing to the floor, they wrestled and grunted, rolling in a deadly ballet for control.

With a twist, Josie turned and elbowed James squarely in the face. He made an angry noise and in a blur of movement, brought the side of his hand across her ribs that knocked the air out of her, and also sent her flailing across the floor.

Gasping for breath, Josie curled inwards briefly, and remembered her krima for the first time. She dug at her wrist, was about to whip it out and fling herself at James, when a sharp rap across her head had her world going fuzzy and jittering with bright colors. She tried to focus—turning to see—barely making out a shape that looked like Ho, who raised his arm to give her another swipe across her head. She brought up her own arm in reflex, waiting for the blow to come down. It never did. When she risked another bleary look, James appeared to be holding Ho's arm and urgently speaking to him.

And then her world sputtered and went dark.

~ * ~

Surrey never thought himself to be a hero, nor did he think himself to be particularly brave. He did what was expected of him because he believed that to do his job, and do it well, was the greatest honor a person could do to those he'd been charged to protect and defend. His duty was to protect and defend the Citadel, the president and his wife, the citizens within the Citadel, and, the world at large. And if it meant that he died in order to protect and defend them, he would gladly do so and think nothing of it. In fact, if he didn't die, he would've been offended—but grateful that he could live another day to protect and defend those that he'd been charged with.

In his head, he composed music, and when he had time, would give birth to that music on his antique harp. His thick, callused fingers would move across the fine strings with amazing grace and dexterity.

When Simon gave him the order to return to the Citadel—as soon as possible and by whatever means he could—he did as he was told without question. And as he walked the underbelly of the Scrap Yard to access the docking bays through a series of crawl spaces and air ducts, the music coursed through his head with orchestral precision. It rose to great crescendos, skipped to allegros and slowed to andantes...

Surrey never did anything in haste, yet he was never sloth in his movements. He always thought things through with caution and care, using his music and logic to keep time and pace. And when he fought in combat, his actions were direct, precise, and accurate—and with a tinge of regret. He didn't like fighting, but he was good at it, like his music. Without one, the other didn't exist. They seemed to go hand in hand. As a boy growing up on the rough streets of inner city Hong Kong, he fought because of his music. He'd been teased unmercifully because of his love of the classics. He'd learned to survive, to dodge, beat, and sometimes kill the thugs that lurked the streets between home and his music. To him, music and survival were the same. There was no separation.

And life in the military was merely the platform for his orchestra to perform on.

He stole onboard a small single-manned shuttle docked in one of the emergency escape chambers that lined the perimeter of the docking bays. Quietly, he manually ejected away without detection and programmed the coordinates, heaving the controls to full throttle, he bolted his way back to Earth.

When he was fifty-eight minutes into his return trip, and saw the massive gunship heading straight to the Scrap Yard, he considered the odds. The music in his head had hushed to a slow and rhythmic adagio accompanied by a mournful aria. The sight of the gunship filled him with utter despair.

It would take him nearly a full day to return back to Earth, given the small size of the shuttle. The gunship would reach the Scrap Yard in less than twenty minutes. Chances were that no one knew it was coming, expect those trying to take control of the space station.

And him.

If he could duck under its radar and steal onboard, it would save everyone the trouble of having to deal with it—considering how full everyone's hands were at the moment. After he sabotaged the gunship, and if he lived, he could then continue on and return to the Citadel where his president needed him. That was, after all, the logical thing to do.

With a crash of cymbals and a change of pace, Surrey made up his mind and maneuvered the tiny craft until it was directly beneath the massive ship. He aimed a harpoon towline, fired it then, killed the engine. Once the harpoon-tow embedded on its mark, Surrey flipped a switch on the cockpit dashboard and towed himself in slowly.

He was surprised that the gunship hadn't noticed him, but then, they were probably too busy concentrating of getting to the space station as quickly as possible. A brief, tiny blimp on their radars was nothing of importance. They could very well think it was a bit of space junk that got sucked up in its wake. He hoped that they thought so. With deft skill, Surrey aligned the craft until it locked itself to one of the ship's holding bays, where it was then scooped inside into an inner holding dock and sealed off from the outside.

So far, so good.

He just hoped that this particular holding bay would not be used to deploy their fighter jets once they were within range to attack the station. Normally, these holding bays were for garbage and recycling, but it wasn't uncommon for some gunships to use them to hold additional fighter jets.

He put the music on pause and opened the cockpit, it hissed, released, and popped open. All was quiet. If, indeed, they stored additional fighter jets beyond the service doors, he'd be the first to find out. There was absolutely no way he could avoid being rammed into oblivion once those doors opened up and the jets shot out.

Nineteen

My head spun. I reached up tentatively to touch the sore spot—right at the back—and felt a knot. Whatever Ho used to hit me, it was something reassuringly hard.

A groan spilled out of my mouth, making me feel nauseous. I swallowed hard and brought the hand from my head to my mouth. My nose hurt too, where Lee smacked me in the face. It felt twice its normal size.

Whether it was the knock on my head or the time-out in blackness that brought me to my senses, I wasn't sure. But I felt like an idiot. I acted impulsively and foolishly, putting myself, Aline—even the unsuspecting Dr. Maines—in serious danger. Everything that I'd learned and had been taught to do in times of danger, I threw clean out the window.

I wasn't sure how long I was out, but it was long enough. When I could finally focus clearly, I saw that I was piled up in a heap in a far corner with Aline. She sat on her haunches next to me, both hands resting on her knees, the fighting ready-stance while sitting. Her face, bloody, she was in a decidedly sour mood. Her left arm had bled and dried where the knife had nicked it. She gave me a considering look that made me feel worse.

"Sorry," I croaked out.

"As I said before," she said through clenched teeth, curling her lips tightly to resemble John that it was scary. "It is never a dull moment with you. If you had waited a few more minutes, that creature called Lee would have assisted Ho, and they would have been distracted for a moment. Consider yourself lucky that the

Rogue used his head and stopped Ho from slicing yours with his krima."

The final bits came back to me.

"Oh, yeah," I replied helpfully. "I'm sorry. I lost it."

The Rogue stood before us at an angle so he could see what we did, as well as what Ho and Lee were. They appeared to be packing up their gear. Ho had just slipped something into his breast pocket, a strange expression on his face. Lee bled freely from a gash on his face and every so often, dabbed at it with the back of his hand.

"By the way, the Rogue, James," I said quietly. "He gave me back my krima."

Aline whipped her head to me and gave me a glower. "So why in hell did you not use it?" she hissed out.

"I...forgot."

She made a resigned noise.

"James," I continued. "I think he's trying to help. Don't ask me why, but he is."

"He's still on Ho's payroll. Do not trust him and kill him the first chance you get. Do you understand? He is a Rogue and they only help themselves or the ones that pay them."

I nodded reluctantly. I didn't like the idea of killing James; it didn't feel altogether right. But surely Aline knew more about Rogues and their temperaments than I did. Who was I to argue with that? I'd already done some fairly stupid and thoughtless things as it was. I promised myself to follow Aline's lead and behave. But, I couldn't help myself.

On impulse—again—I called out to Ho. He snapped his head distractedly at me.

"How do you plan on getting past the security here?" I asked and made an attempt to stand. My world swayed slightly.

Ho pushed past James and looked at me, the odd expression still on his face. He seemed...spooked.

"The alarms have stopped or did you not hear? My men have overpowered the security here—I've just received word. We have a clear path back to the shuttle. Your luck will keep you alive long enough to get us out." He looked at James. "Be ready in five."

With that spooked look, Ho started to turn, paused, and looked at me. "It would appear that we are more closely related than we realized."

"Do tell," I replied and inched forward slightly by pretending to stretch my stiff neck. I heard Aline rise to her feet and noted James stepping back a pace. Yes, he *was* helping!

Ho smiled. "Our dear, Dr. Zara Soz..." then paused as if uncertain how to continue. "She left us a message. I've only just looked at it briefly."

"And?" I prompted—another step closer—and brought my hands before me, clasping them innocently as though I were about to receive a pat on the head.

In a rare moment of uncertainty, Ho rubbed a hand over his brow and frowned.

"She is—was, your niece," he said. "Fern."

I heard him the first time but blinked anyway. He was lying through his small little teeth. To what purpose, I didn't know. And I wasn't about to be fooled by him twice. The betrayal I felt with Margeaux still stung me like nettles. How stupid did he think I was?

"Nice try." I snarled, and with that, whipped out my krima, engaged it, dropped low then jabbed.

Ho jerked backwards in surprise. My krima caught the end of his jacket—it hissed and smoldered. He spun, reaching into his pocket for his own krima, engaged it and there we stood, face to face, brandishing our weapons between us.

A blur of movement told me that Aline had already launched herself at James and tumbled to the floor with him. With a loud smacking noise, James' head cracked sideways as her foot used it—how? I don't know—as a jumping pad to piston her straight into Lee.

From where I stood, Aline looked like a nimble gazelle. Leaping from rock to rock, lining her body into an arrow as she dove into Lee, fists out before her like a diver, slamming into his chest. He cried out in winded pain and fell. She somersaulted off, landed on her feet, snatched up a chair and brought it down on Lee's unsuspecting head in seconds. The crack was loud and solid—the result...effective. Blood was just starting to spurt in rhythmic pulses from a gaping rupture in Lee's forehead. His eyes rolled up into his head, stared out blankly, filling up with blood. A single finger on his left hand trembled into a rictus curl then lay still.

Ho spared himself a quick look at his dead body-assistant as we circled each other like dancers. James, shaking his head to clear it, closed in on Aline. She held the chair before her like a weapon, daring him to make a move.

"I should have killed both of you earlier," Ho hissed at me. "Consider yourself fired," he called out to James. "You have proven to be useless!" Ho glared at my krima.

James stopped mid-way, comically, and looked back at Ho with a bemused expression. "I was given a better offer."

"By who?" Ho spat.

"Madam Lancaster, of course. We had much to chat about while we waited for you at the hotel."

"Did you, now?"

I played along. "It's true. Never trust a Rogue."

Ho seemed distracted enough so I lurched forward with my krima. He hopped away and swung his full-length krima at me. I cursed and dodged to the side, feeling the air crackle beside me. I didn't stand a chance with his full-length compared to my micro-sized pocket version. What was I thinking? It was like trying to fight a mammoth with tweezers.

Speed. I had to move quickly so he couldn't pinpoint me. I leaped sideways again, jumped over a desk and brought it between us, then jumped up—kicked out—sent the desk shooting out at Ho. He stopped it easily with a foot, did a sort of upward thrust, a twirl, and sailed over the desk, swinging the krima in a wide arc. I felt it clip my overcoat, right by the collar, before I had a chance to back-flip away. The smell of burning fabric stung my nostrils.

That was too close, I thought and ran left, pulling chairs, tables, equipment, and whatever else I could grab in my wake. Ho was in pursuit, feet away, jumping over with ease the obstacles I'd knocked over.

"Give it up, Josie," he called out. "I am too strong for you. Too fast!"

In desperation, I threw a stack of vials at him. He deflected them with a shrug as glass broke like transparent snow about him. From the corner of my eye, I saw Aline and James regarding each other with wariness, circling. She still held the chair.

Ho leaped over a fallen piece of equipment, I vaulted up and over a low glass partition and scrambled over a desk. Bottles and vials rattled and fell to the floor. I'd soon run out of places to go. Turning, I saw Ho smash his way through the glass, swinging again with his krima. In panic, I yelped out and ducked.

Up again, practically leapfrogging backwards, I dodged another attack. His krima hit a metal cabinet, sparks and stray beams showered over me, peppering my face and hands with stinging hot embers. Again his krima swung out, making a low whining noise as it glanced off some shelving and then it came hissing down across the front of my coat. I pushed back wildly, my own krima useless in my hand, and crashed solidly against a wall.

Ho moved in for the kill, I lashed out blindly in desperation—heard him roar. He staggered back, bloody murder in his eyes. I'd somehow managed to swipe him across his right thigh. It wasn't deep but I could see it stung him badly; the fabric around it was smoking.

Without wasting another second, I bolted up, kicked out, and felt it connect to his hand that snapped out to block my foot. Twisting in mid-air, I dived across the floor, ignoring the broken glass that sliced my palms. Rolling away until I was on all fours, Ho a short distance away, I scrambled for safety. To my right, the opening to one of the vaults, it was large and deep, but would hold no place for me to hide. To my left, Aline and James, still squaring off.

Safety in numbers, I thought, and flung myself left towards them at a dead run, hurdling over upturned chairs and tables. Something hit me, smack in the centre of my back. It took the air out of my lungs and dropped me like dead weight to the floor. Rolling over and writhing in pain, I barely registered which end was up.

And then, an explosion ripped through the air—blasting us with scorching hot air—hot enough to singe the hair on my skin. I yelped out, balled myself tightly, imagining my skin puckering and bubbling like pork crackling.

It took ages, it felt like ages, before the air cooled. I could hear tiny cracks and pops, then a gurgling noise, followed closely by the pressurized hiss as jets of icy cold water blasted from overhead.

Someone shouted—frantically. I recognized the voice immediately.

John!

A hand grabbed a fistful of my hair, hauling me to my feet. Through the pelting water, I saw the light of the krima—my krima—close to my face. I froze.

"Come any nearer, and I will kill her," Ho called out from behind me.

John looked like a caged wild animal let loose without having been fed. Though the water poured overhead, he kept his head dangerously low, his shoulders bunched, ready for the pounce. He spared me one quick look, then, directed his unblinking feral eyes at Ho.

"Release her," he hissed out, "and I might let you live."

Ho laughed, the laser end of the krima shook with him. I sucked in the squeak that nearly escaped from my lips, imagining for a moment what it would feel like if that lethal end touched my face.

"You might let me live," Ho replied. "How very considerate of you."

A commotion could be heard nearby, I barely noticed, but it sounded as if Aline had belched out orders to someone. I couldn't hear what, nor did I care at the moment.

"It's too late, John," I mumbled out. "He's got it already. The code—he's got it. He doesn't need me anymore. I'm dead already."

"Be quiet, Josie," John ordered, never taking his eyes off Ho. "You need her to get out of here. You've no shuttle left—I made sure of it. Give it up Ho. You can't escape."

"Then I'll just have to use yours," Ho chuckled.

I could feel his heart beating against my back; surprisingly even, thumping solidly. Now I knew for certain that the man was insane. Mine, on the other hand, crashed against my chest. No matter how hard I tried to force it to calm down, it refused.

"You're outnumbered. You cannot win," John continued. He'd moved closer, stalking. He carried no visible weapons. His hands were empty, fingers loose and curled beside him. He meant to use his bare hands and beat Ho to a pulp. That much was certain. Seeing this, it bolstered my spirits. If John—surely this was a dream that I he was here?—could fight with nothing but bare hands, then so could I.

"Stand back!" Ho gave my head a quick jerk, angling it so

that my neck twisted sharply and I could feel it strain. If any more pressure were applied, it would surely snap. I let out a strangled noise but noted that John didn't stand back, nor did he stop. But his face grew darker and even more dangerous.

We shuffled across the floor, slowly inching around in a wide circle. Our general direction appeared to be the exit doors, which was now one massive, jagged hole, smoldering and sparking with pops of lights and smoke.

If we got closer, maybe, just maybe, I could run up the side of it and push Ho backwards. But what about the krima trained at my face? I'd have to find a way to grip his hand and keep it away, and then maybe, John could move in. For the moment, both my hands were free and submissively raised. I'd have to be quick—very quick. I gave John a meaningful look, trying to erase the literal panic I felt. He wasn't even looking at me.

John, I called out to him mentally, willing him to look. *Please, look at me!*

We were closer to the gaping doors now; I ordered myself to breathe calmly. Another three feet, and we'd be close enough.

I flicked a look at the krima, it poised by my right cheek, about five inches away. If I was quick, I could grab his hand and push it away, then kick off from the side of the door.

Another foot, and we'd be close enough.

They talked again, but I couldn't hear, every last bit of concentration was trained on the timing of my move.

A foot closer. I took a breath.

Now!

I wrapped both hands on Ho's right wrist, dug into pressure points with my fingernails. I craned my neck back, yielding to the tilted angle it was already in. Tightening my abdominals, I curled in a crunch and whipped my legs out to the side of the door.

And pushed with all my strength.

We were airborne, falling. I heard Ho grunt, his hand tensed automatically, bringing the krima dangerously close to my face. I made a noise to match, and pushed his hand away with determination. I felt it give a little, enough, and pushed some more. His other hand released my hair—possibly to reach back and break the fall.

When we hit the floor, the crash took my breath away. His body, hard and odd-shaped under me. And my body, already at a strange angle with my hands outstretched before me to keep the krima as far away as possible, felt every jarring bump. Ho turned quickly, dragging me in his wake. He squirmed and rolled under me, wrapping his arm around my waist.

I saw John float through the air. He landed inches from me, grasped Ho's hand with the krima—my hands were trapped beneath his. John twisted, turned, and kicked Ho's arm. Ho shrieked out from under me and dug his fingers into my side. I yelled out in pain, wriggling frantically.

And then, Ho released me, practically flung me off him. I crashed into John, who caught me deftly with one arm, the other still in a tug-of-war with the krima.

John let go the moment he was sure I was safe and together we spun away like dancers. Ho came to his feet in an instant, the krima on the floor, useless. He held his right arm with his left and snarled like a rabid dog.

It happened in a flash. Ho dipped his supposed injured hand into his breast pocket and before we could even focus, the knife flew out of his hand. It came directly for me, not John. We were too close—too close to react, to dodge, to deflect. It sank with amazing accuracy into my shoulder, missing my heart and lungs—even my neck—by inches. But the sudden pain that shot through, nearly crippled me. It froze the scream in my throat, brought my back up into a rigid line as I teetered on my feet.

John shrieked out, clutching me as I fell—sank—slowly to my feet. I barely noticed that Ho no longer stood before us. He'd vanished.

"Get him!" I croaked out to John. He seemed unable to hear me. His hands were suffocating me as they gripped my face. "Get him!" I tried again.

"He's gone," he managed to say hoarsely. "Josie!" His hands now fumbled over my chest, prodding and feeling, his voice tight with panic. "Where're you hit?" The overcoat was thick and heavy; it made his inspection difficult.

"I'm fine," I replied weakly and felt something hot spread across my chest. It was almost as if I had peed myself. "It's up high…" My head dipped, my world tilted. "It's fine—he's getting away. He has Fern…"

And I fell into a darkness.

~ * ~

When John saw his wife, he thought his heart was about to stop. Her face, pinched tight and covered with bits of soot. The explosion was necessary, it had been the only way those solid doors would open. Ho's men had rigged it so that it was unresponsive to normal override commands—and he wasn't about to waste time trying to hack into it. Blowing it out had been the only way. And it also gave him a feeling of satisfaction. He'd only hoped that the people inside were well away from the doors when the blast took effect.

Seeing that she was alive, for the time being, settled the angst he'd been feeling. He pushed aside whatever fears he had in order to deal with Ho. Who now had her firmly in his grasp—pointing a krima to her face!

He'd made his decision long before he blasted his way into the room. If it came to a fight, and Josie was in danger, he would let Ho go. It wasn't important at the moment, Josie's safety being the only thing that mattered.

The dance for control only stoked his anger. He saw Josie suffering from terror—it seemed to clot her mind, make her babble. He hoped she could focus. If Ho meant to take his shuttle, he'd use her as a shield. The moment it was no longer necessary, he'd kill her without a second thought. Yes, Ho could run away, for now, just so long as he let her go unharmed.

When John saw the obvious intent on Josie's face, that sudden flash of determination—he knew. She was about to do something rash. He'd be ready for it. He'd let her—give her—a free rein. To get in her way would only make things worse.

It happened quickly, but it happened smoothly. Her actions were swift, sure, and effective. It toppled Ho, making him lose concentration for a split-second. John's only worry was that she wouldn't be able to keep the krima away from her, or fall onto it by mistake.

Then he saw his opening—and used it.

Trying desperately to keep the dangerous laser away, he

gripped at Ho's arm and felt the moment Ho had decided to give her up. He was ready when Ho threw her off. Her body hit his with a reassuring thud. He clutched her hard, firmly, and backed away immediately.

And then the knife came and his heart stopped. He felt the moment it hit her, her body tensed in his arms. All he could do was hold her—it was too late to do anything else. He didn't know where it hit, only that it sunk easily as if she were made of air. He heard her breath catch, felt her sinking. He roared out in horror.

Whatever she said he barely heard, only his need to find where the knife found its mark.

Please, he begged, not the heart. *She would be dead already, if it were,* he argued with himself. *Please, please, please.*

Her overcoat—*Where had she gotten it from? It wasn't hers. Why was it so thick?*

She spoke again, he answered automatically. It didn't matter about Ho—who was he again?

John called out her name, more to assure himself that she was still alive. And then she fainted.

"Aline!" he cried out. "*Aline!*"

All he could think of now was to grip around the area where the hilt of the knife protruded. Beneath his fingers, he could already feel the slick oiliness of blood, hot and angry in its rush to escape her body.

Aline, beside him now, took control. Reluctant to release his grip, she had to forcibly remove it and push him away. He moved, but stayed close.

Josie made a small noise, her eyes fluttered, and the vibrant green of her eyes were clouded over. Her hand twitched, John grabbed it immediately and held on tightly. She made another small noise, she sounded very, very tired. Her head came up and Aline eased her back, crooning softly to her.

"This will have to be done here, immediately." Aline said to her brother. "I can't risk moving her, it might make things worse. I think it's already nicked an artery—too much blood."

He nodded without thinking. Aline moved quickly, clearing away a desk with one sweep of her hand, sending items crashing to the already littered floor. She gathered up bits of medical supplies along the way.

"Bring her here, gently," she instructed John.

The moment Josie was placed on the desk, Aline began cutting away at her clothing. Beneath the heavy coat, her chest was awash in bright red.

John had seen a lot in his day and was no stranger to it, the amount of blood and gore a person could release. But this was not just any person. This was Josie—his wife. *His*.

He barely suppressed a gasp. She was semiconscious, moaning, moving her head back and forth and muttering incoherently about her long dead niece, Fern.

Aline stripped her down to nothing, exposing her bare chest. The coppery tang of blood filled the air. She sprayed a numbing antiseptic solution around the wound, then, placed a handheld medical scanner over it—her face tight with concentration.

"Hold her steady," Aline instructed again. "It'll be fine, but it's stuck in under her collarbone. It might take a few tries."

She wrapped her hand around the hilt of the knife, gripping hard, and pulled. Josie made a high-pitched whine but otherwise, remained pliant. Aline tugged again, felt the knife give a little. She took a breath and pulled hard, it gave some more and then slid out with a wet sound.

More blood welled up immediately and spilled over as Josie groaned thinly. John ran his hand soothingly over her clammy forehead. Her face was nearly white and had a pasty tinge to it. Her eyes fluttered, trying to focus, and swiveled around the room. A hand flew up in reflex to touch the wound.

"Hold her steady." Aline said again, agitation in her voice. She held the scanner over the wound now, and with a thin, silver tool, started rooting about inside the opening as she muttered to herself. "Got it," she said. "Good, good…"

After a moment, Aline pulled back, smiling as she dabbed the open wound with thick gauze. The blood seemed to be slowing now. She reached for some skin sealer and sprayed the area liberally. It bubbled and frothed white, cleared, and sealed the wound. All that remained was a nasty pink line about two inches long, just under Josie's collarbone.

"She's lucky I was here." Aline ran the back of her hand

over her brow, smearing it with Josie's blood. "An artery was nicked—the bone prevented the knife from moving—but it was close."

"Thank you Aline." John let out a breath, reached out to grasp his sister's arm.

"Ho got away but he forgot all this equipment. Here," she handed John the remains of the overcoat. "Better cover her up. Keep her warm. I'll go see if there's any antibiotic patches."

Delicately, John wrapped the coat around his wife. She appeared to be sleeping, fitfully, but already deep in the clutches of a bad dream. He scooped her up and for the first time, allowed himself to take stock of his surroundings.

It was a mess. The room was littered with upturned tables, shelving and equipment. Glass everywhere, mingled with charred pieces of debris. The water sprinklers had stopped at some point but inch-deep puddles formed at his feet.

Kakuta, off to one side, stood guard with a large pulse gun in the crook of his arm. He'd carefully averted his eyes away from the emergency surgery, and instead, stared dispassionately at a cowering man who whimpered uncontrollably under a table.

"Who is that?" John called out, walking closer with Josie safely—protectively—clutched in his arms.

Kakuta shrugged, risked a quick look to make certain that Madam Lancaster had been decently covered up before facing John. "Possibly a Dr. Caleb Maines—head of archives."

"It is." Aline hauled up Ho's forgotten computers from the floor, tucking them neatly under her arm. "Come, let's move." She looked at Dr. Maines with consideration. "I'm sorry for all this trouble. I will speak to the directors personally. This is no fault of yours."

Dr. Maines didn't appear to have heard any of this, he merely continued with his whimpering. Aline frowned, staring at him a moment longer before turning to John.

"The Rogue has gone as well. Something curious…Josie said he was helping." She shrugged. "He said he made a deal with her."

"Did he now?" John looked down at his wife. That was interesting. Rogue's didn't usually change sides so easily—unless it was *after* the contract was complete.

McLinney appeared at the doorway—looking harangued—followed closely by a bevy of Hontag-Sonnet security. They looked excitable and most definitely offended. At the sight of the president, they froze and fell silent.

Explanations would have to come later. For now, they needed to leave. Quickly. John put on his most stern face and barreled his way through, followed closely by Aline. In their wake, McLinney could be heard giving sharp orders to the security team who seemed to all babble at once to him.

As they left, Aline saw evidence of John's passing. Bodies of men were dotted—dead—along the corridors. One of them, she noted with pleasure, was that of the wiry man. It was difficult, but she resisted the sudden urge to kick the dead man as they walked by.

Twenty

The blast knocked them off their feet. The room shook with tremendous force, making everyone wonder if they didn't, in fact, spin clean out into outer space.

Simon shook his head to clear it, his teeth hurt from the shockwaves and he heard a loud ringing in his ears. He felt slightly nauseous. Whatever that last explosive was, it was designed to have maximum effect on humans. Most of the equipment in the room juddered and made static noises, then resumed normally. The men and droids were only just peeling themselves off the floor. One man retched up his dinner.

They're using Rumble-Bombs, Simon thought quickly.

Just before detonating, the bomb would emit a pitched tone to unbalance the inner ear, followed immediately by the explosion. Most droids used a balance chip to keep them upright, making them susceptible as well.

Smart, Simon mused to himself.

Before they could collect themselves, the room was surrounded by a swarm of soldiers, wearing headgear and protective body armor. They didn't say much, but their intent was clear. Simon and his team were outnumbered three to one. Resigned, Simon raised his arms in submission. The others, taking his lead, followed suit.

"You will move out into the storeroom. Now." A woman, clearly in charge, bellowed. For effect, she let out a quick burst from her automatic rifle. A spray of bullets peppered the ceiling, sending down a shower of metal and plastic fragments. Someone yelped out in surprise.

Madds sent a quick glance to Simon, who shook his head a fraction, then, gave a small nod towards Ox.

Ox took note, purposely puffed his chest out, and cleared his throat. "You cannot do this!" he barked out with feigned indignation.

"Silence!" the woman snapped back, marching up to Ox. "Are you in charge here? Are you Mwenye? If so, instruct your Junkies to stand down and—" she looked down at his black uniform, the crimson trimming. "*Elites.* I should have known." Darting a glance about the room, she tagged Madds and Simon and snorted in disgust. Minnows stood hidden among his taller counterparts.

"Weapons, in a pile on the floor—right here!" she pointed to the middle of the room. "Do it, now."

Reluctantly, weapons were tossed in the centre of the room, but not before a quick scuffle ensued with a couple of Junkies, who considered it a personal insult to be removed of their weapons. Simon made a great show of relinquishing his pulse gun. It didn't matter since he still had his hidden weapons about his person—and his fists. If everyone played along submissively, they might still have a chance. He gave the Junkies a gimlet eye in warning.

The woman turned to beckon someone, a reedy looking man with a ferret-nosed look about him. He brushed belligerently past Ox and darted quick, black eyes over the mainframe controls. From his pocket, he extracted a key card—*the* key card with the fake code. He inserted it into a slot, tapped in a few commands on the console. He frowned, making his beady little eyes contract to slits.

"Where is the tech?" he called out without looking up. "Bring him here, now."

The others were being directed by gunpoint to a small storeroom on the right. No one, technician or otherwise, responded to the ferret-faced man. All the Junkies directed murderous looks back, itching to start trouble. Simon had given them specific instructions that Ox was the only 'tech' that was to deal with the enemy.

"That would be me." Ox stood his ground.

The thin man cocked his head. "An Elite? A tech? Will wonders never cease?"

"What is it you want?"

"What've you done with the commands?"

"Nothing."

"Where is the Governor?"

"No idea."

The woman rammed the back end of her weapon into Ox's back. He grunted, jerking his large frame but held steady. He turned to her and smiled. "A little higher next time. It's still a little itchy."

"Idiot!" she slammed her weapon again, this time, aiming for Ox's head, but he ducked and easily whipped an arm out to grip the weapon. A surge of men pressed forward, training their guns onto him. Ox calmly released the woman's gun and resumed this impassive stance.

"Why isn't it working, Cerevetto?" the woman demanded.

The ferret-faced man, Cerevetto, shook his head. "Someone's been tampering with the commands. It's open, but it seems to be buried somewhere. If I touch anything else, the system will go into shut down mode.

This code is useless!" With that, he flung the key card to the floor in disgust.

"Where is the Governor?" The woman rounded on Ox and barked into his face.

Ox shrugged mildly. "I think he may have been killed. In that first wave of attack."

"Liar!" The woman turned to one of her men. "Find him," she instructed. "Start with the upper chambers—the escape pods. Now!"

A communicator beeped at her chest, she wrenched it out, rammed it into her ear and spoke into it with acidity. "What? Good. How long? Good." She thrust it back into her breast pocket and strode up to Ox. "Unscramble whatever it is you put there or people will start dying."

"Can't." Ox shrugged again. "I didn't create it nor did the Governor. It's all computer generated. Sorry."

Cerevetto whirled around. "He lies! Forget it. Let me at it." He hunched himself over the controls, tapping furiously at keys on the pressure pad and uttering commands.

Simon and Madds had purposely lingered, allowing themselves to be the last to be forced into the store room.

"What is the purpose of all this?" Madds called out, buying some time. "Ho will not get very far in his plans to take over this station. We're not the only Elites here, and more are yet to come."

The woman darted a cold look to Madds, her eyes were a hard grey, like balls of steel. "Why don't you ask him yourself? He should be here within the day."

"Oh, that's good. Was he successful then, in Iceland?" Madds replied. "Yes, we know about that already."

She glared back at him for a moment. "Very." She turned to Cerevetto. "The moment you have control, begin separation. The gunship is in position."

Gunship? Simon thought with interest. Did they mean to blast one half of the station? He spared a moment's thought to John before being shoved into the small storeroom, hoping he had made it to Iceland in time.

By the looks of it, it didn't look so.

~ * ~

Surrey was somewhere near the engine room. He could smell it. The thick, oily scent filled his nose, mingling with wafts of metal and that distinct smell of petrol.

The engine rooms in gunships were located directly under the captain's bridge. It saved time, should something go amiss, and freed up space in the rear where they held the majority of the fighter jets and ammunition. Unfortunately for Surrey, the recycling hold was also located at the rear. It took nearly an hour for him to steal his way through the ship—the crawl spaces and air ducts being his preferred route. He'd learned a lot from Simon.

Time was precious, but stealth was imperative. Besides, Surrey reasoned, once the ship moved into position, they wouldn't engage in combat immediately—not when their own were still onboard the Scrap Yard.

The reassuring hum and rhythm of the massive machinery melded and kept time with his music. It spiked and dipped, keeping tune with the sounds of people speaking. He heard at least five distinct voices—one a woman. Her high pitch told him she was quite young. Three men sounded older, their voices held knowledge by the fullness of its sound. The last voice was further away, he barely spoke and when he did, it was short, precise, and clear. He was probably the chief engineer.

Surrey surfaced from his hiding place from amid the narrow crawl spaces along the walls that led technicians to various maintenance points within the ship. Like Simon, and the underground electrical ducts, he easily managed to bypass the engine room doors. He didn't make a sound as he slipped between two turbine casings.

He gave himself to the count of twenty, slow tempo—adagio—to bring down all five. By the way their voices traveled and resounded off the walls of the large room, they were positioned in a line. One, the chief engineer, was off to the right by a few feet. The three that were closest, he would need to bring down quickly and silently, without alerting the remaining two.

With his right hand, he dug a knife out from his belt, with his left, his krima. It was close quarters here; he made a quick adjustment so that the krima only sent out a single beam from one end instead of the usual double-sided beam. And then he moved, even-paced and silent, his heart rate never increasing, his mind keeping note of the time with beats of music.

The first man, about sixty years old judging from the deep wrinkles in his face, had enough time to glance up from his task of sipping coffee from a mug. The krima sunk through his throat with ease. Surrey deftly snagged the mug by its handle with the tip of his knife, letting it slide down the blade. Hot liquid sloshed out but he barely felt it as it scalded his hand. The man sank slowly to his feet, helped along gently by Surrey.

The next man to die turned his head at the movement, a smile still on his face when Surrey flung the mug off the knife and sent it flying his way. Instinctively, the man reached up to catch it, realizing his mistake a second too late when the knife sliced across his stomach, followed quickly by an upwards jab under his chin. His intestines spilled to the floor before he died, still holding the mug like a precious jewel.

The woman sat, bent over some controls, her right side to Surrey. She raised her head slightly to sniff the air with a frown. The sudden stench of fecal matter thickened the air. Before she could turn to pinpoint the source of the stink, Surrey flitted by and impaled the back of her head with the krima. The deadly laser came clean out of her forehead. She slumped forward with a jerky twitch, her fingers scratched over the console in spasms.

The fourth man met the same fate as the woman. Clearly unaware that anything was amiss. His back to Surrey, he manned some controls, busily entering data into a log and doing a solo jig to some music only he heard. When he died, he slumped down onto his knees; the top of his head leaned forward to rest on wall.

Surrey shifted right, down a grated walkway and came face to face with the chief engineer. Wide brown eyes met Surrey's with surprise and brief confusion. The communications unit he held in one hand dropped to the floor, the other hand made as if to go for a weapon at his side. But Surrey was quicker; his knife flew out of his hand and found its mark—straight into the heart. The man gasped out and staggered. Surrey turned, half-pivoting and brought his krima sweeping down to lop off his head.

Surrey didn't like people to suffer unnecessarily. Death must be swift.

He had counted to twenty-two. The coffee mug had thrown him off by two counts. But the obstacles were out of the way and he could get to work—undisturbed.

~ * ~

Josie awoke with a jerk. Her head snapped up, she let out a strangled shout.

"Ho!"

Then, she groaned.

The room spun and something clutched her across her waist. *Ho!* His fingers were digging her there—she twisted and struggled, trying to wrench herself free.

"Josie. Hold still—easy now."

A hand pressed firmly on her shoulder. She growled in panic, bucked and twisted away.

"Let go of me!" Josie yelled out.

John held her face, willing her to focus onto him. Her eyes appeared glazed, fevered and extremely angry. She snarled and shook like a feral animal.

"Josie!" he said more forcefully. "Josie, look at me. It's me, John."

Through her grunts and the haze, she could barely make out

John's worried face—it was sheet-white, his brow creased. She glanced about wildly, confusion settling over fear. She was in a shuttle, strapped in. Aline's face hovered nearby.

"John?"

"Shh-shh. You're safe, now. Just lie back." He tried to smile but it looked more like a grimace.

A dull pain throbbed close to her neck, she felt it now and let out a low groan. Her left arm tingled with pins and needles.

"What happened?" She reached out to touch her left shoulder; John's hand caught it and held firmly. "My neck's hurting like a bitch. Ow! Fuck!"

It came back to her quickly. The fight with Ho, the struggle, the knife...

"Holy fuck! He stuck me!" Josie looked ready for another round with Ho.

"She sounds *much* better than she looks," Aline called out helpfully. "That's a good sign. In any case, she still needs to be transfused with some blood."

"Damn it, Josie," John muttered weakly. "You're going to kill me one day." He leaned in and pressed his lips to her brow. "Remind me to chain you to our room. You're never to leave it again."

Josie welcomed his lips. His breath was warm and comforting against her face. She sighed and leaned against him. "Only if you promise to be chained up next to me." Managing a weak smile, she looked up at him still feeling fretful.

He looked as if he'd aged. Dark circles bruised under his eyes and the normally predatory look, now nothing but a spooked and hollow stare. He hadn't shaved for some time; his stubble covered his face like dark, grisly moss.

"You look like shit. Is this how you come to my rescue?"

John laughed, the tension in him visibly evaporating. "Speak for yourself." He brushed her face tenderly.

"I'm sorry." She smiled back.

"What for?"

"Everything. For being an idiot, for getting myself kidnapped—for putting you in danger. Everything."

"Josie," John dismissed her with a grin. "Will you just shut up?"

"I let Ho get away," she continued.

"Shut up, now. You're babbling again." He kissed her mouth to silence her. His lips trembled slightly like he restrained himself from swallowing her whole. He pulled away reluctantly.

"Don't, not yet," Josie said softly, reaching out to hold his neck, bringing him close. He smelled like home, like waking up to find all your favorite things around you. She gripped him tightly. "You took ages and ages to come."

"I'm sorry. I tried." John pulled away gently. "I nearly beat the girl senseless to find you. I'm sorry but I—"

"Margeaux!" Josie jerked back. "She's Ho's daughter! My God, I have to tell you, John. The girl, Ho—"

"I know, I know. It's all right."

They both listened in turn as they exchanged their discoveries. Aline chipped in, filling in some blanks. She glanced to Ho's computers. The others followed her gaze.

"Turn it on," John instructed. "It might tell us something. Ho did not seem too concerned about losing it. He must have made a copy."

Aline rose to set up the computers. Josie touched a hand to John.

"What will happen to Margeaux? Do you think Ho will go back for her? Try to get her out? Or will he go straight to the Scrap Yard?"

"I don't know." John's face seemed to be returning to normal, he'd worked his mouth into a line, grinding his teeth thoughtfully. "He waited this long to get that data. He knows we won't harm Margeaux. My bet is that he'll go to the Scrap Yard. I haven't been able to reach Simon. In fact, I can't reach anyone—complete radio silence. Things don't look good."

"Do you think he'll send someone to get her instead?" Josie thought of James. He confused her. She put that thought aside, or so she thought.

"Like another Rogue?" John cocked a brow, slid his eyes sideways to her. "Speaking of Rogues…"

"I made an offer to pay him more than what Ho was going to pay him. He didn't bite, then. So I've no idea why he changed his mind later. He gave me back my krima, for Christ sakes." Frowning, Josie glanced at her wrist holster. It was empty.

"Did he try to…" John couldn't finish. But something clearly bothered him.

Josie frowned up at him. "Did he what? Oh! Shit, no. *No*. He didn't. But…" she considered something. "I wouldn't put it past him, if he had the chance."

After a moment, John let out a small sigh. He looked relieved.

"Sorry Josie. With you, I always seem to think the worst." John smiled sheepishly. He looked extremely tired. "Never mind, forget I even asked."

He dug into his pocket and pulled out Josie's krima.

"Here," he handed it to her. "That's the second time someone's tried to kill you with it. Try not to lose it again or I'll glue it to your hand."

She broke out into a wide grin and snatched her favourite weapon from his hand, holding it possessively to her chest. "I won't lose it again. I promise. And I won't fuck it up next time, either. I lost my head earlier. I panicked. It won't happen again. I'm too pissed off for that, now."

"And what makes you think they'll be a next time? I've already ordered a length of chain from maintenance." Though he was serious, he tried to sound casual, even raising his brows comically.

"Because, I know you're going up to the Scrap Yard first chance you get." Josie leveled her eyes at him. "And I'm going with you."

"No, you are not," he replied flatly. His face changed to a stern scowl.

"Hey, the little shit has messed with my head long enough. I won't let him get away with it."

"Josie," John's face grew dark in warning. "Don't be foolish. I'll not risk getting you hurt again."

"And you think I'm going to let you go? Let you get hurt? No fucking way."

"This is not something we should even be arguing about."

"Who said we're arguing?" she retorted. "I'm going with you. Ho is mine."

"Ho is much stronger and more dangerous than you think." John gripped her hand, urging her to rethink her stupid behavior. "You can't defeat him. Look at what he's already done to you."

"Yes, I can," she said, seething. "Especially, if I take Margeaux with me. And threaten her life. I know he cares for her—he practically idolizes her."

"That is madness, Josie. What will you hope to achieve by doing this?" John shook his head. "I can't believe what I'm hearing. You're no better than he is!"

"I'm not going to *actually* hurt her—don't be insane!" Josie scoffed. "But Ho doesn't know that. He just knows I'm pissed off and likely to do anything."

Glowering at her, John studied her a moment. He opened his mouth to say something—probably mean and small, Josie waited with a squint—but shut it again. Thinking.

"She thinks he's dead—that I killed him," he said eventually. "Don't spoil it for her."

Josie shrugged, one shoulder only. "Then we'll tell her she'll be going to his funeral."

It came out cold and icy, uncaring, which was so unlike her. She heard it and felt shocked by it. This was revenge she spoke of so casually, of killing another human being out of sheer spite. That was wrong. Killing was still killing, no matter the circumstances. Yes, she'd killed before—had to. But now, she planned it, wanted it. Setting a trap…

"I want him dead." She said quietly, her rage tasting bitter in her mouth. "I don't care if he's my…my *nephew*…" she spat the word out. "He's no family of mine. He never will be. And nor will that little bitch he's trussed up to look like Fern."

"Josie, I understand how you feel. But let me do this. Let me stop him."

"No. You can't fix everything for me, John. And you don't know how I feel."

"I do and I want to."

"So do I." Josie sat up despite the wave of dizziness. "He's *part* of me. And the way I feel now, I'm pretty sure it's my gene that started all this madness. Who else could it have been? Look at me? I kill people."

"Stop it." John reached out and held her face roughly; his lips thin in anger, his voice harsh and vicious. "Stop it. You are *not* like him. Do you hear me? You have had to kill to protect people—to protect me, and yourself. Don't even soil yourself by comparing yourself to him. Ho loves no one but himself. He cares for nothing but greed and power. You are nothing like him!" He shook her once and saw the fat tear that spilled out from the green depths of her eyes. She sucked in a breath. He swiped the wet streak with his thumb.

"Will you at least take me with you?" she croaked out angrily. "I need to be there. I need to see it…to see it end. It has to end. Please? I need to be there."

John brought her face to his neck, pressing her close.

"All right," he said.

John closed his eyes, letting out a long, strained sigh.

"All right," he said again, pulling her back to look her in the eye. "But you follow my lead, understood? And only, *only,* if Aline gives you the all clear."

Josie nodded vigorously. Tears still poured out of her eyes uncontrollably but not once did she cry out. She was ashamed of herself. John was right. She was nothing like Ho. How could she even let herself think like that, to sink that low?

Remembering what Adam had said about murder sobered her up. He'd felt power and control by committing murder, by taking a life. She'd always felt sick, regret. She still remembered the feeling of it, the way it happened, so quick, so final… So…*undo-able.*

But if it meant doing it again, to protect John, herself or anyone else that she cared for? Yes, she could do it again. And even though she still felt like killing Ho, craved it, it sickened her that she could want it so badly.

"But if he tries to hurt you," she whispered hoarsely. "I *will* kill him. Even if I die trying."

"I know you will." John's heart sank as he whispered back. "And expect the same from me."

It was against all his better judgment, against everything that was sane—but, yes. He would take her there. He knew her well enough to know what it meant to see it to the finish. He would, too, want—no, need—to see it end. They were very alike in that respect.

And he also knew that if he didn't take her, she'd find a way to get there on her own. He'd rather keep her close to him, under a watchful eye, than have her let loose to her own devices. He was this close to losing her. He was not about to let that happen again.

~ * ~

Aline gave them a moment—they would need it. She needed it.

They'd been whispering fervently to themselves, oblivious to those around them. It looked for a while like a heated argument, yet they clung to each other as though their lives depended on it. Though she and Rand were intensely bonded, she envied the bond between her brother and Josie—they were so alike. And their connection was like a livewire, grounded but bucking and kicking with unexpected twists and turns.

To give them some privacy, she engaged Ho's computer, scrolled
through to the downloaded data and felt her blood chill to the bone. It wasn't the research data that chilled her—fusing machine to man, going past the normal realms of fusion was abhorrent in itself. It was the message embedded at the end that had her momentarily clutching her stomach.

She darted a quick look to Josie, whose mental state seemed fragile at the moment. Would she be able to handle this? Should she simply delete the message? It was tempting...

No, that was wrong. Josie needed to know. She needed to know. Needed to see, for herself.

"John," Aline called out. Her voice sounded hollow and flat, spooked. It brought John's head whipping around to her, his tired face momentarily transformed to that of a savage wolf about to protect its mate.

"John," she continued. "Hold her close, will you. She's going to need you."

Aline brought the computer and placed it before them, instructing it to play back.

She saw Josie's face cloud over with a frown. It grew dark and blank as the message played. Josie seemed nearly transparent, as if any moment she would float away like mist.

Aline gripped her hands together and brought them to her

mouth. Maybe, if she prayed, Josie wouldn't lose her mind.
   So she prayed.

Twenty One

In the year 2034, Fern Bettencourt was five. For as long as she could remember, her father had spoken to her about Aunt Josie. And for as long as Fern could remember, Aunt Josie lived downstairs in the cellar.

Fern had seen her countless times, floating serenely like an angel, her hair framed around a sleeping face like a halo. And her father, lovingly wiping away any dust that would settle upon Aunt Josie's "bed." Sometimes he would talk to Josie's sleeping form. Sometimes, he would simply sit in silence and watch her.

Fern's father had said that Aunt Josie slept because she was very, very tired. Fern was never allowed to touch the bed, nor was she ever, ever allowed to tell anyone. Especially that! It was a big secret.

Sometimes, Fern nearly forgot herself and would tell her friends. Sometimes, her older brother, Conrad, would quarrel with her and say that she talked too much. Sometimes, she would sneak downstairs at night and watch her aunt's sleeping form, and wonder what it would be like to be always sleeping.

She wondered, too, what sort of person her aunt was. Was she a nice person, a bad person? But whatever the thoughts, the one Fern dwelled upon the most, was that Aunt Josie never seemed to age. Only her hair and nails grew, and grew, and grew.

When Fern was eight, she heard her father speaking with her mother. They argued and argued, very angrily, about Aunt Josie.

Mumma screamed and threw things around the house, she didn't want Dadsie to wake up Aunt Josie. Mumma kept saying it was far too dangerous; someone would find out and kill them all. Then she used terrible words—bad words—to describe Granddadsie and his stupid experiments.

The next day, Mumma left and didn't return for a long time. Fern went straight downstairs and hit Aunt Josie's bed until her small fists hurt. Then she said she was sorry, and lovingly stroked her aunt's sleeping chamber. It wasn't Aunt Josie's fault—it was Dadsie's.

He wanted to wake her up.

Fern hated Dadsie after that. He'd made Mumma leave. Aunt Josie was blameless; why didn't Dadsie just leave her alone and let her sleep. She wasn't troubling anyone. She was just tired. And Fern hated Conrad, too, and told him that she hated Dadsie. Conrad told her to grow up and to shut up—that she knew nothing.

Fern was eleven when her father decided that Aunt Josie needed to wake up. It had to be done, he had said. Then he used words like "safe" and "another prototype" and "government sanctioned." It had already been ten years and people had begun to forget about Granddadsie and his work. It was safe, Dadsie kept on saying. It was safe...

The day Dadsie chose to awaken Aunt Josie, Fern decided to stop him. She liked her Aunt Josie sleeping. She wasn't bothering anyone, so why wake her? While her aunt slept, Fern could pretend Josie was anything. Josie had become Fern's best friend. She could tell her anything—and everything. And, what if, when Josie woke up, she was really a bad person? What if she was scary? What if she didn't like Fern? Maybe that's why she was put to sleep.

But Dadsie was insistent, and despite all of Fern's protests—she'd started to sound very much like Mumma—he ignored her and went downstairs. Fern followed and pushed Dadsie down the stairs. She'd only meant to hurt him, maybe give him a broken leg, like in the cartoons.

But when he fell to the floor after slamming and bouncing off the steps and narrow walls, he didn't get back up again. And his head was on backwards.

Conrad came after she screamed out. He didn't ask what

happened even though he was older and knew a lot of things that she did not. He told her that they needed to call the ambulance, but first, they had to cover Aunt Josie. No one must know she was there.

After Dadsie died, Mumma came back and looked after them again. It was good and Fern was very happy. She had Mumma back, and Mumma wanted nothing more than to keep Aunt Josie sleeping. Life had returned to normal again.

But sometimes, Fern did miss Dadsie. Very much.

Fern was a smart girl. Extremely bright, she excelled in sciences, just like her Granddadsie.

She was only sixteen when she was accepted into university and, just like her grandfather before her, she decided to study genetics, but a new subject attracted her like a magnet—a new and radical subject—called bio-fusion. It wasn't unheard of, as it had been accepted and used in medicine routinely, but people still raised an eyebrow over it.

Fern loved bio-fusion, and for a while, forgot all about Aunt Josie, even though it had been her aunt who'd inspired her pursuit of these subjects. Fern had become obsessed with not aging and immortality. Aunt Josie never aged. Fern wanted that, too. So she studied hard and did very well.

At twenty-three, Fern was in an accident. She lost control of the car she'd been driving, slamming into a pole late one night. She lost her left hand and received a new one through the first primitive methods of bio-fusion. Despite the loss, she found that her new hand was stronger—and it gave her the first spark of inspiration. For the next ten years, she dedicated her life to the study of mechanics and cell-fusion. It became an obsession.

Conrad looked after Aunt Josie, now. He'd never dared to wake her—he didn't know how. Like his father, Kellan Bettencourt, all he knew was potatoes. Many times, he asked Fern to help him wake his aunt, but she never did. Fern always had more important things to do. So Conrad waited.

Fern's mother, Verity, died of a massive stroke when Fern had just turned thirty. It was triggered after she uncovered the sheet that hid Josie. Verity had simply forgot that Josie still lay there. She was said to have shrieked and shrieked until her throat rang ragged and hoarse—even the farthest neighbor heard the screams. Then

Verity collapsed and died on the spot.

Conrad didn't mention to Fern what really happened, but she found out later. Instead he'd said that Mumma's death came from the constant worry of keeping Josie hidden. Fern laughed at him, told him he was silly. He'd promised Fern that he would look after the house and their aunt. He would take over from Mumma. No one must know of Josie's existence.

Sometimes, Fern would visit her aunt and spend the whole night just staring at her. Some days, Conrad thought that Fern was losing her mind, but he said nothing. Fern had a violent temper these days. He didn't dare try to remind her that their aunt needed to awaken. Sometimes, Fern looked just like Mumma, just before she died. It scared Conrad.

And then one day, Fern disappeared. It made the local news. *Prominent geneticist goes missing* it had said. *Believed to have been abducted by a new breed of extremist organizations* it went on.

What they didn't know was that Fern had already, secretly, constructed her own stasis-pod and entered it. She'd programmed it to awaken her in exactly one hundred years. Fern had grown frustrated with the limitations that science offered her now, in her century. And, above all, she didn't want to grow old. Thirty-four was already too old.

Conrad lived until he was eighty-nine. The year 2115, and the world teetered at a different place from where it was when Josie went to sleep. The beginnings of a massive economic recession were about to take effect, people panicked, ran scared. But Conrad was too old to care. The only thing he ever cared about was his aunt.

He worried over her. What would happen to her if he died suddenly?

He was old-fashioned. He didn't care about life-prolonging medicines or vaccines, nor did he care for physical enhancements. All he ever wanted was a quiet life, and maybe one day speak with Aunt Josie again. But that day seemed likely to never come. Instead he poured his thoughts and his heart out into his journals as though his life were a detailed account of growth spurts and pest infestations, like the potatoes he grew.

Conrad knew about potatoes and how to make them into food and fuel; people wanted both of these right now. But he'd grown very tired—old. He wanted to die and forget that he'd lived. Fern was lost—gone—and there was no one else in his life. And no one remembered who Dr. Peter Bettencourt was, or his daughter who disappeared nearly ninety years ago. It was ancient history. A history that seemed to be repeating itself now that Fern, too, had gone missing. Yes, Conrad was very, very tired.

Conrad never married. How would he ever explain to any future wife about Aunt Josie? He'd no one to pass her onto, now. But, he made arrangements. Before he died, he left the entire house to the farms' overseer, the kindly Arthur Cutts and his family.

Arthur Cutts was rather simple, but he was trustworthy and loved a good secret at the best of times. In fact, Arthur Cutts hoarded a lifetime of secrets. Conrad knew that he would be the perfect man to care for his aunt.

In his will, Conrad insisted that should an opportunity ever come, Arthur Cutts or his descendents must try to awaken Josie—if, by then, it wasn't too late. And if it was, to make sure that his aunt had a proper funeral. He'd also told Cutts everything he remembered about his aunt, and why she'd been put to sleep in the first place. The threat to her life had long since passed, but the dangers in trying to wake her after all these years were far greater. He begged that Cutts find someone capable and knowledgeable enough to risk an attempt, but he must not make it public. It was a secret. And if Cutts couldn't find anyone suitable, then could he please keep her safe for as long as possible.

In 2163, Fern awoke. The world was indeed different—and dangerous. A war had come and gone, famines and strife. Another war brewed on the horizon, but science had advanced in leaps and bounds. And what was available to her now, was unimaginable in her time. Fern was happy—deliriously, happy. But first, she needed to become someone else. So she changed her name and became Dr. Zara Sozanski, borrowing the names of her two adversaries from university.

Fern continued to experiment on herself, using money she'd hoarded away in a bank vault and from clever investments she'd made a century ago. She even began to make a name for herself again.

Aunt Josie still lay sleeping, in the care of some simpletons who treated her like a ghost—the ghost that haunts the cellar downstairs. Fern didn't have any trouble buying back the farmhouse from them. They'd been more than willing to give it up—they even threw in the ludicrous story about the ghost in the cellar for free—and tossed in the last will and testament of Conrad Bettencourt, along with the deeds to the house and some old disks that were his journal, which she read with disdain before tossing them in a corner.

Potatoes were no longer in demand; farming was a dying trade even though people needed to eat. Money was more valuable now than it ever was. And whoever had it, had power. And Dr. Zara Sozanski had lots of power.

In the safety and privacy of her old farmhouse, Fern began her transformation into a strange entity. She experimented on herself with abandon, becoming more and more machine than human. Her basement offices and lab had begun to look like a clinic or a sophisticated butcher's shop. All the while, Josie lay sleeping in a corner.

The final step, for complete immortality, Fern reckoned, was to clone herself—how ignorant she'd been then. It was against the law to do so; there had been strict guidelines for scientists to refrain from its research. Unstable and unpredictable, *abominations,* the authorities ranted. Ungodly and sinful, the religious groups had said. But people still did it in secret. All the technology was there, needing only for someone to actually do it—and succeed.

So she did it. It took time, many experiments, many failures that resulted in discarded test tubes with mutated cells and hideous half-human fetuses. Until finally, Fern reached a decision that she'd been avoiding. She impregnated herself with her own cloned egg, "fertilized" by a process of cell-mutation and the removal of any foreign DNA strands other than hers. She embedded the egg in her uterus, the most natural vessel to carry her clone—Mother Nature's own test tube. And waited.

But something went wrong—terribly wrong. Instead of a girl, instead of herself, she gave birth to a boy!

Even as she screamed and screamed in horror, the silent farmhouse shattered with the unthinkable that had unfolded within its walls. Bloodied and torn, she lay mesmerized at the creature she'd given birth to.

Herself—but a boy!

As a cruel joke, she named him Brandon. She was tempted to abandon the creature, throw it away immediately, down the recycling chute. She didn't want it. She was eager to try again, fix her mistakes. But curiosity had her intrigued, mesmerized. Besides, it rhymed. Abandon—Brandon. She laughed at that. She laughed and laughed, uncontrollably. She laughed until she cried and cowered fearfully into a corner, watching the baby tremble in shrieking cries of hunger and the need for human touch. Something inside Fern revolted…repulsed.

And when finally she put the baby to her breast to feed him, she cracked completely, pulling her hair out one by one until her *son* drank his fill…

~ * ~

Brandon had been a strange boy and he grew up unloved and distant, like the science experiment that he was. At school, the other kids teased him because his mother was the mad scientist, and they lived in that tumbled-down old farmhouse. No one ever came to the farmhouse. He had no friends. Brandon was very strange, sullen at times, charming and beguiling at others. But his moods were, at best, dangerous.

He was a violent boy and he loved violence. Eventually, the military attracted him, as it did for many others at that time. The world had fallen head over heels into another major war, over food, money, and power. The causes and the reasons were simply too great or too obscure to specify. War was the answer, and Brandon loved it. He had even found love, or so he thought.

He married the woman, a corporal in the military, just like him. Though she managed to calm him, however slightly, they were the same—violent. For a while, they seemed at peace, content.

They had three children in quick succession, and Fern studied her "off-spring" with distant interest. They intrigued her, and they frightened her. They looked normal, but they looked too much like her.

One day, Fern quietly took their DNA samples and continued with her experiments. But she no longer wanted to clone herself; it was too risky, too scary. That horrible night alone in the farmhouse, the night she gave birth to herself… The memory still haunted her, and the small part of her that was still normal—sane—was repulsed.

No, she decided, she would simply keep herself alive, forever. That way, it would only ever be her. Just her…and *no one* else.

Then one day, Brandon lost his head, literally. He got up and decided to kill his wife and children. He'd grown bored with them, he didn't like them anymore, and he didn't like himself either. They talked too much, they wanted too much. They didn't care what he wanted. No one ever cared what *he* wanted.

And something wasn't right with him—he knew it. He talked with the military psychologists and therapists. But no one seemed to understand.

He felt sick, his head always hurt and hurt. His memories, meshed and mixed with events and places that he had no recollection of being in—or people he'd ever met. He didn't know if it were real or not, whether he'd dreamed of these people and events, or merely imagined them. He complained to his mother, she always seemed to know what he talked about. Like she'd *been* there too, seen what he'd seen. She always *seemed* to understand. But she never helped.

Sometimes, he wanted—badly—to have sex with other men. He ached with lust and yearning in parts of his body he knew did not exist. He touched himself all the time—checking, feeling, making sure he was really a man. It bothered him and confused him. His wife never *felt right* to him. His penis felt odd when he was with her, no matter how many times he'd rammed himself violently into her, it didn't feel right. Instead, he wanted to be rammed, wanted to feel helpless and open—reamed into oblivion…

And still his head hurt…

So he picked up his military-issue gun and killed his two oldest children, his wife, then put a bullet through his offending penis, and then his head. He'd forgotten about his youngest daughter—simply forgot her.

Fern attended her "son's" funeral with something like mild relief, feeling as though a secret had finally been hidden away for good. Safe and sound, never to be seen or heard from again. For the first time in a long while, she finally drew an easy breath.

Then, she put Brandon out of her mind, and walked away.

Fern was nearly half-machine by then. People began to notice her erratic behavior, her un-aging face. And they talked about her. In her time, she'd made important and successful advancements and discoveries in sciences, which benefited both herself and the medical community. But still they wondered about her. Eventually, she attracted too much attention without realizing it.

On paper, she was close to sixty-five, though in reality, she was a hundred and sixty-five. Yet, she had no wrinkles, no greying of hair, not even a tilt to her posture. People commented that she used her own enhancements and life-prolonging products. She ignored them or chose not to hear.

But years passed, and still she looked the same.

Brandon's youngest daughter, Ann, having been raised by her mother's parents, grew into a beautiful woman with mesmerizing hazel-green eyes. One day she married and had her own daughter. Fern grew even more intrigued by this new baby. Again, she saw the child looked a lot like herself. Technically speaking, they were *all* her own daughters. But that was her secret. One she must never tell.

When Fern's records said she was seventy-four, and the calendar year was May 2203, she vanished again. Some speculated that she'd died in her dilapidated farmhouse. Other decided she'd disappeared during her daily commutes between Prince Edward Island and Montreal, murdered, for all the research she'd been hoarding and working on. These were vicious times and any advancement to power was sought after with vengeance.

But generally speaking, those in her area of expertise and her peers didn't really care. They'd considered her a mad, mad scientist—a recluse at the best of times. Fern—Dr. Zara Sozanski—had been known to ramble on about her precious experiments that she'd hidden from everyone. Her secret work, the complex key she'd made to keep it hidden. Even Ann, her own granddaughter, thought her to be strange, as Fern constantly muttered and rambled about secrets upon secrets—she'd grown to be an embarrassment at family gatherings. Ann soon forgot about her.

But Fern—Zara—had still made a name for herself as the top bio-fusion expert in Canada and that could not be forgotten, regardless of her erratic behavior. Her research and findings blew everyone's mind. Her suggestions were radical, extreme—and yes, mad. However, no one had time to consider these findings right now. Another war had broken forth, a vicious, terrible war that would last a very long time. It was a war, which by the end of it would spawn a brutal tyrant by the name of Dane Lancaster.

In the paranoia that had been riddling Fern's mind, she imagined being constantly ridiculed and pursued by unidentified "people" who wanted her research, her discoveries, her creation. She *did* discover something. She'd created an immortal being. Herself. Yes, she could die—but she could also live forever. But the imaginary people who chased her; they needed to go away. She needed to hide her work, and keep it safe, just like Aunt Josie.

So Fern made a key, a special key that only she could access and use. To make it even more difficult for those "people" trying to steal her work, she would need Aunt Josie's help. Though Josie's stasis-pod was ancient and primitive, Fern was smart and she knew the mechanics of these pods. It didn't take her long to obtain a small sampling of her aunt's blood—she didn't even lose a single drop of the embryonic fluid that Josie floated in.

Before Fern buried the data, she made a rambled and disjointed message. A taunting, gloating confession from a deranged mind. Though her face remained smooth and untouched by the stains of age and time, and her eyes a perfect pale and glassy green, the finely molded lips and sculpted bones, it didn't hide the vapid madness festering within her.

Or the eerie, half-human control she had over her body movements.

~ * ~

Fern was beautiful. There could be no mistaking that. I vaguely remember what I did, other than to stare at her image as if my life depended it on it. She looked like me, and she looked like my brother, his wife, and…like Margeaux.

But it was all Fern. It was all her. I remembered her vividly though she'd only been a young child when I last saw her. There could be no mistaking it.

And her confession…

Before I awoke from my own sleep, I could've sworn a thousand times over to anyone who asked, that the world was a normal and straightforward place to live in. That black was black and white was white. That rain fell from the sky and the water was blue from its reflection. That people ate, slept, woke up, and did things they'd done the day before, as they'd always done them. That ghost stories and horrors were for around campfires and late night scare-fests with your friends. They didn't happen in real life. And if they did, they happened to someone else, not you.

But that had been before I woke up from my own sleep.

I heard John make a sound beside me, it sounded far away, remote. I wanted to look at him—I needed to—but I simply couldn't tear my eyes away from the image of Fern. I felt his eyes, heavy and troubled, rest upon me. And still I couldn't look at him.

He touched me, it felt like a branding iron and I flinched. He drew his hand away and made another sound. I couldn't tell what it was that he said, it sounded familiar, even comforting, if that were at all possible at the moment. To be honest, my mind was blank of all thought, but I could feel an oncoming cloud of torrential rains and violent storms.

I took a breath, because that's what people are supposed to do. I took another. The first didn't seem like enough. In fact, no matter how much air I took in, it never seemed to be enough. I gasped for air, and instead of the image of Fern, I stared up at the ceiling of the shuttle we were in.

Hot, scalding hands smothered my face, pressing me down.

Surely, I was going to die now—was I not stuck by a knife? I remembered bleeding a lot, so much that I felt light-headed and cold. Yes, that was it. I was dying. I have to say goodbye to John because he'd never forgive me if I didn't.

Where is John? Had he come to rescue me, yet?

Why did I feel so cold, and why did people have such hot hands? I needed to close my eyes, they hurt and they were very tired.

I was very tired.

Twenty Two

"I don't care if she's able to dance atop a roof, she's not going anywhere!"

"John," Aline said with a warning tone. "Going might be the best thing for her right now. She needs a distraction—I sure as hell need one."

"You're supposed to be a physician—act like one."

Aline swiped a hand through her hair, squeezed her eyes tightly, and muttered under her breath. "I definitely used to live a normal life. It's never been a dull moment since the day she came to stay."

"Pardon?"

"Hmm?" Aline furrowed her brow innocently. "Nothing. Look, just let her go. It will do her more good than moping."

"No." With finality, John glared at his sister.

He remembered with some horror the look on Josie's face. The way her eyes, those brilliant green and beautiful eyes, went blank and empty. They seemed to have retracted into themselves—*she* retracted into herself. Far, far inside where he thought he might not be able to reach. And he wanted to reach in and drag the Josie he knew back out, but feared she might not recognize him.

He remembered, too, that barely a year ago, she'd retracted into some inner world when her mind had shattered from shock. It took long months before she surfaced and became herself. But the shadows from the horrors of the night her mind broke still bruised her for months later. And now, just when he thought her life would finally be normal. This…

It scared him, her silent and blank manner. And the way she behaved right now, like nothing happened, as though everything was normal and as it should be. That she didn't just have a fight for her life at the end of a knife or discover that her niece, her *real* niece, was in fact still—was the one who...

He couldn't even finish his thoughts. He couldn't even wrap his mind around it for the moment. Maybe he was the one—this time—whose mind had broken.

True, he'd seen a great many things in his life. Great things, terrible things, horrific things! But, *this?* He didn't even know what category it fell into, if indeed, a category for such madness existed. Yes, madness. That was it. Surely, that was it. And surely it was him that had lost his mind. Surely...

"As her physician, I'm telling you, John—let her go. It will help her. She needs it. Like she said before, she needs to see it end. Let her see it." Aline's voice, soft, calm, and very tired.

Aline stood watching as her brother turned and stared at her. His dark eyes grew large with worry and horror. He looked even paler than he had before.

They were in Aline's offices with Josie, just down the corridor, being treated and transfused with her own blood.

A part of John was impatient to get onto The Bullet and head straight to the Scrap Yard. Two, heavy-artillery cruisers were already being rerouted from the military space stations to rendezvous with him at the Scrap Yard. They had a six-hour head start already. But he didn't seem able to move at the moment. His place was with Josie. She needed him more, and if it meant that he couldn't go to help Simon, then he wouldn't.

He felt torn in half.

Aline read him as easily as a book. She snorted weakly which earned her a look from John. "You have to go, regardless. So go. Simon needs you, too."

"I can't risk taking her." John knew there'd be no point arguing with Aline; his voice lost its earlier conviction.

It was a losing battle. He knew, too, that the only way he'd feel completely at ease was if he took Josie. Kept her close. Absurd as it was, but he needed her just as much as she needed him. And, it was a poor excuse, though the Citadel stood safe enough, someone—

still—had walked right in and taken her. He wasn't about to let that happen again.

"She'll be fine. Trudesson is with her now—she'll be armed and shielded to the point you'll need a tank to roll her out of here. But she'll be fine. She's very angry now, let her use that the get her through this. Her rage needs to come out. Why not let it come out...constructively." Aline shrugged and turned to look at her door.

A harassed looking—if that were at all possible—Loeb strode in, rapping his knuckles twice on the door before entering. He nodded to Aline but directed his reliable brown eyes at John.

"Sir," he said. "Vice President Tretyakov's been briefed on the Iceland situation. She's fielding calls now. She's not amused at what you have been up to. The media has gotten wind of it. Some reports indicate that Madam Lancaster is dead after trying to stop extremists from destroying the DNA banks. And they want to know why there is a DNA bank that the general public is not completely aware of."

Loeb paused, took a breath, and continued. "Her presence there, too, is raising all kinds of questions. Mainly that she was actually the one destroying evidence of her past, considering the recent events. The Scrap Yard situation has also just broken. It is not as major a news item as that of Madam's. And...in another matter, The Americas want to break free from our alliance. There is also talk that Argentina does not agree and will declare war on the rest of The Americas if they do part ways."

John stared at Loeb as though seeing him for the first time. He'd heard him, had understood every single word, but was just unable to process it normally in his head. He blinked self-consciously.

"Sir?" Loeb prompted with a frown.

To cover his utterly blank mind, John turned away to direct a brooding look at the floor. With his customary bowed head and hands clasped behind his back, he looked as though he were deep in thought.

"Tell Argentina," he said, finding himself a little hoarse. He cleared his throat and continued. "Tell Argentina that they can declare independency from The Americas, and they can remain in our alliance, should they choose to do so. But if it's war they want, it won't be with The Americas, it will be with us. I'll not have them taking pot-shots at the rest of the world just because they still want to hide under mother's apron. And, ask them too, if they have suddenly become ignorant." John turned sharply in a blaze of anger, his eyes glinting dangerously like icy points. "Remind them that sixty years ago, they were once a strong and powerful country on the brink of world-wide control. How easily they forget to walk on their own. They have enough resources and money to break free completely from both The Americas and us. Tell them to use their heads and think rationally. And remind them that a war with us will only destroy them further."

Loeb nodded solemnly, mentally checking off his 'to-do' list by briefly closing his eyes.

"And, tell the media that my wife lives. That she was injured by a madman going by the name of Michael Ho—a madman, who, at this very moment, is hell-bent on taking control of the Scrap Yard. All because he wants to be immortal," John all but spat out. "Spread that far and wide. He'll find no refuge anywhere in this world, should he live."

Loeb looked hesitant. He wasn't fully aware of Josie's true connection to Ho, and he was too much of a professional to ever ask. However, he took a bolstering breath before he spoke again.

"Shall I say—instead—that she was, and has been investigating and seeking out Ho since his involvement with the recent siege? Which led her to track him to Iceland, where she uncovered a plot to terrorize the world? That the incident in Iceland is indeed linked directly to the current situation on the Scrap Yard, and, that Ho was not destroying, but stealing DNA samples, which he plans to use for his misguided scheme of cloning and cell-fusion with the droids?

"From there his intentions are to infiltrate these droids into society and eventually take over the world? And your presence there, as well as Dr. Lancaster's were all orchestrated by Ho, who kidnapped you all. First to gain access into the facility by Dr. Lancaster's association with Hontag-Sonnet, and to obtain a sample of your DNA in the hope he could clone you into a malleable, fake president that he could control for his own devices? And Madam Lancaster followed to foil Ho's plans and attempted to rescue you both. This will put further credibility to her loyalty to you."

John stood gaping at Loeb. He nodded eventually and reached out to grip his trusty aide on the shoulder. "You mix lies with truths with such honesty. Loeb, have you ever considered going into politics?"

"I prefer to work with you, sir, where things always make *perfect* sense. In any case, I lack the charisma," Loeb replied with a bland expression.

John managed a short chuckle and considered something with a frown. He looked briefly at Aline, who sat on the edge of her desk, mildly watching the two men. Her face looked puffy and sore from her encounter with Lee. She rubbed it absently as a man would, checking for stubble.

"Loeb," he said. "It's against my better judgment, but...while I attend to the situation at the Scrap Yard, confer with Adam on any matters of a political nature. He's good at that. Only if you think you need advice. I'm sure you're capable of managing yourself. If not, brief him on Argentina and The Americas and listen to his advice," he paused and pursed his lips. "But do not necessarily act on them. Use your own judgment."

Loeb nodded and turned to go. If it seemed confusing, he didn't let it show. If it shocked him that Adam was still alive, he didn't let that show, either. Instead he smiled. "No wonder Madam Lancaster still speaks of Adam in the present tense before correcting herself."

John merely raised a brow and slid his eyes to Aline, who suddenly seemed to find her fingernails very intriguing.

Loeb stopped short of the door with a worried look that creased his smooth forehead. "Madam Lancaster is well, I take it? Will she be accompanying you to the Yard?"

"She will, yes. And she is...well, enough. Thank you."

When Loeb left, Aline smiled motherly to her brother. "You're going soft, allowing Adam to help. I can see Josie's influence on you. But must you confuse poor Loeb by telling him that Adam still lives?"

"Loeb is not stupid. And with that...imagination of his, he would've figured it out eventually. I do admire his discretion—he's a rare kind of person. One day, he'll make a good president, if he's so inclined." John spoke lightly, then, pressed his mouth into a tight line. "And I'm not going soft. Adam is the one going soft."

He turned and headed for the door where he paused, frowning. "Besides, he's a good strategist and he can be of some use rather than talking to imaginary dinner guests."

John walked out of Aline's offices and headed straight for Josie's room, walking with purpose. He would try again to dissuade her, but his heart wouldn't be in it. She'd make another fuss, but, to be honest, he just wanted her near. He was so close to losing her already—it frightened him.

~ * ~

Josie had never been in space. To be perfectly honest, she wasn't even sure if she was going to like it, either. Aside from countless tiny dots that were stars, it seemed riddled with endless bits of junk. Lots of junk—scrap metal and bits of flotsam and jetsam from centuries of man polluting the great vast ocean called space. Every so often, the shuttle would jerk slightly to avoid these floating bits of junk. Larger crafts would simply repel them with their shields, or blast them away with their guns.

And then, getting there, or through it, was tedious enough. Hours upon hours with nothing but endless blackness around you—strapped into a small, uncomfortable chair with nothing but a nagging husband for company. She could think of a hundred other things she'd rather be doing than sitting here now, next to him.

Granted, he wasn't particularly nagging at the moment. Just being overly polite and concerned, that it drove her ape-shit mad. He treated her as if she were made of very thin glass.

"Please, will you have a little more?" he said again, offering her a rehydrated steak sandwich.

The Bullet was a bare bones, no-nonsense, moving vessel stripped of all its niceties. And that included the food choices. Josie had no inclination of eating another morsel of the tasteless, rubbery, artificial sandwich than she did for wanting to step into a pile of shit. No matter how hungry she was.

"No, thanks." Josie replied slowly as if speaking to someone hard of hearing.

"You've barely touched it."

"I don't eat shit."

"You need to eat something."

"I notice *you* didn't eat it."

"I'm not hungry."

"Because it tastes like shit."

"Josie..." he sighed.

"John..." she mimicked. "What *is* your fucking problem?"

"Might I remind you, you've just been injured—not four hours ago. You need to keep your strength up. You're going on nothing more but pills and adrenalin."

John had been trying very, very hard to keep his voice level and calm. It was very, very hard. His teeth hurt from clenching them tightly together for the last two hours.

"I'm fine! Have you never heard of, of—oh, here it is—feed the fit and starve the injured?"

"Josie..."

"I'm *not* hungry—not for *that*, anyway." She looked around inside the "lunch box" before them, a large metal container crammed full with suspiciously bulky packages in silver-foil wrappings. "What's this one? Why don't they just tell you what's inside instead of putting stupid numbers on them? What's number six? Feels like a log of shit."

John sighed again. It appeared she had shit on her brains. "Six, means juice."

"This?" Josie whipped her head to stare at him in disbelief. "This turd-like thing is juice? *How* are you meant to drink it?"

"Add number one to it." John rubbed a knot at his brow. "Water."

She rooted around in the box until she found a bulbous packet labeled '1.' Then, she stared at both packets in her hands, looking left then right with a screwed up face.

"How the fu—"

"Oh, give it here." John seethed with impatience, taking both packets from her with force. He pulled at a corner from 1, extracted an extendable straw and used it to punch a hole at a red dot on 6. He squeezed 1 and let it fill 6, the silver-foil wrapping expanded like magic. With an angry tug, he pulled the straw out of 1 and left it sticking out of 6. He pinched the end of the straw, shook the packet a few times and handed it to Josie, who watched with great interest.

"There," he muttered, and under his breath, added: "Try not to choke."

"I heard that," she snapped out.

"Hmm?"

"*What* is the matter with you? You know, not everyone knows how to read this military-food-shit thing."

"I could ask the same of you. What *is* the matter?" John turned in his seat to regard her with his sharp stare, hoping that by doing so, it would prompt her into talking.

"Nothing's wrong with me," she slurped up some juice, made a face and nearly spat it out. "Holy fuck! That is bad. It tastes like—"

"Shit, I know."

She glowered at him for a moment. "I was going to say piss. Look, if you're going to behave all snippy like this the whole way, you might as well put me off right here."

The temptation was great. So was the temptation to grab her by the neck and shake her until she talked, or her mood changed, at least. Annoying was but an understatement.

"Josie," he said angrily. "Do you not want to talk about it, at least?"

"No, I don't!" she said flatly, raising her voice. "What's there to talk about?"

"Josie, you've just found out—"

"That I'm a freak. Read my lips, a total, fucking freak. I've always been one, from the day I woke up. My whole goddamned, fucking family are freaks. I mean think about it? Oh, wait—what's there to think about? It's just too bizarre to even wrap your head around. Look at us! Mad as fuck from the cradle to the grave! And, and, that business with the cloning, giving *birth* to yourself? I mean, who the fuck does that kind of thing? That's just sick! It's just...wrong. Christ, John, if, if you want a divorce, I don't blame you—nor will I stand in your way. I would divorce me in a flash." She muttered irritably to herself then made a sound of disgust. "Dig a ditch and just chuck me in while you're at it."

She flung the vile-tasting juice across the narrow confines of The Bullet, it hit against the back of another chair with a wet splat. She folded her arms across her chest and scowled sourly out the window—her mood as black as the fathomless space around her. And the juice sat acridly in her stomach.

After a moment, John cleared his throat and tried to sound as unperturbed as he could manage. "I don't want a divorce. I quite enjoy being married to a freak."

He waited for a reaction; she twitched a corner of her mouth. A hand found its way up to it and fisted itself there. Her shoulders shook slightly. She was either laughing or crying. He wasn't sure which.

"Fine," she said airily, her eyebrows flying up high. "Then I don't want one either. I enjoy being married to a nagging, stubborn-assed man who can't let things alone."

Impulsively, he caught the fisted hand, pulled it towards him and kissed it firmly. "*I* need to talk about it," he mumbled into her fist.

"Oh, you're such a weepy *girl* sometimes, you know that?" With a tone of mock exasperation, Josie finally turned to face him. She wasn't scowling anymore, her face had softened and, in fact, her eyes were a little watery. Maybe she had been crying.

"Honestly, John," she said with a serious tone. "I don't know what I'm feeling. Sick, for one thing. Shocked and horrified. I don't know. I just want it to go away—to end. Pretend it never happened, that...that, I'm just a normal person. Not a three hundred year old relic, with a fucked-up niece who's gone and copied herself and went off in the head and..." she sighed, slumping back in her seat. "Fuck."

He nodded and chastised himself, cupping a hand to her face. He shouldn't have pressed her so. "I do, too. It makes me sick after what we saw—found out. It's also just unbelievable, I still cannot bring myself to make it make sense."

"Imagine how I feel, then. It's all fucked to hell up. I'm beginning to see, now, where and why Ho is so messed up in the head. And Margeaux."

They linked hands and pressed close together, shoulder-to-shoulder, head to head. For a very long time, they were silent. Time seemed to stand still, with nothing to remind them that it passed but the constant sound of the engines and the floating space debris.

Josie turned, studying his face as if committing it to memory. He watched her watching him, and knew with a certain feeling of dread, that her next words would squeeze his heart with suffocating pain.

"If I die—not that I'm planning to, just yet," she added quickly. "But if I do...will you promise me that Margeaux is cared for?"

John didn't reply immediately. He needed a moment. He sat, looking back at her with thought, barely breathing. He couldn't imagine a life without her, would not. But recent events seemed insistent that he faced that truth one way or another.

"I promise," he said eventually. Even to him, he sounded far away.

"And by taking care of her, I don't mean committing her to some mental asylum."

He scowled. "I know. But she's been brainwashed from very young. The damage may be irreversible. And considering her family history of, well...*inbreeding* is too gentle a word. I didn't mean you, by the way," he added as he saw her face cloud over.

She shrugged it off. "She's still young and with the right sort of guidance and direction, maybe..."

"She *will* try to run, you know that. First chance she gets. She's not the sort to sit quietly and let fate take over, regardless of her so-called dedication to her religion. She's a schemer, a manipulator."

"I know."

"I thought you didn't care for her anymore." John frowned at her.

"She's still a part of me," Josie replied quietly, but her face showed distaste. "Like I said, she's still young and there's still a glimmer of hope she might...change."

John nodded, understanding. He knew she still cared greatly for Margeaux. "Do not worry about her now. There's time for that later."

"But, what if something happens to—"

"If you dared to die, Josie, rest assured, I would kill you myself. Don't speak so foolishly...please."

In fact, thinking of Josie's dying made him very, very uncomfortable. It scared him cold. Though he knew that life was unpredictable, he planned to keep Josie alive for as long as it was humanly possible—himself, included.

She'd made him normal, made him alive. If he could help it, no way would he let her die. Unfortunately, he knew, too, that if it were the other way around, she'd do the same. It seemed they were both fated to kill themselves before they could allow the other to die. He wished he were a different person, that they lived a different life. One that wasn't riddled with dangers and rife with fear and uncertainty. Then he realized that he couldn't picture their lives any other way.

"Well, the same goes for you." Josie scoffed as if offended. "So don't go around doing heroics like you usually do." She sighed deeply. It sounded sad and tired.

"What is it?" he asked softly.

"I know it's pointless to blame anyone, right now. But I can't help thinking—wondering—that if I hadn't been around, down in their basement, then none of this would be happening. Fern wouldn't have become obsessed with immortality, of doing those...*things* to herself. Of giving birth to...to... You know."

"I wondered that, too. You can't change it, Josie."

"I know."

"And, I also thought if you hadn't been there, with them, you might not be here now. Despite everything, they looked after you. They made sure you lived. Fern, however twisted her mind had become, cared for you. Well, you mattered to her in some way." John squeezed her hand and softly whispered in her ear. "She brought you here, to me. So I have to be thankful for that."

Josie smiled warmly, some color returning to her face. She sighed again and made a helpless noise. "I can't believe she killed my brother—her own father. Kellan. I always thought maybe they were all killed—you know, by the people who killed my father. But all this time, all this fucking time...it was her." Her breath caught in the back of her throat, she swallowed hard. "And Conrad. Poor, little Conrad. Dying all alone, old and forgotten. All by himself and no family of his own. And she spoke of him as if he were—what's the word? Collateral damage. Jesus. What a cold bitch. Oh, God."

"Josie." John gripped her hand and brought her closer.

"I wanted to know what happened. Now, I do. Every single question answered. John, I don't feel so good. I think I might puke."

"It's all right. Just take a few breaths. Space travel does that to some people."

John comforted her, trying to distract her. She looked pale again, her face clammy with cold sweat mingled with tears. He wanted to crawl inside her and beat the sickness; the pain and confusion—whatever it was that troubled her—bludgeon it and fling it far away.

They sat quietly again, resting against each other. Time ticked away, they didn't speak, just sat comforting the other in silence.

Eventually, Josie took a small breath. "Do you think she's still alive? Somewhere, sleeping? Is that possible?" She gazed out the window again. Her face slack, tired-looking.

"Until I met you, I didn't think much about things that were too far-fetched. But now, I'm not so sure." John let out a breath. "Josie, if she's still *out there;* you do realize that she's so far gone from the girl you once knew."

"She's a fucking lunatic, I know." Josie let out a weak chuckle.

She felt a little better. The queasy sensation, the light-headed vertigo; evaporated as John's solid presence bolstered her like a revitalizing tonic.

Space travel, my skinny ass, she snorted to herself. *It's that chalk- food and putrid juice.*

She guessed that by talking about it, hearing it out loud, made it more believable, more real. She pushed the thoughts away with force. It only made her head hurt—confusing things. She didn't need that right now.

"Okay, I shouldn't think about it now. I don't need to," she said, more to herself and inhaled deeply, angrily swiping the tears from her face. "Right," she cleared her throat. "What's the plan once we hit the Scrap Yard? Who goes in high, who goes in low?"

John let out a long laugh—a rare moment, as he hardly ever allowed himself to laugh as long and rich and unabashedly open like he did now. The tension that had been visible on his face evaporated like mist in sunlight. He wrapped his arm around his wife, hugging her tightly until she squeaked in pain. She pulled back, rubbing her sore shoulder with an amused frown.

"You know," John knocked his forehead gently against hers. "You lied. You're not really a freak. You're the most annoyingly normal woman I've ever met—soon you'll be knitting. I want a refund."

She grinned then laughed, her mood lifted like his. "You're such a soppy idiot. Hey, ever heard of the mile-high club?"

John's face screwed up in an uncharacteristic expression of ignorance. "Eh?"

Twenty Three

 The mechanics of space travel kept you grounded like you were on Earth—but it left you with a strange sensation in the middle of your stomach. A vague fullness, like you'd eaten something and then went straight into a pool of water. A strange compressed feeling, as though your stomach was somewhere between where it was supposed to be, and where it was not. It took some getting used to, but considering that my stomach had been fairly empty to begin with, at least the puking sensation went away eventually.

 The smells were also very distinct. Not that space itself had a smell since I never got the chance to actually stick my nose out a window to find out. Who would, as that would be the last thing I ever did before being sucked out like a vacuum and tumbling breathlessly into the black void. By smells, I meant inside the vessels we traveled in.

 Aside from the constant metallic tang of machinery, and the oily smells of fuel and lubricated engines that mingled with the dull undertones of fabrics, upholstery and disinfectant, it was the distinct and surprisingly earthen smells that lingered in every single corner.

 People. Crowds of people. Different kinds of people, all crammed together for extended periods, festering together despite the mandatory hygiene washes and cooled air—the cooled *recycled* air.

 It stank sometimes. Eventually, I suppose you got used to it, which I did in the end—somewhat—as I had other smells on my mind. It helped, too, as I became more and more distracted that I eventually forgot to take notice. But initially, I couldn't help but wonder if my lungs weren't festering slowly from the vile fumes of human b.o.

While I could pick out John's smell from a mile away, whether he'd been scrubbed clean or unwashed for days, I knew his scent to the point it struck me first among a crowd. It smelled of home. Safety. Something I'd grown so accustomed to that sometimes I barely noticed it—until it was among others.

His was the clean scent of male sweat, mixed with the complex spice of his cologne. Compared to the other human smells around me, his was like a breath of fresh air. At least I didn't gag when he was near. I couldn't say the same for the swarm of space cadets that surrounded us as we boarded the heavy-artillery space cruiser, *The Sloop*. Even breathing through my mouth, I thought I could taste them.

Space travel, no, it wasn't everything it was cracked up to be.

We were escorted straight to the observation deck and given an impressive view of the Scrap Yard. Between us, floating like an aerodynamic dick, a stocky yet luxuriously sleek gunship—a sci-fi fanatics wet dream. Riddled with mounted guns seen and unseen; at this very moment their guns were aimed at us, and the Scrap Yard. From the looks of it, we were in stalemate.

"How long has it been like this?" John asked the captain.

The captain, a sharp man dressed in severe black, wore something like a jumpsuit with knee-high boots to match. At his shoulders, thick molded guards extended down to his elbows, and a sort of neck guard framed the back of his head like a scalloped hood. These protective guards also ran down the center of his spine to his tailbone. At his waist, he wore a thick belt with every conceivable gadget, weaponry, and compartments imaginable. It seemed to be attached to a sort of twin-tailed guard-flaps that curved seductively between his thighs—to protect the arteries there, I was told later. Along the front, across his chest, more of the protective material fanned out like a mesh. He wore black gloves too, lined with the trademark Lancaster color of midnight blue; the wrist guards had barbs like the back of a lobster. He was the living, breathing specimen of what one would imagine a futuristic space marine would look like.

I made an audible gasp. Sexy outfit aside, he was very

handsome. Dark-haired and sharp featured with a hawk-like nose that fit his face perfectly; he had blazing blue eyes that seemed to see everything at once. His mouth, firm and straight, and to top everything off, a wickedly jagged scar ran from his left cheekbone to the side of his nose. The angle of the scar and its color were just right, making him both ruggedly handsome and vulnerably romantic at the same time. His name was Captain Sandvik.

There were more like him. Dedicated to the defense of space, much like those privately funded Space Junkies that I'd heard about, only these were Lancaster-trained and government approved Space Marines. They were the space version of Simon's Elites. And Captain Sandvik was the best of them.

"We came and found them already there." Captain Sandvik had a careful, calm way of speaking. For a moment, he reminded me of John, only a brutal and wilder version. And much like John, he had a tone in his voice that suggested he was accustomed to people following his orders.

"We've tried contacting the Yard, but there's no answer," he continued.

"Did you hail the gunship?" John asked, not looking at the captain.

Sandvik shook his head. "No reply."

"Can we get inside the Scrap Yard without them tagging us?" John scrutinized the controls before him. He flicked his eyes from the wide observation window to the consoles, glancing at the faces of the deck personnel, taking everything in detail.

Sandvik regarded him with a look. Sensing eyes on him, John did a sort of inward scowl and with a calming breath, turned slowly to return the stare. They stood at eye-level and appeared to be evenly matched in body weight and strength. But at the moment, I feared that despite Sandvik's imposing array of weaponry, and distractingly attractive uniform, he didn't stand a chance to the all-consuming authority that was John Lancaster. And I knew how fast John could move. The air seemed charged with static, as if two bull elephants were about to clash heads and wrangle tusks. Even the crew surrounding us sensed the tension and were mindfully subdued.

I began to dislike Sandvik as quickly as I'd been taken in by his appearance. He seemed to be struggling with the fact that we were civilians, ignorant of war and tactics, intent on hampering his authority. And of his ego being rubbed the wrong way. I longed to see John swat him over the head like an annoying fly.

Outwardly unmoved and unfazed, Sandvik continued to look at John. But I could see some inner struggle briefly flit across his features. A rapid blinking of his eyes, a subtle roll of his tongue within his mouth, as if he tasted something bitter.

"I cannot risk your going in," Sandvik said simply, no doubt guessing John's intentions of stealing onto the Scrap Yard.

"The risk is not yours to take," John replied casually. "Captain."

Sandvik held his stare a moment longer. "They're looking straight at us. It would be hard to slip away unnoticed. Your shuttle is too big to pass as space junk."

"Then we must make our intentions clear." John turned away to look out the massive window. "Advise the *Renwick* to ready their guns."

The *Renwick* was the sister ship to the one we were currently aboard. It presently flanked the gunship from the other side.

"The gunship carries shield-penetrating missiles. I cannot risk—"

"Then maximize our shields and target those missiles first." John turned to face Sandvik again and spoke matter-of-factly. "If you have a problem, tell me now. If not, prepare to engage. We have hundreds of civilians on board the Yard—including members of my Elites. The objective is to save as many as we can and stop Michael Ho at whatever cost—as soon as possible. This is a warship. And there are two of us to their one."

If Sandvik was upset, he didn't show it. Instead, he inclined his head curtly and signaled a similarly attired woman beside him.

"The Yard is still under the control of the mercenaries and they've blocked all coms. We've no way of assessing what the situation is actually like. May I ask how you plan on getting past them, once you have cleared the
eyes of the gunship?" Sandvik asked.

"We have a special surprise for a certain individual on board."

Sandvik flicked an icy blue stare at me, then back to John.

"You intend to take your wife with you?"

"I do," John replied casually, idly circling the confines of the observation deck, his eyes still darting everywhere.

"It is impractical to risk both your lives. You are already two civilians more than I care to be responsible for."

"My wife is not a civilian, and neither am I." John turned his head to give me a mild look. "And she is not your responsibility. She is quite capable."

"I cannot allow it, regardless. You are the President of—"

"My wife's place is by my side." The tone suggested that no one should argue with that. I certainly wasn't about to. "And I am Commander In Chief of the Space Marines. As you well know, I did not acquire that title by my name alone. Prepare your guns, Captain. My shuttle is ready and waiting."

We left Sandvik to mutter his orders to his subordinates. John looked grim and sour after his encounter with him.

"You don't have a plan do you?" I asked mildly as we walked on, passing military personnel who curtly sidestepped out of our way.

"Brute force," he replied with a small curl to his mouth. "Sometimes, that's the best way."

"So how does very dead sound?"

"I don't plan on dying today and neither are you." He half-turned his head and gave me a sly wink.

We entered to a sort of hospitality room filled with some more members of the Elites including a few I remembered seeing in Iceland. They'd followed directly behind us in another Bullet.

Waiting among them, Margeaux. Her expression matched that of John's.

I hadn't had a chance to speak with her since the last time I saw her. Her eyes flicked across my entire body with curiosity. On her wrists, were two—not one—security bracelets, gleaming brightly as if daring her to run. I felt a certain gleeful smugness seeing them, remembering the time I had to wear one.

"I thought you were injured—badly?" she asked me with that clear, high-pitched voice of hers.

The Elites, sensing a family reunion of sorts, discreetly parted and shuffled to another part of the room. I could hear John muttering his orders among them.

"I was," I replied pleasantly. "Want to see it?"

She tossed her hair and allowed herself a small pout, pitching her voice to sound bored, "Why am I here?"

"To attend your father's funeral. Were you not told?"

I stood before her, for once glad that I was armed to the teeth, trussed up with a body-shield and weapons secreted away about my person—dressed to kill. It was a poor excuse, but it somehow made me feel safe around her. It buffered me from any hurt she could inflict upon me. Protected.

"I don't believe you. You are not good at lying." Her quick eyes darted a look to John. "Does this mean that Father is not dead, as *he* says? You tricked me. Congratulations. Touché."

Her voice turned sour and clipped. I could sense her hatred towards me.

"Your father's been dead for a very long time," I replied mildly. "His body is about to catch up."

"I knew it. You cannot kill him. He is too smart for you. And I'll get you back for tricking me. You'll not get away with it. You plan to trade me, aren't you?"

She took a small, purposeful step forward, daring me to react, to move. Behind me, the Elites fell deafeningly silent. I could feel several pairs of eyes crawling along my back. And John, I felt him close to me. His strength radiated from him, I could feel the heat of it. Yes…protected. She wouldn't dare make a move on me here.

I gave her a long look, up and down her body. Purposely studying her clinically like a specimen of a strange new species.

And, I no longer felt anything for her but pity. The care I'd felt earlier was quickly pushed aside the moment I laid eyes on her again. It was a strange sensation. Despite the blood-link, the ingrained notion of keeping your family first, I basically saw a complete stranger.

Essentially, she was a by-product of all of this madness. Her role, however key it might've been, had been purely for distraction. Her intentions and her mind, those were purely of Ho's. Brainwashed from birth into believing everything he'd said to her, taught her. He was just like Fern, using his own child to mold to his own purposes.

Yes, I only felt pity. I wanted to help her, but at the same time, I wanted to erase her image from my mind, from my presence. Was she dangerous? Yes, very. Could I, if I had to, stop her? I'd consulted myself many times on that, trying in vain to look inside me to see if I could raise a hand and stop her. I didn't have an answer just yet. But I kept reminding myself that her youth and her so-called innocence shouldn't distract me. Danger came in all shapes and sizes, and in all manner of beauty and innocence. And even now, in this surreal future, it was like my own time. Children were used to fight wars, side by side with their adult counterparts. And they hefted arms to wreak destruction and death just as easily—and willingly. It wasn't particularly brainwashing, or forced. It was just a way of life, like falling in step to keep up.

Besides her obviously excellent command of childishly subtle persuasion, I didn't know what else she was capable of. Danger signals flashed all over her, like a mine-riddled field. How I felt now, empty and hollowed out by a sick betrayal, I supposed I could do just about anything. So, it didn't surprise me when I opened my mouth to answer her.

"I'm only dishing out what you've already done to me. Tricks. Isn't that what this has all been about? And," I seethed out with venom, "I plan on doing whatever I want with you."

Anger boiled inside me like a pressure cooker. The insult of being tricked—fooled—and the ugly sting of the hurt she'd caused spilled over. The very sight of her smug face seemed to stoke my rage. I saw her draw back slightly with a look of surprise, a respectful sort of surprise.

"You want to kill me, don't you?" she said mockingly, curling her lips into a sneer, a nasty gleam in her eyes. "You don't have it in you. And I know how to fight back."

With a speed and reaction that startled even myself, I whipped out a hand and wrapped it around her small neck. A full head taller than she was, I used it to my advantage like a schoolyard bully. With my body, I pushed, slamming her against the wall and pinning her there. My left hand had already made a quick flex, drawing out the krima stick, which I then pointed threateningly under her ribcage. One flick of the thumb and the laser would engage, driving itself into her liver.

The temptation was ever so great. It was wrong, it sickened me and I had to restrain myself with effort.

"Think again," I whispered close to her ear, surprising myself, even shocked that my heart rate was level. "You little fucking shit. You and your father, you may be connected to me by a few random genes—but that's all. Trust me, it's not enough to keep you alive. If you only knew the half of it…I saw your father after he found out the real truth. He looked sick, and so he should be. I thought he was going to lose his mind. Oh, wait—its already lost. The whole lot of you are mad as fuck."

I could feel a pulse at her neck pounding under my hand. She didn't seem scared, just angry. Her small face had turned white with rage and pinched up in a snarl, exposing her small even teeth. Those glassy eyes were riveted to mine; whatever evil thoughts passed through them was plain enough to see. She meant me harm and nothing more. She despised me, hated me with a menacingly dangerous passion. I could see it written all over her face. I disgusted her just as she disgusted me. Maybe it *was* too late to help her after all.

I released her with a final shove, knocking her sideways to her knees. She flung her head up to me with a vicious snap.

"I *will* kill you," she hissed out.

"I'll be waiting." I whirled away from her and met John's dark eyes, looking at me with a steady, cautious stare. We stood a moment regarding each other; I half expected him to berate me for being so impulsive. Instead, he nodded with a tiny twitch of his mouth and took my arm, pulling me away from Margeaux.

"You never cease to amaze me," he said softly, directing me through the Elites and out the door. "Remind me, when we have children, I'll be the good parent."

I glared at him, my anger still, not quite managed. "Children?"

"Yes, dear. But not just, yet. We're at war."

I blinked suspiciously, seeing him smirk.

"Or would you rather Sandvik father your children?"

"What?"

John could pick the strangest moments to vent his jealousy. If I weren't in such a vile mood, I would've laughed out loud at his question.

"You seemed quite taken with him," he replied mildly, shooting up an eyebrow.

"That egocentric, trussed-up, piglet of a man?"

John grinned, looking very much like a young boy up to no good.

"You and he have got a history together, I take it." Remembering the tension between them earlier.

"Mmm, ancient history," he replied mildly, suddenly sounding remote. The smile was gone.

"Do tell."

He clicked his tongue distractedly. "When we were in the Academy, it involved his younger sister."

"You and her had a thing going on?" I asked with a raised brow.

He frowned in thought but gave me a reassuring squeeze on my arm. "No, but I cared for her. She was only ten. She was mentally challenged and I simply reminded Sandvik that he had responsibilities that needed fulfilling. He ignored me and told me to mind my business. She followed him everywhere, their parents were both dead and he was the sole caregiver. But she was always smart enough to slip away from her minders. One day, she followed him onto a training field...I couldn't stop her in time."

"Oh, shit." I gave John a supportive nudge as we walked on. I felt shock and horror and formed another mental picture of Sandvik, seeing him in a different light—a different and decidedly ugly light. "I'm so sorry. What an asshole."

"Let's just say that we exchanged words among other things. This is the third time I've seen him since that day." John shrugged to shake the memories off.

"How old were you?"

"We were both nineteen. He'd been jealous of me, and my family, all his life. Always out to prove he's better. As you can see."

"And you just love to prove him otherwise."

"Life's small little luxuries," he smirked but it wasn't from his heart. "She didn't have to die that day if he'd allowed her to live at the Citadel like I suggested. It was a waste of life. Nothing about her was evil. She was pure and good."

"You've been a knight in shining armor since the day you were born, haven't you. Don't know why people think you're a tyrant," I rolled my eyes dramatically.

My mood had changed somewhat. John's story reminded me that life was full of uncertainties. That a good person could die for no reason at all, while an evil one could wreak havoc with abandon, and live, seemingly, forever.

I thought of Margeaux, and again wondered what I'd do to stop her. I wanted to help her, not kill her. But I knew that if she left me with no choice, I might not be able to stop myself. I knew it was my repulsed hate for her that drove me to think this way. I felt ashamed and tried hard to muster up some compassion. It was very hard to do, considering.

John spoke again, distracting my thoughts.

"So, do two sound appropriate? Three is ideal, coming from a family of five, myself," he grinned from the corner of his mouth. Memories seemingly pushed far away into that private, secret corner of his mind that I sometimes coveted to find and unlock.

I stared back at him. He seemed to be enjoying himself. War *did* agree with him. I remembered him light-hearted like this on another occasion, during the siege. He was frighteningly calm.

"Two will do fine," I replied with care. My eyebrows felt as though they had flown off my face. "Any more than that, and my ass will spread like a balloon."

He flashed his teeth at me, evilly. He looked deliriously happy. "I like big bottoms."

"Fuck off, John," I hissed back and elbowed him. "We're at war!"

~ * ~

Agnes could feel her life slipping away from her. The entire lower half of her body had gone numb. Even her fingers started to tingle with pins and needles and she worried, when the time came to start shooting again, that they wouldn't cooperate.

She hadn't been able to move, save a few controlled twitches of her legs, for nearly an hour. The last few hours were merely a dull series of waiting, listening, and waiting some more. Her heart felt strained, pumping out an ever-lowering supply of blood through her body. Waves of dizziness sometimes washed over her. Even her lungs felt smaller, tighter.

The emergency first-aid kit that contained three small tablets of adrenalin was gone. She could feel the last of its effect ebbing away from her. So much for the rush, she thought. She shook her head to clear it, wondering erratically if she'd said it out loud or merely thought it. She wasn't sure. Again, she shook her hands to fling off the pins and needles that settled in them.

Simon had said the metal shard in her thigh would keep the blood from spilling out. What he didn't know, what she didn't tell him, was that the shard had pierced clean through to the other side. She now sat in a puddle of blood. The smell of it made her sick. She knew it was bad the moment it happened. She wasn't stupid; she knew the risks. But they were her risks and her own choices. Simon, he didn't have to know.

The fact that no one had come to relieve her also meant that the situation hadn't improved. Either Ho's men had taken over, or Simon was unable to send support because he was either captured or dead. It didn't matter anyway. She knew her time now was limited.

She had no regrets dying. She never put too much thought into it. In her line of work, the dedication to protect, death was expected. But she was still human, and at the brink of oncoming death, she struggled with the idea. The will to live took over in urgent shockwaves. Panic began to set in. She even starting to hear noises—was it real or imagined? She wasn't sure. She couldn't remember if the Space Junkies she'd sent to man the elevators were still there or not. So did she just imagine all of that? Surely, not. Or did it all happen already and it was all over? So why were people not coming to help her? No, that wasn't right.

She kept hearing noises, so again she shook her head to clear it. The world swam before, clearing briefly, then, clouding over again in a fevered haze. The back of her neck was peppered in icy cold sweat. The edges of her awareness seemed dulled.

When the noise came again, she cocked her head. It sounded like a herd of elephants thundering into a very small room. They crashed and banged about clumsily, their bulky forms sliding against each other in their intent to get across the room. She flexed her numbing fingers and shook her head, again, to clear it. She'd be ready for those noisy elephants.

They came in a rush, nearly tumbling on top each other. Agnes was glad that when she could still focus, she'd rigged all of her remaining weapons into one. They were connected electronically now by a series of 'tricky-triggers'—her term—where all she had to do, was punch a control pad next to her like a drum-set keeping time. By doing so, her weapons would change automatically as the control pad sent out a remote signal via the, now, networked system. All she had to do was keep the trigger pulled on any gun of choice, and aim.

She was armed with an enormous pulse gun, straddled between her legs. Mounted beside it on either side, a heat-seeking automatic rifle and two Elf missile launchers, strapped together. And, as a final resort, several explosives attached to her body like medals.

From her corner against the wall, hidden in the semi-darkness, Agnes pulled the trigger, cutting down the first wave of the elephant-hoard with her pulse gun. Shouts could be heard amid the smoke and confusion. She punched the pad with the heel of her palm, it switched to heat-seekers; more fell dead, piling on top each other. She could smell blood and roasting flesh filling her nostrils.

Die, you stinking elephants! she imagined shouting. *Die!*

She felt something stinging her arm, her face, her neck. The elephants had turned into bees! They were stinging her all over her body. Oh, what she would give for a flame-thrower just about now.

Angered, she punched the control pad again—Elf missiles. A series of small, compact, self-contained missiles shot out and exploded in muted pops. Elf's were specifically designed for the use in space combat, where minimal damage to the surrounding areas were imperative, but offering the maximum damage to humans. It sensed biological matter within its range and latched onto it like magnets.

The bees bit into her shoulder, making her arm fling away; she felt it drop useless at her side. She shouted in rage. Digging out explosives one-handed from her chest, she flung them wildly before her. More pops and screams, but still the bees stung her. With the last of her strength, she emptied her missiles, then manually switched to the heat-seekers and emptied that as well.

When something hit her head with the force of a sledgehammer, she felt her heart trip and the deafening noises around her immediately hushed. Her last thoughts, as she slumped backwards against the wall, looking like the delicate fallen angel that was her trademark look, was that she'd forgot to pull the last explosive on her chest.

It was the explosive that would set the rest of them off and blow nearly half the room into oblivion.

~ * ~

Simon stood, legs apart, hands behind his back considering the storeroom door. It was solid but simply made, and breakable.

Until a few minutes ago, he'd been consulting with Jane, having secreted her away into a fold of his jacket. With her undetectable fingers feeling around the networks, he'd managed to access the communications system that Ho's mercenaries used.

Agnes was dead and the upper escape chambers had been penetrated. Governor Mwenye would be captured soon enough and brought down to the mainframe to unlock the sequence codes he'd created. Torture was a strong possibility and the chances that Ho would perform them were high.

Ho was now onboard. Sometime during the last three hours, he'd slipped in and now ran the show. And something else, too. Two warships now flanked them, causing great agitation among the mercenaries. He imagined a few of them already had encounters with the Lancaster's special Space Marines.

Simon wondered for a moment if Surrey had managed to get back safely to Earth or maybe diverted and gone to one of the military stations. A likely possibility, but it was too soon. John, he thought. He'd be on one of them, Simon could be sure of that. All was not lost then. He consulted his memory. Sandvik, surely he too would be in board. No space engagement, especially of this magnitude, would slip by him.

He turned to Madds, who propped against the wall, chin resting on a fist.

"How much do you reckon this door weighs?"

Madds gave him a noncommittal shrug and looked at the door. "It's not the weight of the door you need to consider, it's what's on the other side."

"True enough," Simon grinned wickedly. Madds was a philosophical man at the best of times. "But I'm just itching for a good brawl. Are you game?"

Russell, the Junkie, came forward. "It's about time. What're you planning? My men are with you and they're more than ready."

"A good, old-fashioned fist-fight. However, the bitch is mine."

"That's cheating, she's got a weak right arm and you know it," Madds said as he flexed his shoulders, readying himself.

Minnows sniggered in the background, nervous, but ready.

The technician in control of activating the droids in Distributions cleared his throat. "Half are online and waiting, sir. I've finally managed to remote access them," he patted his personal unit like an obedient dog. "It's taking some time, but…in another hour, I should get the other half activated."

Simon nodded with a stern smile. "I'll leave you in charge, but make it thirty minutes, no pressure. Once they're activated, have half proceed directly to the docking bays to assist in the…clean up. Alert them that they are friendly warships waiting outside, target only mercenaries. They're wearing green. The other half, direct them throughout the Yard to assist. In both cases, they are to use extreme force. Are they fully equipped?"

"Yes, sir."

"Good. And when you're done, destroy that unit. We wouldn't want it falling into the enemy's hands so they can gain access."

Earlier, Simon had opened the access code briefly, using Jane as the carrier for the signal commands, so the technician could slip through using a personal unit. The technician had the good sense not to ask how this was possible, looking at Jane with a glazed look of interest. It took hours of slow plodding work, but finally, the tech gained full control without raising any alert flags.

Simon turned to the others, ignoring the technicians for now.

"Are we ready? It should take two good kicks and the door will be down. When that happens, we pounce in a stagger-formation. Understood?"

Madds stood before the door after giving it a few prods with his finger. "Simple metal door, nothing special, standard pressure lock," he could be heard muttering.

Considering it was just a storeroom door, and judging from what was in it, nothing of any great importance. Just basic, everyday supplies, the door stood more as a partition to block the room off from the mainframe.

Madds rolled his shoulders like a boxer. He turned to Simon. "Make that one kick."

The door gave in—or out—depending on how you looked at it, with ease. The force with which it flung out knocked down one man, who stood guard just outside. It slammed into the back of his head, knocking him out senseless before he even hit the floor.

The three Elites ejected out as a mere blur. Simon arrowed out first and directed himself, fists outstretched before him at another guard standing a little to the right. The guard literally gaped in horror by the time Simon's fist slammed into his face; the other fist broke his sternum with an audible crack.

Minnows jumped out, sailed over the short flight of steps in a tight ball, and pounced to the floor like a cat. From his boot, he pulled out another krima, already engaged and whirling around the room like a dizzying kaleidoscope.

Madds was the last out, having ducked low after kicking the door, allowing the others to soar over him first. He had small, marble size pellet explosives hidden in his crotch. He flung them out in a spray into a small group of armed men, where they popped like firecrackers, distracting them. He dove straight in, barreling two down in his wake.

The Junkies followed suit, swarming out the little storeroom, they knocked down whatever stood in their way. Three headed straight to the pile of weapons, still on the floor in the middle of the room.

The woman in charge shrieked in rage. She hoisted her gun and took aim at the first person she had in her sights—the flash of his red hair catching her attention. Simon. She fired. The heat-seeking bullet found its mark, and though the last minute dodge saved him from a bullet to the chest, it still ploughed through his side and out his back.

With a grunt, Simon crashed to the floor, sliding across it on his own blood. Before the numbing pain speared through him, he did a quick mental check as he rolled away and ducked behind some console stands.

Left side, no major organs—kidney might be damaged.

He smelled his blood and bit back an oath. Aside from the rich, metallic tang of copper and the heavy musk of open wounds, the air was tinged slightly of fecal matter. The intestines! If he wasn't treated, and treated soon, he could go septic and that would kill him for sure. Rage filled him instantly. He wasn't about to die in space. Not if he had something to say about it.

He risked a quick look—his side rang in such pain it nearly dulled his vision. The mainframe was in utter madness. Everyone fought everyone else like a heaving sea of wriggling worms, tumbling atop one another—a medieval war where bodies clashed with bodies. Shouting, yelling, even gunfire amid screams of pain and flashes of light as krima sticks materialized everywhere. He saw Minnows airborne, twisting and turning, diving into a group that parted away from him as he cut them down. Madds had just finished breaking a man's neck, flinging him sideways like garbage; his expression calm, serious. And Ox, taller, larger and stronger than anyone else, sweeping his arms out like a fan as he pivoted and kicked, crushing anyone who stood in his way.

Simon braced himself. Gritting his teeth, he hoisted to his feet, and jumped into the fray. Then saw his mark, screeching her head off and swinging her gun wildly about her. In a few jumping strides, he was upon her, hooking the crook of his arm around her neck, and slamming her to the floor. But she was made of rubber, it seemed. She flexed, twisted, and slipped from his grasp. In an instant, she was on her feet and swinging them out at him. One foot caught him on his shoulder, the other he caught, twisted it and sent her spinning out onto her back. She grunted and made a noise as she pounced back to her feet and headed straight for him.

She's like a spring, he thought and managed a quick back flip; despite the narrow space he had to work with. Other bodies bumped and nudged him as they fought. The woman, falling short of her intended target, crashed instead into one of her own men. She wrenched him away with force and headed straight for Simon.

He was ready. He judged her stride, noted that she was left-handed by the way her body was aligned, and weaponless.

She struck out in a lunge, her left arm swinging, the fingers curled into a tiger's claw. Simon dipped right, snagged her by the left shoulder when the swinging arc was complete—he used her momentum and heaved her to the right. She toppled and slipped to the floor. He spun, driving a foot into her spine, she screamed out as it broke.

That was too easy, Simon thought. He'd expected her to bounce back up and give him a better fight. To end it, he hopped to his other foot and sent the other into the back of her neck, breaking it clean. She lay, facedown. The last of her dying reflexes made her fingers twitch, curling inwards to her wrists.

Simon's side throbbed from the exertion. A quick inspection told him he'd bled quite badly during the fight. His hand came away slick and oily with dark blood. Madds caught him as he swayed; he had two pulse guns and handed one to Simon. Then, they pushed themselves into a corner.

"Bad?" Madds asked quickly and he fired a few rounds.

"Very. I'm losing blood like a stuck pig." Simon gritted his teeth. "But I'm not done yet."

"That's the spirit." Though Madds made light of the situation, he noted the pale color of Simon's face. He looked worried. And the smell about the wound...

It took another few minutes to get the room back under control. Ox, towards the end, had the ferret-faced Cerevetto in a permanent headlock the entire time as he fended off two men with one hand.

But it was Minnows who saved the day. His aerial acrobatic skills no match for the solidly grounded—and sometimes gaping— mercenaries who witnessed him flying through the air before their bodies were lopped in half.

The stench of blood was everywhere, the floor slick with it, causing people to slip and slide. As it stood, among the dead and dying were several Junkies, and some technicians that decided to lend a hand. A few of the mercenaries still alive had the good sense to surrender. The injured hobbled about looking grim, but definitely satisfied.

Russell dripped blood from his head, arms and neck, but still stood defiantly. He spat out blood as he directed his men to stand guard at the gaping hole that was once the door. A few security droids were still functional as well, those that didn't perish earlier. Russell instructed them to stand guard with his men. He seemed to thrive in chaos. The technicians stood vacantly, shell-shocked. He grappled one by the scruff of his neck and pushed him to the consoles, snagging Ox and telling him to coordinate with them. They needed to get the droids out of Distribution and into combat—fast.

Simon left Russell to organize and pulled out Jane, finding a quiet corner to sit while Madds treated him with a quick and rather painful first-aid. It would do until he received proper medical attention. Jane took a while to route herself onto a secure network but once she did, John's face swam into view.

"Christ on toast! Simon. What's happening?"

"We've taken back the mainframe—for now," Simon explained, gritting his teeth. The pain made him feel nauseous. He filled his friend in on the recent events. "We're hoping once the droids are deployed, we can open up the docks manually. Dock 4 is open; that's their entry point. Best place in, is there. But I reckon it's heavily guarded. How bad is the gunship situation?"

"They've got some serious fire-power. We may just manage, but I can't risk them opening up on you lot." John creased his brow, studying his friend. "Simon, you're injured."

"Just a small ding," he waved John off with a hand. "Mwenye is under threat. Agnes is dead. Renna is on her own with Junkies and droids—trapped in the escape chambers. I'm not sure how long they can hold out. Ho seems to have an endless supply of men. We need to cut him off from his men—shut down Dock 4, do you hear me?"

"I've a little surprise for Ho," John grinned with wicked glee. "I'll organize to concentrate attacks on Dock 4 once we've cleared the gunship. Prepare for battle, give me an hour."

Simon grinned back. "An hour, he says. Take your bloody time, I'm not going anywhere."

When he broke transmission, Simon realized that he forgot to ask about Josie. He took it she was all right, given that his friend's face wasn't overly distraught. Tucking the thought aside as things to ask about later, if he made it, he ordered Jane to transmit another call.

This one was to Deidre Moorjani.

~ * ~

The first wave of attacks riddled the side of Ho's gunship. Bright flashes of light popped along like Chinese firecrackers before being sucked out by the airless space around it. Josie had just enough time to witness this before she was dashed away into the waiting shuttle.

Margeaux was already there, secured to her seat, face white with fury.

Ignoring her, Josie dropped into a seat beside John. Captain Sandvik, nearby, spoke in a low tone to two of his six men. The rest were Elites. In total, there were twenty of them, not including Margeaux.

John busily performed a weapons check, which prompted Josie to do the same.

"I want you to stick close to me—at all times," he said quietly.

She nodded back making sure the four reload cartridges for her Snare Gun 3 were still at her belt. Check, she nodded to herself.

He snaked out a hand, caught hers. His face dark and serious. "Understood?"

"Yes," she frowned back in annoyance. "I'm not a total idiot, you know," then rummaged through the pockets of her many-pocketed trousers.

Contact explosives, she counted ten. Check. Throwing knives—three. Check. Digging into her shoulder holster, she pulled out a small handheld heat-seeking gun. Cocking the barrel, she peered through it to see if it was clear. Check. She patted her other pocket for the reloads. Check...

John watched her with a mixture of fascination and anxiety. A year ago, Josie had never even picked up a weapon, let alone known how to use one. She'd been a scared and gangly, sickly-thin woman he'd picked on unmercifully. And now, look at her. Strong, sure, determined, and ready. She was capable of things even she didn't know she could do. Her courage made him admire her, just as it scared him cold.

"Stop staring at me," she hissed without looking at him.

"The girl is watching."

"Let her watch. It might teach her something about human decency."

He was well aware that Margeaux watched them. How could he not feel the weight of those glittery, evil eyes, taking in every single move they made? He was also aware of the eyes of the others, his own men included. Staring bashfully with mesmerized awe and surprise at his wife, casually doing a weapons check as if it were an everyday occurrence.

Though men and women fought side by side now, it still brought a raised eyebrow when it came to the President's wife being among them. He noted that they looked not with hesitation or reluctance, or even mockery, but with respect. He could see, too, that many would willingly stand before Josie to save her life—if only for the mere fact that she was here with them now. And, it hadn't taken long for the news of the Iceland incident to reach the ears of his team. Loeb was right, her loyalty to him, as well as for those on his side, was clear and evident enough. And his men knew it. He'd even heard snatches of their whispers, talking of Josie being knifed brutally by Ho, yet here she was, standing among them. Ready to fight. His men were more than impressed—they were almost fanatically honored.

Doing what she did now with a sure confidence others would take years to acquire, she seemed oblivious of the attention. Her mind seemed fixated on her task with a sense of calm determination, with conviction. Almost as if she'd always been destined to be sitting here, next to him, ready to fight. Courageous—that wasn't the word for it. Not even bravery. It was more a sense of purpose for her. Something that she knew she had to do, and face, in order to get past and onto the next phase of her life. She may not like it, may not even want it, but she did it without complaint. Her life in this future was a far-fetched and stretched existence from the one she grew up in.

If it were him, could he be so calm? He wasn't too sure, nor could he imagine. Because, aside from the physical evils she had to fight, there were the phantoms that plagued her mind. And fighting ghosts wasn't the same as fighting a real person.

He knew she was scared, terrified. But she pushed that aside, knowing that it would hinder her—and him. Instead, she used her anger to push herself on. A surge of pride swelled up inside him.

"Give us a kiss, then," he said softly. The room had blurred, he saw nothing else but her. He didn't care who saw.

"What? Now?" Josie gaped. "Jesus, John. Now's not a—" She stopped suddenly, catching the look on his face. It was, in a rare moment of public display, wide open with concern and love—and a silly, goofy smile.

She bit back a giggle and felt like the total idiot she claimed she wasn't. Here they were, about to jump into the certain jaws of death and she couldn't even give her husband a kiss. It could very well be the last kiss between them, and she was making a fuss.

Josie leaned in and held his face tenderly in her hands, and gave him a heart-wrenchingly soft and slow kiss. She heard his breath catch, felt him holding back with a fierce, determined control; and felt herself falling as if from dizzying heights.

With great effort, they parted and rested their foreheads together.

"Are you ready?" she whispered.

"Yes," he sounded hoarse.

"Then, so am I." She grinned wickedly. "Let's go fuck up Ho's day."

"You're so charming, only your husband could love you," he grinned back.

"I know. Have you seen him lately? He'd kill me if he caught me kissing some lovesick, weepy girl of a man."

Twenty Four

Renna Djankovski knew when she was outnumbered. But more importantly, when the other side had bigger guns. With reluctance, she lowered her weapon and indicated to the Junkies to do the same. When Governor Mwenye didn't immediately comply, she glared him down with her doe-eyes.

"Unless you plan on using it on yourself—stand down," she ordered under her breath.

Affronted, Mwenye curled his wide lips into a sneer. "Are you suggesting I kill myself? It would save us all a great deal of trouble, wouldn't it?"

She raised a brow mildly and looked away, seeing no point in answering a redundant question.

It took less than ten minutes for Mwenye to be dragged away from his sanctuary. Despite Renna's attempts—and a burgeoning black eye she received in the process—she couldn't follow. Simon's orders had been precise. Mwenye must not leave her sight. But sometimes, orders were very hard to follow. Simon would understand.

At least, she thought to herself, Mwenye's captors still didn't realize the mainframe was no longer in their control. And in any case, they didn't appear to be the smartest individuals, either.

Bright flashes caught her attention through the escape shuttle's windows. Several people holed up with her were already hissing with interest at the sight. They'd all seen the arrival of the gunship with a feeling of dread. Then came the two heavy-artillery warships, emblazoned with the Lancaster military colors of midnight blue. Junkies and techs, even Mwenye himself seemed to breath easier at the sight. But it seemed like ages before either warship planned on doing anything productive.

Now, finally, the warships had initiated an attack on the gunship, pelting it down from both sides with barrage after barrage of gunfire. Unfortunately, the gunship had maximum shields, so the damage was minimal. It returned fire with the same intensity.

With nothing else to do but wait, Renna, along with the others trapped inside, watched the show. Simon's last order, while he still remained inside the storeroom, said to wait.

She felt useless.

~ * ~

Mwenye, in a desperate attempt, tried to run. It earned him a solid blow right between his shoulder blades and knocked the air out of him. He'd thought, while his captors argued amongst themselves, that he could make a quick escape. After all, he knew this place like the back of his hand. It was clear they didn't.

He was in the company of five men; the rest stationed in the reception area of the upper deck, keeping guard. Judging from their disjointed conversation, Mwenye had determined that it had taken them a good few hours to find him.

First, they'd gotten lost and ended up in an observation tower on the far side of the upper decks. Then, backtracking down, they crossed to the other side where they met a couple of Junkies manning the entrance to the upper deck elevators. It had been an all out massacre. Some deranged woman with a stack of weapons had cut down the majority of them. Thankfully, as Mwenye listened to their agitated conversation, they'd managed to kill her. But the encounter still left them so spooked that every noise they heard had them jumping anxiously. Then, they'd had to wait for reinforcements to arrive, which took forever. After that, it was the long task of deciding which escape chamber Mwenye might be hiding in.

With each wrong turn they made, they encountered more hiccups and resistance from Junkies, droids, and techs alike. And now, their quarry found, they argued and bickered amongst themselves. Each hotly insisting their own suggestions, which were better and much sounder than the other, should've been followed in the first place.

Despite the throbbing pain in his back, Mwenye chuckled to himself. There seemed to be no respect among mercenaries. And no order.

First and foremost, Mwenye was a military man. He understood order and he understood respect. To witness an insult to both repulsed as well as inspired him. All was not lost. And he knew well enough how to create disorder and lay the seeds of mistrust.

They'd just cleared the upper-deck foyer when he acted again. This time, Mwenye used words rather than action.

"Why are we going to Distribution?" he asked as if perplexed, pitching his voice to sound tired and half-uncertain of his fate.

One man cocked his head at him in annoyance. Another told Mwenye to shut up. A third snorted and said: "This isn't the way to Distro. He's talking crap."

"Sure? We passed this before, right?" a fourth asked.

"Idiots," Mwenye muttered under his breath. "Fine, let's go to Distribution, then. I assume you need me there to place official seals on the boxes?"

The group paused briefly, looking at him suspiciously.

"He's talking fool to save himself. We're going the right way."

"No, no. We came up from the other side. I don't remember this paneling on the wall here."

"They all have this paneling. Are you running this, or what? Last time I checked, Ming was heading our team."

"Ming got his head ripped by the bitch, remember."

"Where's whats-his-name? He should run this—he can take the blame. That Ho guy's not right in the head. I'm not taking heat if this gets messed."

"I'm running this now so it's me that'll get the bonus."

"Since when? I've been doing this longer than you have, you runt."

"Listen, stop wasting time. Let's move. And bonus is being split five ways. Deal's a deal."

"Other way. Distro is this way—any idiot can see that."

"Listen to the runt. It's this way, I tell you. Don't listen to him."

"Five-way split, remember. Or I walk out and take my men with me. This show's been a cock-up from the very beginning."

"Go ahead and walk, idiot. You can't even find the exits. Means more money for the rest of us."

Mwenye listened as they argued, surprised at how easily they doubted themselves. It gave him hope. These were not the smartest, even though they may be the strongest. Nor were they particularly loyal to the cause. Ho obviously needed as much muscle he could get—intelligence and allegiance were not key factors in his goal to take over the Scrap Yard.

He didn't have a plan, but Mwenye had every intention of continuing what he did. Anything that prevented him being taken anywhere near the mainframe, helped.

~ * ~

If birth could be likened to a spark of light switching on to illuminate a darkened room, then nearly five thousand sparks of light ignited in the eyes of the droids. A dull orange that ebbed to red, dramatically flashing to green to indicate they were online and fully functional. The green light juddered and flickered briefly to suggest their instructions were being downloaded into their central processing units, upgraded into their existing software, and saved.

With sleek and menacingly strong bodies and limbs, gleaming with silver metal, they turned as one. Their faces were wide and oval; smooth, dark, tempered glass—featureless save that single green light, dead centre.

These were the SD-M 3.1 security droids, designed and designated specifically for the military—fully equipped with heat-seeking weapons, explosives, and super-human strength, speed, and agility. Their bodies were made of modified, lightweight titanium casings to enhance their speed and their ability to withstand extreme heat and pressure. Full shields also encased them—though they weren't indestructible, many wouldn't linger long enough to find out.

In a matter of minutes, the droids blew a hole in the locked door of Distribution and filed out; their feet drumming the floor like a thousand drops of rain on a tin roof.

Once their targets were in sight, they plowed through, opening fire with such canny precision that none were left standing for too long. Damage to civilians and Scrap Yard military—nil.

~ * ~

Surrey knew he'd made a mistake. Though it had been a necessary one, he told himself, along with an admonishment for not thinking it through with more care. He realized that there'd be no way to sabotage the engine *and* get out in time to save himself. He'd weighed the odds carefully, even trying to think of an alternative solution. He found none. There was no other way.

Furthermore, he was too far ahead now to turn back. He'd spent close to two hours rerouting the engine room commands to suit him, and now, everything was on track and ready. They were even sounds of engagement. It was time. Before long, the engines would overheat with the excess energy being routed to the shields. He'd shut down the coolants and extractor fans. And with each new volley of weapons fire the command deck ordered, the engines had begun to overheat—even the air seemed charged with concentrated heat. He'd disabled the safety alarms as well. No one would know when the engines reached critical mass.

Since returning to his small vessel was pointless—it would be too late anyway—Surrey stayed in the engine room, to make sure all went well, he told himself. The music in his head was positively deafening—it was the greatest composition he'd ever composed. With some regret, he knew it would never be put to paper, to be played again for others to enjoy, even if it were only to himself.

With a matter-of-fact sigh, he pulled out his communicator, sent out a call to Simon, and left a message. He reasoned that once communications were back up and running, Simon would retrieve his messages. In Surrey's message, he apologized that he'd been unable to follow his orders and return to the Citadel. He explained why and then thanked Simon for the honor to have been able to serve under him, to have been selected as part of the Elites…and now he would die as one.

He signed off with a bowed salute of humility, and prepared himself for death.

~ * ~

Under the cover of artillery exchange, the shuttle slipped out from the far side of *The Sloop*. With their attention concentrated on what lay in front of them and right beside them, the gunship seemed uninterested in the shuttle, now stealthily wending its way in a wide arc towards the Scrap Yard.

John stood, braced in the doorway of the cockpit, his eyes riveted on their progress. Captain Sandvik himself piloted the shuttle, trusting no one to skilfully maneuver the craft undetected as well as he could.

Josie sat on the edge of her seat, her heart thudding not from fear, but from mounting excitement. She couldn't even explain it herself, the lack of fear. Surely, she should feel some trepidation about going headlong into the arms of sure death. But it seemed that the aura John emitted was catching. Though his eyes were dark and dangerous, and the line between his brow deep; he curled the side of his mouth into a wicked smile.

"Coming into view," the young co-pilot, Lieutenant December, muttered next to Sandvik. She flicked and tapped at some control. "Weapons are online and ready."

"Begin engagement in thirty seconds. Target bay doors—*wait.*" Sandvik inclined his head to the right. "They're open. Use scatter-shots to draw them out. Then target as we approach."

John nodded, remained silent but watched everything in detail. As if remembering something, he turned his head once to glance at Josie. She twitched her mouth in a quick smile. Though his expression was serious, he gave her a half-wink before turning his head once more to the front. His hands gripped the sides of the doorway, his body held taut—waiting for impact.

Seeing the stance, Josie copied and held tightly to the sides of her seat. She tightened her abdominal muscles, pressed her back against the seat and slightly inclined her head forward.

"Engage," Sandvik ordered, calm and cool as though they took a scenic tour of outer space.

The shuttle seemed to vibrate with some wild and uncontained force. Beneath her seat, Josie felt a rolling tremble as six successive rounds of scatter-shots barked out. It sounded muted, a sound very close to hitting a pane of glass with a hammer—repeatedly. Sandvik thrust engines, the shuttle shot forward with a jerk, it pulled against her neck muscles but she held it rigid.

A series of return fire rocked the shuttle and its passengers like a washing machine. Josie grunted and risked a look at the walls, imagining them to have ripped open from the attack. She grimaced as the sound of the shuttle's shield hissed and spat like a cat. The air felt slightly charged with static.

Lieutenant December switched controls and brought online the missiles, letting them target in clusters of three before firing. She looked calm and seasoned, despite the youthful plumpness around her cheeks, the only part of her face visible from under the gleaming black helmet she wore.

The missiles ripped through Dock 4's defense posts, scattering man and metal every-which-way. The shuttle zoomed through the narrow passageway of the docking bay, targeting more defense posts along the way. Hovering to a halt, December brought online manual weapons control, and like an all-too-real computer game, began firing at moving targets one by one from the mounted rotary guns. Her thumbs moved in a blur on the trigger, her wrist twisting and turning erratically at the sensor-joystick. The shuttle resembled a strobe light as gunfire spit out in all directions.

John whirled around, sweeping a glance at his Elites and nodding. Snagging Josie's arm, he marched down to the exit doors, pressing her close to him, possessively. He let his Elites swarm around them. Two positioned themselves in front—McLinney and Kakuta—they exchange wicked looks, each trying to out-smirk the other. Whatever the joke was, John seemed to know it, and he too, grinned. Behind them, two more held Margeaux between them. She'd been silent since they left *The Sloop*, her expression unreadable.

The shuttle landed with a dull thud. Sandvik flung out of his chair and crossed the distance to the exit in big strides. Outside, explosions and gunfire, and the general sounds of discord could be heard. December remained in her seat, still firing. Occasionally, the shuttle vibrated and its outer skin coughed and rang with shock as gunfire pelted its body.

"Wait for my men," Sandvik barked. His arms beckoned his men in his wake. He stopped before John with a glower, the first real sign of annoyance.

"I cannot let you engage before my men. The risks are too great." He gave an irritable—somewhat disdainful—glance at Josie, before addressing John again. "Please, allow my men a ten-second advance."

John inclined his head politely, casting a look to McLinney and Kakuta, who stepped back without argument. They did, however, look slightly disappointed.

Sandvik and his team poured out of the shuttle amid a rain of gunfire. The noise was deafening. Without consciously thinking, Josie began counting off ten seconds and curled a hand over her Snare Gun, the other held fast to John's hand.

"Ten?" McLinney's solid pug features looked expectantly to John.

"Must be by now," John replied with a grin. He turned to whisper into Josie's ear. "I'll be needing my hand, if you don't mind. Stay close, always to my left. Don't forget."

She nodded, and without hesitation, turned her head and kissed him soundly. "Try to walk a straight line then," she grinned back to his reddening face.

"On my mark," John called out after clearing his throat.

They sprang out of the shuttle like bouncing balls. Each going a different direction, but decidedly fanning out to keep the central balls, that were John and Josie, protected. Margeaux was shoved among them in the centre, being dragged along now by one Elite. However reluctant she looked, Margeaux obediently followed.

Josie spared her niece a quick look, more to make sure she was still with them, then sidled into position at John's left side, a step behind.

It was an agreed formation for when Simon wasn't with them. John, right-handed, needed that arm free and clear in case of combat, in case he needed to protect her. It wasn't a submissive move—but a smart one. He had his whole life perfecting the art of combat, compared to her mere year of befuddled training. He'd stated plain enough that he trusted no one else but Simon or Josie to watch his back. They were, after all, driven to protect him, and each other, from love, not duty. While he could train eyes to his front, they would always, without thinking, watch his back, allowing him to concentrate on the task at hand.

As if to unwittingly emphasize this point, Josie slid narrowed eyes back to Margeaux. Their eyes met, locked. Whatever thoughts passed through their minds, unreadable. But both carried an icy glare that spoke multitudes in warning.

The docking bay was a mess, a wrangle of chaos, noise, metal and smoke. Tucking her head low, Josie followed John as they dashed across the littered dock floor, nipping behind smoking parts of shuttles, fallen equipment, boxes, and whatever else they could find to seek refuge. Before them, spread out strategically, Sandvik and his team mowed down those still left standing from December's wake, trying to clear a path. Still in the cockpit, December could be heard shooting randomly at those still resisting.

Sandvik made a quick motion to John, who nodded. Like pieces on a chessboard, they moved forward in increments, taking up new positions. Their aim, the docking bay exits doors.

Leaving four men behind, including Lieutenant December to secure the docking bay, Sandvik forged ahead.

"It will take us roughly ten minutes to get to the mainframe. Providing we're not detained." Sandvik spared a look behind him as he spoke.

"Understood." John, well aware of that fact judging from his terse tone, sent a quick glance beyond the exits doors with tight expression.

They stood about twenty feet from the glide elevators that would run them up along the arm to the main body of the Yard. Two of Sandvik's marines could be heard neutralizing a small attack on them by a lone mercenary still hiding behind the leg of a shuttle.

"Hail the *Renwick*," John continued. "Get Captain Grosjean to deploy. We need them within to hold this docking bay."

"My lieutenant has already done so. They should be here shortly. Her scans indicate a large mass ahead of us, just outside the glide doors in the reception area. Approximately twenty to thirty men, armed. Be ready as the doors open."

John nodded and readied his weapons.

They were sixteen-strong, armed to the teeth. With luck, they'd stand a chance. He glanced at Josie who stood grim-faced, reined in tight like a coiled spring—ready. He shook his head slightly, catching her eyes. She should not engage, it said.

Josie inclined her head with something like relief washing over her face.

"On your mark, Captain." John nodded again to Sandvik.

The group marched swiftly out, stepping over fallen bodies,

blood and gore, and into the waiting glide. Margeaux made an audible noise, a choking sound. Her eyes riveted to the dead.

"Not feeling well?" John asked mildly. He pressed himself to the sides of the elevator, towing Josie in his wake.

Margeaux made no response but a scowl, which failed to mask her obvious horror at what she'd just witnessed. She tossed her hair, wiped her features blank and regarded him in cold silence.

"Cheer up," he continued with a flash of teeth. "It doesn't get any better. Death is a messy business. Either you're ready for it, or not."

"Barbaric." Margeaux muttered under her breath and turned away from him.

Josie cocked an eyebrow high up and turned to stare at the girl. Before she could form a scathing remark, the glide sounded its arrival and the doors slid open.

Sandvik's men were ready. Crouched low, they opened fire at the mercenaries before them who scattered like birds, flapping for cover amid yelps of surprise. The Elites followed suit, John included.

John pressed a hand back, shoving Josie further into the corners of the glide. Had she been able to see amid the smoke and stench of weapons fire, the crackling static as body-shields repelled bullets and projectiles, she would've joined in. Maybe. But it was safer to mind John's warning. She had no business engaging in war when it wasn't necessary.

Margeaux stood hunched in the corner opposite Josie. Her hand fisted over her ears, her face tight with discomfort.

Someone in the glide yelled in pain then dropped to the floor, followed by another who curled into a ball. There were grunts, shouts, and directives. Josie focused through the confusion to see who had fallen. She knew it wasn't John; he stood at her right flanked by McLinney and Kakuta. It was a marine and half his left shoulder was gone, those who stood behind him were covered in his blood. Roughly, he was dragged aside, inspected briefly to determine his condition—dead—then shoved away. The other man who had fallen pushed up but listed heavily to one side; he crawled into position once more. He'd not lost hold of his gun once during his ordeal.

Another fell, an Elite. His body-shield sizzled and sparked

with smoke and pops of light as his chest ignited with fire. An Elite who stood nearest, flipped him over, snuffing out the flames. John cursed in rage as he called out the fallen Elite by name. Margeaux gagged. Josie shut her eyes and took a breath, ignoring the smell of roasting flesh and blood. She knew she could never erase what she'd just seen: it would stay with her whole life.

War was a messy business, it was expected. But still, she needed a moment.

The exchange of gunfire was over in three minutes. It seemed like half a day. Three more were dead, a total of five—two Elites and three marines. John was splattered with blood and bits of gore. Even Josie, tucked away in the corner, didn't escape the spray of blood as it released from the body at high velocity. She had bright red splashes across her arms, neck, and face. She wiped them roughly, stamping down the rush of nausea by reminding herself that they were from men. Men who had been alive just moments ago, fighting and giving their lives to defend what was theirs. Josie forcefully memorized their faces to make herself better able to deal with having their blood on her.

Margeaux had thrown up at some point, she was sheet-white, her eyes slightly glazed over, staring at a point somewhere beyond the glide doors.

The other side didn't fare well in the least. Sandvik himself could be seen trudging through the bodies, mercifully killing those that had no hope of living—who screamed to be put to death from their mortal pain. Those that lived were hustled together, secured, and dumped in a corner for later retrieval.

John flicked a glance to his wife. She nodded and they filed out, slipping in blood and skirting the worst of the dead until they reached the far side of the reception area. The Elite followed, dragging Margeaux. Part of his pant leg smeared with her vomit, which he seemed oblivious of.

In silence, they proceeded through a door and then onto another elevator—a direct ride to the mainframe. Their scans indicated another cluster of men waiting just outside, not as large as the first. It also indicated the telltale signs of a swarm of security droids quickly advancing to their position at inhuman speed.

John pulled out his communicator and called Simon.

"Not quite a hour, we're ahead of schedule."

Simon grinned. His face looked pale and clammy. "John. It's about bloody time. Ho's making a move—he's got Mwenye and heading this way. How far along are you?"

"About seven minutes. A batch of droids will intercept some unfriendlies before we exit the ride. Be ready for us. Where is Ho now?"

"Judging from the communications, he's coming in from Distribution. There's been a bloodbath there with some of our droids. Mwenye was the only one left alive, but he got caught trying to head back to the escape chambers." Simon shook his head. "Ho is alone, it would appear. The droids didn't kill him because he wasn't wearing the merc colors. A slight oversight, which is being corrected as we speak…" He glanced to one side, no doubt admonishing the technician with a look.

"Simon…" John clamped his mouth into a line, unable to finish. He exchanged a look with Josie, who stood close.

Josie watched John studying his old friend's face, taking note of the pallid appearance, the sickly sheen. Lowering his voice, he seemed to beg to Simon. "Wait for me."

John pocketed his communicator and looked to Josie again. She gave him a small smile and leaned in closer to nudge his left arm with hers. He leaned back to her, relaxing slightly.

"This time tomorrow, we'll be home having a great big feast with Simon and Trudi and everyone else. You'll see." Josie whispered quietly into his ear, heard him softly snort out a chuckle.

"I'm scared for him," was all he said.

"Yeah. Me too."

Twenty Five

Captain Alanis Grosjean scrubbed a hand roughly through her short dark hair and directed cold brown eyes at her lieutenant.

"Repeat that?" she barked.

While Sandvik was calm and collected, choosing his words with care regardless of his forceful nature, Grosjean was his opposite. She was loud, brash, and scathing—a live wire, crackling and bristling with energy, an unexpectedly deceptive temperament, belied by her delicate elfin features, her flyaway eyebrows, heart-shaped face and creamy complexion. Her voice, smooth and feminine, rang with subtle tones of a Euro-Gallic origin, yet crude with authority. Her height, average, her build, slight, but she carried herself as imposingly as a giant.

"The bay doors are jammed, sir." The lieutenant shifted uncomfortably. "That last barrage was a direct hit. We're grounded."

"Goddammit!" Grosjean shouted, flinging her helmet to the floor. It bounced high enough that another space marine had to dodge quickly from being knocked in the shin. "What about the secondary doors?"

"No, sir."

"As in what? Have they been jammed as well?"

"Yes, sir."

Grosjean braced herself against the weapon's room wall, pinching her fingers over the bridge of her nose. "Is there *any* place we can use for an exit at this moment?" she tried to ask calmly.

"No, sir."

She inhaled loudly. "Fine. Hail December, explain."

"Yes, sir." The lieutenant replied, then, cleared his throat. "*Yes?*"

"We could deploy from the rear escape pods. It will take some time, and we won't be able to carry as much weaponry—but it's an out. Three to a pod, should take about forty minutes for us all to reach the Yard."

"Then what're we standing here discussing it for? Ready yourselves—we leave in five. Scramble!" Grosjean snatched up her helmet and thrust it onto her head. "Minimize weapons for maximum effect, necessities only. Now!"

Grosjean began discarding her own gear, throwing down extra explosives and weapons that were considered too bulky or heavy for the lightweight escape pods. It pained her to do so, but she had no choice. It pained her too that they wasted precious minutes, preventing them from reaching Sandvik and the President as quickly as she'd hoped.

Goddamn those mercs!

She'd like nothing better than to pull the trigger that blew that gunship into the next universe. Oh, how she'd love to witness it.

Harm my ship, will you? Ground us like simpering school children? We'll see about that. Grosjean flung down the last of her explosives, ignoring the flinches and tight expressions of her men as she crudely discarded the volatile items.

~ * ~

When John clapped eyes on his friend, blood drained from his face, drawing it nearly as white as the one before him.

Simon half-stood, propped heavily against a shelving unit with Madds hovering nearby. Both obviously relieved to see John. Following close at John's heels, Elites, Sandvik, and the marines.

"Fucking hell, Simon!" It was Josie who spoke first, barreling forward to inspect him. The bandages wound tightly around his waist were already soaked through and he was on his third saline patch. The painkillers and the antibiotics seemed only to dull Simon's awareness that he considered tossing his next dose. But Madds had lingered nearby, refusing to leave him alone. Her voice crackled slightly as emotion took over. "Are you about to drop dead on us?"

"If you'd let me, but something tells me that I won't be

allowed," Simon managed a smirk.

"Sit." John finally found his voice, gripped his friend's arm and urged him to a seat, a cushioned office chair on wheels.

"Yes, Mother." Simon muttered, allowing himself to be seated.

Madds snorted and stepped away. "You'd sit for him," was all he said. Relief washed over him as he strode over to Sandvik to brief him on everything that had happened since.

"How bad is it?" John asked quietly. He appeared recovered from the shock of seeing his friend so pale. "A gut wound?"

"Mmm. I'll do for now, but I'll need immediate medical as soon as possible. Any ideas on when that will be? No pressure, just wondering." Simon spoke matter-of-factly, trying his best to keep his voice mild. But the beginnings of panic could be heard. Not about dying. "See, I forgot to kiss the wife and kid before leaving." He smiled weakly.

"You're not meant to get injured," Josie accosted him, looking ready to smack him had he not been hurt already. Her eyes were round and wide with worry.

"No fair, I hear you got stuck—that's not meant to happen, either."

"That's different. I wasn't ready for it."

"And you think I stood still and drew a bull's eye to my belly?"

"Will the two of you shut up," John hissed quietly. "Now where is this Jane? How is it she's tracking Ho?"

Simon pulled out Jane and explained to them. "She's latched onto the Yard's security cams—don't worry, she's invisible. We've tracked him leaving Distribution about thirty minutes ago. It's slow going since the droids are hampering them from going the usual routes. They're in control of the communications and still in command of the control room. We've directed the droids and Junkies there as we speak. Minnows is with them, along with a Junkie called Russell—solid man. Now that you're here, I need someone to spring Renna. She's still trapped up in the escape chambers with a group of about thirty and close to fifteen unfriendlies on guard."

"I'll spring her," Josie offered.

Having studied the schematics of the Yard during the quieter moments on her journey, she knew exactly where it was. And judging from the reports, Ho and his men pretty much ignored that area, now that Mwenye was with him. All eyes seemed to be trained on the mainframe.

"I could take a few Elites with me."

"You will not," John warned. "I will. You stay here with Simon."

"With him? Why me?"

"Let me go." Madds approached them. "If they see you two strolling through the Yard, that's like double the pleasure for Ho and his lot. Best not let them get the advantage any more than they already have."

"Makes sense." Josie nodded wholeheartedly. She stamped down the sudden hysteria that rushed into her, hearing John would trundle off on his own—without her—clutched her heart with icy fingers.

"Fine," John replied. "Take two more. Keep out of trouble. Contact me as soon as you've got Renna out via this." He cocked his head to Jane and read off her signature code.

Madds left immediately, dragging two more Elites with him, hopping over the makeshift barricade, formerly the entrance doors. Junkies stood guard there, mixed with a few marines and droids.

Sandvik marched up to John. "Grosjean is fifteen minutes away. Once her team is in, we'll rendezvous at the control room. Instruct the droids to hold fast until then. I'll send her here with a few of hers to assist."

"Grosjean is coming?" Simon mused idly, sounding drugged. "Things should be quite interesting. Josie, I'd hold your tongue if I were you. She's...what's that term you like to use? A bitch on wheels, that's it. Good woman, but hot-tempered..." Simon clamped his mouth shut immediately with a frown, realized he was rambling. He gave John a meaningful look, half apologetic, that said his time was near.

John took note of Simon's expression and cast a worried look to Josie. He turned back to Sandvik with renewed anger.

"Take two of mine as well," John instructed. "I'm counting on you to take back the control room." He turned to McLinney and Kakuta. "I want you two to find a way to the Prosthetics Labs. Once there, make ready the remote surgery and hold steady until we open back a link to Earth. I'll alert you immediately. Once we're back online, open a link directly to my sister—get the techs there to assist and prepped for surgery. I'll send Simon in a moment so she can operate on him. Be quick and be invisible."

"I forgot about that," Simon muttered.

"I want no arguments from you," John growled at Simon. "McLinney and Kakuta will clear the way. I'll have to send Josie with you if you can't walk. But you *are* going."

Josie gaped at him but said nothing.

"And what, leave you here having all the fun?" Simon grinned. "And can you please stop shouting, you're giving me a headache on top of everything else."

"Simon, I'm not pissing about here. Aline can help via the remote surgery link. Just get there!" Real concern and fear was etched on John's face that he leaned in close to Simon. "I'll not see you dead, not if I can help it. Josie will keep you safe," he glanced to her with a pained looked. "I want you both out of this mainframe."

"Fine, fine. But I can get there on my own, thanks. Going with her would only kill me further. Just give me a moment, will you. Let me catch my breath some." Simon sighed, sobering slightly, then tugged John's sleeve and spoke quietly. "I've informed Ox that Ho is after the cloning technology. He's been trying to create a virus that once—should Mwenye fail and talk—the files are accessed, will target that alone and destroy it. Unfortunately, it will leave control of the droids wide open."

"There's not much we can do about that, right now." John glanced about the room with a scowl.

Too many people stood shuffling, uncertainly awaiting instructions, too many civilians.

John looked to Kakuta. "Get these people out of here. Anyone that's not military—out. Escort them to a safe point. Then straight to the Labs."

"Where did all this blood come from?" Margeaux spoke for the first time. Her voice sounded a bit strained and thin. She stood with her Elite escort, tentatively looking at the floor.

Simon turned to face her. He seemed to need some focusing to see her clearly. "Your father's men. They're in the storeroom above us if you'd like to pay your respects. Some might still be alive to hear you."

"I think not, thank you. Once my father comes here, you'll be sorry."

"I think not."

"You're going to die just like those you killed. My father will see to it."

"Just shut up," Josie marched up to her. "No one wants to hear how superior your daddy is to the rest of us. He's a twisted, murdering bastard because his genetics have been screwed over and—"

"Josie," John warned. There were too many ears, wide open and listening. "Sandvik, take your men and wait at the rendezvous. The rest of you stand guard at the door. No one who's not supposed to be here is allowed in. Understood? Ox, hold fast."

"As soon as Grosjean comes, I'll send her here." Sandvik gathered his men together. "Good luck," he inclined his head to John with some reluctance, then left, his men falling in behind him.

The room cleared, leaving just John, Josie, Simon, Margeaux, Ox, and the bland featured Elite, a man called Parker. Three Junkies and two droids manned the entrance, the marines having joined Sandvik. As a courtesy to the others, Parker sidled to one side and joined those at the door. But he faced inwards, watching the girl.

"Am I missing something here?" Simon asked quietly.

"A great deal." John moved closer, poked gingerly at Simon's midsection, sniffing the wound. Simon grunted with a wince, his shirt was rolled up and tucked up around his chest. "I'll tell you in a minute. Let's change this dressing, it's sodden."

Simon sighed. "You just love to make me suffer. Josie, hold this. Do not let it out of your sight." He handed her Jane, then reclined as John began cutting away his bandages, shifting his body so his left side was slightly raised.

Simon groaned in pain and squeezed his eyes shut. "If it pings," he continued, nodding towards Jane, "it means Ho has reached the outer doors. We'll probably have the advantage in numbers, but he has Mwenye. I'd rather he didn't get hurt, even if he is a tight-ass—Ah, careful!" Simon glowered at his friend. "You've the delicacy of a bull in a china shop!"

"Let me do it, for Christ sakes." Josie pushed John away. "You go deal with what you need to deal with over there." She waved him away, squatting next to Simon.

His wound looked hideous. It was about two inches wide, gaping open to reveal pink muscle tissue. Further in, it was dark and rank with thick blood and fecal matter. Blood oozed slowly. The outer rim was charred, curling the skin away like a gnarled tree root. The antiseptic skin-sealer had slipped away from too much blood getting under it. It slopped to one side like a discarded, wet plastic bag. She pinched it away and let it drop heavily to the floor. Beside her, a box of medical supplies, some familiar to her, others not so familiar.

"You'll have to talk me through this, as you've more experience with things like this," she said as she sprayed her hands with disinfectant.

"Well, then," he grimaced. "I think you'd better deal with the back end first. Because I don't think I can keep this position for much longer."

"The back? It's gone through?" Horror etched her face. "Jesus..." she couldn't finish.

Sucking in a breath, she nudged him gently so he turned, and gasped. The exit wound was twice as large and looked as if it was torn to shreds. If there was any skin there, if it was once part a back, she couldn't tell. And a section of an intestine poked through, pinky-grey and peppered with clots of blood. She paled, but held fast.

Ignoring the smells, the blood and stench, Josie decided to quietly recount all the events since Simon had left to come to the Yard. Her kidnap, James the Rogue, Iceland, the fight with Ho, the revelations about her past—Ho's past—everything. Speaking of it helped to steady her mind and the task at hand, pausing only momentarily to listen to Simon's instructions. It helped. Soon, the horror before her eyes no longer affected her.

Simon listened with care, absorbing every word as if his life depended on it. The obvious pain was still there, like a gigantic pressure resting upon him. But listening to Josie now, he nodded and breathed easier, seemingly managing his pain.

Working as quickly as she dared, following Simon's

instructions, she sanitized the area once more and sprayed more skin-sealer as he grunted in pain. Then she applied a pressure bandage and wrapped him tightly, trying her best to avoid the injury at the front as she did so. Once his back had been dealt with, she repeated the process at his stomach.

The moment she finished, Simon exhaled loudly and struggled back to a sitting position. He smiled weakly as he leaned forward. The pressure from reclining had him in excruciating pain and waves of dizziness threatened to cloud over him. The pain had weakened him further that he gasped for breath and was drenched in sweat.

"Hand me another patch, that one with the blue on it."

Josie handed him a saline patch with bloodied fingers, surprised how steady her hands had been. If she didn't know any better, she would've thought she was a veteran combat medic. Even the blood on her hands didn't bother her. It was, after all, Simon.

"Here, these I know." She offered him two painkillers. He made a face, almost waved them away but caught the look on her face. Her expression was of sheer concern and affection. "I'll get you some water."

"No…no. Bad idea."

"Why? You need them."

"I've a hole in my gut, remember. Use the syringe instead—stick me in the arm. It'll work faster."

"Oh, right. You mean I get to stick you?" Josie tried to sound pleased. When she drew out the syringe pre-filled with painkillers, she hesitated. She couldn't do it. "I…" she said and looked up at him blinking. "You'd better do it."

"Josie, you disappoint me. I thought you'd be first in line for a chance to stick me with a needle. Does this mean you're in danger of being nice to me?"

Taking the pressure syringe from her, he fumbled as he placed it over his arm. Josie watched, gritting her teeth, thinking a two-year old could've pulled the trigger easier. Simon was weakened to the point that even that had become an effort. Finally, he pulled the trigger, it hissed and ejected its solution. With a groan, he slumped back, breaking out in a fresh batch of cold sweat.

The thought of hurting him further by injecting him tore at

Josie's heart. Even watching him struggle with the syringe had her swallowing hard.

"There, see. You did it much better than I would've. You know how bad my aim is." She shrugged, more to hide the embarrassment. "I might've stuck you in your eye instead. I'll get you good and proper when you're up and running again. Bad sport of me to do it when you're already down." She laughed nervously, stopping abruptly, fussing unnecessarily with the bandages.

Simon reached out and patted her arm, his fingers felt cold. He didn't actually say it, nor did Josie expect him to, but it was a good enough substitute for a thank you. Josie smirked back. She really wanted to wrap her arms around him and comfort him but decided the horror of the act would kill him for sure.

"By the way, you look paler than I probably do," Simon grinned and flicked his eyes to her shoulder. "Hurt much?"

"My neck's stiff as a dick and my shoulder aches constantly. I get light-headed now and again, but that's probably from the space travel."

"No it's not. You just can't help it. Nothing's in there, so…"

"Ha-ha. I hurt, I ache, and I'm pissed off. Other than that, I've been better."

"Yeah. Me too."

She got up and flexed her limbs. Turning, she met Margeaux's cool stare and unreadable expression.

Beyond that, John stood watching them.

She didn't doubt that Margeaux had heard every single word she'd uttered to Simon. Something in the girl's eyes glittered with new knowledge, new understanding.

"Here," John called out with a bottle of water in his hand, but his eyes were still on the back of Margeaux's head. "Wash some of the blood off."

Josie walked past the girl, took the offered water and rinsed her hands as best she could. "It looks really bad, John," she whispered to him.

"I know." He stroked her arm in comfort. "You did good."

"Do you think he'll make—"

"Shh-shh," he shook his head to silence her. "Simon is a strong man. His will to survive is even stronger."

"He can't die on us."

"Death comes to every one."

"I know, but still. Simon…"

"You love him just as much as you love me, I know."

"I do not," she muttered quickly and spared Simon a look, ignoring the fact that Margeaux still watched her. Simon could be seen steadying himself with deep, controlled breaths, his eyes closed. "But he's grown on me."

John smiled, then, took a small breath as he looked at his friend with a pained expression.

He turned to face Josie. "I don't care what he says, you have to escort him to the labs. You know the way. It should take you less than ten minutes."

"John, that's madness. I can't fend off an army on my own. He can barely raise his arms to hold a fucking syringe—"

"You were ready and willing to free Renna," John scolded her with a glower.

"Yeah, with a bunch of Elites as backup. But he's too weak to fight."

"He would if you were there. And by being there, you'll keep him alive—keep him going—long enough for Aline to get to him. Please, do this? For me? I need to be here. You know he cares for you more than he cares for himself."

Flustered with emotions, Josie scrubbed a hand through her hair. "Then Margeaux and Parker are with me. I'm not leaving that girl alone with you. She's watching you with murder in her eyes."

"As she was watching you just now. Still is. You think I'll let you take her with you? Ho needs to see her."

"Fine. I'll give Simon five minutes to catch himself, then make ready." Josie sucked in a breath and cleared her mind.

Chaos flooded her with wild thoughts about leaving John alone. Panic, sheer panic, numbed her limbs and her injured shoulder flared with pain. She willed herself to calm down by reminding herself that John probably felt the same way. And both of them couldn't afford turn into a puddle of mess at the same time.

"Right. Okay. How is Ox coming along?" she took a steadying breath.

"Ox is running into trouble. It's tricky work, what he's

doing. Mwenye's a bloody magician. He may have rigged it so that he alone can work it, but Ox is talking about layers and sub-layers," John shook his head in incomprehension. "I think he's about to have an orgasm in praise of Mwenye's genius."

Josie craned her neck to stare at the large man hunched over the controls. His head rocked from side to side and he muttered appreciatively over something. It sounded a lot like "wicked" but she couldn't be sure.

"Any plans for when Ho gets here?" she asked.

"Hold him here for as long as possible until we get more reinforcements or find a way to kill him." John shrugged. "Either way, he will be stopped."

"You think using Margeaux will loosen his mind up a bit? You think it'll work?"

"He cares for her. If I'm here to make the threat, he'll believe it more. He may reconsider; he may not. It's a risk. But we've no other cards to hold. We need to stall, wait for Grosjean to come."

Jane pinged, causing Josie to jump with a yelp.

"Fuck!" she managed to croak out. "Is he here? Already?"

"In position, now." John had already grabbed her by the arm and swept her across the room, taking position behind a large console.

Parker had crossed the room swiftly, gripping Margeaux by the scruff of her neck and retreating with them to the side near some shelves. The girl's eyes glittered with excitement, her head practically swiveling around her.

Simon struggled and found he was unable to stand without being washed over with dizziness, so he slumped back down shaking his head. Resigned, he dug in his heels and wheeled himself and the chair until he was closer to Ox.

His appointment with Aline would have to wait for now. They had no plan whatsoever, but he reasoned that if he were to die, he might as well make it look as if he went down fighting—if only he could see straight and his hands weren't so cold.

~ * ~

Michael Ho was livid with fury.

Mwenye had tried to run. Twice, Ho had to use brute force

to subdue him. Twice, Ho had gotten a fist in return to his own face. Now, nose bloodied, his lip cut, he was in no mood to show civility any longer.

The delays he could live with, but the presence of so many droids disturbed him. He was aware of the two deep-space war cruisers, but not overly worried over them. Once he had control over the mainframe, all the droids were his and his alone.

And the cloning technology would be his. For him alone! He would be unstoppable.

But the droids—so many of them—that meant someone controlled them from the mainframe. That meant his mercenaries were no longer in charge there. He cursed. He couldn't depend on anyone to do anything right!

When he turned the corner and saw the destruction in the anteroom to the mainframe, his heart skipped a beat. A split second of hesitation faltered his movements. He tightened his grip on Mwenye, wedging his pulse gun firmly under the governor's throat.

The three Junkies barked out orders for Ho to halt—he ignored them.
What would they do? Shoot him while he had Mwenye's life in his hands? Junkies were loyal, but they were not stupid. If anything, they were stupid because of their loyalty.

Without a word, Ho merely pressed the pulse gun firmly to Mwenye's throat. He allowed himself a wide smile and ignored the sting of pain it caused his split lip. The droids shifted—assessing the situation and running probabilities in nanoseconds. They wouldn't shoot unless ordered to, nor would they so long as their Governor was under direct threat. Droids, dependable as ever...

"You shoot, I shoot," Ho called out in a singsong tone, never once stopping as they picked their way over the wreckage.

"Do as he says," Mwenye instructed calmly. He too sported a bloody nose and his left eye puffily squeezed shut by a brilliant bruise.

"I've more men behind me. You cannot win." Ho spared a moment to wonder what kept them. "So stand aside and let me through."

"Let him pass," Simon called out from inside the mainframe. "Let's get this thing over with already."

"Simon," Ho beamed back. "What a pleasant—" His eyes darted to John, then Josie.

They stood together, their stance almost identical, ready.

"Surprise," Josie called out. Her krima, already released from its holster, slid into her hand. "I'm still alive and ready to kick your ass."

A struggle in the corner, to Josie's left, caught Ho's attention. He froze as his eyes shifted to see.

Margeaux wriggled and twisted in Parker's grip. He had the good sense to clamp a hand firmly over her mouth.

"What is she doing here?" The crack in his composure at seeing his daughter seemed to catch him by surprise. It was too late to pretend he didn't care. Instead, he snarled and aimed his fury at Josie. "*You* brought her here!" Immediately he cackled in laughter. "You think you can work a trade? Don't be ridiculous!"

"I can play just as nasty as you. After all, we basically come from the same tree, do we not?" Josie smiled, taking a step closer. "Bring her here, Parker."

If John was displeased, he chose not to show it. He exchanged a look with Simon, who nodded a fraction then nudged Ox.

Ho looked from Josie to Margeaux, rapidly. He was shocked, yes. Scared? Maybe. The sudden pang of fear he felt when he saw his daughter rattled him. He cared for Margeaux a great deal, she was, after all his only daughter. His. But, he reasoned again, she knew the risks, the dangers—she understood. She knew. But still. To see her here, right now, when he'd thought she was safe and secure in the Citadel. It...upset him.

And this wasn't how the plan was supposed to go!

A setback. A mere setback, he told himself. He stared hard at his daughter. She looked back at him with relief and confusion, and some thing else...accusation.

~ * ~

"What's the matter, Ho?" Josie taunted him with a scathing tone, watching him closely. "Afraid?"

"Let her go. She is no longer a player. Her role is done. You should not have brought her here."

"Oh, how touching, how you care so much about her, isn't

it?" Josie flicked her eyes to the girl.

Margeaux's eyes were riveted on her father. Reaching out, Josie yanked her by the back of her collar and dragged her closer, companionably wrapping an arm around the skinny neck. Josie's arm tightened in a vice-like grip, a warning to make sure Margeaux knew that to run was useless. The krima, hidden in the folds of clothing and their bodies, was pressed into the girl's back.

"Yet, you can cut her just as easily." Josie spoke with a mocking tone. "Bet you didn't expect him to do that, did you?" and nudged the girl with a smile. "Oh, wait, I forgot. It was your idea that he cut you. What's wrong with you, girl? And what kind of father would *actually* do it? Surely, not a real father, who's supposed to love and care for his only daughter. No matter what, a real father would never listen to any suggestion as horrible as that. Hurting her, cutting her so viciously unless...he's insane, mentally unbalanced, and he just can't help himself. Just like his daughter, two peas in a pod. How sweet."

Silence.

"I know you heard every word," Josie whispered coldly into Margeaux's ears. "You know all about your genetics, your history. Look around you, look at this madness. You helped cause this and it has to stop. Tell me you don't give a damn. Tell me what you feel when you see him."

"It's a lie!" Margeaux spat out, her body rigid, breathing hard. "It's all lies! You would say anything now to save this stupid man and his stupid station."

Margeaux wriggled angrily in Josie's arms, snapping a leg backwards to kick her shins. Josie dodged neatly away, tightening the grip around the girl's neck. Margeaux jabbed out her elbow, caught Josie square in the gut. Josie grunted and buckled slightly, gritting her teeth. Margeaux's other hand swung wide, causing her body to twist, she caught Josie's injured shoulder and dug her fingers in. With a yell of pain, Josie knocked the hand away with her right hand. Still holding the krima, as Josie's hand retracted, she smacked Margeaux solidly across the face with the back of her hand.

The desire to engage the krima and slash Margeaux's angry red face was great. Instead, Josie snarled in controlled rage and gripped the girl even harder.

The scuffle ended as quickly as it started, and Margeaux was back in her headlock; seething with such fury that spittle flew from her mouth as she snorted and grunted with anger. She made a high-pitched growl that sounded like a whine of utter frustration heard only in young children—a sound Josie heard with delirious happiness.

John stepped forward, shifting himself so he stood before them. "Release the Governor and we will return your daughter to you."

Ho laughed out again. "Such ridiculous promises. Do you really expect me to believe that?"

"Believe what you want, the choice is yours." John lowered his head some more, changing the angle with which he looked at Ho. "Either way, you will lose."

"It's all lies!" Margeaux persisted, her voice high and angry. "They want me to believe that we're abominations! Genetic freaks! Descended from a clone!"

Ho snapped his head to stare at his daughter, a half-grin on his head, frozen. He blinked but said nothing. Mwenye struggled once in his grip.

"Enough of this bartering!" Mwenye said. "It's getting us nowhere. You want what's in my head, don't you? No one else needs to get hurt. If you want it, then release me and I'll give it to you. You have my word." He looked to Simon. "Too many have died—I won't have any more dead because of me."

Ox shifted slightly, casually glancing at Simon. With an imperceptible nod in return Simon eased back to regard Ho. "Ox, stand aside for the Governor."

Mwenye glanced at John. "I'm sorry, sir."

"Just like that?" Furious, Josie looked at Mwenye. "You can't be serious? You're meant to protect that code!"

John inclined his head. "This is not your fault, Governor. But I'm afraid the girl must stay with us now that the situation has changed."

"I'm sorry," Mwenye repeated.

"The Governor is right. Too many have died already." John's tone rang with finality. With that, he yanked Margeaux from his wife's grasp and curled his hand around the back of her neck. It was done so quick, so unexpectedly, that both Josie and Margeaux gasped in surprise.

"The station is yours, Ho. Allow us clear passage out of here, or I *will* hurt her. You know I will. And then I'm coming after you," John continued in a low voice, directing his glacial stare at Ho, already walking purposely towards him. He held no weapon, just Margeaux's neck. Her eyes were round like balls, staring out with disbelief, her breathing tight to suggest the pain he inflicted on her was excruciating.

"I will kill you all if you do not release her." Ho hissed in anger.

"No you won't. You want your daughter alive, but you want the access codes more. It's in your nature to want what you cannot have. You crave it because you and Fern are one and the same."

Ho blinked, distracted. "Fern…?"

Josie followed John's lead, trailing behind him, partially hidden. Disbelief still in her eyes at what Mwenye was doing. How did the plan shift so unexpectedly?

As they neared the console, Josie snagged the back of Simon's chair and pushed him before her. She heard him mutter something weakly—barely hearing.

"You *believe* that nonsense?" Ho laughed again. It sounded pitifully deranged. "You actually believe that drivel? It's preposterous!"

"It's the truth, and you know it." Josie called out from behind John. "I saw the look in your eyes. Didn't it make you feel ill? It did me."

Ho shook his head, inching closer to Mwenye who now sat heavily in the chair once occupied by Ox. He shoved the pulse gun to Mwenye's ear, causing him to flinch. "The codes, Governor. Now."

Mwenye made a great show of fussing over the console, tapping keys and opening files with methodical care.

John walked a wide arc around Ho with Margeaux pointedly placed before him like a shield. Parker and Ox fell into step. By the doorway, Junkies and droids had their weapons trained onto Ho, shifting and angling themselves—ready.

"Father," Margeaux sounded offended, and in mortal pain. "Make him release me."

"He will not hurt you." Ho scoffed in distraction. His eyes were riveted to what Mwenye did. "So long as I hold a weapon to this one's head, you are safe."

"He *is* hurting me, Father. My head has gone...numb." She seemed sluggishly immobile, as if her spine was made of liquid, her limbs like jelly as they flopped uselessly at her sides. "Make him stop. I can't feel my...my legs..."

Ho spared his daughter one look. "Silence. I will fetch you later. Do you realize how close I am? All that we've worked for, it is here, now...it is *this* close."

Margeaux gasped. "Father!"

"He doesn't care for you," John crooned softly in her ear, a wicked smile curling his lips. He batted his dark eyes, making him look as innocent as the devil. "After all you've done for him, all you've been through. He cares not."

"Do you even realize what I have, right here, at my fingertips? The knowledge and genius of unfathomable research and uncharted science! To mould together man and machine beyond anything ever tried before? Do you even know what that means?"

"Abomination," Josie enunciated with care.

"No!" Ho snapped back. "Progress. The elimination of disease and death, the insurance that man will live forever!"

A loud disturbance could be heard in the anteroom. Gunfire and shouts erupted like some random street riot. Ox and Parker shifted—eager to join in. Ho cocked a head gleefully in the direction of the noise.

"My men are here," he grinned. "Hurry up!" He jabbed the gun into Mwenye's ear again.

Mwenye inhaled deeply. "It takes time. If it's not done carefully, everything will be lost. The sequence must not be broken."

Mwenye's hands may have been steady, but his mind jumped erratically with confusion. Someone had tampered with his files—it was expected. He would've risked a look at Ox, but feared that would only alert Ho that something was amiss. His only choice was to delay things. The actual sequence-code was still in place, but from what he could see, there'd been a half-completed effort to sabotage the cloning information with a virus. But the droids were wide open for take-over. If he could, without being caught, finish the job then things would swing into their favour. It was a delay, not a long one, but a delay all the same. He had to work quickly.

"Something is wrong," Mwenye said, hoping he sounded confused. "Someone has been tampering with my files."

"What do you mean?" Ho directed a cold look to Simon.

"I mean that maybe your men have done something to it. It will take longer than I expected."

"But you can retrieve the commands, can you not?"

"Of course, I can!" Now Mwenye sounded genuinely offended.

"Father, please. Make him release me." Margeaux's voice sounded thin and weak.

John, with Margeaux before him, had now rounded Ho completely. Gunfire still came from the doorway.

"Quiet, girl. I will not have any—"

A low rumble vibrated the room like an earthquake. Ho nearly lost his balance, as did most everyone else. An odd silence followed, as everyone stared questioningly at each other. Like deer in the forest, they paused in the face of imminent danger to listen with frozen bodies, ears rigid with strain, eyes large and alert, noses flared to catch the scent of danger.

"What...?" Josie couldn't finish. Her hand gripped the back of Simon's chair. The soles of her booted feet tickled by the vibrations—her toes instinctively clenched.

"Something quite big," Ox muttered quietly beside her and put a large, steadying hand on her shoulder. "Very, very big."

"Let's hope it's not your gunship, Ho." John curled a smile. "If it is, you're trapped on this piece of floating metal. But, no worries, you'll be immortal soon."

"True enough. It will all be irrelevant once the technology is available to me." Ho waved an uncaring hand. "The droids will be under my control very soon to protect this station from you and whatever army you send my way. I am unstoppable. The gunship has served its purpose, in any case."

"As your daughter has? Call off your men outside so we can leave unhindered."

"You cannot leave here."

"Watch me."

"You cannot leave." Ho ground the gun into Mwenye's ear, heard him grunt.

"It's a stalemate, Ho." Simon called weakly. "Or have you not noticed? If one of us doesn't give an inch, we'll be here forever. Once the codes are unlocked, the Governor is no longer needed and you can kill him at will. Have you not noticed that he understands this and has resigned himself to it already? But we'll have the upper hand by holding your daughter. And trust me, I will not hesitate in killing either of you! Now, something blew up out there—could be yours, could be ours. Aren't you just dying to find out? I certainly am."

If Ho cared, he didn't show it. All he wanted, all his adult life, was what was before him. He was this close. He had the research—he just needed the facility and the information for the cell-fusion cloning. And everything he needed was all right here, in this very space station. Just a few more minutes and everything would be his. All his.

It didn't matter if his gunship was destroyed, or if it was the Lancaster warships. Nor did it matter if they held Margeaux, they wouldn't hurt her. They were not barbarians; she would be safe. He was so close...just a few more minutes and all he'd every wanted would be his.

Yes, all his.

Twenty Six

Just before Ho's gunship exploded into a hundred million pieces of phosphorescent light, it glowed brightly then undulated like a belly dancer.

The gunnery sergeant on board the *Renwick* paused briefly with his finger poised over the holo-trigger, frowning. In *The Sloop*, its sergeant opened his eyes wide, thinking that the gunship looked like those old stories of Jack-O Lantern's. But whatever the cause, both agreed later among their friends over some space-brew beer, that something massive within the ship ignited in that split second with the brightness of a hundred billion candles. Night had turned to day it would've seemed, in that moment, far out in the depths of space.

No sound could be heard, unless you were on board the gunship itself. But the shockwaves that followed rocked both deep-space warships and their inhabitants like driftwood in a vast ocean.

From the stingy little cockpit window of her escape pod, Captain Grosjean gaped in awe. The magnitude of the blast was enough to suck small satellites in its wake. A tiny escape pod, puttering along with all its might across space wouldn't stand a chance.

Having deployed her team before her, she and two lieutenants brought up the rear. Grosjean rammed her controls to full throttle, heard the small engine whine in protest, and screamed out orders for her passengers to hold fast.

While the gunship's gravitational mass wasn't big enough to cause the explosion to turn into an implosion, it was still big enough to disrupt space like a giant washing machine. If they didn't reach the Scrap Yard's docking bay before the shockwaves hit them, they'd be catapulted into the far reaches of space—or disintegrated from the impact.

They were literally on the outskirts, with less than a minute before they reached the Yard. When the blast hit, it was like being sideswiped by a train. Grosjean and her lieutenants lurched sideways in the opposite direction. The small craft rocked and juddered like mad, the engine hissed and crackled, desperately trying to move forward. Grosjean tried her best to ride out the storm by angling and swerving to keep on course. She snapped out her arms and braced them against the pod's frame.

Something ripped away from the outer shell with a tearing noise. One of the lieutenants made a desperate sound; he flailed helplessly but could do nothing, wedged like a piece of luggage in the back seat.

"Bay doors within range!" Grosjean yelled. "Come on, just a little further…" She punched the thrusters, the controls blinked rapidly to indicate overload.

"Within range for what?" her other lieutenant shouted back with something like rampant panic pitching his voice high. Grosjean's reckless reputation was known throughout the known space system.

Ignoring him, Grosjean spared a moment to worry over the fact that they might not reach the Yard in time. If she were to die as collateral damage, it sure as hell wouldn't be like this, flicked helplessly out into space in a puny rowboat!

"*Grapples,*" she roared out and slammed her palm over the release button for the grappling ropes.

"Grap—It'll rip us from the inside out!" the lieutenant shouted back with horror.

"Then secure your helmet, engage tanks, be ready to eject and pray to whichever god will listen!"

The grappling ropes shot out like two projectiles, making a hacking sound they spiraled towards the docking bay doors and embedded within seconds. The small craft snapped forward with a horrendous jerk. Grosjean shrieked out a snarl, gripped her arms tightly around her chest, the seat harness dug into her.

Within moments, the outer shell of the craft ripped away, slopping off like excess water—metal and glass disintegrating. It rocked and jerked sideways, the shockwaves pulling it one direction, the grapple tugging it the next.

The craft was nothing but a stump with gnarled bits of the metal framework around it. The base from where the grappling ropes were connected was still intact. Designed to pull the craft the moment they were deployed, they would slowly start to tow. Used generally for piggybacking or being towed alongside larger crafts, it wasn't designed to withstand the pressures and speeds of high velocity shockwaves from explosions. The central structure was the strongest part of the craft, fused together to the main chassis were the seats and controls, now useless, save for the automatic reeling mechanism below their seats. The seats itself could eject manually, but to do so now would cause them to be sucked straight out into open space.

They'd have to ride it out, exposed as they were like literal sitting ducks in open space, until the shockwaves subsided.

Grosjean judged it to be another thirty seconds before space righted itself and returned to normal. She'd once experienced the destruction of a deep-space war cruiser. That had taken exactly two minutes and forty seconds from the moment it exploded until the last of the shockwaves abated. All that was left of the cruiser was a small piece of metal, wrangled and twisted beyond recognition. The rest of it simply evaporated, its crew included.

Her ears almost popped but finally, with a sort of sharp jolt, it was over. They were spared the shower of debris, but she felt windblown and charred all the same.

She turned to look at her lieutenants. They appeared to be alive; it was hard to tell with their visors down.

"Are we still together?"

One nodded, the other lifted a hand somewhat reluctantly.

"Very good." Grosjean grinned widely behind her visor then whooped loudly, causing the lieutenants to jump. She hadn't had this much fun in quite some time. "Prepare to eject, on my mark!"

~ * ~

I wasn't sure if we'd manage to get away as well as stop Ho at the same time. From the look of it, John seemed quite determined to get the hell out and forget about Ho altogether. But I knew him better than that. If anything, he wanted us safe and away from danger, just so he could go back and finish the job he'd come here to do.

I looked desperately down at Simon; he slouched lopsidedly in his seat. The top of his head bobbed as I slowly pushed the chair as we inched along to keep time with John. I couldn't see his face, but I reasoned it must be even paler than before. He needed to get to the Labs—urgently. I began to panic, thinking that may never happen.

Ho spoke like a maniac—practically blathering on and on like a very mad, mad scientist. The battle sounds from the anteroom could still be heard, not as urgently as before. The Junkies shouted directives for the other side to stand down, they responded with gunfire.

Whatever John had done to Margeaux, rendered her insensible. He'd probably latched those clever fingers of his onto some pressure points at her neck. She looked like the walking dead. I couldn't say it gave me pleasure to see, but like her father, she wouldn't shut up. Pleading and whining for Ho like a baby. It had become distracting and annoying. However, a small, mutinous part of me felt pity and concern for her. I wanted to tell John to stop hurting her, whatever it was that he was doing.

Mwenye still sat hunched over the console, it looked like he was biding for time. Or maybe, just scared shitless and bumbling about. Simon said something to Ho, goading him. Ho wasn't really listening.

"We are walking out of this room. Order your men not to shoot or your daughter gets harmed," John said.

He'd already shifted, back towards the door. I moved automatically with him, covering his side. Ox and Parker now stood by the door, their weapons directed into the anteroom.

"Stay where you are!" Ho snapped out. "No one is leaving this place until I say so."

If I didn't know any better, I'd say he was torn between his daughter and the prize at hand.

It happened very quickly. While Ho busily yelled at us, Mwenye stood up abruptly and slammed his fist into Ho's face. Ho staggered back in shock. Mwenye reared up his large body and did something like a jump-kick, straight into Ho's midsection. John flung Margeaux to me—I caught her automatically, wrapping my arms around her tightly. She grunted and her knees buckled and she fell like dead weight in my arms.

John launched himself at Ho, who'd just righted himself with bloody murder in his eyes, his attention split between Mwenye and John. He dived away like a nimble monkey. From the corner of my eyes, I saw Ox and Parker dive into the anteroom, guns blazing.

"Get him out of here, now!" John yelled at me with fire in his eyes. "Go!"

"I won't be able to get past the anteroom!"

"Just go!"

With a growl, I turned. Clutching Margeaux around the waist, half-hoisting her like a sack, I pushed Simon's chair and barreled myself to the door, keeping my head low. From the anteroom, desperate gunfire and yells could be heard. I caught sight of Ox on the floor, bracing himself on his knees, shooting at something. He grinned like a fool.

Looking back, I saw John and Mwenye, both hopping over an upturned desk in pursuit of Ho. They could probably run circles all over the mainframe room until they dropped down dead from exhaustion. There was nowhere to hide, just run.

Parker shouted something, he looked right at me, eyes wide with urgency. Trying to focus, I barely caught him saying *"Down!"* before he dove straight towards us. He caught Margeaux and me, pushed us down back into the mainframe. Still airborne before we crashed onto the floor spread-eagled, I saw Simon jerk himself sideways with a grunt.

Lights flashed brilliantly, something boomed into my ears. My world shook violently; the injury to my shoulder screamed with blinding pain, even my teeth ached. I'd barely felt the ground come crashing under me—barely saw anything around me. Parker lay like a ton of bricks upon me, forcing the air in my lungs to come gushing out.

The explosion blasted through the already wrecked anteroom. Hot, blistering air rushed out. For a moment, I forgot where I was, only that I was alive and on the ground. Margeaux wriggled beside me, screaming—shrill and high—at the top of her lungs. It brought me to my senses. I shook her roughly hoping she'd stop—it made it worse. She cowered in a fetal position, practically losing her mind by the sounds of it.

"Josie!" I heard the panicked shout. John.

"I'm fine!" I yelled back, uncertain which direction he was.

Parker hiccupped in spasms beside me. Something quite long and metallic stuck out from his back and parts of his clothing smoldered.

"I'm fine," I repeated. Acrid smoke filled my eyes, stinging them viciously. Blinking rapidly to remove the sting, I coughed and spat out grit.

Scrambling to my feet, I looked wildly about. John crouched low on the floor, about thirty feet away, frozen beside a table. His eyes were riveted to mine. I nodded back. He broke away and turned to seek Ho again. Mwenye had just emerged from behind a cabinet and spared John a look before he resumed his search for Ho. Ho was nowhere to be found, even though I knew he couldn't have left the room.

Simon! I turned frantically, found him still sitting, facing me with a grim look. He'd turned his chair at the last moment, the back of it taking most of the impact. It too was smoldering like Parker's back.

"What happened?"

"Some idiot launched a regular explosive in a contained area, that's what happened," Simon replied with a grimace. His voice sounded weaker—resigned.

"Ox?" I called out. No reply. "Ox!"

I turned back to Parker, he groaned, his eyes rolled up in his head.

"You can't save him," Simon spoke through gritted teeth. "Shut the girl up and let's move it. I feel like a sitting duck."

"Oh God!" I nearly wailed.

Parker was dying before my eyes—I had to do something, anything. Reaching out, I touched his face. He seemed oblivious to my presence. His whole body hitched and jerked, his breathing erratic and strained, his face red with exertion. Blood kept pouring out of his mouth and nose as he gagged. The projectile, the leg of a metal chair by the looks of it, had pierced him from the back into the lungs. To pull it out would kill him for sure, to leave it, the same. In desperation, I slammed my fists repeatedly into the floor and yelled. Why did the idiot have to save my life? Why did he jump before us?

I didn't even know what to do. Watching the man die before me, helpless to save him, helpless to even ease his pain. Instead, I blindly reacted. Grabbing the still screaming Margeaux, I shoved her face to Parker's and screamed down at her to watch. Watch, while he died. Watch what madness she and her father had created, had caused. Just watch...

I shook her as violently as she trembled. I could see that her eyes were large and round, staring with manic desperation at Parker. And still I shouted to her to watch him.

If Parker knew we were there, he could never tell me, but when he died at last, it was like a release. His face relaxed and his body slumped. Did he know what was happening? I would never know. I didn't even know myself. Why did I drag Margeaux to make her watch him die? I probably would still question myself for years to come.

But at last, she stopped screaming.

"Josie." Simon spoke to me, softly. "Come, we must go." He looked at me with a strange look and offered me his hand.

I nodded, not even aware that tears ran freely down my cheeks until I rubbed my face in agitation. I stared at my wet hands for a moment; they were covered with dirt and blood. With effort, I dragged Margeaux, stood, and looked back to seek out John. I saw the top of his head darting around a shelving unit. Pushing the chair and Margeaux, I bounded into the smoking anteroom.

Ox lay unconscious, two Junkies were dead and ripped apart. The droids were barely functional and one Junkie coughed amid the smoke—alive but bleeding from his head. He appeared dazed and incoherent. Across the room, I couldn't tell if what I saw were dead bodies or a scattering of body parts. The roasting stench was enough to have me swallowing hard. It looked like Ho's men were all dead. I heard Simon repeatedly telling me to keep going. Not to stop, just keep going.

Behind me, John shouted. He said something to Mwenye. Mwenye replied. Ho could be heard laughing. I faltered in my steps, wanting to stay behind. But Simon needed me more. Simon, I had to help. I couldn't with Parker, but I could—hopefully—with Simon.

Margeaux now simply fell into step, walking beside me. I held her arm, more to guide her through the many twists and turns that were to come. She didn't say a word. A quick glance showed me a girl that was pale, her hair disheveled and uncharacteristically unkempt. She blinked automatically, her breathing tight and strained causing her thin shoulders to rise high and fall low. Something inside me tugged with pain at the sight of her. I felt horrible at what I'd done to her—what I'd been doing to her. I treated her no better than her own father had. He at least loved her. I didn't. I wasn't even sure if I could. But—I had to admit—I did care.

Pushing Margeaux out of my mind for the moment, I looked down at Simon and pushed his chair forward with determination. Right now, Simon came first.

We had to use alternative routes. Thankfully, the Prosthetic Labs were on the same level. I couldn't imagine having to haul Simon up stairs as well as drag Margeaux along.

"Josie…" Simon spoke, he sounded winded and far away. "Tell Trudi that—"

"Tell her yourself," I snapped back. What was he trying to say? I refused to hear it. I didn't want to hear it.

"Listen to me. I may not be able to—"

"I don't care! You are and whatever you have to say, you'll say it to her in person. I'm not going to pass along some mushy-fuck to her. Don't be disgusting." I heard a catch in my voice and swallowed. Simon wasn't allowed to die!

"I might not be able to, given the current circumstances," Simon replied mildly. "I feel myself…slipping."

"Just…shut up!" I did whimper then, so I clamped my teeth together, glad he couldn't see my face. My mind filled with images of John, Margeaux, all the dead…I shook my head to clear it and ordered myself to focus. I couldn't bear the thought of losing Simon, not right now.

"Josie, please listen to—"

"Look, you and I don't do mushy, okay? Haven't you gotten that through your head yet?"

You can't die on me, please. Don't make me carry messages

to Trudi, or Yumi. I can't do that! I won't do it. How can I? What could I possibly say to Trudi? How do I say it? Or your daughter... What the fuck am I going to say to her? Don't make me do that—don't, don't, don't!

I refused to think it, even though I could sense the cold clutches of death pulling at him.

"Josie." He sounded as if he were grinning. "You're really one of a kind, but I must ask you this one favor. Please."

Looking backwards nervously, straining my ears for sounds, I wheeled him furiously down a deserted corridor; the back of my neck prickled with nerves and steeled me with purpose. I no longer felt like dropping to my knees and bawling while Simon slipped further and further away.

Shaking my head, I swallowed. "No. Simon, don't make me do this. I can't."

"Josie."

"Goddammit! I said, no—just forget it. I'm not your errand girl."

"Josie, you're beeping."

"What?"

"Jane."

I pulled out the device with rattled emotions, absently handing it to Simon. We cleared the corridor, and with a sense of relief, navigated around a particularly devastated area. Part of a wall partition had fallen down, blocking most of the passageway. Lights sparked here and there, the walls were charred, but otherwise, all was quiet.

Another few minutes and we'd be in the Labs. As if sensing that time passed quickly for Simon, I pressed forward with renewed urgency. Simon seemed distant and moody—and shivering—like death drew close and he was at a point where he was about to accept it, embrace it, with gratitude.

I dug my heels and practically sprinted the rest of the way.

~ * ~

Ho fired a shot; it missed John by inches as the compressed air of the pulse gun ploughed past his chest. Angered, John returned fire but found only an empty space as his target.

Like a trapped wild animal, Ho began to panic. They'd

already run around the mainframe twice—dodging and hiding, seeking and pursuing.

John, like a feral wolf, kept his head low, his scent trained on Ho. It impressed him how quickly his prey moved. Margeaux was right; Ho *was* very skilled. John was even impressed with Mwenye. Decades on a space station hadn't dulled the governor's abilities.

When he'd seen Josie fall in the explosion, his heart had nearly stopped. But she rose without a scratch and relief had washed over him, despite knowing Parker was mortally wounded. The pain of that, and blind anger surged into him, spurring him forward, eager to sink his hands into Ho and squeeze the life out of him.

"It's too late," Mwenye called out to Ho. He crouched low near John beside a length of consoles. "I've transferred commands from here. I'm no longer in control of the droids."

Ho laughed. "You would say anything to save yourself." He inched his way stealthily towards the doors. "So if you don't have control, who does?"

"My assistant."

"And where might this assistant be?" Disbelief rang through Ho's voice. "Stop playing games, you and I both know that it can't be done. The commands are locked into the mainframe. To transfer that information would take time—you could not have done that just now, so quickly."

"She is safe."

"She?"

John glared hard at Mwenye. By his expression, he demanded to know what the Governor was up to. By telling Ho that the information was now with Jane would lead him directly to Josie. And that was something he would not allow.

John's communicator beeped. He snatched it out—saw Simon grinning despite the death mask he wore.

"We're back in business," Simon said. "Just got word from Sandvik."

Keeping his voice low, John nodded. "How far are you?"

"About to go into surgery. Aline is prepped and ready..." Simon looked as if he wanted to say more. Instead he nodded absently then ended the call.

John looked expectantly at the blank screen. His heart was

being tugged in all sorts of directions. He couldn't afford to think about Simon right now. He had to be comforted by knowing Aline was with him now. And that Josie would goad his friend on—keep him alive if only to direct a nasty remark at her.

"You've lost command of the control room, Ho." John called out evenly, a calm tone, full of the authority and power that he'd spent a lifetime perfecting. He stood, unafraid. "Give yourself up. This way, I won't have to kill you."

Ho emerged from behind a charred shelving unit peppered with debris and blood from the recent explosion. His small, dark eyes glittery with anger, his face white.

"It's you who'll be killed," Ho spat out. "You have no idea—none at all—of the time I've spent in search of this research. You will not stand in my way."

"I don't care." John saw Mwenye shifting his position, circling around to sneak up behind Ho.

"A lifetime! And I *will* finish what I've started. I've not come this far to watch it evaporate before my eyes."

"For what? For immortality?"

"Not immortality! Do not confuse me with my...with Fern."

John laughed, wicked and taunting. "Even *you* cannot stand to call her your grandmother!" He moved slightly, changing his stance. "If not immortality—what?"

"Power! What else is there?" Ho raised his gun as if to emphasis his point. "Power—ultimate power. To perfect the fusion of man and machine will make me the richest and most powerful man in the universe. Do you know how many people will want that? Will want to *buy* immortality? Thousands! Millions! It's already there, the technology, the know-how. You have it, *right there*," he jabbed a finger at the consoles, "and you have stamped it down for generations. Why? And Fern—Zara—she only wanted to give it to the world."

"Give it? You're confusing yourself, Ho. Fern wanted it for herself."

"She was a genius."

"Is that why she experimented on herself, you think? Don't be foolish, Ho. She was unstable—insane. And why do you think we've controlled it? To save people from what it does to them. Look what it did to her, and now, to you."

"She was a genius!"

"Genius?" John snorted. "Maybe. But can you not see what it did to her? We have laws in place to prevent such things. *Look* at what she's done! Cloning herself. My God, she gave *birth* to herself. And it was an abomination in the truest sense. And you come from that. Can't you see it frightened her, too? She didn't try it again—no. She realized the hideous nature of her experiments. Instead she tampered with her own body, making herself machine. A cyborg. Not because she lost a limb or needed a new heart—no. But because she wanted to live forever, to cheat death that is due to everyone. And where is she now? Hiding somewhere! Sleeping, cowering from her own natural fate. Prolonging her life, yet again. Is this what you want to sell to people? Unnatural living—life? You can't cheat people of their deaths. You can prolong it, make them healthy and whole, but everyone has to die someday."

"People would kill for a chance to live forever. Can't you see? I'm giving people a chance—a choice!"

"For a goddamned price!"

"This is what Zara…Fern wanted. She saw the bigger picture. She was genius," Ho insisted. "You practically use some of the basic elements of her work for your cell-fusion technology. She helped create some of the said 'advancements' that make it possible to attain what you have now. How else can your prosthetics fusion be so successful? She's helped you countless times. And just think how much more, how much better… A new skeletal frame—your body will never deteriorate. And skin. Synthetic skin! She had spent her entire life perfecting the fusion of biological skin with synthetics. Did you not see her face? After centuries, how young she looked? Did you not see?"

"I saw madness."

"She was genius," Ho repeated reverently. "And I have her research—all of it."

"So why not take it with you and build your own bloody lab? Don't steal from me."

Ho laughed—high, unsteady. Desperate. "Steal? Come now, I am an opportunist. Did Adam not clarify that point to you? He did to me. I saw a chance to create something more, a dream I saw unfold right before my very eyes. I saw this place as an opportunity, where I could utilize the resources already here, already in place. I saw how to make it grow, progress—develop. So I took it. *You'll* never use it to its full potential and you'll never allow another to be built while this still exists."

"It's still stealing," Josie said from the doorway.

Both John and Ho snapped their attention to her. She stood, with a calm sort of fury, holding her krima in one hand and Margeaux with the other. She looked sickened by what she heard.

After seeing Simon safely received into the mechanical hands of Aline via the remote surgery link-up, watched over by McLinney, she and Kakuta, with Margeaux dragging reluctantly along, practically flew the distance back to the mainframe. Kakuta now crouched over Ox, trying to revive the concussed man.

John, with disbelief etched on his face didn't speak, but gave her an angry look. She ignored him, keeping her eyes riveted to Ho.

"Josie, my dear," Ho grinned, collecting himself with a series of rapid blinks. "You've come to return my daughter. How very thoughtful of you. Blood *is* thicker that water, after all."

"Sorry to disappoint you." Josie strode forward, Margeaux in tow. "I've come to help my husband kill you and make her watch. Ask her what she's seen. Oops, I think she's in shock right now. My bad."

Ho grinned. "You'll have to catch me first."

A sudden flash of light flared—bright, blinding, painful—followed by thick smoke.

A crash, a pulse gun discharging—*phut*—and John's angry cry.

Instinctively, Josie slammed Margeaux against the wall, pressing her behind her back, her krima engaged and at the ready.

When the smoke cleared, Ho was gone. In his place John, rapidly looking around for him. On the floor nearby lay Mwenye, clutching his arm in pain.

"*How* did he do that?" John demanded in rage.

"I told you," Margeaux said sullenly from behind Josie. "He's very skilled."

Not even Kakuta, who stood in the doorway, saw Ho pass him.

"Governor," John bent down to help Mwenye to his feet. "Are you able? Hail Sandvik and instruct him to shut down this sector as fast as he can. Ho does not leave this station. Understood?"

"Understood." Despite the obvious pain, the jagged hole in his arm, Mwenye sat at the console, his fingers dancing over them with agility. "The closet exits will be the upper chambers. That's where I would go, if I were running."

"Then that's where you'll find me." John already swirled around. One look to Josie was all that was needed for her to peel herself from the wall to follow.

"Kakuta," John called. "Stay with the Governor. When Grosjean arrives, follow me to the upper decks. This ends here—today."

"Yes, sir."

Ox was groggy and insensible, but Kakuta had him firmly by the shoulders and a thick dressing pressed to his head.

Twenty Seven

Renna had a premonition. She saw herself dead. She always had premonitions and they were always of her dead. She reasoned that her subconscious told her of dangers to come, warning her—keeping her alive.

In the most recent vision of her death, she lay on her back staring vacantly up at a black and starless space after someone had shot a hole into her chest. At very close range. The thought made her pause and touch her chest—it ached.

"What's wrong?" Madds asked.

They walked briskly back to the mainframe, stopping briefly to witness the destruction that Agnes had caused a floor above. Madds had tried to contact John but there was no answer. Either he was busy killing Ho or...

Madds didn't wish to think about the alternative, so he quickened his steps and urged Renna forward. Agnes's death and her torn body seemed to further darken the mood Renna was already in. It may also have been prompted by the bloodbath they'd caused in their attempt to free the occupants in the chambers. Three dead techs. And twenty-two dead mercenaries, foolish enough to draw weapons upon them. Madd shook his head mentally. They'd been warned, but did they listen?

Madds gave Renna a considering look to prompt her.

"Nothing." Renna sounded as if she spoke from a long way off. "Just that—wait, Madds. Wait a moment."

Renna frowned, her hand still to her chest, gingerly touching her sternum. She massaged the dull ache of a phantom pain.

"Rens, what is it?" Madds reached out to touch her arm.

"Shh—listen. Someone's coming. Scatter!"

They faded into their surroundings. Madds seemed to dissolve into the shadows of a recessed part of the wall, while Renna crouched low near a water dispenser, twisting her body so any shadow she cast would look inhuman.

Seconds passed, slowly. Madds would never question Renna's psychic abilities, but he began to wonder what was keeping the oncoming danger. Then he heard it, the unmistakable soft shuffling of someone walking quietly and lightly—and quickly.

Renna smiled to herself. *Yes, right again.*

It had felt as if her mind had stepped out of itself and shook her violently to rouse her, begging her to heed. She never doubted it before, so heed, she did.

She slid her eyes towards the sound, counting the footfalls. Another four seconds and whoever came would be seen.

Ho appeared around the corner, looking agitated and angry. He moved swiftly but kept turning his head back like a man pursued. In his hand, he carried a pulse gun, at his hip, a krima in a holster. Immediately sensing danger, he froze—feet away from Madds and Renna. He seemed to be sniffing the air like an animal.

In a flash, he extracted his krima, engaged it, and took a step back—ready.

Madds peeled himself out of the shadows, faced Ho with a small, tight smirk. "I'm sorry, you cannot pass."

"Then I'll have to kill you," Ho replied, cocking his head. His eyes shifted, sensing the presence of another. "Come out, I know you're there."

Renna stood and pushed off from her hiding place, her body braced and ready, her mind sharp and wary. She may still be alive but the danger was still there and practically sending her senses haywire. And, to make matters more unsettling, they were in an oval shaped observation gallery that connected to the elevators, which took you down to the central levels. Above them, clear tempered glass with a vista of the endless black space all around them. She wanted, very badly, to touch her chest again, more as reassurance.

"Trying to run, are we?" she asked calmly, belying her frazzled senses.

Ho smiled, lazily flexing his wrist so that the krima turned mesmerizingly; the double-pointed lasers glowed in evil amber. Deliberately, he touched the wall with one point, sending a crackle of light spitting out like fireflies. Then he was airborne, literally scaling up the side of the wall with his feet, slashing the krima as he did so. From his other hand, the pulse gun coughed out at Madds, who stood closest.

Renna dived to one side. Madds dipped low. Ho catapulted off the wall, twirling in the air. The krima nicked Madds on the shoulder, just as he hit the ground in a roll ready to twist over to shoot at the flying Ho. He'd just enough time to see the upside-down Ho slash with the laser. Madds hissed out in pain then, his right arm went numb and useless, and his weapon clattered to the floor. He continued the twist, still on his back, rolling away into the shadows.

Ho landed on the ground, back-flipped once, lined his sights on Renna; he extended his arm to shoot. He pulled the trigger—*phut*. She bounced up and mimicked his back flip. The shot went wild, missing her by feet.

She landed and quickly sent her arms snapping out before her—two contact explosives flew out of her sleeves and aimed their way to Ho. By the time Ho landed, they would sink into his exposed torso.

Ho seemed to sense that he'd have to move quickly. The moment his feet touched the floor, he pistoned up as if on a trampoline. He saw the contact explosives whiz by under him. He turned in midair, aiming with his gun again. The explosives landed behind him, made contact with something solid, popped like balloons.

Renna was ready for the second shot, anticipated it. She turned her body sideways, feeling the disruption of air as the shot passed her.

That would've been the chest-shot...

Ho aimed again, fired. She dodged that as well—calmly, serene like a fluid dance move, her arms sweeping out like water reeds to keep her balance and momentum. Calm had returned to her. She knew the danger had passed. She would live today.

Madds dug out his own contact explosives. Using his left-hand—his right clutched close to his body—he threw them from his prone position. The angle was wrong, but he didn't have time to correct it, Renna was in imminent danger. The explosives flew; one snagged the edge of Ho's pants—who forever moved making it hard to pin him down.

The explosive popped—Ho snarled as stinging pain shot up his leg. It embedded into the flap of his pant leg and would've maimed him for life if he hadn't moved as quickly as he did. Instead, only one leg of his trousers smoked. Angered, Ho twirled through the air, then, in a bright flash and smoke, Ho once more vanished and Renna clutched her head as something hard slammed into it. It felt a lot like someone's foot, but with all the smoke and dizzying lights, she couldn't be sure.

At least I'm still alive.

She sniffed the air; it seemed heavily laced with a sweet narcotic smell. It would account for the slight vertigo she felt.

Smart man, she mused, still rubbing her head. *Small dose of a disorienting drug to ensure dizziness.*

John found them minutes later, still prone and coughing away the last of the bitter smoke. Josie crouched by Madds, inspecting his injury. The topmost part of his right shoulder was slashed and scorched black. Blood was just pushing past the singed area and soaking his shirt. He'd administered a quick first-aid on himself but without much luck. She helped as quickly as she could.

"I've had much worse. Go. Get him!" He struggled to a sitting position, looking at John. "The man is full of tricks. Be careful."

"That I know already," John nodded, sparing a quick glance at Renna.

She clicked her tongue and gave him a wink, a hand still holding her head. John had known Renna all his adult life. Her clicking her tongue meant she'd messed up and would probably berate herself for a long time to come. He shook his head in reassurance before sprinting away.

Josie, followed. Margeaux trailed behind her, no longer needing to be towed. Something like desperation clouded the girl's eyes, like someone seeking the truth, at whatever cost to her sanity. Suddenly, she looked very much like a young child—scared, alone, and seeking comfort.

For the moment, Josie had forgotten all about Margeaux. Her mind still buzzed with chaos. Too many people she knew and cared for were hurt or dying, if not already dead. She'd had enough, the stench of it, the feeling of fear, the nearness of death...of war.

It had to stop—it just had to.

~ * ~

We found him, just about to press a button to open one of the doors to the escape chambers. We were in the launching area, having passed the reception foyer that was scattered with dead mercenaries and Scrap Yard personnel. It was ripe with evidence that much shooting and destruction had taken place there earlier. Maybe Madds and the other Elites did this. I wondered for a moment where the others were. Madds had taken two others with him and they weren't with him when we passed them in the corridor.

The place was deserted. Two wrecked droids were in pieces near Ho, and made humming noises. Like a kid caught with his hand in the cookie jar, he simply looked at us with a slight gape. Behind me, Margeaux stood poised, a bird about to fly. I could hear Renna making her way cautiously to join us.

Ho smiled, recovering quickly from his surprise. He pressed the button. The door slid open with a soft hiss. He put one foot inside.

"Father!" Margeaux jumped forward.

I whipped my hand out in reflex, snagging her shirt, holding her tight.

"Father, you can't leave me here!" she screamed, nearly hysterical.

Ho lingered, watching his daughter. He looked as though he were about to say something, then, changed his mind with a series of rapid blinks.

I wasn't sure why but found myself walking straight to Ho. I heard John call out to me once, felt his hand pull me back. I jerked it free and kept closing the distance to Ho. In my other hand the krima, which I held poised near Margeaux's neck.

Ho backed into the chamber, reaching out to close the door. I lurched forward, standing in the doorway. He jumped backwards with the pulse gun trained on me.

We stared at each other.

Margeaux's ragged breathing vibrated through her. What was I doing? Had I gone mad as well? Was I really going to kill this girl just to stop Ho? Was that even going to stop a man like him anyway? I wasn't sure of anything anymore, but I wanted Ho stopped—badly!

"I can't let you leave." I spoke evenly, quietly.

Ho, still backing up, edged his way to the control deck and grinned. "Step inside, why don't you. We can have a family reunion of sorts. I'm about to leave this place, myself. I must say...I am very disappointed."

"Things not going your way? What a shame."

John's hand gripped my neck. "Josie, step back. Let him go."

The escape chamber was basically a very large shuttle. Once you entered from the tail section, which was attached to the station, it opened into a wide central area, uncluttered but for guardrails. Beyond the rails, lined along the walls, seating. Spaced evenly at four points on the sides exits doors bracketed a wide expanse of tempered glass windows. At the front lay the control deck, navigational consoles and cockpit. Through a large and impressive domed window, one of the deep-space war cruisers was visible, squatting like an obese bullfrog at the water's edge.

From this position, the chamber—one of many—sat poised for take-off. These chambers ringed the central launching area like pins in a pincushion.

"No, I can't," I replied to John without looking. "It has to stop."

"I agree, but not like this." His hand squeezed my neck in comfort. And in a whisper, "We don't have to give him the girl. We can still use her to bargain with. He's lost; he knows it. Let him go."

So long as I stood in the doorway, Ho couldn't engage the engines—this much I knew. It was a safety mechanism on all shuttles. But the moment I stepped away, the door would slam shut, and lock.

"Yes, listen to your husband. Let me go. And give me my daughter." Ho extended a hand, beckoning Margeaux. She cried silently, her thin shoulders jerked up and down.

"We both know that as soon as I hand her to you, you'll kill us. I'm not as stupid as you think. The girl stays with us...unless..."

"That is true. But as you are family, I might reconsider. Killing *you*, that is."

"I'm touched." I allowed myself a few steps forward, sensed John bunching up close behind me. He stood guarding the doorway now.

"But I just can't do it," I continued. "I can't let you continue with this madness."

"It's a gift I am offering to the world. Can't you see that? Your niece wanted that for everyone."

"No, sorry. I don't see it. And I can't recall ever hearing her confess to wanting that in her ramblings. She was selfish and greedy. She wanted it all for herself. She didn't want to share anything. Why do you think she hid all her data?"

I stood ten feet from Ho. John still braced by the doorway. I looked back at him, saw his face tight with concern for my safety, and a little bewildered at my behavior.

Turning back to Ho, I continued. "You see; I knew Fern. Granted, she was still a small girl, but you could still see her personality. She was happy, she was loved and she was gentle. Somewhere along the line, something inside her changed—snapped. It may have always been in her or it may have been caused by outside influences. I don't doubt that my presence in that basement helped much. But I can't change that. She had a choice when she was older. She chose, instead of a normal life, an unnatural one. It consumed her—it destroyed that little girl I once knew. She's now a stranger to me. The Fern I knew, no longer exists. She's created a madness that people have been craving since the beginning of time itself. And then you come along and want to sell this madness to people—that's just wrong.

"I mean, yes, I hear your logic. Like I said, people have been after the fountain of youth for eons! Fuck, I nearly did it—not for that, but...you see what I mean? Even stasis pod technology is risky, dangerous, more so to the mind. People can get carried away, like how Fern did. And where will it stop? When you've got millions of forever-young people populating the world, never dying? And what's to stop you from doing it on yourself, just so you can keep making your millions? Keep getting richer? And, on a real personal level, if the blame for Fern losing it points back to me, then all the more reason why I can't let you do this. You're like a branch on a tree that needs clipping off when it stars to rot."

Ho shook his head with a laugh. "Don't be so high and mighty with your issues on morality!" He raised his gun, aiming it at me. He had a clear shot—Margeaux would never be harmed as I towered over her. "You bore me with all this. Now, I am pressed for time. Hand me what's mine."

"No," I persisted. "I won't."

"Stop it!" Margeaux screamed. "Father, is it true? About Fern, about her cloning herself—that we are the outcome of her own clone? Is that all true? Please tell me!"

Distracted, Ho waved his hand. "Of course it is. What of it, girl?"

"But you didn't know about this before, did you? I mean, how could you, right?"

"No, he didn't," I replied for Ho. "And when he found out, one would think it would've brought him to his senses...but it didn't. Because, he is just like her."

"Look, enough of this." Ho took aim.

I tensed, holding Margeaux closer and my krima nearly touching her neck.

"Don't do this, Ho." John spoke from behind me. He sounded much closer. I didn't dare turn to see.

"Margeaux stays with me," I said. "Put the gun down."

"No."

Ho fired.

I could literally see the disruption of air—it curdled into vibrating coils before it jetted out towards me. I twirled sideways, flinging Margeaux away and dropped to the floor like dead weight. The pulse shot over me; I heard it slam into the wall with a hacking noise.

John had vanished from the doorway, he was airborne, soaring high above me, twisting and turning like an acrobat—aiming straight for Ho.

They connected like a battering ram does a thick and solid wall, and hit the floor, locked to each other like lovers. Twisting and rolling, they sprang apart, keeping low and tensed, fighting cats eyeing one another.

"Are you hit?" a low voice behind me.

I spun around and clapped onto yellow eyes. It froze my mind.

James!

I blinked in shock, snatched myself up off the floor, bringing my krima forward.

"You! What—How are you here?" I looked beyond him. *Renna! Where is she?*

"She lives. I hit her again." He shrugged, grinning like a cat as he easily read my thoughts. "The first time to save her life, the second to save mine."

"I don't understand. Why are you helping?" I snarled. Anger, at the very sight of him and his smug face, speared through me. Even now, at such a critical time, when danger and death seemed imminent and all around us, he didn't hesitate in dragging his gaze about my body. Lingering at my chest, my crotch...

He shrugged again, seeing my hostility. "I do this for Griet."

"For—*What?*"

I heard a loud crack, John was on the ground with pieces of the control console scattered around him—and blood on his face.

"No!" Forgetting James, I dived straight for Ho.

I caught him by his mid-section, saw the surprise on his face, heard him grunt as we crashed to the floor. The impact jarred my senses momentarily. Ho wriggled under me as I sank my fingers into his neck, my other hand fumbling to re-engage my krima. He bucked, dipped his hands under mine and pushed me off as if I were nothing but a fly.

I landed on my backside, the krima nearly dropping from my hand. Ho was on his feet, slightly winded, staggering like a drunk. I heard John clambering up from the floor. He made an angry noise and I vaguely heard him curse Ho.

I vaulted up and shifted sideways without taking my eyes off Ho.

"One of you will have to die," Ho grinned from a bleeding mouth. "Which one is it? Ah, James. Good of you to join us. I take it you've remembered which side your loyalties lie, after all?"

If John did a double take, I didn't notice but for the jerking motion he made. But I could sense him bristling with rage.

James approached cautiously, eyeing John warily, his body tense but submissive. "Actually, I've no side at the moment. But technically, I am still under contract by you. Speaking of which, there is a question of payment?"

"Stand back," John warned as James came within range of us.

Again, James turned his body away to suggest he didn't mean any threat to us.

"You dare ask for payment after you failed me? Don't be ridiculous," Ho spat out. "Just kill one of them and we'll talk financials later."

James shrugged. "It was worth asking." He glanced sideways at a tautly alert John. The two looked very much like sparring animals. "Do not fight me. I mean you no harm. I've come for the girl."

John frowned, as I did.

"What do you mean?" I asked.

"He means that I've charged him to protect her. Not so?" Ho swiped a hand across his sore mouth. "I always knew you were soft on her."

James merely shrugged.

John twisted his mouth into a snarl. "Then either take the girl and leave or stand aside. Which is it? Or did you mean to help us?"

While they spoke, I inched forward slightly. My krima was engaged—ready. Ho, distracted, looked shiftily from James to John. He'd lost his pulse gun and seemed to forget he had a krima at his hip.

"I cannot help while still under contract, technically." James looked apologetic.

"Then stand aside," John hissed angrily.

Ho laughed wickedly; I inched forward yet again. Then, I ducked low—quickly—feigning an attack. Ho's eyes flew to mine. He braced himself rigid; about to jump backwards, his arms low to counter the blow he thought I was about to give him.

Instead, I snapped out my leg, bringing it up and around in a spinning move and kicked him squarely in his unprotected face. I heard a dull crunch, his nose breaking. He let out a high yell as he flipped away. He landed a few feet to my left, his eyes watering, his face brilliantly red. And he looked livid with fury.

Not hesitating for a moment, I was on him again. Twirling my other leg, I brought it low this time, catching him on the side on his knee. He buckled sideways. The look of surprise was evident, as well as the insult that he'd been caught unawares twice. As I saw him go down low, I sprang up into the air, straight as an arrow with arms outstretched, and did a backwards flip.

I'd been practicing that move for a short while, never managing to master it as I did just now. When I landed, my breath labored only slightly, but the pain in my injured shoulder was suddenly sharp and painful. I pulled out my Snare Gun 3 from the holster at my chest. Left-handed as it was, I managed to quickly put him in my sights. And fired.

Ho was no longer where he'd been standing. My explosive barb-shots uselessly embedded into the wall behind him and popped like firecrackers.

I saw him ducking around the navigation consoles and John sliding over them to reach him. James was nowhere near and I couldn't spare the time to look.

"Two against one, Ho!" I shouted. "You can't win. Give it up."

"You don't understand!" he shouted back. His voice slurred with a mouth full of blood.

Another crash rocked the shuttle. John's foot connected squarely into Ho's back, sending him flying across into the cockpit area. A curse, a yell, and two bodies locked together in the small room. Then John catapulted backwards, back towards me. He landed heavily on the navigational equipment with a painful groan, and toppled over to the side.

I rushed forward to check on him. His face contorted in pain, his hand clutching his left hip. He'd landed on his old injury and the pain seemed to cripple him.

I sensed movement behind me. Whirling, I saw Ho bearing down on me with his krima, now fully engaged and burning evilly like his eyes.

If I moved, John would be hit. If I stayed, we'd both be hit.

I froze for a split second before I re-engaged my krima—my

Snare Gun was lost somewhere.

I'd have to meet him head on.

Rearing up, I braced my body for attack, keeping my centre of gravity low in the event that I had to throw him off me. I knew I'd be seriously injured from the angle of Ho's advance, high, nearly airborne. But I had to do it. I had to do something—*anything*—to keep him away from John.

The object that flew between us knocked me sideways as it slammed into my left arm. It was a square emergency medical kit; large enough to service the entire escape chamber's passengers, and heavy enough to explode onto the floor and belch out its contents. It hit Ho's side with a reassuring crack, knocked his krima out of his hand and sent him crashing to the floor.

On my belly, I spun my head around and saw James just straightening from a spin. He'd either kicked or thrown the kit at us. Margeaux stood rooted next to him, her mouth gaping.

Ho screamed in anger and stood shakily to his feet, holding his side. Blood poured out from a gash on his right temple.

John rolled to his side, reached out to me. My left arm had gone numb with pain, but we were still alive. He grabbed my leg and jerked me to him, away from Ho.

It happened like a dream, where the events were real enough but watched as if from somewhere above. I saw Ho pull out a dagger and for a moment wondered when he'd retrieved the one he put into my shoulder. He lurched forward with it poised over his head; he held it by the blade as it gleamed wickedly at me. One flick and the knife would sink right back into me.

John yanked me to him—I felt myself slide backwards as I stared mutely at Ho. Then, a loud crack. My ears nearly popped inside my head, my eyes blurred from pressure. I could feel every blood vessel inside me being rudely tugged out of my body. And then the air exploded with confusion, a rush of stinging wind and biting cold. A sound of a million wailing cats deafening me until it hurt to my very core.

I saw Ho stand rigid, his body bending backwards and then he was in the air. With a look of complete shock and surprise, he sailed across the room and out through a gaping black hole.

John and I shot forward along the floor as the black hole

pulled us. I screamed out though my lungs burned, grabbing at anything I could sink my hands into to keep from being sucked out. I even stabbed my krima into the floor, hoping it would slow our progress. Instead, it sent showers of blinding sparks every-which-way.

Margeaux torpedoed over us, her hair spread out around her as she spun head over heels. Her arms were crossed neatly across her chest, and in the briefest of moments, I caught sight of her face—it was an expression of absolute smugness. And sheer, uncensored anger as her eyes scorched into mine.

And then the blackness swallowed her whole.

Before I could even dwell on the fact that something horrible had eaten her, a wall slammed down before it and silenced the screaming cats.

My ears rang in the silence, my face—my entire body—stung with pins and needles. I felt glued to the floor, barely noticing the vice-like grip of John's fingers as they dug into my ankle. He lay on his side holding onto part of the railing that circled the room, staring at me with relief. He slumped onto his back and expelled a long sigh, closing his eyes.

I looked up to see James peeling himself off the wall on the far side of the shuttle. His hair mussed, his face uncharacteristically grim. He straightened up and ran a hand through his hair, giving me a wink.

"What the fuck just happened?" I said weakly, still on the floor, my stomach nearly raw from being dragged along it.

"I couldn't stop her." James put a hand behind his neck, rubbing it he shrugged. "I am sorry."

"What do you mean?" I fumbled to sit up. "You mean..." I had to swallow. "You mean *she* opened that door?"

John on all fours now, crawled tiredly towards me. He curled a hand around my arm and helped me to my feet.

James shook his head. "I did...to stop Ho. She hit me, not hard, but enough to distract me. Then...she just...jumped into the air." He seemed to be thinking to himself as he gazed at the point we last saw Margeaux, before she was sucked out into space. "...let herself go."

"What—why would she do that?"

"To be with Ho," John said softly and ran a hand over his hip. "Her father."

John, still favoring his left leg, put a hand to my cheek and brushed it gently. It stung and I automatically touched it with a wince. How I cut it, I couldn't say.

"Why would she do that?" Remembering the hate on her face, I swallowed.

James shrugged. "Why do we do anything?"

Twenty Eight

"What did you mean earlier? You said you came for Griet," Josie asked, even though every bone in her body ached and begged for her to sink to the floor so she could curl up and hope a coma would take hold of her. Her injured shoulder throbbed with nauseating pain. By everything that was logical and sane, she should be tucked away in her bed, recuperating with a pile of painkillers and lots of chocolate covered pastries.

John turned to stare at her, then to James.

"Yes." James shrugged again, making Josie think that it was an unconscious habit of his, regardless of his mood or answer. He looked at John and nodded. "*That* Griet. Your mother."

"I don't understand." John narrowed his eyes and regarded the Rogue with a suspicious look. "Speak with care."

"Your mother taught me everything there is to know about being a Rogue. It is true." He grinned, flashing brilliant white teeth. "Surprised?"

"Your mother teaches Rogues?" Josie gaped.

John had clamped his mouth into a thin line. "I did not know."

"Well, it is not like she advertises it," James continued. "I was her first. She took me in off the streets in Brazil. I was about seven. A bit old to train, but…it was either that or be killed by the men I stole from. I had to eat; I was hungry. So I stole…among other things. Your mother came across me quite by accident. It was around the time she had been exiled. You see, I was always odd, a certified sociopath or sorts—I hurt others without a care. I also had narcissistic tendencies—so they said—and clinically confirmed with a delusional disorder. That's why my mother abandoned me. You could say...I had problems. Your mother knew, but she saw potential in me. She asked for no payment, only that once my training was complete, that I would develop conscience. You see, each of us was given a goal to aim for—like a lesson we needed to master. Mine was my conscience.

"She taught me how to think past my sick little box—developed me, so to speak. She instilled in me the conscience that I seemed to lack, that I seemed to have ignored all my life. But she knew I would never be a saint, I knew that too. She knew that my path in life would be that of a Rogue. We Rogues do not require hindrances like a conscience. So, she taught me to be one, and she taught me well. She kept reminding me that regardless of my profession, that I should always use my talents for good. She did not beg it of me, but she made sure I did not forget. I guess, somewhere along the line, I lost it—forgot. But...it came back when I realized how close to home this was. Forgive me." He looked to John. "But I consider your mother as my mother. She is, after all, the only mother I've ever known."

James paced the chamber, an idle saunter. "She contacted me—oh, she knows just about everything that goes on. Told me to fetch the girl and bring her directly to her. Margeaux was too old, I told her. Too unstable, too far gone. But Griet insisted. She could help her and hone her skills. Mend her." He faced them, shrugging. "She's helped many others by breaking them first before she fixes them. Reconditioning them, so to speak. Some are Rogues like me, and some...well, they do something else. And believe me, some were far worse than Margeaux, and me, for that matter."

John listened. He'd heard every word said, yet found it hard to understand. He vaguely felt Josie's hand curl around his, squeezing it reassuringly. At first, he thought to dismiss these revelations, but the more he heard, the more believable they became. And it was just like his mother to do something like that. It was so...*her*.

"She never once mentioned any of this," John said quietly. He laughed suddenly. "Why would she? She always does exactly as she pleases. My mother," he shook his head. "A Rogue Master."

"Among other things," James added helpfully.

"Is that why you helped us?" Josie asked. She still held John's hand; it gripped hers like a vice despite his bemused face. "Because of Griet?"

"Yes and no," James shrugged. "The connection to Griet, of course. But...I liked you. I won't apologize for staring—I mentioned before I had a delusional disorder. In my case, certain words, looks, or situations, all trigger me to think that you *like* me...and, I you. Well, some habits are very hard to break. I'm not a pervert, nor a rapist...just obsessive." He flashed another brilliant smile. "It appears I am not cured."

John gave him a warning look.

"But, yes. I do like you. Honestly, I do. And truthfully, it is more from admiration. Also, because I kept making mistakes since the day I met you. I took it as a sign."

"Mistakes?" she frowned.

"Oh, yes. Failures. Unfulfilled contracts, missed deadlines...very embarrassing for a Rogue. My conscience kept returning just when I had conveniently forgotten about it. And with it, those painful memories of the lessons Griet taught me—I felt...ashamed."

"You're a very strange man. Look, I *really* don't like you, but, thanks for saving my life." Josie made a small move as if to shake his hand, but John subtly reined her back with a firm grip.

The Rogue saw the intended gesture, pursed his lips. "I only helped. I did not save your life."

"Well what do you call that business with the medicine chest and opening the emergency exit? How about not fighting with Ho, and, if you go a little further back, you conveniently left my krima in that overcoat pocket."

"Oh, that," he shrugged again. He actually flushed darker in the face, causing Josie to squint suspiciously at him.

"I think what my wife means to say, is thanks for *helping* to save her life, our lives." John wouldn't offer his hand, but inclined his head courteously. "I agree with my wife, of course. I don't like you, and I can't say I ever will. But obviously my mother has seen something in you that is moderately good. And she is never wrong. So, I thank you."

James tentatively watched them. The two men then eyeballed one another a moment longer. A small smirk touched the Rogue's lips, like a cat pleased with the outcome of the day, as he basked lazily in the sun.

"Fine, then." James smartly tucked his hands behind his back. "I shall be leaving. No need to see me off, I know the way."

"Before you go," John raised his hand to his chin. "I need a little assurance."

"Hmm?" the Rogue replied with a cocked brow, his yellow eyes turning beguilingly innocent.

"What you have learnt here, about my wife…"

"Oh, what's one more wild rumour about her going to do?" James smiled. It was, for the first time, warm and genuine. "Do not worry. We Rogues have terrible memories. And I won't insult Griet by exposing you."

~ * ~

"He's still a perv," I said.

"I agree. I don't like how he looks at you."

"Jealous?"

"If I were jealous, there'd be no men left to roam free in this world," he replied airily.

"Well they do seem to be dropping dead around us quite quickly." I smiled broadly, feeling smug. "You're jealous."

"Very."

"Even from a delusional pervert?"

"They are the worst kind."

We walked briskly towards the Lab. John, so eager to see about his friend that he forgot all else, even ignoring a summons from Captains Sandvik and Grosjean respectively.

I had to admit, after the events that transpired in the escape chamber, all else paled compared to whatever the captains had to say. And, from where I stood, the imminent threat was gone—flying breathlessly out into space like flotsam and jetsam.

At the thought of Margeaux, a sharp pang of guilt shot through me, racked with sadness. I couldn't even admit to myself, yet that she'd sacrificed herself—*willingly*—to spite us. She hated me so much and I really couldn't blame her after the way I'd treated her. A hot sting of shame dashed across me as her angered expression burned into my mind. Her hard, cold face, it said clearly that she'd won some sort of game. That she chose to die with her father rather than face the consequences and that she didn't care about her own life as compared to their plans.

A small, hopeful part of me thought that maybe she finally saw the truth—saw things clearly. Maybe it was guilt, and remorse. Or maybe, like the Rogue, her conscience racked her. I doubted it, and now I'd never know. I could never ask her.

John, sensing my mood had suddenly dipped, curled his fingers through mine as we continued to walk, hand in hand.

Simon had gone through his surgery, as well as anyone could, considering the circumstances. It was by far better than any field surgeon could've done or asked for. The Prosthetics Labs were, after all, fully equipped and designed specifically for the remote surgery procedures they performed. Normally it was the other way around, where the patient was on Terra Firma, with only the rare occasion that an actual live patient would be lying exactly where Simon lay now.

Simon reclined in a large, vacuous room, riddled with close to ten or more of these surgery tables. All others were vacant, save for one terrified looking patient at the far end, bound up in bandages and strapped in with what looked to be his new legs. Though he'd been partitioned away by clear tempered glass, he strained with desperation to hear what the latest news of the Scrap Yard's fate was.

It surprised me to find Simon wide-awake, a little sluggish and out of sorts, but alert enough to give us his trademark smirk. He was hooked up to various bags of colorless liquid, blood, and other medical paraphernalia that beeped and flashed with sound and light.

Simon was still inside the remote surgery chamber, the mechanical arms gingerly moved across his mid-section, putting the final touches to a dressing. Beside him, McLinney stood suited up in a blazing white smock that covered him from head to toe. Even his pulse gun had a plastic covering over it, which he'd slung loosely over his arms. Nearby, another man stood, dressed similarly, sans gun, and spoke to Aline as he assisted her. A holographic image of Aline danced overhead. At this moment, she peered intently down at her work, her mouth drawn into a thin straight line, causing her to look so much like John.

I noticed a series of micro-thin needles dotted around Simon's stomach and various parts about his body. Acupuncture needles. Aline had a fondness for using them as a method of anaesthesia and pain inhibitors. Having been the recipient of these needles myself, on numerous occasions, I realized they would account for Simon's general alertness and lack of pain.

"All is well, then?" Simon asked a little hoarsely. He still looked like death.

John nodded, relief that his friend was still among the living had him grinning foolishly. "You could say so. Aline," he nodded to his sister.

"When you're done being space cadet, John," she muttered, not even bothering to look at him, "don't forget us down here and your duties as President. But then, Loeb is doing such a fantastic job that no one seems to realize you're not even here. But our Vice President is about to have an apoplectic fit and is demanding advice about Iceland and how best to contain the situation. She said other things but none were pleasant."

Aline fussed with the dressing some more, then, sternly accosted Simon. "Right! Bed rest for you. There will be absolutely *no* gallivanting around and chasing mercenaries for *at least* two solid weeks. Understood? You are the *luckiest* man on earth! How you're not dead, is beyond me. I suspect your sheer ill temper is what kept you alive. My God, a hole in your stomach, front and back..." she shook her head with weariness. "What do I tell Mrs. Trudesson? She'll have a conniption when she finds out."

"About that, ahh...if you could hold off on tell—" Simon said sheepishly.

"I'm not finished," Aline snapped back irritably. "If I even *hear* you've been out of bed to do god-knows-what misadventure you boys gets up to, so help me, I will tell on you. You are not made of metal, Simon, so stop acting as if you are! To even think I actually could have married you at one point. It would have been *me* worrying my head off like Trudesson is now."

I gaped, looking at both an embarrassed Simon to a foul-tempered Aline. John chuckled, already dragging a chair nearby to sit beside his friend.

"You and...Aline?" I continued to gape.

"It was years ago, Josie," John said helpfully. "Simon had a fascination with older women—and an interest in medicine."

Aline snorted loudly. "Medicine, he says. Is that what it's called now?" She flashed a look at the assistant. "Go find something to do elsewhere."

The man practically dropped everything on the spot and bolted out, leaving McLinney to idly meander to another part of the room. A kaleidoscopic picture display seemed to attract his attention as he cocked his head and stared at it with absolute fascination.

"Josie," Aline looked at me. "I've a message from Mrs. Patel."

"Mrs. Patel! Shit, I keep forgetting her!"

"Right. Anyway…she had to leave. The Rogue, that James character, returned her husband. I saw no point keeping her detained any longer than was necessary. My God, she talks a lot. She's back at the estate in Britain, watched of course." She flicked a quick look at John in response to the quick intake of breath he made from annoyance. The look suggested that she was still a Lancaster, and knew how to handle things. It also said that John ought not to question her judgment in the matter.

Aline continued, "She left you a message that the estate is now yours. Lorcan Wellesley, before the siege last year, made arrangements and transferred ownership of the estate to you. She remains caretaker, if you please her to be. Oh, and he's apparently left you all his remaining assets and monies. How is your shoulder? You don't look so good."

I felt the blood draining from my face, it made my head swim. Had I really heard right?

"Why…why would he do that?" I managed to mutter. "Why would Lorcan do that? It should've all gone to his son, Max. He didn't know then what Max was…so, why me?"

"You forget," John said softly beside me. "That by then, Max was made to disappear. To transfer his property to him would draw attention to the fact that Max was somewhere close. Remember, Lorcan thought Max's life was in danger. He would not have done something to threaten him any further. He knew that you, at the time, would benefit more if you had money and a place to live. And, I suppose, he cared enough about you to make sure you had someplace to go. To call home." John nodded appreciatively. "He was a good man."

"Yeah, he was," I mumbled.

"Mrs. Patel also said that she tried a few times to contact you," Aline continued. "After your arrest, she was also arrested by an ill-faced Inspector Narayan. Ah, I see you've heard of him, then?" Aline nodded once as I snorted in temper. "Well, her connection to Wellesley got her detained indefinitely by the London police. And after we took you away from them, Narayan thought she knew things, but she wasn't saying anything to harm her boy. It was weeks later before she was released. Wellesley's attorney's worked very hard to have her released and her name cleared. I believe it was around that time that Wellesley transferred everything over to you. By then, you were here and impossible to contact, as you were a prisoner of sorts yourself. Then, a few months later, the siege, and soon afterwards, you were married and any appointment with you was practically impossible. So she waited and hoped you would check your messages. She'd apparently left several over the past months."

"She did?" I looked to John, to Simon. They both shrugged. "Why haven't I gotten any of them?"

Aline answered patiently. "Josie, you're the President's wife. You are not expected to respond to every single message that is addressed to you. That is why you have aides."

"I do?" I frowned. "Well, remind me to fire them. I should've gotten those messages. How do you ignore stuff like that? Didn't my so-called aides think to inform me of any of these?"

"Well, that is your problem, not mine. I've delivered *my* message. Now, Simon," Aline returned her attention to her patient. "Your hunch was right. Moorjani says that Ho had two, possibly three, other individuals helping him. For an operation the size and magnitude as the one he's staging now..." she slid her eyes to John, who nodded. "Correction, the operation he *has* staged, he would have needed considerable resources and money. He may have been wealthy enough on his own, but he would have needed more. Moorjani has two confirmed names that are linked to him directly. There are being apprehended as we speak. One is a cosmetics conglomerate with five directors—all involved, and all have come clean to save their skins, claiming it was all Ho's idea and he was blackmailing them. The other is a wealthy private individual; he's been tracked down in Sydney. The possible third, well, on several occasions, the searches have led back to Adam…" Aline trailed off and looked disturbed.

"What did you say?" John leaned forward in his chair then glared at Simon quickly. "You suspected this?"

Simon nodded weakly, beginning to look tired. "It was just too much of a coincidence. It kept bothering me. It all started with Adam, so to speak, and Ho. How did he know that Adam was still alive? He practically insisted on it. And, why even mention Adam in the first place, if it wasn't for the fact that he could be involved? Which he was, to a certain extent, or so we were being led to believe. Distractions…illusions. It was nagging me to no end. I started seeing things more clearly when I thought I was dying."

"But Adam knew nothing of this." I jumped in to defend him. "And how could he contact Ho? There's just no way!" I shook my head. "There's just no way Adam is involved. He's lost the will to fight. He's given up. For fucks sakes, the man talks to imaginary people!"

"Did Moorjani say how old these connections to Adam were?" John asked Aline through gritted teeth, his face in turmoil. "Were any…recent?"

"She didn't say. It's all very sketchy and vague as it is. To be sure, she's done a thorough sweep of his quarters and surrounding areas—nothing out of the ordinary. No electronic signals, nothing. Adam once owned about three companies that connected him to Ho. To the best of our knowledge, he's relinquished or sold ownership of all his businesses. We saw to that, remember? He's clean. I have to agree with Josie. I don't see how he could have done it. His heart is just not in it anymore."

"A leopard doesn't change his spots," Simon warned.

"Nor do they like being in a cage." John sounded far away. He seemed to be thinking of something, a tight frown knitted his brows and his lips pursed.

"You don't seriously think he's involved, do you?" I asked fearfully, thinking of the man I'd spent many hours in conversation with. The man I'd made a point in getting to know, to understand.

"He used to work with Ho, in business. We knew that. That's where the connection comes from obviously. How the hell can he still be working with him? Moorjani said there's nothing to indicate that he could communicate with the outside world. Yes, Adam loves money—craves it, almost. He was right about Ho's motives being solely for money and power. But Adam, he...he just isn't Adam anymore." I looked helplessly to John, to Simon, and then Aline.

"I don't doubt you, Josie," John replied quietly. "I've always trusted your judgment and I agree with you that Adam has lost the fight. I've seen it in his eyes. The fire is no longer there; the hunger is gone. But if, by some slim chance, he is still manipulating us—deceiving us—then I will find out and make him pay."

"I don't doubt you would," I snapped at him angrily, saw him narrow his eyes at me.

I was angry, yes, but a small niggling feeling of doubt ignited in me. Could Adam be so cunning and deceptive? *Anything is possible,* he'd said to me when we discussed how Ho could've known he was still alive. We suggested that Ho had tapped into the security droids memory banks, but of course, that possibility was too far-fetched. Or was it? Maybe Ho *did* have help—from the inside. Maybe Adam wasn't really talking to himself, but talking to Ho. How? Anything is possible... Adam did, after all, kill his own father. And, if a chance to live forever were to present itself, without ills and a deteriorating body—why just stop at killing your own father?

"What are you thinking?" John asked quietly. He'd been studying me intently ever since I snapped at him.

"Nothing." I needed to sit. My head began to swim and my eyes went out of focus. "Only..." I took a breath. "Only that, out of all the people, Adam had the most to gain should Ho succeed."

John had already pulled me into a chair. "How so?"

Aline answered. "He wants to live forever."

Twenty Nine

After we left Simon, John disappeared to speak with Sandvik and Grosjean. I envisioned another few hours before I saw him again so decided, against my better judgment, to help with the injured. Though I was deathly tired, my shoulder lanced with pain, and my head swimming in dizzying circles, I helped.

A part of me needed to, rather than find a quiet corner in which to cower and hide. I wanted to see the destruction and the bloody mess which, inadvertently, I too, helped cause. After all, I wasn't completely blameless.

Though it sickened me, I joined Renna and Minnows and helped to retrieve the fallen and injured soldiers throughout the Scrap Yard. The sights were hideous and will stay with me for the rest of my life. But essentially, it helped ease the tightness, the guilt and shame that had been building up in me since this whole thing started.

Like the morbid curiosity that drives people to watch a horrific accident unfold, I heaped on the dead and injured, feeling the wet, oily ooze of their blood soak my hands and clothes as I carted them away. I listened to the wails of the hurt, the final sighs of the dead, and the grate of broken bones beneath their bruised skins. I slipped and skidded in trails of blood and gore, felt the crunch of bone fragments under my shoes, and the unbearably earthen smells of death.

When it was over, I looked worse than the dead themselves. Borrowing a Space Junkies reserve uniform, I showered and changed with the rest of them. Renna stayed protectively close, but more to have someone to talk with as we cleaned ourselves up.

She had a certain hollowed look about her; I probably looked no better than she did. She seemed distant and remote, but like people who've been through the worst, we grinned like idiots and made light of things, exchanging jokes and silly stories.

Before five hours were up, the Prosthetics Lab and adjoining clinic were completely filled with the injured. For the dead, we used a docking bay to lay their shrouded bodies. Ho's men were also laid there. Later they would be DNA-tagged for identification, and, mostly likely their names, if they went by any, would be scratched off some special mercenary list that I knew John kept handy somewhere.

It would be hours yet before we could leave the Scrap Yard. A rigid lockdown was in effect. The last of the last of the mercenaries were hunted down or killed, whichever was preferable. Many escaped in the final confusion as the battle to take control of the Scrap Yard came to an end—fleeing in tiny escape pods that lined the lower decks, to take their chances in the great vast void of space.

Sandvik and Grosjean's marines could be seen everywhere, restoring order. A rumour rapidly flew around that Grosjean single-handedly brought down a particularly aggressive group of unfriendlies. She began by firing on them with her weapons, then abandoning these altogether to fight with her fists. Exaggerated or not, the story went on to say that she was found by her surprised lieutenants atop a three-deep pile of prone mercenaries. With one hand, she was wiping a bloody mouth, the fingers of her other hand were firmly wedged up a man's nostrils like she was about to go bowling with his head. The story made me chuckle and I wished I had a chance to meet this infamous Captain Grosjean. But Renna's adamant headshaking and insistence that Grosjean was a loose cannon had me reconsidering.

With nowhere else left to go without getting in the way as normal activity slowly began to resume, I found myself back in the Lab sitting next to Simon. He slept soundly apparently unaware I sat there. But with Simon, I could never be sure.

John found me there nearly falling out of my chair, my head nodding with exhaustion. I felt his warm hands brush the hair off my face; he leaned in to plant a kiss on my forehead.

"You look half dead," he said quietly.

"So do you."

"We've another ten hours or so before a transport shuttle comes. The Governor has given us a small hospitality room to rest in. Can you stand, or shall I carry you?"

"I can stand." I got up wobbly, mortified by the thought of John carrying me helplessly through the Yard, for all to see and gape at. But, knowing his tactics to get me on my feet, I smiled back. He did look dead-tired himself, and he seemed almost relieved that he didn't have to carry me.

"You smell clean."

"I washed," I replied. "I needed it." I looked sideways at him. He was covered in blood and suspiciously foreign bits of glob. But he seemed otherwise unperturbed by it. "You need one too."

"Mmm," he replied.

It was slow going towards the hospitality quarters two floors above us. We encountered many people along the way busily repairing or assisting sections of walls and rooms that were destroyed. Most were service droids who ignored us altogether.

"I'm glad it's done. Too many have been killed or injured, but it's done." He sounded pained. "Surrey is dead. He rigged the gunship to destroy it. I must tell his mother when we get back."

"Agnes, too. Madds is up and running, though. His injury is bad, but he'll be okay."

"Good." He pulled me in automatically as we sidestepped a fallen panel of a wall in the corridor. "Agnes was a good operative. Simon will miss her badly."

"I think Renna wants to retire." I recalled Renna's face. "Did you know she just had a baby?"

"Mmm, I thought so. That's too bad, though. She's exceptional at what she does. Do not worry about her. She'll not stray too far from this kind of work." He shook his head to clear it. "Enough of this for now, Josie. Let's get some rest. I'm about to fall on my face and my hip is killing me."

The hospitality room was small, extremely, but it at least had a bed, bathroom facilities, and a window that showed the vastness of space. Ignoring the view, we crashed headfirst onto the bed, hearing our joints crack and moan with blissful relief, our spines creaking like rusty hinges. Before we could fully appreciate the luxurious sensation of being off our feet, we fell fast to sleep.

~ * ~

Trudi was among the additional physicians, military personnel, and support crew that arrived with the transport shuttle. She headed straight to the Prosthetics Lab, looking murderous.

Before seeing her husband, she gruffly slapped a crumpled envelope into Josie's hand. It looked a little frayed and dog-eared around the edges, had numerous creases and folds marks, but the seal remained intact. By the looks of it, it appeared to have lived for the last year, safely and in the trusted sanctuary of Mrs. Patel's ample bosom. It even smelled of her, sweet and floral like her signature perfume of tuberoses and gardenia.

Allowing Trudi and Simon a little privacy, John and Josie lingered back for a moment before entering. Her voice could be heard high and clear through the open door. It sounded, most definitely, pissed off.

Simon had been removed to another cubicle, one that had clouded privacy screens and soundproofing. He lay uncharacteristically timid on the bed, staring up at his furious wife with something close to fear on his face. When Trudi finished with her rant, mostly threatening him with bodily harm should he ever decide to become near-mortally wounded again, she smoothed back her short hair and flexed her neck muscles to relieve the tension. Satisfied that her message had gotten through, her face was once again its usual pleasant self.

"Sorry to interrupt, Mrs. Trudesson," John said, a little timidly himself. "Just need to brief Simon on a few matters. What news of home?" He gave Simon a personal unit. His friend snatched at it like a lifeline.

"Nothing out of the ordinary. Loeb is holding his own quite well. Aline said he declined your suggestion of using Adam as an advisor. I believe he's resolved the matter on his own. Media houses are still clueless about the real deal here on the Scrap Yard. That may change as the civilians on board call home. Loeb already has damage control in effect when news of this breaks."

John nodded with relief. Trusty Loeb. He made a mental note to give the man a raise.

"That's from Patel." Trudi nodded to the still unopened envelope in Josie's hand. She settled herself by propping a hip on the side of Simon's bed. "Aline told you that we had to let her go. We've a two-man team watching her as we speak. But she's clean and just relieved to have her husband back." Despite her business-like manner, Trudi quickly flicked her eyes in the direction of her own husband, who studiously read over some information on the personal unit that John had handed him. "She's been holding that letter for you all this time."

"I can tell." Josie wasn't sure she wanted to open the envelope; she still reeled from the latest news of her newfound inheritance. The envelope wasn't addressed, but she knew that inside, contained a message to her from Lorcan.

"Sit here." John offered his wife a chair, running a reassuring hand along her back.

With her heart pounding in her chest, Josie ripped the seal open and unfolded the single sheet of paper within. Seeing Lorcan's handwriting made her breath hitch. It was like reading a message from the dead. For a moment, she could scarcely see as tears quickly obscured her vision.

Hello, Josie, the letter read, neatly written in Lorcan's engineer-styled print. *If you're reading this, then you must know that I am dead as I've left Mrs. Patel with instructions that this finds you. I'm sorry. There was much I needed to say when I was alive, much that needed saying but I was too stupid to realize it at the time. A letter alone seems insufficient now, but I have no choice. I was going to send a recording, but I thought you might not be able to stand the sight of me, considering everything that has happened. But this way is better, as I've a secret that you must memorize and then destroy.*

Before I get to that, you now have a house, somewhere to call home. Mrs. Patel would have forwarded you all the necessary documents. Max is on his own now and he has funds that I've saved for him over the years. You need not worry about him. Regardless of whatever happens to me, know that you have someplace to go. I've left Mrs. Patel as caretaker, and she has assured me that you will be looked after. She also knows some people who can create an identity for you. Trust her, Josie, she's like family. I've also left my remaining assets and funds that I have saved over the years, all to you. It is a little too late, but I hope it is enough. It is the best I can do. This is my gift to you.

Now on another matter, a very important matter, I've something very precious for you. It's a secret that I have learned while on my quest to learn the truth about Uron Koh. Alas, at the time of writing this, I still have not discovered who he is. You are now being held in the safest place in the world, the Citadel. But for how long is uncertain. When last I saw you, you were a prisoner and it pained me to see you like this. But you are safe, and that is all that matters. Should you be set free, it is my hope that you head straight back to North York, where you belong. Whatever you do, do not tell anyone, as I came by this secret quite by accident from Michael Ho. I am hoping, by the time you do see this, you will no longer need it to keep you alive and that things have been resolved. You see, by stealing it from Michael Ho, it ensures that you live—should I not be alive to protect you. It was my insurance policy for you. I am hoping you will never need to use it against Ho, as he's a powerful man and a very dangerous one. Be wary also of The Expert, Mr. Jones. I do not know the full extent of his involvement. He appears harmless, a mere consultant, but be cautious with him. He knows much about many things. And he seems well connected to many powerful people as well as Uron Koh himself.

At the time I stole it from Ho, Mr. Jones was in close contact with him and I overheard discussions on the matter. What I give to you is a secret code that unlocks the entire controls to a space station, ST-Cy 15, also known as the Scrap Yard. It houses every known command and directive for all the droids in the world. It is Ho's intention, one day to steal onboard and take control—but not for the droids. He intends to take the cell-regeneration and prosthetics sections of the station. I believe, he is experimenting with cloning—humans. He seems quite obsessed with the idea, and for years, has been running hugely funded investigations and research into this area. Use this knowledge against him should you need it, and go directly to President John Lancaster. I loathe saying this, but whatever Lancaster is, whatever he may be or what I have told you about him, he is the only one that can stop Ho and The Expert. Use every advantage to save yourself.

It is my hope that you will never need this, but it was also my *hope that you and I could have a future together. I think, at last, I am over my battle of devotion to my beloved Carmen. But, now I am dead and I've left you to fend for yourself. I am truly sorry. Will you forgive me for this?*

It was signed simply 'L' and as a postscript, a series of numbers and letters and symbols that took up two lines.

Josie inhaled quickly to ease the sudden sharp pain she felt in her chest. John had a hand pressed firmly at the back of her neck to steady her. He was silent, his mouth a grim line. She looked to him, then, handed the letter to Simon who scanned it quickly, grunting when he finished.

"He suspected Adam, as well." Josie's voice came out in a hoarse whisper. Instinctively, she reached for the spot where her pendant, the one Lorcan had given, once hung. "My God," she croaked out. "If only we'd known all this before…"

"I know." John stroked her hair. "We can't change that now."

"It would also mean that Adam might have known who you really were from very early." Simon's voice was flat and angry. "And if he managed to keep that to himself with a bold poker face, there is no limit to the lies he's said to protect himself."

"What if he really did not know?" John said softly.

Both Simon and Josie whipped around to goggle at him. John was the one who doubted the most, who suspected the worst. To hear those words nearly knocked the breath out of Josie.

"How could he not?" Simon replied cautiously. "I mean, he and Ho were—according to this new revelation," he flapped the letter still in his hand, "speaking in detail about the Scrap Yard, and specifically, the cell-fusion aspects."

"Merely speaking of it, yes, but not specifically talking about Josie and her past. If Lorcan overheard, surely there would have been some mention of that fact. And if he heard, then surely he would have done more to ensure that Josie was safe. He would have killed Ho and Adam on the spot."

"That may be, but it says nothing of what Adam would or would not have known at the time. Yes, Ho may have been keeping it quiet, after all, it's his own family history he was talking about." Simon shrugged and thoughtfully ran a hand gingerly over his injury.

"As it stands, Lorcan only stole the code to make sure that Josie and her connection to him did not get her killed."

"True." John looked to his wife with a preoccupied expression. "Has he ever touched you?"

"Pardon?" Josie blinked. "Who? What do you mean?"

"Adam. If he knew who you really were, he would have choked on the spot at seeing you. His phobias, remember. You would be considered unnatural in his eyes."

"Oh," she nodded. "No. He never touched me except maybe lightly touched my arm or something. If that's so, why has he managed to be near me *after* he found out? But wait, wait... He *knows* I'm a pod survivor."

"Yes, but not a three hundred year relic."

"Is there a difference?" Josie sneered at his favoured use of the word relic.

"It's because he's in love with you," Simon replied casually and snorted as John and Josie stared at him in surprise. "And," he continued, "you've not been in contact with him since he's learned of it. You forget your little kidnapping incident."

Ignoring his first comment, Josie got up and stood akimbo. "I was standing right there when he found out, and to the best of my knowledge, he didn't choke up and keel over in fits." She paced now and in her mind, the room seemed to be shrinking. "But no, I've not been in contact with him since."

"Fine," John spoke again. "Let us pretend that he didn't know—or suspect. And let us pretend that he was not a key player and funded Ho. Ho, we know was fanatically involved for obvious reasons, but he still was not a foolish man. He'd have made sure he had enough resources and funds before he acted, and very possibly used some of Adam's funds as well as others. We know, too, that Adam perhaps had the most to gain by the success of this entire operation. And if he knew who Josie really was, he would have avoided contact with her—regardless of his...affection for her. I know him, at least the extent of his phobias. They are too strong, too ingrained in him. He would have been revolted."

"Unless love has rendered him senseless." Trudi, who'd remained silent for the entire time spoke up. She wasn't up to speed on events, but her quick mind seemed to rapidly fill in the blanks. "It happens."

Josie stared at her. In her mind, she rewound and reviewed events from the last year. In her heart she knew Adam was smitten with her. Yet, he'd always remained respectfully distant and treated their relationship as nothing but friendship. A small part of her recoiled from the thought that Adam might be in love with her, it was somewhat creepy, knowing his history as she did. A manipulator, liar...murderer.

"So, what now?" Josie asked with a heavy heart.

"Good question." John stood to pace as well. "We can't very well accuse Adam without any proof other than this letter. I don't doubt Wellesley's word, but still."

"And what happens next if there is enough proof?" Trudi asked, straightening a corner of Simon's blanket. "He's already in exile. The public thinks him dead."

"Good question." John mused over something. His first impulse was to have his brother executed on the spot, regardless of the proof. If the public thought him dead, he might as well comply... No, he wanted solid proof of Adam's involvement. If it took a day or if it took another half century, he would find it and make Adam suffer for it.

"John," Josie brought him out of his reverie. "Why don't we just ask him?"

"For him to lie to us again?" Simon snorted. "He's lied before to protect himself, he won't stop now. No matter how remorseful he is or appears to be, sorry, he won't be getting any favours from me. I don't trust him. I've said this before and I'll say it again."

"But Ho is dead, the research exposed...he's lost any advantage he may have had," Josie pressed on. "If he knows that we know, maybe he'll confess or something. How else will we catch him? How are we going to get to the truth?"

"I don't know." John replied for Simon. "But I'll find a way. He may have covered his tracks well and good, but everyone makes mistakes. It's human nature. And the last time I checked, dear brother Adam was still very much human."

Yes, John thought, he'd find a way to prove Adam's involvement in the matter. This had Adam written all over it. It literally stank of it. It would be just like Adam to play his little mind tricks and drop hints and suggestions, making them run around in circles, confusing the issue more. He'd find out—one day—he most definitely would. If it was the last thing he ever did, it would be to find out the truth.

~ * ~

"You think she's out there?"

"Margeaux? She'd have died instantly, Josie."

"No, idiot," Josie clicked her tongue in annoyance. "Fern."

John nodded silently, rubbing a knot at his neck. "You want to find her, don't you?"

"It has crossed my mind."

"You do know that—"

"I know, I know. She's some mentally twisted creature, I know. But still… I want to find her. She's the last link, the missing link."

"You intend to find her and kill her?"

"No! Jeez, what do you take me for?" Horror had her eyes wide that she goggled at him.

"Well, the way the conversation was going and you on about last links and all. I just assumed…" he shrugged mildly in defense.

John spared a moment to think about it, he'd have found her to kill her. Probably. These last few days had been nothing short of confusion for emotions and nerves, and he seemed to be still jumping with remaining adrenalin. If someone offered to pick a fight with him, he'd fly out of his chair and beat them to a pulp—with a wide grin. He also felt extremely horny.

"Will you help me? Find her, that is?"

He replied carefully. "Yes. If that's what you want."

"It's what I want." She tilted her head to him. "You don't think it's a good idea, do you? You can't protect me from every hurt that's out there, you know."

"You seemed bent on proving that fact to me. I've aged these last few days more than I would have in twenty years." He reached out and cupped her face. "I'll help, you know I will. For however long it takes to find her, I'll back you on this."

She smiled back warmly. "Needle in a haystack, that's what it'll be."

"Hmm," John grunted and settled back in his chair. "More like a speck of dust in a vast desert."

"So anyway, I've been reading up on Margeaux's religion." Josie said suddenly, changing the subject as abruptly as he would have. She still looked weary and tired, but also wonderfully alive—as though a burden had been lifted from her body.

"Have you now?" John gave her a bemused look. "You've figured out how to use the personal units' download feature? It's about time."

"Ha-ha, funny."

They sat companionably on their stingy observation deck, the vast emptiness of space around them. Each had their feet propped up on the window ledge; all that was missing was some space-brew beer. They made do with a flask of water.

"Anyway, its quite interesting," she continued.

"Are you thinking of converting?"

"Nah," she flexed her arms and tucked them behind her neck, leaning back into her chair. A small pout formed on her mouth. "But," she continued. "As you didn't give me a ring on our wedding..."

John frowned. "You never asked for one. Did you want one?" He felt, suddenly, that he'd done something terribly wrong. A memory of his father flashed through his mind. His father had forever muttered about women and their trick questions. This sounded a lot like a trick question.

"Well," she looked at him as through he were the biggest moron in the known universe. "Duhh. I mean, yes, but...no. What I mean is, I didn't ask because you people don't seem to wear rings anymore. In this century, that is."

He replied carefully. "Some still do—traditions die hard. It's a matter of preference. And rings are bothersome in times of combat. They get in the way..." He sounded too much like a man making excuses so he clamped his mouth shut.

"Well, I didn't know that. Besides, Simon doesn't wear one, or Trudi. I just didn't want to ask stupid questions and sound like an outdated idiot." Josie scowled. "But that's beside the point now."

"It is?" He didn't sound relieved in the least.

"Mmm." She grinned suddenly and took note of his

suspicious squint. "As I was saying, this Buddhist thing... There's this endless or eternal knot thing that I quite liked the sound of. It's all about things overlapping with no beginnings and endings. Like endless wisdom and compassion, harmony and simplicity and balance, continuity and cycles. How everything is interlaced and connected and linked with our fates all bound together with our karmic destiny and—"

"I get it. Your point?"

Josie slid a quick, sheepish look at him.

"My point is—what I mean to say is, that... The endless knot design looks really cool and the meaning behind it, the symbolism and all, well...I thought we could have matching tattoos instead of rings, of the endless knot—on our fingers. You know, considering how rings get in the way of combat, as we seem to do quite a bit of that of late." She blinked innocently across at him, her features bland.

John spared her a similar look, purposely silent for nearly fifteen seconds.

"Why didn't you just say so in the first place?" He nearly snorted and turned to face the window again, a crooked smile nearly bursting to erupt on his face. "Instead, you went on and on with some philosophical ranting."

"Idiot!" she swiped the back of her hand on his arm. "I take it that's a yes?"

He sobered. "It is. I think it's an excellent idea. Rather permanent, don't you think?" he added with a raised brow. "I'm not sure I want to be stuck with you for all eternity."

"*Big* fucking idiot!" She laughed now as she swiped her hand out at him again. "You're stuck with me forever, whether you like it or not."

He caught her hand and dragged her closer. "I suppose you'll have to do, then. You have proven to be quite brave and your loyalty is without question. And you've finally started dressing respectably enough, so yes. I suppose." He grinned widely. "But that cursing of yours, now...you've got to—"

"Fuck off you big—"

His mouth covered hers swiftly and stamped the words right out of her mouth. She didn't resist and her giggles became a long sigh. When they parted, they rested their brows together.

Josie smiled lazily, nuzzling his cheek, at ease, content, and at peace. "You're still a big soppy girl, you know that? If you start to titter and squeal like one, I'll open that escape hatch and jump out."

"Then I'll have to scream like a girl."

Josie snorted out a laugh, it sounded light-hearted. She looked at him with a purse of the lips that slowly became a wicked smile.

"So, you still want to know about that mile-high club?"

John sighed with patience, then chuckled wickedly. "Josie, we're in outer space, I'm not sure a mere mile qualifies at the moment. But, I've something better," he skillfully pulled her onto his lap. "Forget mile-high clubs, I can show you a whole new universe."

About T.K.

TK was born and raised in Barbados where she currently lives with her husband. For the last twenty-odd years, she has been working as a freelance graphic artist. Writing has always appealed to her and is something that she'd eventually like to do full-time. Early in 2008, she decided to just jump right in and make a start with *The Lancaster Rule*, the first in the trilogy. Since then, books two and three have been written in quick succession. And, still more books wait to be written.

Visit our website for our growing catalogue of quality books.
www.burstbooks.ca